T0363034

TWO SHANES

'Tulloch has always shared Armistead Maupin's skill for writing quirky characters…[she] has an infallible bullshit detector.'
Sydney Morning Herald

'A timely novel…a witty piece of social observation'
Sunday Age

Lee Tulloch is the bestselling author of *Fabulous Nobodies*, *Wraith* and *Two Shanes*. A long-time resident of Manhattan, she returned to her native Australia in 2001. Lee now lives on a Sydney beach with her husband Tony Amos and daughter Lolita.

LEE TULLOCH
THE CUTTING
A Nullin Mystery

 Text Publishing Melbourne Australia

The Text Publishing Company
171 La Trobe Street
Melbourne Victoria 3000
Australia

Designed by Chong
Typeset in 12.5/15.5 Baskerville MT by J & M Typesetting
Printed and bound by Griffin Press

First published 2003
This edition published 2004

National Library of Australia
Cataloguing-in-Publication data:

Tulloch, Lee.

The cutting : a Nullin mystery.

ISBN 1 920885 19 6.

1. Murder - Investigation - Fiction. 2. Villages - New
South Wales - Fiction. I. Title.

A823.3

For my sister, Coral

She'd got herself dolled up for him. That's what her mother called it. Getting 'dolled up'.

'What are you all dolled up for?' she'd say, like it was a crime or something. Not 'you look pretty'. Never 'that's nice makeup' or 'I like your top'. Always 'go scrub that black gunk off *now*' or 'has the cat been chasing a mouse through your hair?' Not that she would have accepted a compliment from the frustrated old bag. If her mother had ever actually *liked* her hair she would have gone straight back in the bathroom and wet it down. Her mother had no idea at all. She wore curlers at night, for fuck's sake. She had yellow toenails like horns that she never painted. God knew how her father could sleep in the same bed. Probably ran for the couch the moment the door was closed. Staying together for the children. Yuck. He was no looker either. She's seen his balls sagging in his grey Y-fronts. Chicken skin. Yuck again.

How did they produce her? Could she be adopted? She often thought so. They were ugly. She was gorgeous. The mirror didn't lie. Boys' hands didn't lie. She *did* look like a doll if you thought about it. Big clear blue eyes like one of those supermodels. Whatsername. She didn't pay attention to names. It was like not important, your name. You could change it if you wanted. She would change it when she went to Sydney and got a job. Maybe a model, everyone said she could be one, but if not a makeup artist in a store. She would *live* in nightclubs and drink cocktails that were blue.

Soon. She would cut loose soon. Get out of this crappy little town with one cinema and nothing else to do except burn yourself to a crisp on the beach. Then the bitches at school would be laughing out the other sides of their faces. They said she couldn't get him. That's why she said bring the knife. I want you to cut me. I want them to know. They won't believe I bled between my legs, we have to show them something.

She had been sucked and squeezed and come home with bruises inside her thighs but she had never given it up. She was proud of that. Her mother might call her a slut for the weal on her neck but she didn't know the truth. Her love was something pure and wonderful. She was his. He was marked for her.

It was her idea that they meet, tonight, on the old Speculator Road. It would be romantic up here in the whispering bush. She didn't want to do it in Nullin, not the first time. She wanted them to be free of all that. If he wanted to do it in his car, that would be OK too.

The whispering bush was howling now. The scented candles she'd brought would flicker out in the wind. She hated the cold. It was November, it should have been nice out, but the wind whipped around her bare legs and messed her hair. She'd carefully selected her seduction outfit, a scooped-neck pink tee-shirt with *Kylie* in glitter on the front and a miniskirt that showed her sexy knickers when she bent over. But she'd had to wear her parka and it spoiled the look. She had her arms wrapped tightly around herself now, but as soon as she saw his headlights, she'd tear it off and he'd never be the wiser.

There were no cars on the road this time of night. It didn't really go anywhere anymore. Sometimes the kids would ride it as far as the Void, the big old quarry cut into the mountain and they'd park there, fuck on a dare. It was scary down there, all right. The stones were cold under your skin and it was black as Satan. She'd almost gone too far one night, for a lark, and only got away because she convinced the stupid fuckwit he needed some light to see her tits. Never again. She lost a good shoe that night. Her mother had called her a tramp when she crawled in afterwards. But she wasn't one.

The Princes Highway crossed the road and she could see the rise and fall of headlights behind the trees. Occasionally a big beam would fill the horizon and her heart would leap at the thought it was *him* swinging the corner and coming for her. But it would only be a truck, driving through the night on the lonely Sydney–Melbourne route. She liked to sit up high in the cabin of trucks and swing her legs. The truck drivers liked it too. They were mostly nice to her. Mostly.

She paced up and down on the bitumen. She wished she had brought her fags. She was getting jack of waiting, if the truth be known. She had chosen sandals with high cork wedges to make her legs look longer but the soles of her feet hurt. Not to mention her ankles, which kept on twisting on the uneven road. She could hear things in the bush scratching around. She hoped they were only possums and silly old wombats. Not snakes, she never did much like snakes. But snakes only came out in the sun, didn't they?

There were stars. She paced and filled the time by trying to name the constellations. Everyone knew the Southern Cross. There was that pot thing. And something that looked like an arrow pointing straight at her heart.

Gradually she realised that one beam at the end of the road had not moved. The beam was low, a car or a truck with its headlights dimmed. It did not turn back to the highway or come towards her. Maybe he'd thought she'd be there, not by the old milepost like she'd said.

She waved, then realised that the moon was not bright enough for him to see her. If it wasn't so windy, she could light a candle. And then she thought of her cigarette lighter, always somewhere in the bottom of her bag. She found it and clicked the flame, her hands cupped around it. It went out once or twice, but she kept clicking.

3

She felt like a spy. A little quiver of excitement shot through her body.

The car didn't move. She flung the lighter back in her bag and started tripping along the road towards the beam, unzipping her parka as she quickened her pace.

She was close now. She couldn't see the car or its driver through the arc of diffused light. Then she heard the engine start up. The lights dipped and then brightened. She had to shield her eyes with her forearm. The car crawled along the road towards her.

She stood in the middle of the road and dropped her parka at her feet. Hastily, she pulled at her cleavage and stood there, hand on hip, bosoms thrust out, like a vamp in one of those midday movies her mother watched.

The car stopped.

She wobbled a bit on her shoes.

Heidi hoisted her massage table into the back of the Kingswood and slammed the tailgate with a curse. She should have seen it coming. She'd been living in this coastal town only four months, but already she'd lost her city smarts.

The client had looked innocuous enough when he'd opened the motel door. Mid-thirties, fair hair wet from the shower, scrubbed pink skin. She'd given him her usual speech to make absolutely certain he knew the terms of their arrangement. He told her he'd developed a sore back on the drive up from Melbourne. She said no problems, I can fix that, and he'd let her in.

But she hadn't liked the way he sat on the bed, legs open and short towelling robe gaping, or the way he'd watched her as she set up her table. She liked even less the way he moaned as she worked on his back.

The way he said 'please nurse' and 'oh, that's good'.

The thick erection she covered with a towel when he turned over.

The hand that shot up between her buttocks as she oiled his leg.

She'd wriggled away, told him the massage was over.

He'd called her an 'Asian bitch' and lunged at her.

She didn't even think about the danger. She flipped the side of the table up and over, forcing her weight behind it and tipping him between the table and the bed. She was slight and the table was fragile but she had the advantage of surprise. Quickly, she kicked the table legs to fold them and gathered her things. He staggered to his feet but didn't try to stop her.

'What the fuck did I do?' she heard him bellow as she slammed the door behind her.

She started the car, grateful for the engine's roar.

There was no way she was going to tell Beckett about it. Things were difficult enough between them without him going ballistic about her work. He'd ban her from doing it altogether. And she loved it. Not as much as she loved him, of course. But he didn't make it easy.

From now on, she'd stick to lady pensioners.

She put the station wagon into gear and pulled out onto Eden Street, Nullin's main drag for a hundred years. The area around the post office and cake shop still had a bustling authority, but that soon petered out as the road shot in a straight line south and narrowed to a wasteland of weatherboard bungalows with brown lawns and deflated kiddie's wading pools.

She turned into Jade and followed it to the Princes Highway. Her humour started to return as she reeled off the street names in her head. The municipal powers had endowed this shabby neighbourhood with the names of stones—Emerald, Turquoise, Aquamarine, Sapphire, Peridot and Citrine—that reflected the colours of the Tasman Sea, tantalisingly out of sight a kilometre away. In another part of town, the same authorities had named streets after the local wildlife—Osprey, Whale, Penguin, Platypus—that shrewdly stayed well clear of Nullin human beings. And around the Koori Health Centre, out back of the football field, some committee had felt guilty enough to name the cul-de-sacs of the new housing development Barunguba, Wallaga and Bemeringal.

The highway opened up immediately, a ribbon of bitumen winding through shoulders of verdant hills dotted with spears of red bloodwood and spotted gum and the occasional assembly of cows. The rainforest had been cleared generations ago to make pastureland for dairy farms, but still thrived on the other side of the rise, humming with life, waiting for the day when it could reclaim the soil that tumbled to the sea.

She drove across the steel span bridge over the Bilba Inlet. Below, the tide left boats stranded in silver mud. The town's biggest employer, the Sea Pride cannery, sat on a pier where the river met the bay. She could see a cluster of men leaning against the jetty railing. She checked her watch. It was 11.30. Lunchtime for the blokes who stripped the skin off tuna.

The road hugged the coast, green hills on one side, pebbly beaches and rocky outcrops on the other. The bitumen road to the caravan park shot off to the left, its plastic sign touting hot showers and off-season rates. In the parking area alongside Hapless Bay, where explorers' ships had been lost to the reef, a tour bus was parked on an alarming angle, its white-haired inhabitants disgorged in search of the grey kangaroos that sometimes obligingly came down to the water. It was late April, past Easter, not prime tourist time.

As the road curved away from the sea again, she floored the accelerator. She kicked her sandals off and drove with bare feet. The apple-green Kingswood rattled up a steep hill and roared down the decline. She punched the radio buttons but nothing happened. Damn. She felt like something soothing. Enya. Moby. Music Beckett would hate.

In the distance, a black four-wheel-drive pulled out to pass a milk tanker grinding up an incline. Behind it, several trucks headed north in the direction of the 'big smoke', Bateman's Bay, which boasted 30,000 inhabitants, or further to Sydney, which was pushing four million. Trucks were the things she hated most about this road—the tankers taking dairy products to the big cities, their drivers already semi-comatose from long hours on the road, the furniture vans that bore down on you, the flat bed trucks, hauling trunks of once-magnificent hardwood trees, their carriages so long and rigid they swung out across the opposite lane at every tight turn.

The four-wheel-drive was taking forever to pass the milk tanker, its macho appearance compromised by its obvious lack of horsepower. Heidi eased her foot off the accelerator to put more distance between herself and the struggling vehicle. She quickly checked the rear-vision mirror and started when she saw the gleaming hardware of a huge Mack truck right on her tail.

Shit! If she needed to brake, she'd end up with a necklace of headlights and twisted metal.

She struggled to concentrate on the road. The black vehicle was coming straight at her, the driver just a halo of brown hair and two hands rigidly on the wheel. Heidi thumped at her horn. The Mack behind her joined in, its belligerent bullhorn making her skin crackle. She could feel the electric shock of it in the white hairs that fizzed on top of her braided head.

Back off. She willed the milk tanker to slow, to stop...anything to get the four-wheel-drive out of her path. But it was too late. The black car flew at her. The outside world was reduced to a roar.

She flashed on an image of herself flung from the car, lying crumpled on the verge, neck broken, skirt ridden up over gravel-scraped thighs and Beckett standing over her with a bunch of white daisies.

The country life snatched away from her before she'd even begun to enjoy it. The home they were making never finished. The children they would love never conceived. Their turbulent mattress exchanged for the clots of rotting earth that would make her bed.

No more kisses at night, under the Southern Cross.

Get a grip.

With seconds to spare, she swung her steering wheel hard to the left. The back wheels of the Kingswood slid in the gravel by the road. She squeezed the brakes, drove through the loose stones, gripping the wheel, praying to a higher authority she never associated with traffic direction. The car lurched towards the verge, straightened, then thundered directly towards the stone wall of a narrow bridge at the bottom of the hill. She pounded the brakes again, yanked the wheel, slid in the gravel and spun sideways, stopping a metre from the wall. The massage table thudded against the back seat as the truck ploughed past, its horn blaring. The nose of the Kingswood jutted into the lane. No one stopped.

She reversed off the road and jumped out of the car. Only then did she falter, dropping to her knees in the long grass. She let herself roll down to the water's edge. It was damp on the banks and in the back of her mind she thought of snakes but she lay there, arms outstretched, until calm returned.

She was mesmerised by the sounds in the gully—the faint tinkle of a bird, the hiss of running water, the shivering leaves, the way her breath rose and fell.

The dull, scraping noise of metal being dragged over stone.

She tensed. Slowly, she rolled back onto her knees. She held her breath, listening intently, watching for movement. The tree ferns grew along the bank like dipsomaniac attendants, leaning this way and that. But the only activity was the fluttering of small birds among the ruffled umbrella foliage, in rhythm to the defibrillation of her heart.

Nothing.

She sighed and stared at the shallow water, darkly rippling under the shade of sassafras and yellow stringybark. And then she saw it. On a smooth rock across the creek some child had forgotten a stuffed toy. When she had been four, she'd lost her poodle pyjama case—kicked into the gutter from the seat of a car was the adults' final verdict—and she still remembered the pain of it. She couldn't bear that another child was crying over a lost toy. If she waded across the water she could reach it, maybe hand it in at the local police station and hope that the family was local.

She carefully entered the stream, mindful of the slippery

algae that coated the larger rocks. The water was icy, the stones were sharp on her soles. She had to wade around a branch of stringybark that had snapped off from the canopy above, holding on to its tip to steady herself. The current was deceptively strong.

As she reached the other side, something silver swished off a rock and away through the long grass and her heart flipped again. A ute roared past on the bridge, the inevitable blue heeler in the back pacing and barking. She felt a rush of fear. The stuffed animal lay just out of reach on a wide, dry rock. She pushed herself up onto a flat stepping stone and bent over it. Her brain, having decided 'toy', did not take in the full implications of what she was seeing.

She touched the velvet tentatively and then circled it with her hands. It felt sticky, heavier than she expected. It was only when she turned and lifted it that she realised what she was holding.

Beckett had been dozing down by the stream when Heidi appeared on the back verandah, calling his name.

Startled, he pushed the straw hat off his face and guiltily swung his crossed legs off the edge of the wicker table where they'd been propped.

'*Beck-ett!*'

She had an arm in the air. He waved back. He expected that she would turn and go back into the old cheese factory and make them some tea, as she usually did when she came back from town. Instead, she stepped over the splintery wood of the collapsed top step he'd been meaning to fix—along with the thousand other things he'd been meaning to fix—and scrambled down to the lawn.

He glanced at the screen of his open laptop, which had long since gone into standby, and snapped it shut. If she asked him about his morning's work, he would tell her he had made progress. As far as he was concerned, any sentence that contained a verb was progress.

Now she was running down the rough path he'd hacked out of the grassy slope, her feet, encased in those ugly Birkenstocks she'd swapped for her city high heels, sliding on the patches of mud. As she hurtled towards him, he saw that she held a white bundle closely to her chest. A baby? His stomach felt heavy with dismay. It couldn't be, unless she'd become impatient with his procrastinating on the subject and snatched someone else's infant from outside the Nullin Hot Bread Shop.

He jumped up from his chair and she tumbled into his arms, the white towel pressing against his chest. She let him hold her for a moment. The top of her head only reached his breastbone.

'Hey,' he said, squeezing her shoulders.

'Look at this!' she demanded, pulling away, but he couldn't take his eyes off her face. After six years of marriage it was still like this when she returned to him. The heart shape of her face, the sharp cheekbones, the way her hazel eyes were folded under long, heavy lids—all these features were unmistakably the gift of her Chinese father. He supposed there were other Eurasian women with skin as creamy as anything the local dairies could produce—the milkmaid skin she inherited from her Celtic mother—but he doubted there were many whose noses and cheeks were also splattered with a galaxy of pink freckles. And then, to complicate matters, there was the white scar slashed across the bridge of her nose—a mystery she refused to speak about. 'I'm a freak,' she had told him the night they met, but that didn't inhibit her from making more of a point of it by bleaching her coarse dark hair white and wearing it on top of her head in braids, a parody of her storybook name.

But now, colour stained her cheeks, a bruised scarlet he knew signalled extreme anger. 'I can't believe someone would do this,' she said and thrust the towel at her husband. It was cold and the weight of a small cat. He took it gently and placed it on the grass. Kneeling, he unwrapped it.

'Wow. I've never seen one of these up close before.'

'What do you mean, *wow*?' She stood over him, hands on hips, the white nurse's uniform she wore when giving massages hoisted fetchingly above a pleasing stretch of thigh.

He dragged his eyes back to the animal. 'Well, I've seen them at the zoo of course. Are they endangered?'

'For God's sake, Beckett, they're going to be endangered if people go around cutting their throats!'

'Its throat has been cut?' He took a closer look.

The platypus was laid out on the towel on its stomach like a display in a natural history museum. The fur looked sleek, slightly mangy near the flat tail as if it had been in a fight. The front feet were tucked under but the back paws were splayed, the webbing evident between the toes. The wide bill looked like it was made of grey clay, stuck onto the fur like a party mask. 'Freaky,' he said, poking the bill with a finger.

'Turn it over and look at it!'

He turned it gently. Despite the towelling it was cold. 'Shit.'

'See what I mean?' She crouched down beside him. 'It looks like someone has slit its throat.'

The mammal's fur had been slashed from beneath the bill to its chest. Beckett could see the yellow layer of fat under the skin and the congealing viscera. But there was blood on its tail too. He blanched. 'I think it's been skewered on a stick or something. Where did you find it anyway?'

'You know the creek that crosses the highway? I went into the gravel to avoid some soccer mum overtaking a truck and ended up near the creek. I saw—*this*—on a rock. *Bastards!*'

'Maybe it was kids or a poacher. The locals do have a more straightforward attitude to death than thou and I. You've seen those dead possums stuck on fenceposts.'

She shuddered. 'Don't remind me.'

He stood and nudged the mammal with his toe. 'The closest thing I ever came to killing was a cockroach in our Balmain bathroom. I couldn't do it.'

'That's crap, Beckett. What about all those animals your father slaughtered in his butcher shop?'

'He didn't slaughter them. They arrived slaughtered. He just cut the carcasses into pieces that didn't resemble animals to make the customer feel better about it. Anyway, it had nothing to do with *me*. I stayed well clear of it, so that he wouldn't rope me into the family business. What are we going to do with this thing? Bury it?'

13

'No way. I'm taking it to the cops.'

'The cops won't care. They're too busy writing speeding tickets.'

She took a corner of the towel and folded it across the dead animal. 'I'll make them care.'

The Nullin police station was a cream brick, 1950s house at the northern end of Eden Street, squeezed between a small court-house and a weatherboard bungalow, with a lump of plaster, possibly representing a dolphin or marlin, in the middle of the brown lawn.

Beckett parked his 1964 Volvo Amazon along the kerb behind a white Ford Falcon wagon with POLICE across its back doors. Heidi slid her feet into the gutter, the platypus in her arms. She stood on the nature strip, less nature and more man-made neglect, while Beckett locked the car door. 'Don't know why I'm bothering to do this. They don't have any crime in Nullin do they?'

She looked at him critically. His green cable sweater had holes in the sleeves and the cord trousers were crusted on the cuff with mud. His dark hair straggled to his shoulder blades, under the frayed Panama hat he wore when he wrote. 'I like your country squire look, but do you have to wear that hat?'

'What's wrong with it?'

'You look like Buddy Ebsen in "The Beverly Hillbillies".' When he didn't respond, she shifted the towelled bundle to her other arm. 'Come on, let's get this over with.'

The duty officer was a slight young man in a short-sleeved blue shirt. He was sitting behind a counter, drinking a milkshake through a straw and reading a magazine. He looked up when Beckett and Heidi walked in and closed his magazine furtively.

Beckett strode up to the counter. 'Reading the *Women's Weekly* I see.'

Heidi nudged him. *Be serious.*

'Research, sir.'

'What?' Beckett said, craning his neck to look at the cover. '"New Looks for Every Body and Budget"?'

'It's Mum's sixtieth,' the cop said. 'I'm looking for something to cook.'

'Pavlova?' Beckett asked hopefully.

'I was thinking poached quince tart with lemon myrtle creme anglais myself.'

Heidi was impatient. 'Sergeant—'

'It's Constable. Constable Brendan Barton. How can I help you?' His fair skin was sunburnt, the skin peeling to reveal a fiery cyclamen nose, but he looked a little paler when he noticed Heidi's bundle. 'What's that?'

Heidi stepped forward and put the towel on the counter. She started to unwrap it.

'Do you have to do that here?' Barton asked warily. 'It isn't a baby, is it?'

'Get lots of abandoned babies?' Beckett asked.

'Had one a month ago. Poor little bugger. It was twelve hours old, the social worker said.'

'Well, this is a *platypus*,' Heidi announced. 'A dead one.'

The cop looked at the unwrapped corpse. 'Thank Christ for that.'

'I wouldn't sound so relieved if I were you. Someone has slashed its throat. What kind of creep would do that?'

'Same person who did the other four, I reckon,' he said.

'There have been *five* platypuses murdered?'

'Nah, not platypus. This is the first one of those. Let's see. We've had a sugar glider. Then a grey kangaroo. Bastard got an echidna last time. Don't know how he did that. They're prickly characters. Rare as hen's teeth too.'

'You know who did it?'

'Not really. I'm speaking figuratively. Could be anyone. Could even be a girl.' He smirked at Heidi.

'Well, what are you going to do about it?'

'Can't do much unless we catch the bugger red-handed.'

'But that's ridiculous! Surely you can do something?'

'Don't have the time. There's four of us, but the others have all pissed off to the caravan park, where a bloke's holed up with a shotgun and his wife as hostage.'

Beckett put a hand on Heidi's arm to calm her. 'Where were the other animals found, constable?'

'I'll have to bring up the file. But a couple of ferals brought in the echidna. They found it up near their commune or whatever they call it. I had a hard time convincing them it wasn't the farmers done it just to upset them.'

'Where are these ferals?'

'Back in the national park, about six kilometres deep. You just keep following Chinaman's Creek. Shouldn't be there, of course, but we don't have enough manpower to keep them out. The post office even delivers to their mailbox on the highway. Gondwana is their name. Means something in Abo. But they're all white. Trust-fund kids, you can bet on it.'

'The great southern land,' said Beckett.

'That's right. Well, I better take your details. I can get a bloke over from Parks and Wildlife to look at it if you want.'

'What will he do?' Heidi asked.

'Nothing much. Toss it in the incinerator.'

She flinched. 'No thanks. Can I take it home to bury it?'

'Suit yourself.' He ambled over to a table with a computer monitor and sat in front of it. Heidi and Beckett squeezed onto small vinyl chairs.

'Sorry about the chairs,' Barton said. 'We got them from the kindergarten. Have to wait until the next budget for some replacements.' He tapped on the keyboard. 'OK, here's the file. Ringtail possum found strung up on the population sign, south of Nullin. Echidna found on the turn-off to the Gondwana camp. Fruit bat behind the Harding house. Sugar glider behind the Leagues Club. Grey kangaroo on the golf course. Let's see, eighth hole. Tricky one, that. You should see the sand trap.'

'Can you find any connection between those sites?'

'No. None.' He tapped a few more instructions. 'OK. I'm going to need your names.'

'Heidi Go.' She spelt it.

'Unusual name.'

'My father's Chinese. My mother's directly descended from the convicts.'

'We had a lot of Chinese here once,' Barton said. 'Then they made their fortunes and cleared off. All except for Simpson Cheung. Owns most of the fishing boats.' He nodded at Beckett. 'Your name?'

'Beckett Versec.' He spelt it.

'Versec?'

'It's Serbian.'

'Oh yeah? Like them refugees from Bosnia? We had a few of them down here at the old quarantine station a few years back. The poor buggers didn't want to go back when the war was over. Who could blame them? You're a Muslim, then?'

'Both my parents are Catholic. My mother's Irish.'

'Didn't think you looked dark enough.'

'Not all Muslims are dark,' Beckett said patiently. 'But, yes, I have my father's black hair and my mother's green eyes.'

And your father's cynical take on everything, combined with your mother's overactive imagination, Heidi thought. She could see Beckett was enjoying himself, his long, reed-slender body slouched down in the tiny chair until he was almost horizontal with the floor, his ratty old straw hat pushed back on his head.

'Address?'

'We moved into the old Nullin cheese factory around Christmas.'

Barton smiled. 'So you're the city slickers who took on that white elephant? You paid too much for it, mate. They would have given it away. No one's been near it for years.'

'That's what I like about it,' Beckett said.

'Yeah. Well you've got your work cut out for you. It's got holes in the floor the size of the Nullin Void.'

'The Nullin Void?'

'Old quarry out back. You renovating the thing yourself?'

'With a bit of local help.'

'My husband fancies himself as a bit of a handyman, constable,' Heidi said and put a hand on Beckett's thigh. 'But I just fancy him.'

Barton cleared his throat. 'They say you have to live in a house for a while before you do anything to it.'

'Exactly my point,' Beckett said.

'OK.' The police officer looked back at the screen. 'Now tell me where you found the platypus.'

Heidi filled him in.

'So you didn't notice anyone lurking around when you found it?'

'I'm sure he would have been long gone.'

'Not necessarily. The animal doesn't show any signs of being infested by larvae or attacked by birds. It was freshly killed.'

She looked at him with new respect. 'I didn't think about that. You mean, he could have been behind a tree, watching me?' She remembered the scraping sound she'd heard as she lay there. A muscle twitched in her neck. She reached to rub it.

'I reckon. He's going to get off on your reaction.'

'And you're not worried about this guy?'

'I didn't say I wasn't worried about him. I just said I didn't have the resources to catch him at it.'

'So you *do* have some idea who it might be?'

19

'I might.'

'Can't you tell us? I don't want to end up in his house giving him a massage.'

Barton looked up. 'You're the lady who advertises those massages in the paper? I was thinking about giving my mum one for her birthday. Do you think she'd like it?'

'She'd love it,' Beckett said. 'And my wife will give your mother a massage for free if she tells all her friends about it and you do too.'

Heidi looked sharply at her husband. She was having a hard enough time making money without him giving her work away. He never took it seriously. 'You don't write screenplays for nothing.'

'Shut up,' he whispered back. 'It will be good for business. Cops know everyone.'

'Well, that's really nice of you,' Barton grinned. 'Of course, I'll have to pay you something, otherwise it's corruption, you know. How about half price?'

Beckett put his keys in the ignition. 'That Constable Barton might be useful for my research.'

'I wonder how he got so savvy so fast,' Heidi mused. 'He must be all of twenty-five.'

'He's not that savvy. He's just opportunistic. Shit, have you forgotten the city cops?'

'I, unlike you, had nothing to do with them. And, thanks, by the way, for devaluing my services. I'm only making about two hundred dollars a week as it is. I'm going to have to give blowjobs at the back of the Leagues Club if this keeps up. Take that as a warning.'

'How much?'

'How much what?'

'How much would you charge for a blowjob? At the back of the Leagues Club, home of the Nullin Whales?'

'Twenty?'

'What about a blowjob in the front seat of a car?'

'More. Danger money.'

'I could find a back street.'

'They're all back streets in Nullin.'

'Do you give family discounts?'

'No. Only to cops. Half-price for cops. You were the one who set the price.'

'I'll throw in a dead platypus.'

'I'd rather you threw in a kiss.'

4

Heidi lay in bed with her arms behind her head listening to the kookaburras mocking the morning. The cool April light slipped under the fold of the old chenille bedspread she had strung across the window. Beckett was turned towards her, his hands clasped under his chin like a praying seraphim. Whenever she woke, he was always facing her as if he couldn't bear to put his back to hers.

A few dark locks of hair swept behind him as if a gust of wind had blown across the flannel pillow. She rolled onto her left side, pushed herself up on one elbow and reached over to tuck a stray hair behind his ear. He flinched but didn't open his eyes. His face, even in repose, had an intense expression, as if the strong angles of his brow, cheek and jaw were frowning at the tip of his long nose. She ruffled the short hairs that grew across his cheek in a roguish attempt at sideburns. Lately, she noticed, a few of them had turned pure silver, whether from the shock of finally reaching forty or the anxieties of uprooting his urban soul to the country, she did not know. She rubbed her finger against the grain but still he did not stir.

He had thrown the bedding off during the night and now one leg straddled the featherdown quilt while the other stretched underneath it. The exposed leg was wearing baby-blue cotton pyjamas, but the top had been pulled off and lay scrunched under his back. She ran the back of her hand down the deep crease on his cheek to his neck and bare chest, which was rising and falling with the rhythm of his breathing. The air in the room was frosty, but his skin felt clammy. She toyed with the gully of black hairs trailing down his abdomen. He was still golden from a summer of digging paths and demolishing outhouses, which he had sometimes done without his shirt on. His neck and arms below the biceps showed the faint tan line of the occasional tee-shirt. She touched the arm and followed the ropy veins from elbow to upper arm. She grasped the hard muscle and squeezed gently. He did not move.

Slowly, she sat up and slid out of her peach silk slip. A whisper of cold air ran over her body. She moved closer to him, sliding under his arm, pulling it over her hip and pressing her warm skin against his length. She found the place where her curves fitted his valleys. She pushed against him more insistently and felt his heat against her thighs. Her hand slipped down his back, under the elastic of his pyjamas. She could feel his buttocks clench beneath her touch, but his leg, his arm were dead weights.

She slid her hand over his hip and brushed his belly. She hovered for a moment, delicately teasing at the hairs below his navel. There was movement where she wanted it now. Definitely.

She untangled herself from the weight of his arm and pushed him gently onto his back. His arm flopped heavily on the mattress and his head rolled. She kicked the quilt away from between his legs and straddled him, the sharp bone of his hip grazing her inner thigh. She reached down, freed him from his pyjamas and abruptly took him into her.

His arm shot off the bed and onto her right breast. 'I thought if I lay still long enough you might do that,' he smiled, eyes still closed.

She put her hand over his and squeezed his flanks with her knees. At that moment, there was the crunching of tyres on the drive outside and the sound of an engine cutting out near the front door. Heidi stopped moving and listened. A car door slammed.

'Shit.' She pulled herself off him.

Beckett groaned and grabbed her wrist. 'Don't stop.'

But she was already off the bed, pulling her black velvet 1920s wrap tighter around her. 'Wait,' she said. 'I'll get rid of whoever it is.'

She walked through the kitchen to the front verandah. A muscular young man in stretch jeans, navy singlet and yellow workboots was pulling a ladder out of the back of a rust-red ute.

'Damian,' she greeted him, not knowing whether to be dismayed that the builder had interrupted them or overjoyed that he had finally turned up. 'It's been a long time since you've graced us with your presence.'

He propped the ladder against the car and sauntered over to her. 'Yeah, well, I finished at the Leagues Club. Thought I'd get going up here before the rain came. Knew you folks would be pleased to see me.' He gave her the lopsided smile that no doubt had made him a raging success with all the local lasses since primary school.

She noted he said 'get going' not 'finish'. She pushed her unbraided hair behind her ears. 'You're up early.'

'Can't waste good daylight. Besides, I have to leave at 2.30 to pick up the kids from school.'

'Kids?' He looked barely out of his teens.

'Kirrily and Kyle. She's six. He's seven.'

'Exactly how old are you, Damian?'

'Twenty-eight. You're thinking I'm too young to have kids? I reckon this way I can retire in fifteen years. They can both get jobs and look after me.'

'What about your wife. What's she do?'

'Don't have one of those.'

'Oh?' She was thinking—his teenage sweetheart's dumped him with the kids and run off to the big smoke.

'She died.'

'Oh, I'm sorry.'

'Yeah, it was bad luck. She went in the water off Nullin Point. A shark, they think.'

'That's terrible,' she said. 'Can I make you a cup of tea?'

'Nah, I better get started.' He looked up at the rust-scarred roof and sighed. 'Don't know why you came to this lonely old place. Most of us'd kill to live in Sydney. Don't you miss it?'

Heidi made a face. 'Not its superficiality.'

'Yeah?'

She could tell he didn't know what she meant. 'I do miss my friends. But they all promised they'd come and visit.'

'That'll be the day. Nullin's on the road to nowhere.'

'That's not true. Besides, it's beautiful. It's peaceful. You can live a simple, honest life.'

'I suppose.' He didn't sound convinced. 'It's good for raising kids. You got any?'

'No, not yet.'

'Didn't think I'd seen any around. If you don't mind me saying, you better get a hurry on.'

She did mind him saying. She was thirty-four and children were an unresolved issue between she and Beckett. Well, Beckett was resolved—not to have any until they'd finished the house. And that might never happen, she reminded him. If they relied on Damian, it certainly wouldn't. 'I could say the same thing for you. You better get a hurry on. Before the *next* football season.'

'I like a woman with a sense of humour,' he said, and gave her a whack on the backside before ambling off to the truck.

She put a hand where he'd smacked her and watched his cocky walk. She was outraged at his familiarity but more outraged with herself and the fact that she hadn't been *quite* as outraged as she should have been. No one had flirted with her in months, if you didn't count her husband, who *didn't* count because he was her husband. And Damian was a good-looking boy. There was always something to be said for trade.

He walked back past her, smiling, with the ladder over his

shoulder. He leaned it against the wall. 'Can I use this old rag?' he asked and picked the rolled-up towel off the old church pew, where she'd left it last night.

'No!'

He'd already unfolded it. 'Shit.' He blanched at the dead platypus.

'I'm sorry. Give it to me. I was going to bury it yesterday. I found it by that creek that crosses the highway. Someone pushed a knife or a stick through it and slashed its throat and chest.'

'No kidding? I've heard about these dead animals. Must be seven or eight now, all in the last couple of weeks.'

'The constable said six.'

'No, more than that. Not everyone who finds one would bother to tell the cops about it.'

'Why not?'

'Well, it's obvious who done it.'

'You mean, you know?'

'Of course I know. It's one of them Blackpeters. They're a family live out in the bush. Generations of them in the same old shack. They just keep on adding to it. It's their land, fair and square, but they live off poaching and selling the fur. I've been out there once, their place is a tannery. Stinks to high heaven.'

'But if they make money out of selling fur, why would they leave perfectly good kills around for other people to find? It doesn't make sense.'

'Maybe they're leaving the town a sign. They never did get on with anyone in Nullin. Way back, they say the great-great-grandpa mated with a Koori, got some Abo mixed in with the family blood. That's why they're *Black*peter, get it? I'd put my bets on Spaz Blackpeter, he's in his twenties now, the mentality of my Kyle.'

'His name's Spaz?'

'Yeah. He's a sorry case. A bit of a retard. Over the genera-tions there have been dozens of them, breeding like rabbits, all as thick as wombats. Grandpa's name was One, and his brother was Two and his kids followed that, but after Nine they couldn't count any further. Spaz's generation all have nicknames, like Dingo and Shank. There's one called Sniffy, got a petrol habit. And Crock, for crock of shit. Most people in town call them the Seven Dwarfs, because there's seven of them and most of them are short and built like brick shithouses. Spaz's the different one, he's the beanpole of the family. Not one of them has been to school, except Joey, she's the youngest, and she didn't last long. Every few years the social services send some old spinster to come after them, but the kids hide in the bush.'

'God, that's amazing,' she said. 'I didn't think people like that existed in real life.'

'The town don't tolerate them. They scare the tourists.'

'Why do you think it's Spaz and not one of the others who's killing native animals?'

'Because the cops got his big brother Sid in prison and the moron loves him. It's a protest or something.'

'What's Sid doing in prison?'

'Aggravated assault or some shit. That's Sid as in Sid Vicious. You could say it's a descriptive name.'

'If you know all this, Damian, why haven't the police made an arrest? The cop I spoke to didn't say anything about Blackpeters.'

'What did the cop look like?'

'Young, fair, tanned...'

'That'd be Brendan. He doesn't like to upset the Blackpeters. Shit, I wouldn't either. I try to stay on the right side of 'em.'

'But killing a platypus is so cruel. Who's going to stop this Spaz kid?'

'He'll stop by himself when Sid gets out of jail. That's in about five years but.'

'I can't believe the cops won't do anything. I feel like going up there.'

'Hey,' Damian said, raising both his hands. 'I wouldn't have told you if I thought you'd go after him. You stay away. Your tits are far too nice to be carved up by that crowd.'

'My tits?' She felt herself blush.

Damian pointed to where her velvet wrap had strayed open at the front.

'Good morning, Damian.' Beckett was standing inside the wire door. 'Are you molesting my wife?'

5

Heidi ran some warm water in the kitchen sink and washed. Modesty precluded her using the outside shower while Damian was around. It was getting too cold, anyway. They'd managed showering outside through the summer, but now it was time for Beckett to find a plumber to make them a real bathroom.

Beckett sat at the kitchen table and watched her. 'I don't know why you won't come back to bed. I'll put a chair against the door to stop Damian barging in.'

'I've got a massage in town in half an hour.'

'You should be working on *my* flesh.'

She quickly patted herself down with a towel. 'I'll cook you dinner and work on your flesh tonight. You'll have to wait.'

'You can't cook me dinner. There's the debutante ball.'

Heidi groaned. She had forgotten about it. Beckett's enthusiasm for authentic local culture embraced everything from the monthly sausage sizzle at the bowls club to the cake stall outside the opportunity shop on Saturday mornings. He'd been beside himself at the news that there were Masons in town, and Masons who still held coming-out balls to boot. 'We don't have to go.'

'At forty dollars a ticket, are you mad?'

'I've made my offer,' she said. It came out more sharply than she meant.

He took it the wrong way. 'Maybe I should just leave my ticket on the table for Damian.'

She started to say something reassuring and then shut up. He was being unreasonable. The move to the country was supposed to have enveloped them in bucolic bliss. But it had just made Beckett crankier. The old factory was falling down around their ears. He was so overwhelmed by it he couldn't get his screenplay done, which meant they were running out of money.

He had even taken to complaining about the peace in the same way he'd complained about the noise in Sydney.

Then, most irritatingly, he would get these little enthusiasms about debutante balls or bingo at the RSL. And he'd go off on tangents for days, his writing neglected, the bathroom situation ignored.

She wrapped herself in the towel and closed the bedroom door behind her. She could hear Beckett get up from the table and fill the kettle.

When she left, he was sitting with his back to the bedroom door, hunched over a coffee. He didn't say goodbye.

Beckett sat at the kitchen table with his third coffee of the morning and lit his third cigarette. He could only smoke in the house when Heidi was out—provided he aired it properly before she returned. He brooded over the sound of Damian scraping the paint off the old wire door. The builder had been at it for a good two hours, which must have been a record. But the scraping set his teeth on edge.

Heidi was supposed to be working on a pensioner but he often wondered if she told him the truth. Maybe she'd really gone down to the Leagues Club to massage a firm fleshed member of the Nullin football team. He wondered if her male customers got erections. She had always smiled enigmatically when he had asked. He was glad, in fact, because the answer would probably drive him insane. He was sure they got hard just at the sight of her standing in the door with her fold-up table in her hand. He usually did.

Damn it, he was restless. Sitting in the small kitchen, which had been the cheese factory's office in another life, only served to remind him of all the work he had to do. The framework of a bench was still waiting for its butcher-block top. The old window needed replacing. The linoleum on the floor was so pitted and scarred he could probably donate it to the local school for use as a topographical map of South-East Asia. There were a thousand repairs to do around the property, but he hadn't the patience for any of it.

And he didn't have the patience for his script. The first draft of *A Small Death in Wollongong* was due in Sydney next week, but the laptop lay open on the kitchen table, untouched since he'd checked his e-mail a couple of hours before.

He'd been writing about Aboriginal deaths in custody—with a few car chases and blondes in bikinis thrown in—but he'd lost his edge since they'd moved to the country. The sound of cows mooing was no substitute for police sirens. He was finding it impossible to get a bead on the urban jungle in the country air.

What Damian had said about those hillbillies in the bush had piqued his curiosity. Maybe one of them could be a model for his hero, Blackie Brown.

He got up from his chair and went into the bedroom, taking care where the floor joists had rotted. Heidi had done her best with bits of fabric but nothing could disguise the fact that the room looked like a salvage yard shed during a fire sale. Tea chests and boxes, hurriedly dragged away from a leaking roof in the next room, spilled their contents onto the dusty floorboards. He rummaged about a bit and then found his heavy suede jacket in the one cardboard box that was still tightly sealed. He buttoned it, he found his car keys on a tea chest beside the bed and wandered outside to the front verandah.

'Damian?'

'Yeah, mate?' The builder put his scraper down. Beckett noted the cut muscles of his arms with distaste. He really was a good-looking boy.

'Don't let me distract you, but I'm interested in those Blackfellas you were telling my wife about before.'

'Blackpeters.'

'Blackpeters. Do you know where they live?'

'Why do you want to know?'

'I thought I might give them a visit. They sound inspirational.'

'I wouldn't if I were you, mate.'

'Why not?'

'For starters you're not going to get further than the front gate. They're armed and they don't take kindly to strangers.' He looked critically at Beckett's cord trousers and suede jacket. 'Especially strangers dressed like ponces.'

'Thanks.'

'Just being honest. They'll take one look at you and *pow!* that pretty wife of yours'll be a widow. Come to think of it, maybe I should give you a map.' The white smile lines etched into his tanned skin crinkled. 'They live out past Speculator. We used to go look for them as kids. Sometimes you could follow the trail of animal parts, you know. What they didn't cook they just left for the birds.'

'Speculator you say?' Beckett took his car keys out of his pocket and rattled them.

'Actually, mate, I was wondering if I could knock off now. Need to get more paint stripper anyway.'

'Could I stop you?' Beckett asked.

There weren't many roads out the back of Nullin. The dairy country soon gave way to the dense forest of the national park, and beyond that rose the slopes of the Great Dividing Range and its snowy plateau. Beckett guessed his best option for finding the Blackpeter camp was to take the sealed road west of Speculator and then explore the network of gravel roads that departed from the bitumen. He knew that one of these was signposted for the

Third Eye health resort. He doubted that there'd be a signpost directing him to the Blackpeter family but maybe someone in the village could help him.

Speculator had a permanent population of fifty-five and most of these inhabitants lived over the National Trust-preserved shops and craft galleries that now were the town's main industry. The petrol station was a vintage pump and a bit of a shack at the highway end of the street. The fellow who manned it was possibly twice as old as the pump. He took ten minutes to shuffle from his office to Beckett's car.

'I need some directions,' Beckett said.

The old boy looked like he'd been around long enough to know the way to the Tower of Babel. He scratched his head. 'If it's around here, I reckon I could help.' He didn't so much speak as croak.

'I'm looking for the Blackpeters' place.'

The old man made a sucking sound on his lower lip.

'I have some…business I need to do with them.'

The attendant looked Beckett up and down for a biblical age. 'One of them big city traders are you?'

Any other answer would be too difficult. 'Yes.'

'Don't know why you fellas buy off them. Personally I think there's too many damn possums and wombats around here. But I wouldn't risk my neck goin' up there.'

Beckett looked at his watch. 'I'm late. Can you give me instructions?'

'I wouldn't worry about being late, lad. Blackpeters don't have clocks.' He chuckled and it came out as a thin creak. He bent down and drew a complicated map in the dirt. 'Take the road to the Void.' The map had so many branches it looked like Beckett's own crazy family tree. He tried to memorise every junction. 'Old granite quarry. Some of the rock was shipped to Sydney to build the Harbour Bridge.' He poked at the map again. 'Don't go as far as the Void but veer off here, see?'

'Thanks a lot.'

'I hope you're armed.'

'Just with my wit.'

The first three turns were easy enough to remember, but at the fourth junction he stopped. The choice was between a muddy track veering right or a muddy track veering left. He'd been travelling along some kind of plateau and the forest was denser up here, the floor thick with bracken and a rambling bush like wild blackberry. The tree ferns and ironbarks crowded in overhead.

He did an Eeny Meeny Miny Mo, substituting Blackpeter for blackfella. The 'mo' directed him right. He travelled a slow couple of kilometres along the track, having to stop to clear it of fallen branches. The sound of the forest was hollow, like the sound at the bottom of a pit. A bellbird tinkled deep inside it.

He was discouraged to see a dead wombat on the side of the road. If the Blackpeters were anywhere near here it would have been collected long ago. He slowed down as he passed it and he could see flies buzzing busily. The animal looked whole but who knew what damage the maggots had wreaked underneath.

The man lumbering down the track was only a few metres away when Beckett looked up and saw him. He slammed on the brakes, even though the car was moving only marginally faster than the dead wombat. Beckett could see that he was quite young. He was very tall, with ungainly arms that swung well below his knees and he ambled along in a flat-footed way, with huge, bare feet pointed out and his knees bowed. He was wearing a faded floral shirt, pulled tight across a pigeon chest. His jeans were too short. If I look like Jed Clampett in this hat, Beckett mused, putting a hand to his old straw Panama, then I think I've just discovered Jethro.

The young man didn't appear to be carrying a weapon but it was possible he had something concealed in his belt. Beckett suddenly wished there were something heavier in his glove box than a chammy and a packet of Sherbies. What was in the boot? A tyre jack, a picnic blanket and a fishing rod and tackle he'd never used.

He wound down his window, but kept his foot hovering over the accelerator. The young man didn't approach. He didn't react to the car or Beckett at all. The youth's eyes were focused on the dead wombat. As he got closer to the lifeless animal he gave a little yelp and his hands jerked in an agitated way. The young man dropped to his knees and bent over the creature. He then started howling, a high-pitched keening sound that scared a flock of galahs out of the trees.

Beckett turned off the motor, put on the hand brake and eased out of the car. The young man was sitting on his haunches, holding the wombat now, the dead weight of the heavy animal hooked in his elbows. His arms were spidery, the skin luminously white and marbled with prominent veins, as if made of wax. Beckett was struck by the length of his fingers, each joint twice the length of his own and knobbly like a crustacean's, the nails like small, shell-white carbuncles.

When Beckett gently put a hand on the youth's shoulder the young man turned to him, tears brimming in his milky eyes. The face was also unnaturally long with pixie-point ears hinged high at right angles. Despite this, there was nothing unpleasant about his face. He had the wide-open visage of many country boys, only in his case it appeared as if someone had tugged and stretched it like gum. The boy's shoulders trembled under Beckett's hand.

'It looks like a car hit it.'

'No!' Did that mean he knew the wombat had been killed another way? Or did he simply want Beckett to move back?

He needed to get the boy's trust. 'I'm Beckett,' he ventured. 'What's your name?' But he already knew. Damian had mentioned him. Spaz.

Before the boy could answer, two men appeared at the curve of the track, trailed by a small child of three or four, sex

35

indeterminate. One had a shotgun wedged under his armpit and another hanging from a finger in that hand. The second had his shotgun over his shoulder. They were both considerably shorter than Spaz. They took one look at Beckett and quickened their pace. They ran remarkably fast, given that both were wearing loose blue jeans in danger of falling off their hips. One was tanned and bare-chested despite the mountain chill. The man with the two guns was wearing a vest made out of animal pelts and a confederate cap.

Blackpeters.

That was about all Beckett could make of their sartorial style. He scrambled to his feet and put his hands up to show them he was unarmed. This didn't seem to make any difference. The bare-chested man flipped his gun off his shoulder and cocked it at him. It flashed through Beckett's mind that he should make for the car. He'd left the driver's door open, but it was several metres from where he stood and he feared any quick movement might be taken for aggression.

Spaz howled and leapt to his feet, still clutching the wombat. He stumbled off into the bracken, crashing through the forest until the trees swallowed him up. The bare-chested one raised his shotgun and pellets exploded into the air. Birds screeched. As if he'd heard a starting gun, Beckett ducked his head and raced to the car. Something hard and sharp smashed against his right temple, momentarily stunning him. Instinct got him to the car door and he fell against it, his straw hat flying off. He used the open window to pull himself up and slid into the seat. Without closing the door he powered the ignition and flicked off the handbrake. The confederate cap was heading towards him, one shotgun raised like a club. He used the butt of it to smash at the Volvo's grill. Beckett's first thought was: how the hell am I going to get a replacement part? Then a rock thudded against his windscreen, cracking it.

He floored the accelerator and reversed down the track,

trying to keep the car from sliding into the soft verge. The Blackpeters came after him, hurling abuse with the stones. At least they weren't shooting. But they'd pulled their knives.

Better get out of there.

He spun the Volvo around in a clearing and in the direction of civilisation. The Blackpeters had stopped chasing him. Confederate cap was standing perfectly still, guns through his arms, watching him, like a rabbit he'd allowed to get away.

The child picked up another rock and threw it.

'What on earth happened?' Heidi had just returned from town and was making tea when Beckett staggered through the door, his black hair matted to his forehead and blood on the back of his hand. She completely forgot their earlier tension. 'God, not a car accident?'

He pulled out a vinyl kitchen chair and collapsed into it. 'A small child hit me with a rock.'

'I told you not to steal candy from the kids at the playground.'

'Very funny. This wasn't a kid. It was the devil's spawn.'

'Hold on. I'll clean that wound.' Heidi wet a facecloth and held it against Beckett's temple. 'OK. Now just press on it with your hand.' She went to a cupboard and pulled out a glass bowl. Then she took two eggs and cracked them on the rim. She peeled the fine film of skin from the inside of each eggshell. She removed the facecloth and lay the egg skins across the graze. 'This will heal it with no scarring,' she told him.

'Oh?' He sounded disappointed. 'I would have liked a scar. A record of my first contretemps with the Blackpeters.'

'The Blackpeters? What the hell have you been doing, Beckett?'

He told her.

'Well, that was bloody smart. Damian said they were danger-ous.'

'I was only driving around. I was going to decide when I got up there whether I'd talk to them or not.'

'They decided that, didn't they?'

'The one called Spaz seemed harmless.'

'Harmless enough to skewer native animals and leave them around to upset people.'

'I don't think he killed that platypus you found.'

'How do you know that?'

'I saw him nursing a dead wombat. He's an odd-looking character. Like something out of *Close Encounters of the Third Kind*. Long fingers, amazingly pale skin for a person who's lived in the bush all his life.'

'An albino?'

'No, his hair was dark and kind of long. Not an albino. Something, though. Maybe a genetic defect? The others looked like your normal ratbag.'

'What makes you think he didn't kill my platypus—or that wombat?'

'The way he was holding it. He was crying like a mother over a dead baby. And then he ran off into the bush with it, like he was trying to get it away from his brothers.'

'You're romanticising again, Beck. Maybe he was taking it away to slash its throat.'

'Here's the tragic part,' he said. 'I seem to have lost my hat. It might have fallen off when I got hit.'

'You'll just have to go buy another one.'

'I can't. It's my lucky hat.'

'Beckett, you're not going back there to get it. That's final.'

'I don't intend to. But it means I can't write until I get it back.' He stood up, feeling a fool for pressing egg skins to his temple. 'I'm going to lie down for a while. Coming?'

The look she gave him made him suggest he better not push his luck.

6

The old Masonic Hall was decorated with clusters of black and white balloons and crepe paper streamers taped to the dark wainscoting. The women's committee had been busy decorating the tables with white cloths and stems of white carnation tied to black-painted driftwood. A dance floor had been cleared and a three-piece band in dark-green suits was playing an Air Supply standard. Someone had affixed a mirror-ball to the centre of the panelled ceiling but had not dimmed the lights enough for it to have any effect.

One elderly couple was dancing. Heidi felt overdressed in her beaded sixties sheath, but Beckett looked completely out of place in the old pair of tails he'd dusted off. It was as if he'd stepped off the silver screen into the audience, like a character in a Woody Allen movie. He fancied himself as William Powell, and she didn't have the heart to tell him what he really looked like was a magician at a Rotary Christmas party. She could see that 'black tie' was interpreted here as anything dark, even leather jackets. A few of the older men had dragged out tuxedos and a smattering of younger men, debutantes on arms, looked uncomfortable in rented powder-blue and bottle-green suits that had probably done the rounds of several local weddings.

Their table was occupied by a ruddy man about sixty in a tuxedo that was too tight across the chest and a thin woman some years younger, presumably his wife, in a ruffled turquoise gown and lots of heavy gold costume jewellery on her hands and wrists.

Her hair was a rigid helmet of chestnut and she patted the flipped-up ends unconsciously as Beckett and Heidi approached.

'Beckett Versec.'

'Heidi Go.'

The man took Beckett's outstretched hand but ignored Heidi's. 'Keith Bankston,' he said gruffly.

'Pleased to meet you,' Heidi said. The look he gave her suggested he thought she was some mail-order bride from Thailand.

Beckett offered the woman his hand. She took it and gave him a wry smile. 'I'm Carmel,' she said. 'I hope you don't mind, but I asked for you to be seated at our table when I saw the unfamiliar names. It's so nice to have some *new* people in town.'

Beckett thought he heard a trace of bitterness in her voice. He pulled out a chair for Heidi. 'Let me find the bar. What would you like?'

'Do you think champagne is too much to expect?'

'For forty bucks a ticket? I bet they're serving Dom.'

She made a face. 'Sparkling wine will do. Don't be long. *Please.*'

Carmel shook her head when he asked her if she'd like another drink. Heidi watched him go then placed her evening bag on the table next to her plate, which was inscribed with the logo of the Nullin Golf Club. 'Interesting flower arrangement,' she said to the woman, to make conversation.

Keith Bankston answered instead. 'Margaret Spencer's responsible. She's the *artistic* type. Too artistic for my bloody taste.'

'You don't like artists?' Heidi asked, against her better judgment.

'They're all right in their place.' He looked at her suspiciously. 'You're not one are you?'

'No.' Here goes, she thought. 'I'm a massage therapist.'

Bankston snorted. But the wife looked interested. 'The beauty salon here is a disgrace,' she said in a husky, cultured voice.

'I have to go all the way to Bateman's to get a proper manicure.'

'Who does your hair, then?' Heidi asked, grateful that at least the woman was sounding agreeable.

'Oh, I'm lucky with that. My daughter-in-law Michelle does it. She's retired now she has children. It works out perfectly.'

'She does a nice job.'

'Thank you.' Carmel tapped her long French-polished nails on the table. 'I suppose they have that stupid no-smoking rule again, Keith. You really should do something about it.'

'It's council law.'

'But you *are* the council!'

'I have to let the others win one occasionally.' He turned away from them and surveyed the room, nodding terse greetings.

'When did you arrive?' Carmel asked, taking a small sip of white wine. 'I haven't seen you at any of these things. And I'm sure I would have noticed that handsome husband of yours before.'

'We've been here four months. We live on Milk Mountain.'

'The old cheese factory? I heard that someone had bought that. *Hippies*, they said.'

'We're from Sydney.'

'Don't they have hippies there?' She laughed. 'I'm a newcomer myself, originally from Melbourne. I've been here thirty-five years. Keith's born and bred. In fact, his family used to own your factory, eons ago. You know Nullin Cheese? That's him. That's *us*. Not that I ever understood the dairy industry. I'm a city slicker through and through.'

'Aren't you bored here?'

'I have three children, all still living at home. If you can call our compound a home. And we have a Cessna. I'm allowed to go to Sydney or Melbourne from time to time.'

'How old are your children?'

'Oh, two are married. Charley, our youngest, is twenty-three and his wife Michelle, a local girl, is the hairdresser. Hair *stylist*, sorry. They have two little ones, a baby and a three-year-old. The elder boy's Peter. He's twenty-five. No children yet. His wife Diane works.' She gave a sniff. 'Not that I'm against it. But she doesn't really need to. And Peter needs a lot of maintenance. He's rather highly strung.' She turned in her chair and looked around the room. A pert brunette in a figure-hugging white jersey gown was standing with a young man in a black tuxedo. They were by far the most attractive young couple in the room. 'There she is. That's my youngest, Elisabeth. It's her coming out. Why we're here. You wouldn't catch me dead otherwise.'

'She's lovely.'

'Yes, she is.'

'What do your sons do?' Heidi asked.

'They work for me,' Keith interrupted. He picked up his glass of beer and downed half of it. 'It's good to keep it all in the family.'

'Oh, we do that,' said Carmel cryptically. She looked up. 'Here's your delightful husband.'

Beckett put two glass cups down on the table. 'The Pimm's Cup is delicious,' he said to his wife. 'Try it. And just think, it's got virtually no alcohol in it.'

'What do you do…may I call you Beckett?' Carmel asked when he was seated.

'I'm a screenwriter.'

'How interesting! Have you written anything I've seen?'

'Not unless you like trash.'

'He's being modest, ' Heidi interrupted. 'He got a co-writer credit on *Dirt Cheap*. Did you see it?'

'Not if it was any good. The program at the Nullin Regal leaves a lot to be desired.'

'I assure you it wasn't any good,' said Beckett.

'Where on earth did you find a *humble* man?' Carmel asked.

'Over a butcher's shop,' Heidi replied.

'Oh, here are the others,' Carmel said, as a group of people approached the table. She leant towards Beckett and whispered, 'Dull, all of them. *Poms*. I think Keith got a package deal.'

'Hi Mummy.' Elisabeth Bankston put her hands on her mother's shoulder and kissed her on the top of the head. Heidi noticed she had burgundy tips through her pixie-cut hair. The young man who was her partner shook hands easily with Keith.

Carmel made the introductions. 'This is our daughter, Elisabeth, and our friend Jack Harding, who is a rising star at Nullin Cheese.'

Jack shook Heidi's hand first and then Beckett's. Beckett cast her a look that said 'very smooth'.

He was about ten years older than Elisabeth, which would put him in his late twenties. He looked more handsome from a distance, possibly because of his relaxed way of holding himself and the careful way his sandy hair spiked on top, in trendy soccer-player fashion. On closer scrutiny, there was not much structure to his face and in sun it would probably erupt in pale freckles. His eyelashes were parchment-coloured and gave him a curious, naked look. But Heidi liked the sparkle in his eyes, although it crossed her mind it may have just been the reflection of the mirrored ball churning above them.

'Come and sit next to me, Jack.' Carmel patted the seat between herself and Heidi.

Elisabeth didn't seem to mind that her mother was annexing her date. Beckett started to get up to give the young woman a seat, but she waved him down. 'Thanks but I've got to go to the loo. Too much excitement.' She said this with an arch of a perfectly formed eyebrow, meaning exactly the opposite. Heidi smiled and Elisabeth caught it. She put a hand on Heidi's shoulder. 'I really like your dress.'

'Nullin op shop,' Heidi said.

'God, that's my favourite place! I get all my clothes there.' She bent and whispered in Heidi's ear. 'Mummy's thoroughly disgusted, of course.'

They all watched her leave, everyone's eyes on the way her gown dipped to the tailbone. That frock, at least, wasn't bought for a few dollars in a charity shop.

'I haven't seen you at one of these things before.' Jack leaned over and whispered in Heidi's ear. He smelled of something bracing, like verbena.

'You mean you have to go to this sort of thing *often*?' she whispered back, in mock-horror.

'Only when it's work,' he said. 'Keith snaps his fingers and we all jump.' He didn't seem to care whether Keith heard or not.

'What do you do at the cheese factory?'

'Bugger all. A lot of travel on expense accounts. They pay me a shitload for it.'

'Nice work if you can get it.'

'Oh, the Bankstons are *very* nice to me,' he said.

'Elisabeth's a lovely girl.'

'She's better than the rest of them. You should meet her brothers.'

'Oh? What are they like?'

'Jealous.'

She wasn't sure what he meant. She caught Carmel's eye, who had been watching them with a hungry look. The older woman had expectations for Jack beyond the cheese factory. For herself or her daughter? Heidi wondered.

Carmel put a hand on Jack's arm. 'I feel like dancing,' she said.

Jack nodded. It was a command.

After a few drinks, Beckett took to the dance floor like a veteran, his ambition to dance with all the women abandoned by partners who had gone off to hang around the bar.

Heidi watched his gyrations with an old woman on a walking frame. She then excused herself from a clutch of Nullin Cheese executive wives comparing notes on Queensland holiday resorts and went in urgent search of the toilets.

A sign led her to a line of debutantes and their mothers fluffing their skirts and applying lipstick in hand mirrors. She sighed at the inevitable long wait. On the other hand, the men's room was sure to be underutilised, despite the copious amounts of alcohol being downed at the bar. She wandered down the hallway looking for it.

The dusty floorboards of the old hall were scattered with discarded plastic cups and limp crepe paper streamers. A boy in a lavender shirt and a girl in a matching dress, both of whom looked to be no more than thirteen, locked braces under a plaque honouring past Worshipful Masters. A young man with a thick neck—probably a member of the local rugby team—came around a corner zipping up his trousers.

Heidi turned the same corner and came across another hallway lined in plaques. There was no one in sight, but a door to the right looked promising. She waited a moment to see if anyone came out. A floorboard creaked, but no one appeared. Thinking she was safe, she turned the knob and slid her head and shoulders through the doorway, ready to make an apologetic exit if needed. But the edge of the door sent something crashing and she instinctively stepped into the room to pick it up.

It was only then she realised she wasn't in a bathroom at all, but in a storeroom or broom cupboard, dimly lit by the hallway light. At the same time she became aware she was not alone. In a dark corner she could make out the shape of a man's back, his face partially turned towards her. Her first thought was that he was a janitor lifting boxes.

'Oops, sorry,' she said.

But then she saw the legs, slender and tipped in white spike heels, that were wrapped around his waist. He began to say something, but the woman with him grasped his head in her hands and turned it roughly back towards her. She pulled herself more tightly to him and urged him back into her.

Elisabeth Bankston smiled at Heidi as she held her partner's bleached head and rode his thrusts. 'You won't tell Mummy, will you,' she whispered between gasps.

It wasn't a question.

Heidi drove home while Beckett lolled on the seat beside her. 'Someone spiked my twelfth Pimm's Cup,' he moaned.

'Serves you right. If you ever get an inkling to play bingo at the Leagues Club, count me out. There's only so much yobbo culture I can take. Did you see the way those debutantes had to curtsy? It's positively medieval.'

'Bingo's not yobbo.'

'You know what I mean.'

'I saw that Carmel woman take your number. So the night wasn't a complete wash-out.'

'I'm going to treat her in the morning. Apparently she always gets a terrible headache after those things. I can understand that.'

'Especially married to that prick.'

'Hmmm. I thought he was creepy.'

'All rich, provincial people are creepy. But you can charge them seventy dollars an hour.'

'What do you think of the daughter?' Heidi asked.

'Cute and bubbly.'

'I thought so too,' she said. 'But guess who I found in the broom cupboard with her legs wrapped around a young man?'

'And you're going to tell me the young man wasn't rising star Jack?'

'Do you always know the end of the story?'

'Darling, I'm a writer. It's my job.'

7

Carmel Bankston had been accurate in describing her home as a 'compound'. It sat on a prime piece of oceanfront property bordering the golf course, its roadside perimeter shielded by Norfolk pines and a high hardwood fence. The house didn't come into sight for another two or three minutes and even then she had to negotiate a long, curving slope to reach what looked like a parking area, where a white BMW was haphazardly abandoned next to a beaten-up Commodore. But all along the route she had been watched by several pairs of eyes—an old gardener riding a mower, a young woman dead-heading roses, a dark-skinned maid in a pale-blue coverall carrying a bundle of linen and a dour middle-aged woman who stopped pushing a young child on a plastic swing and stared.

Heidi parked and considered whether to knock on the door next to a triple garage or to investigate a neat side path that rambled through the garden and led, she assumed, to the ocean-side of the house. The house, from the back, was a two-storey brown brick structure perhaps of seventies vintage, yet across the gravel courtyard beyond the garage she could see an old stable and, further still, a white-painted weatherboard cottage that looked at least one hundred years old.

She took the path, manoeuvring her fold-up massage table so that it wouldn't crush the perfect flowerbeds that lined the passage. Periodically, she would pass under a trellis of meaty vine or have to step around a stumpy azalea or hydrangea bush, pruned back now that it was autumn. Only a manicured lawn and a copse of Norfolk pines stood between the house and the ocean. Where other parts of the coast were rocky cliffs, the land here ran down to a sandy cove that made a perfect natural swimming hole. A heated pool was set into the lawn. She could see the upturned lounge chairs, stripped of their cushions, and the steam shimmering on the surface of the water.

The path led to a long, wide flagstone verandah set with Italian smoked perspex and chrome outdoor furniture, the kind that was expensive back in the eighties and would be again when the interior design mavens rediscovered its dubious charm. Above the front door was a wooden plaque with the words 'the nineteenth hole' burnt in script. The door itself was ornately carved in a Spanish style and gated with an iron flyscreen. Heidi pressed a button and she could hear the chimes play a few bars of 'Song of Joy'.

All hell broke loose. Inside the house she could hear frantic dogs barking. Something large thudded against the door and shook the frame. Adding to the cacophony was a baby crying, a woman's voice calling something indistinct and the clatter of heels on a hard floor.

The door swung open. Through the screen, a young woman stood with a red-faced baby on her hip. Two elegant black dogs jumped at the wire, snarling. Dobermans. 'Bobby! Suzy!' the girl shouted. 'Heel!' The dogs ignored her. 'Don't worry,' she said to Heidi, opening the screen door. 'They won't bite you. Not while I'm here, at least.'

Heidi warily stepped through the door, keeping her table in front as a shield. The wire door closed behind her. The dogs sniffed her feet and one cold nose travelled up under the hem of her uniform, but nothing they found interested them and they wandered away. The baby was mewling now, its damp hair stuck to the hot forehead in ginger ringlets. It wore a navy blue sailor's top over powder-blue towelling leggings. The girl shifted the child to her other hip. 'I'm Michelle,' she said.

Heidi would have assumed she was the babysitter if Carmel hadn't mentioned that her youngest son—Charley?—was married to a Michelle. Michelle who did Carmel's hair with such lavish use of spray. The girl wore her own shortish blonde hair pulled back into a high ponytail, the strands that fell out around her neck darker by several shades. She showed off her deep tan in a halter top and low-slung cut-off denim shorts, clearly impervious to the chill morning air. A stud gleamed in her navel. Heidi tried to take her in without staring. Michelle had the sort of cute that would only last a few years. She wouldn't become interesting until she was forced to do some heavy reinvention.

Michelle kissed the top of the baby's head. 'This is little Keith.'

An unfashionable name for a modern baby, but no doubt grandpa was flattered and the inheritance secured, Heidi thought. Then: damn that Beckett for making me so cynical. 'You've got a lovely house,' she lied. The entrance hall gave on to a large sitting room with hard terrazzo floors, brass-and-glass coffee tables, a red marble fireplace, red, white and lime chintz furniture with matching drapes and a wading-pool sized crystal chandelier that hung from the centre of a too-low ceiling. Expensively claustrophobic and designed to display every cent spent.

Michelle frowned. 'Well, it's not really mine. Charley and me and little Keith and Rebecca live in the white house up the hill. It's nice and cosy out there. Pete and Diane've got the stable—you saw it? Pete's kind of artistic and he's got a studio in it.'

'Keith said Charley works at the cheese factory.'

'Yeah. He's in marketing. Pete develops all the new products.'

'He must be creative then.'

She shrugged. 'Pete wanted to go to art school in Sydney but big Keith wouldn't let him after...' She bit her lip and changed the subject. The baby was pulling at the strings of her top. 'I'll go and see if Carmel...Mrs Bankston...is ready to receive you. Would you like to take a seat?' She gestured at a wing-backed chair and clattered off down the terrazzo hallway. Heidi noticed she was wearing mules with four-inch heels. Heidi leaned her table against the chair and strolled over to the marble fireplace where a dozen or more framed photographs crowded on the mantel. There was a formal picture of the baby Keith. A wedding photograph of Keith and Carmel. She looked very chic in a white pillbox hat and satin coat. Her hairdo hadn't changed in thirty years. Next to that was an older wedding portrait, probably Keith's parents, judging by the woman's similarity to him under her halo of roses. Her bridesmaid stood beside her carrying a basket of lilies. The groom was beefy in a tight double-breasted suit. His best man wore a military uniform she didn't recognise and sported a half-beard, the kind that Scandinavian men wore.

In another picture she recognised Elisabeth in school uniform, noting the way she'd hiked her gym slip up to reveal a stretch of thigh. Heidi had done the very same thing at school. There was a photograph of the three children splashing about in a swimming pool. In another, two young men posed under a Nullin Cheese sign: Peter and Charley. Peter was tall and dark with his mother's fine features. Charley was ruddy and robust, a good six centimetres shorter. She thought she'd seen Charley around, but he had the kind of face that propped up the bar at most pubs. Peter was more pensive, sullen even, unhappy to be posed like that, or there at the factory. You couldn't imagine they were brothers. Elisabeth resembled Peter, making Charley look all the less like a sibling.

Heidi put the frame down next to a photograph of Charley standing awkwardly beside Michelle, who was wearing an ante-bellum-style bridal gown, with too much makeup and a garland of white flowers ringing a teased-up bump of hair. Next to it stood a similar frame of Peter with a tense, slender brunette in a red suit. Diane. She looked older than Peter. Considering the bouncy Michelle and the stern Diane, it seemed as if the boys had married female versions of themselves.

She heard Michelle clattering back down the hall. 'Carmel can see you now. Do you need help with that thing?' She pointed to the table.

'It's fine.' Heidi followed her. At the end of the hall, the floor became thickly carpeted in salmon-pink. She could glimpse a rumpus room with a pool table.

Michelle turned up a flight of stairs. 'Carmel's bedroom is up here. It's nice and private.' She hesitated for a minute. 'I shouldn't be saying this, but Carmel's a bit upset today. I told you she was sick, but she's not really. It's just a family thing. But, you can help headaches, right?'

'The physical symptoms, yes.'

Carmel's bedroom was the second door along a narrow hallway decorated with a set of dreamy watercolours of the sea. 'Pete did those when he was a kid,' Michelle said. 'Just knock, she's expecting you.'

Carmel's voice was loud and clear. 'Come in.'

She was sitting on the edge of the bed in a housecoat made of patterned Thai silk and wearing a towelling turban. She was holding the receiver of a bedside phone to her ear when Heidi entered.

She waved a hand. 'Set up wherever you like.'

'Thanks.' Heidi started unfolding her table at the end of the bed. The room was the same pink as the carpet, with lavender and white touches. Everything in sight was ruffled, padded or quilted. The bed was a double with a shiny new brass bedhead and a cluster of frilled pillows and matching cushions piled at one end. Heidi couldn't imagine the gruff Keith Bankston sharing this bed and she knew instantly that he didn't.

Carmel sighed into the phone. '*There* you are. Didn't I tell you to stay by the phone? All right, I accept that. But please *try*. I'm having a massage now and don't wish to be disturbed. But if she calls, you'll put her on immediately, won't you?' She hung up.

Heidi placed a towel on the table. Carmel stood up. 'I'll just disappear into the bathroom for a minute,' she said. 'If you need to put your oils somewhere, I prefer if you'd use that dresser. Just move the pictures.'

There were three photos on the dresser. In the largest the Bankston children were making a sandcastle on the beach. They were all less than ten, she guessed. Peter was concentrating hard on unmoulding a bucket. Charley was balancing a scoop of sand on a plastic spade. Elisabeth, only a baby, was sitting in the dug-out moat with a bonnet on her head and what looked like a piece of kelp hanging from her mouth. It was one of those photographs possessed by every family, of a moment of perfect childhood contentment, fleeting in real time but preserved by the picture taker's haphazard luck.

As she put it down, the image shifted in its frame. One end was ragged as if part of it had been torn. She shook the frame to conceal the edge again and started laying out her bottles of oil.

'Sweet, weren't they?' Carmel said from the bathroom door.

Heidi turned around. Carmel was stark naked, except for the turban. Her lithe body was in excellent shape. Only a slight softening of the arms and a small belly distinguished her from a woman twenty years younger. 'I assume you want me without my clothes on.'

'That's great.' Heidi disguised her surprise. Her clients were usually more modest. 'Would you like to lie on your stomach?'

Carmel, a veteran sybarite, knew precisely where to lie. Heidi draped a towel over her taut buttocks. 'You've still got that headache?'

'It comes and goes. Elisabeth didn't come home last night and I'm worried sick. She's gone off with some of her school friends from the ball but usually she calls us. Her mobile's not answering. We're ringing around now. I could strangle her.'

Heidi was thinking about Elisabeth's liaison with the boy in the broom cupboard. She decided not to say anything. Elisabeth might turn up at any moment. Besides, it wasn't really her business, despite how rattled Carmel seemed. 'Has she done it before?' she asked.

'Gone off? Oh, sometimes. The young ones like to go down to the beach and hang out in summer.'

'But it's cold now.'

'I know. She'll catch her death in that gown. She wouldn't take a coat.'

'Does Jack know where she is?'

'Jack?'

'Isn't he her boyfriend?'

'Goodness no! She doesn't have a boyfriend. Jack's like a brother.'

'A pretty girl like that doesn't have a boyfriend?'

'She's a good girl.'

Heidi hardly thought that having a boyfriend made an eighteen-year-old a bad girl, but she let it go. She poured some oil into the palm of her hand. 'I'm going to add some peppermint to the oil I use to help shift that headache and I'll mix in some neroli and lavender to help you relax. Do you mind your feet being touched? I think some reflexology would do you the world of good.'

'Go to town. I've been pummelled by experts from Beijing to Barbados.'

Heidi pulled the towel so that it covered Carmel's back. She placed her right hand on Carmel's left shoulder blade and her left on Carmel's right hip and gently pushed them apart. Then she walked around the table and did the reverse. She folded the towel back down again and poured more oil into her hands. Standing at Carmel's head she started to stroke the whole back.

'God, I've needed this,' Carmel said. 'I don't have time to fly to Melbourne or Sydney every week. And the local chiropractor, who's an idiot by the way, insists on doing those terrible cracking things to my neck. There's that health farm out the back of Speculator but its far too hippie for my tastes. They drip hot oil on your third eye, for God's sake.'

'That's maybe going a little too far,' Heidi agreed. 'But there are lots of things you can do to help if you're feeling stressed. When I get a headache I mix two tablespoons of apple cider vinegar with two teaspoons of honey in a glass of water. It doesn't taste as bad as it sounds. My grandmother used to tie a handkerchief dipped in vinegar around her head, close to the eyebrows. She swore it worked. I tried it once.'

'And did it?'

'No.'

Carmel laughed and relaxed as Heidi criss-crossed her hands down her back. 'I don't know what feels better, the massage or the decent company. I never see the boys and I'm stuck with that airhead Michelle and the help all day.'

'She seems very devoted to Charley.'

'She should be. He was quite a catch for a girl like that.'

'What about your other daughter-in-law, Diane? What does she do?'

'She does her best to make sure the prices of property around here go through the roof. She's a pain in the neck. Pete would never have met her if Keith hadn't given him responsibility for selling off one of our properties. She made herself a handy commission all right.'

Heidi leaned over Carmel's body and dragged her thumbs from under the ribcage to the base of her neck. That will fix your pain in the neck, she thought. 'You must have lots of friends in town, though?'

'If you like women who play golf and talk about their grandchildren all the time.' Carmel was quiet while Heidi stroked the back of her legs. 'You know, I'm envious of Elisabeth. She can get married and have a career as well. It's expected now. Keith dragged me out of first-year uni to bring me up here. I was doing law. I probably would have been good at it. I should have stuck to my guns. But I fell in love. And this beautiful place was so seductive. I could have done a correspondence course. We had enough money for anything. But I wanted babies, silly me.'

'What does Elisabeth want to do?'

'She says she wants to be a fashion designer. Keith wanted her in the family business, in marketing, but she just plain refused. And he was soft on her because she was a girl. Ironic, isn't it?' Carmel shifted her hips and Heidi felt her back tense again. 'She gets everything she wants out of her father. So where *is* she?'

8

Heidi drove along the highway experiencing new pangs of guilt about not telling Carmel about Elisabeth. The silly girl had obviously gone off with this boy for the night and was now delaying her return home, wondering how to do it gracefully and minimise her mother's anger.

But Elisabeth didn't seem that silly. She'd seemed composed, fully in control. Even a little bit triumphant. She'd asked Heidi not to tell her mother and she'd been certain Heidi would not.

She slowed down as she drove past the spot where she'd been forced off the road a couple of days before. She shivered as she thought of the ice-cold water, the sound of scraping on stone, blood on fur, the anxious yelp of the heeler going past on a ute. She cast a quick glance at the rainforest gully. Brendan had been right. The animal's killer had been watching her. She had felt it at the time and denied it. Was it really that boy Spaz or some other pervert?

She almost missed the two hitchhikers sitting on a log at the bottom of the hill. She drove past them and pulled up. They picked up their string bags and came running.

'Where are you going?' she asked as she stretched to wind down the passenger's side window.

'Anywhere south along the highway will do,' said the female, leaning in. She was a small, pale girl of about nineteen or twenty, dressed in a vintage slip over army pants and plastic boots, her hair a Medusa's nest of small braids and rainbow-coloured ribbons. The hair was rainbow-coloured, too, in careless patches of lime, hot pink, crimson and blue. She had a stud in her nose and three rings through her left eyebrow.

Her companion was a few years older Heidi thought, although this was difficult to ascertain, due to the fact that his eyes were obscured by tobacco-coloured dreadlocks, bleached at the ends, which straggled to his shoulders. He was wearing a khaki shirt with the sleeves cut out and a mud-print sarong. What she could see of his skin beneath a maze of inky tattoos was powdery white. She wondered how these people kept so pale under the fierce, ozone-depleted sky. A silver pin was threaded under his bottom lip, like the tribal decoration of a primitive witch doctor. It must have been pretty tricky giving him a kiss.

'OK, hop in,' Heidi said.

The girl scrambled happily into the back. Heidi was surprised that her male companion took the front passenger's seat. His manner was too proprietorial for her liking. But he sat quietly, his hands on his knees. The arm facing her was a labyrinth of gothic lettering and latticework.

'This is great,' the girl said as they set off, leaning over the back seat and waving expansively. Heidi could see that her hands were decorated in the kind of lacy henna design that had been a passing fad in Sydney several years ago.

'We usually have to walk back,' the girl explained. 'The truck drivers give us lifts, but the locals are mean bastards.'

'How far is the walk?'

'From Nullin? Ten kilometres maybe.'

'Do you have to come in often?'

'We take it in turns. We grow most of our own stuff. But we need to get flour and seeds, that sort of thing, from the health food store. At least this dump has one.'

'It's not a dump. It's beautiful.'

'Well, the nature is beautiful. But the human beings around here are pretty ugly. You ever had anything to do with those bastards who go out on the fishing boats? They're, like, neanderthal. It's all about greed.'

'The greed of the individual is the greed of the system,' the young man intoned darkly. Heidi could detect a slight accent that she couldn't place. She looked sideways at him. He was watching the road with a slight smile on his lips. Then he turned his head slowly and stared at her. It was disconcerting not to see his eyes. She gripped the steering wheel tighter and concentrated on the road.

When they hit the highway, Heidi cranked her window down. The couple smelled unctuously sweet, a scent she could only describe as 'purple'. She always resented being invaded by other people's fragrances. She had even said so to perfumed women in city elevators.

'Do you mind if we smoke?' the girl asked. Heidi could hear her rustling around in her string bag.

'Actually, I do,' Heidi said. She wouldn't let Beckett smoke in enclosed spaces. She wasn't going to tolerate it from two strangers. 'I don't support Big Tobacco.'

'Fine.' The girl stopped rustling. Then, after a pause, 'What's your name?'

'Heidi.'

'Pleased to meet you. I'm Sara. Without an "h".'

'Hi Sara.'

'He's Klas.'

'Klas? Where are you from?'

'He's from Sweden. He met a few of our family at the IMF demo in Melbourne and stayed.'

'Do you like Australia, Klas?'

'It's the end of the world.' There was admiration in his voice.

'You're not from round here.' Sara said, 'I can tell.'

'I'm from Sydney.'

'Is that a massage table in the back?'

Heidi nodded.

'What kind do you give?'

'A mixture of Swedish, shiatsu, reiki. Aromatherapy.'

'Cool. We get rolfed every week. Martin's really great at it. He's from Taos. Have you been doing massages for long?'

'About five years. But only full-time for four months. I was an actor before. Well, for a few weeks of every year anyway, when I could get work.'

'But you're so pretty. Why didn't you work all the time?'

'There's the question of my slanty eyes. Some prick of a producer once told me I'd be better off in a rock band with my looks. The brotherhood of music is a little more tolerant than the theatre.'

'We don't go to the theatre or watch movies. It's white man's entertainment.'

'I can think of quite a few people with very dark skin who are making millions out of entertainment.'

'Yes, but in the end they have to invest their money with corporations owned by white men. And those white men are busy screwing the developing countries where the black people came from in the first place.'

'I think you're being a bit simplistic.'

'Well, I'm not the best person to speak to. Martin knows everything. He's written a *book*.'

They were quiet for a while. The highway was dense with trucks. Heidi thought again about her accident. Then she remembered something Brendan had said about the Gondwana clan.

'Actually, I want to ask you something,' Heidi said. 'I heard that someone from your...group found a dead echidna the other day.'

'That was us!' Sara put her elbows on the back of Heidi's seat. 'It was *awful*.'

'Where did you find it?'

'At the bottom of the track leading to our camp. Klas and I had gone down to check out the crop and someone had just dumped it on the track, where we couldn't miss it. The poor thing! It had been killed by a spear or something.'

'Do you have any idea who did it?'

'Someone from the town who hates us,' Klas said.

'But do you really think it was directed at you? I found an animal, too. A platypus, stabbed the same way. Just back there a bit, near the creek.'

'You did? How horrible! We took ours to the Parks and Wildlife.'

'What did they say?'

'They said it looked like a trapper had killed it. Someone who knew how to do it. It's not easy catching an echidna. They're rare. And they have all those spines. Look—you can drop us here if you want. This road will take us where we're going.'

'I can take you. It's not far out of my way.'

'If you want. Turn off here. The road gets really shitty a kilometre or so in.'

They crossed a creek and then followed it for a few kilometres. There'd been a drenching of rain the night before and the forest smelled sweetly of sassafras, rough-barked apple and varieties of tangy eucalypt. One of the gums, she knew, was called the Bundy eucalypt. A magnificent tree with the name of a serial killer. They passed a track covered in tan bark. A bunch of leaves, like a wreath, was nailed to a tree. 'Stop here,' Sara said.

'I can drive in.'

'Look,' Sara said. 'We're not supposed to show anyone our camp, OK? We hardly know you.'

Heidi was slightly hurt. 'I'm not going to tell anyone.'

'It's the rules,' Klas said.

'Suit yourself.' Heidi pulled over.

Sara jumped out and slammed the door. 'Thanks! See you round!'

Klas gestured farewell and got out.

Sara popped her rainbow-coloured braids through Heidi's

window. 'Say, if you need any pot, just let Klas or me know next time you see us. We deliver.'

Heidi watched them traipse along the track until the forest swallowed them up. She stared at the point where they disappeared, tempted to follow. It was not that she was particularly attracted to them; the girl was too much of a chatterbox, the young man truly unpleasant. She thought of the way he sat staring ahead with that faint smile on his lips, as if entirely comfortable with being chauffeured around, despite his anti-capitalist doggerel. A trust-fund kid probably. At the same time as he repelled her, she felt something about him draw her in, the seduction of the half known, the need to complete a story she always felt when people closed down on her.

Maybe her urge to follow was the intoxication of the bush, the spicy scent of rotten leaves that filled her senses and, underneath that, just beyond her recognition, the whiff of things animal and newly dead.

9

Heidi thought the way back to the highway would be straightforward. But she was now so far off the main road that she hadn't even heard another car in thirty minutes.

She reversed down the rocky track and took the other fork. The road was rutted and the suspension on the Kingswood almost nonexistent. Her teeth rattled in her head as she drove. She wished her backside were better padded. The car was making strange groaning noises as the road gradually ascended to the top of the mountain. She thought maybe there would be a ridge up here and she could see the lay of the land. But she worried most about getting stranded. If the Kingswood gave up the ghost—now, after all these years of faithful service—she'd have to walk back to Speculator. That is, if she could find the way. She had no water, no phone, no means to judge direction unless she found the creek. It would be a miracle if she stumbled upon a friendly farmer. It was more likely she'd run into an unfriendly Blackpeter, given Beckett's experience. The thought of it made her armpits go clammy and the sweat rise from her pores.

She was getting flustered. Calm down, she told herself, all you need to do is get to the top of the hill and find your bearings. Sure enough, as the rise levelled out, the gravel track made a crossroads with a bitumen road. It was barely narrow enough for two cars to pass and its edges were crumbling into the sandy mountain soil but it looked like it led somewhere. She turned down it.

The bitumen road did indeed go somewhere.

Heidi groaned as she sat behind the wheel, looking down over an abandoned granite quarry. The road had petered out into a muddy parking area about ten metres above the vast, scoured hole in the ground. The bush had been cleared here and also at the top of the other side of the quarry, about half a kilometre away, where a road had been cut into the side of the rock face for trucks.

Way down in the pit of it she could see a jumble of timber and wire, a workman's shack or an outdoor dunny crumbled in on itself. Dark birds circled overhead, lured in search of carrion by the jagged shapes the shattered timber made. The only other living creature she could see was some kind of tall heron, picking its way through the pools of muddy water. She shivered.

She drove forward to get a swing at turning and her attention was caught by a fluttering in the quarry. At first she thought it was a bush turkey ruffling its feathers, or a wounded bird. She engaged the car's handbrake and stepped out cautiously. The wind was stronger up here. She wished she were wearing more than her uniform and cardigan. Her Birkenstocks sunk into a ridge of mud, a tyre track, the wet soil oozing in under her heels. She cursed under her breath, not to frighten the birds.

She crept close to the edge, where the topsoil was crumbly. She could now see that there was a walking track cut into the face of the stone. Halfway down the cutting, stuck on an old tree root, its fringe ruffling nonchalantly in the breeze, was Beckett's straw hat.

'Bastard!' she said to no one, not knowing whether to be absurdly angry with the hat itself or pleased that she had found it. She started down the slippery path to retrieve it, keeping her centre of gravity low and clinging to bracken to aid her descent. She remembered that the locals called the quarry the Nullin Void. Void was a good name for it, she thought.

She slid dangerously a couple of times and scraped the side of one leg on a sharp rock, but it only took a few moments to reach the hat. 'Yes!' she said as she unhooked it from the root. Then she stood, which was a mistake. Vertigo. She was still far enough from the bottom for any fall to be perilous. There was nothing much to cling to here, a few straggly branches grew straight out of the stone yet she doubted they'd be strong enough to hold anyone. She sat down again, feeling the wet through her thin skirt. Rest a moment, she thought. The climb back up was going to be worse.

A flash of something sparkling down below caught her eye. From where she was sitting, she could see the silvery beak of the heron about fifty metres away. A flutter of wings and she realised the heron had strayed to a pool of water across the quarry. What was she looking at then? And what was attracting the attention of the crows? She was staring at something larger than a heron and peculiarly static. It appeared to be a large, furry animal poking a long stick in the ground. A bear? But that was bizarre. There weren't any bears around here. And what kind of bear, outside of a carnival, walks with a stick?

Suddenly, the wind dropped. Heidi was aware she was holding her breath. There was something very wrong.

She tossed Beckett's hat back up towards the top of the path. It did a graceful boomerang and then dropped into the mud. She cursed. Keeping low, she scrambled down the path, grabbing roots and branches where she could. She felt vulnerable and exposed.

At the bottom, water had accumulated in a shallow pool—when she jumped in, it went past her ankles. She didn't think about what was in the bottom as she waded through. It dried up after a few metres and she was able to sprint the rest of the way, muddy skirt flapping around her knees, the soggy suede of her sandals rubbing the skin off her feet.

As she staggered towards the creature, her eyes took in the ghastly picture first, but her brain was several seconds behind. She stopped before it, damp and frozen, wishing she could do something, knowing there was nothing to do.

She knew the hair, crimson-tipped.

'Oh, God, Elisabeth,' she finally said. 'How did you get down here?'

10

Heidi crouched on her heels a few metres from the teenager, hugging her knees to her chest. It was damp down in the quarry, still except for the circling of birds overhead, magpies and crows attracted by the smell of blood. She picked up a rock and threw it at them, but they continued to circle. She could do nothing, either, about the flies that had gathered at the corners of the girl's eyelids, in her nostrils, inside the awful wound at her throat.

All around her, she sensed that smaller creatures were waiting their turn, the worms squirming under the soil, the beetles scratching among the rocks, waiting for the skin to fall off the bones, the bones, stripped of connecting tissue, to bleach and crumble, what was human to turn to soup for a putrid autumn feast. The earth seemed to be buzzing with anticipation. But Heidi was determined to deny them their meal. She sat on her haunches in a puddle, throwing sticks and gravel at predators, alert for the sounds of larger animals come to feast. Like a Roman guard at the Crucifixion, she thought.

Heidi forced herself to look at Elisabeth. The girl's body, wrapped in a fur coat, had been lashed to a timber frame, a few old planks of wood dragged from the crumbling outhouse and arranged roughly into an A shape. The teenager's arms had been twisted behind her through the triangle of the A, the dead weight of the body supported by leather cords pulled tightly across her chest and through the frame, as if she were a hunter's kill tied to a roof rack. Her head lolled to the side in defeat. The hands flapped free like cold little fish. Her marbled legs, which Heidi had last seen wrapped around a virile young man, dangled above the ground, the bare feet tipped, pathetically, with sparkle nailpolish as blue as her skin.

She looked like she was dancing on points. At first this made no sense to Heidi. Although she was small, the girl's dead weight should have been too great for the leather straps and frame to support her. Something helped hold her off the ground. And then Heidi saw.

Elisabeth had been impaled on a long spear, the lethal flint of it forced through her body until the tip of it emerged from her throat, where it had torn the delicate skin in a vertical eruption. The other end of the spear sprang from the pool of muddy water at her feet. The straps and frame had been devised so that her skewered body stayed upright, for what sick purpose Heidi didn't know. She sat back in the mud, the horror of what she was looking at seizing her whole body in a tempestuous rattle. She gave in to the trembling and turned her head away to be sick.

It took her many minutes before she could turn back. Some of the flies that crawled over the wound on Elisabeth's throat came at Heidi and she swatted them away in disgust. There was another odd thing about the body. There was hardly any blood. She would have expected rivers of it, running down the poor girl's legs...

And something else. The fur coat was thick and bristly, its leather buttons done up from hem to breastbone to conceal the girl's body. It was a cheap and ugly thing, not mink, certainly not Elisabeth's. What had Carmel said? Elisabeth refused to wear a coat to the ball.

The murderer had violated Elisabeth unspeakably—and yet he had taken the trouble to do her buttons up, to preserve her modesty. And then he had covered her in fur.

Heidi thought of the dead platypus and started shaking again. She felt the static rise on the back of her neck. Then self-preservation kicked in. She swung around and scanned the rock face. The killer had lured Elisabeth there but he had no need to go to so much trouble for Heidi. She had brought herself there, a sitting duck.

She quickly picked up a rock and put it in her pocket. Then she scrambled across the pit, estimating it would take a good ten minutes before she reached her car. She prayed he wasn't crouched in the scrub above, waiting for her.

She heard a cry and turned. It was only a circling crow, triumphant that she had at last relinquished her post.

She couldn't remember the rest of the climb back up the cutting or how she found her way back to the highway, but instinct and fear had driven her. She managed to pull over by the side of the road and flag down a driver with a mobile phone. The woman, Oona Lewis, the proprietor of a bed and breakfast outside Speculator, also happened to be the sister-in-law of the Nullin police superintendent, Stan Lewis.

Heidi refused the offer of a hot, sweet cup of tea back at the house, assuring Oona she was driving straight home. But as soon as the Camry rounded the bend back to Speculator, Heidi pressed a trembling foot down on the Kingswood's accelerator and took the road back to the Void.

Superintendent Stan Lewis looked remarkably unhealthy for a man who'd lived most of his life enjoying the benefits of sea air and copious sunshine. Scrawny, with a hard nut of a stomach under a concave chest, he had the sour expression of a jockey whose mount had pulled up short in the Melbourne Cup. His multicoloured knitwear supported the impression. He strode toward Heidi like he still had the whip in his hand.

'Who is this?' he demanded when he saw Heidi crouched in front of Elisabeth's body. Three uniformed officers stood behind him. One of them was Brendan Barton, in a wide-brimmed hat.

She heard him mutter something under his breath.

'I found her,' Heidi said, standing uncertainly, a shard of timber in her hand.

'Take that stick off her, someone.'

Heidi handed it over. 'I was just protecting her.'

'Didn't do too good a job. Name?'

'Heidi Go.'

'Never seen you before. Are you local?'

'She's the one who found the platypus.' Barton still hadn't taken his eyes off the body.

'Oh, yes? Finding dead things a hobby of yours? What the hell were you doing down here?'

'I found my husband's hat.' She shrugged her shoulders. 'He lost it.'

'He lost it here? No one's been down here for donkeys.'

'He wasn't here. Someone must have found the hat and dropped it. I got lost and—'

Lewis held up a hand impatiently. 'So you found the body and then came back to wait with it? That's not exactly normal, Miss Go. Most people would get out of here fast. Take down her particulars, Fraser. We're going to need to talk to this husband of hers too. Now all of you move out of the way. Cheryl, Brendan, come with me.' A female officer stepped forward. She had a square haircut and a thick body like a rolled-up futon. Fraser was a beefy man, with a very small face in a big head. He flipped his notebook sullenly and grunted at Heidi.

Lewis took a few steps closer to the body, wiping muddy hands on his trousers. 'Jesus bloody Christ. And just when I've had my afternoon tea. We can thank our lucky stars it's out in the open, not shoved in some old trunk.' He stepped closer again, peering at the flint like a collector examining a case of estate jewellery at an antique fair. 'Recognise the victim?'

'It's Elisabeth Bankston, sir.' Brendan said.

'Are you sure it's Keith's lass? A crying shame that would be, after everything's that happened to them.'

'I think so, sir. It's the hair.'

'God, it's disgusting. Any ideas on the weapon, Cheryl? What's that in her throat?'

'It looks like an old spear. It's been put through her, sir.'

'It doesn't take a bloody genius to work that one out. What else?'

'Is it Abo?' Brendan volunteered.

Lewis grunted. 'Looks more like islander to me.'

'I didn't know you were an expert, sir.'

'I'm not. But I know who is.' He turned around. 'Brendan, take some Polaroids of the carving on the bottom of this spear while we wait for Scientific. Get them over to Octavia Goodhope, pronto. She might have an idea. And watch where you step!'

Barton was carrying a camera over his shoulder on a strap. He approached gingerly and lined up a shot.

Lewis rubbed his chin. 'Anyone know if Miss Goodhope has reported anything missing lately?'

'Do you think she'd even know, sir?' Cheryl Martin said. 'All that stuff.'

'She'd know all right. Smart as a tack at eighty-five.' He rubbed his eyes. 'Come to think of it, Brendan, get on your bike. I don't want anything to happen to her too. Damn the woman for not having a phone.'

Barton pocketed a couple of undeveloped Polaroids. 'Want me to take back-up?'

'What's your feeling?'

'If it's her spear, then she might have disturbed him taking it. She doesn't have a phone. We might need a doctor at least.'

'All right, drag Summerfield off the golf course and let's hope it's a wild goose chase. Not much you can do here. The bastard who did it's probably in the next state by now. You can drop Fraser and the witness back at the station on the way.'

'I want to stay,' Heidi protested.

'Get her out of here,' Lewis said. He turned back to Cheryl Martin. 'Now, let's secure this crime scene while we wait for that ambulance. I don't know how bloody long it's going to take Scientific to get here from Bateman's. Now I need to do the real dirty work.'

'What's that, sir?'

He unhooked his mobile from his belt. 'Phoning Keith Bankston.'

Heidi talked Brendan into allowing her to drive back to the station in her Kingswood. She felt faint, but she needed to be in control of something, even if it was a rustbucket with wornout tyres. Steven Fraser went with her while Barton took the paddywagon. Fraser noted down the rest of her statement in the car while they drove along mainly deserted roads. 'Got footy practice in an hour,' he explained, suddenly cheery. 'Thought I wouldn't make it.'

'Are you a Nullin Whale?'

'Best and fairest last season.'

'I can imagine,' she said, but she couldn't. Why did so many cops have thugs' faces? It must be a very slender gene indeed that separated the will to do good from the urge to do bad.

When they reached the station, she pulled into the kerb behind Barton's panel van. 'Could I phone my husband from here?' Heidi asked.

'You should get a mobile, you know. A young woman like you driving around. There are some undesirable elements around.'

'As opposed to desirable?' Heidi asked, but Fraser was already out of the car.

Inside, Heidi was directed to a phone.

'I found your hat.'

'You little darling. I wondered where you'd gone.'

'But it's in police custody.'

Beckett wasn't so happy when she told him the story. 'You should have cleared out of there. What if he was still around?'

'It might have been a woman.'

'What makes you say that?'

'I don't know. The buttons on her coat were done up.'

'And that makes you feel better?'

'No. It was horrible.'

'Well, come home now and I'll pour you a strong drink.'

'I don't feel much like drinking.' She hung up. Behind her she could hear Brendan Barton swear and slam down his phone in unison with her. He stood up, grabbed his keys, and called over to the duty officer. 'I can't raise Summerfield. He's not at his surgery or the golf course. I've left messages. If he calls here, divert him to me. I'm going to Octavia Goodhope's. I might need a doctor. I've got a bad feeling about this.'

'I'm a doctor,' Heidi volunteered. 'Sort of. I've volunteered in nursing homes, anyway. I can help.'

'You should go home to your husband.'

'I'll follow you in my car, then.'

He brushed past her. 'That won't get you far.'

11

Heidi closed her eyes and wrapped her arms tightly against her body under the warmth of Brendan's sweater. The police speed-boat slammed against the river's waves. It was cold, she was still damp from the quarry, but she had no desire to stop, lie down, sleep. *Ever.* She wanted to keep on pushing into the future because the immediate past did not bear contemplation. The wind in her face took her mentally and physically away from it.

She hadn't really known Elisabeth, but there had been a connection.

I really like your dress. Time-honoured girltalk for *I really like you.*

Brendan said something but it was carried away on the air. Heidi opened her eyes and took in the scene. Until now, all she had known of the Bilba River was its entrance to the ocean, which was clogged with cruisers and the fishing boats that offloaded their catch at the Sea Pride cannery. Brendan was making sure she was getting an education. He steered the boat roughly around the islands of mangroves, whose limbs stretched like the arms of exhausted washerwomen into the river, and pointed out the old mission house located amid a tangle of ruined wisteria vine and other unchecked growth.

'Old Groeber's still here, the last missionary, must be over a hundred,' he called out to her over the burr of the boat's engine. 'He's run out of Aboriginals to convert. They say his teeth have worn down to yellow stumps. His wife died twenty years ago and he got some local bod to embalm her, then built her a casket out of glass from the old conservatory. Or so people said. As kids we used to dare each other to come here in the dark. I never did see the coffin, although my brother swore he did. But that was just to get into Shelley Taylor's pants.'

'Shelley Taylor?' Heidi raised her voice and pulled wind-blown strands of hair out of her mouth.

'My girlfriend Danielle's little sister. They used to have the hairdressing salon together. Michelle's a Bankston now.'

'Oh, yes. I've met her up at the Bankston house.'

'You went there?'

'I gave Carmel a massage this morning. Michelle's very perky.'

'Nah, not a bean on what she was before. Poor Shelley's had the life drained out of her by that lot.'

'I wouldn't be so sure.'

'Well, she dropped Danielle in it. Left her short a good hair stylist. I reckon Carmel Bankston forced young Charley to marry Michelle so she could get her hair done every day for free. I love Shelley, she's almost my sister-in-law, but anyone can see that she's not a brain surgeon. Charley's way out of her league. Danielle tried to talk her out of it. She thought Charley'd get tired of her. But I could see Shelley's point of view. I mean, look at the shitheads around here. Charley's the best catch in the district.'

'Apart from Peter.'

'No, Peter's an odd one. Keeps to himself.'

'I would have thought you were a good catch yourself.'

'But I'm taken, aren't I?' He grinned, a familiar grin she couldn't place.

As Heidi looked back to get a better view of the house through a grove of twisted tea-tree, a plaster grotto rose out of the vegetation, a luridly painted, life-size Virgin and infant against a chalky blue sky decorated with gold stars.

'Creepy, isn't she?' Barton commented. 'Used to scare the bejesus out of us as kids.'

'Her head looks funny. It's twisted.' Heidi winced. Another female figure violated.

'Yeah, some vandal knocked the old head off and so old Groeber had to make a new one himself. He wasn't much of an artist.' Barton gave the boat some throttle. 'Hang on, we've got a clear run up the river now.'

'How soon until we get there?'

'Ten minutes maybe.'

'You're worried about this old woman?'

'I reckon it's her spear. No one else around here has stuff like that.'

'She's got a collection?'

'Wait and see.'

The river narrowed and the mangroves thickened, reducing the sky to a ribbon of washed-out blue. Remnants of old jetties, rotted to stumps, shifted in the speedboat's wake. A flock of cockatoos alighted on the trees, squawked and shot back into the sky. Barton reduced speed as they took a comma-shaped bend and then steered towards a long, intact jetty. He shut the engine down and they rolled towards the steps.

At the end of the jetty, two enormous carved figures, each taller than a man and twice as thick, sat on grotesque haunches, both staring implacably out on the river. Each held a long spear which crossed at the tips over the wooden pathway.

'My God,' said Heidi, looking up at the wooden monsters. 'How did they get there?'

'They say she used to keep slaves. Rumour has it they were from New Guinea or the islands. Others claim the authorities released Japanese prisoners to her after the war—she used them to do her dirty work, kept them in a chook shed and then starved them until they died. Not that there's any evidence of it, except a few Jap skulls inside. She's a nice old dear. An anthropologist or something, way back. Any time I come up here, even as a kid, she'd pour me a glass of this rancid cognac she keeps. A wicked drop. I can't imagine her starving anyone.' He placed a foot on a step and held out his hand. 'Let's have a squiz.'

They moved quickly along the jetty, which was losing planks in places. At the end of the pier, an iron gate, tangled with vine, stood open. 'Doesn't look good,' Brendan said, quickening his pace. 'This is never open. She's very particular about it. Maybe you should wait here.'

Heidi shook her braids. 'No way. You might need me.'

She followed him up a sandy path lined with clumps of dead iris and rusty hydrangea. An old verandah-style house with a pitched gable loomed before them out of the bushes, the timber cracked and silvery where most of the old paint had worn off. The balustrades were encrusted with small seashells and rocks, and giant conches and cowries were placed on the steps, the pink blush of their interiors exposed to the world. The verandah was fringed with hanging things—grass skirts, masks, seed pods, small carved tools and weapons.

'Are they what I think they are?' Heidi recoiled, pointing to several dark brown, fist-shaped, hanging balls.

Brendan nodded. 'Shrunken heads. Not sure they're legal.'

'Are you going to confiscate them?'

'Not on your life.' Brendan approached the front door cautiously. It too was open. He waved Heidi behind him. 'Miss Goodhope!' he called. 'It's Brendan here. Are you all right?'

A sound of tapping came from inside the house. Barton put his hand on his hip. Heidi could now see that he had a gun holstered under his leather jacket.

One...two...three... The tapping sound again, followed by a twisting sound, a creak.

'Stay here!' Barton stepped inside. Heidi ignored him, even though she was terrified. The hollow echo of the tapping and the creaking noise sounded like a body twisting from a rope.

The room was almost dark, the windows shuttered. A strong smell assaulted her senses...dusty violets? She could make out all kinds of shapes in the shadows; there were large, aggressive forms and small, cowering ones; there were softly draped things and tall, pointed things. Objects hung overhead, others were strewn across the floor. Every small step brought a new contact with some object unknown. Her knee banged against a sharp corner. She put out her hand to steady herself and clutched at something large and furry. She gasped and dropped her hand. It was a stuffed animal of some kind, no longer capable of doing her any harm, except the worst harm of all, to remind her of Elisabeth in her mangy fur shroud.

She might have given in to fear if the tapping sound had not started up again and focused her. She heard Brendan mutter something. Now she could make out his shape more clearly as she became accustomed to the dark. He was bending over a table or desk, fumbling.

She heard a click and a small lamp spilled warm light over a table covered in a lace cloth and pile of dusty books. She could now see the outline of a seated figure, clutching a cane and lifting it rhythmically to tap on the floor. It might have been one of the strange objects come to life.

The woman was old but not frail. She filled the chair with huge shoulders, a wrestler with the rigid posture of a sergeant-major. She must have been six foot tall in her slippered feet. She was wearing a robe of dark paisley silk. Heidi could see the embroidery on a black satin cuff as it fell back from wrists the colour of tea, scattered with liver spots the size of tea leaves. Her face was all angles and deep pools of shadow where the eyes should be. Her hair, what was left of it, was a fringe of white on a large skull, which made the vast, crusted blister of blood over her left ear stand out like a clubbed seal on snow.

The thudding stopped. The old woman turned her head towards the light. 'So it's you, young Barton,' she said in a metallic voice. 'What took you so long?'

12

Heidi washed the wound and made a poultice out of cheesecloth. Octavia Goodhope's bathroom resembled an apothecary's lair with its ancient bottles of tinctures and creams. Much of the stuff must have been decades old, though there was a relatively modern bottle of Mercurochrome and plenty of bandages. The old woman didn't flinch when Heidi applied the stinging antiseptic.

'It's not too nasty,' Heidi told Brendan.

'Just when did this happen, Miss Goodhope?' the police officer asked.

'This morning. About six.'

'You've been here like this since *six*?'

'I'm perfectly all right. I got a bit of a shock, I admit. But he only pushed me over. He didn't hit me with anything.'

'You've been sitting here all this time?'

'Of course not. I can move around. I left the wound open to heal. It's not as bad as you think.'

'You might be concussed. I'll call the hospital and organise a bed for you.'

'I'm not going anywhere.'

'They'll only keep you for a night for observation, all going well.'

'All has gone well, young Barton. You and this nice young child have fixed me up. You can go now.'

'I can't do that, Miss Goodhope. He might come back.'

'I doubt that very much. The bank handles all my affairs. I

only keep about fifty dollars in the house. If that's gone, there's no reason to return.' She waved her hand. 'Look under that skull.'

Brendan's eyes followed her gesture. There was a small skull sitting on a mantel, among a cluster of other bones. Brendan moved over to it and picked it up gingerly. He held up a wad of notes. All of them were in small denominations, faded and thin. 'The money's still here.'

'That's all of it. Hardly worth attacking an old lady for, is it?'

'But when we were kids, everyone said you had gold doubloons hidden under your bed. When we asked you, you never denied it.'

'I didn't want to disappoint the kiddies.'

'So maybe he came for that—and took a spear instead?'

'A spear?'

'That's why we're here. A spear has been involved in a violent crime.' He took the Polaroids out of his pocket. 'I wonder if you recognise it?' he shuffled through the pictures and picked out the least distressing one. 'This only shows part of the spear, I'm afraid. It was stuck in a shallow puddle.'

She took it off him and held it close to her face. 'Ah, yes. That's the black palm from Wewak. It's in the Sepik province of New Guinea. A beautiful place. Orchids climbing all over the trees. It's one of mine, I recognise the carved clan head. Where did you find it? Stuck in some unfortunate roo by the look of it.'

'No, I'm sorry. It was used in a murder.'

She sat forward in her chair. 'Whose murder?'

'Elisabeth Bankston. She was found in the Nullin Void this afternoon. The spear...well, it was the murder weapon.'

'Elisabeth? My great niece?'

Barton went pink. 'Oh, shit, I'm sorry. I forgot.'

'It's a wonder you young ones even know. I haven't talked to Lydia for decades.'

'She's Keith's mother, isn't she?'

'And a nastier piece of baggage never walked on this earth.'

She put a brown hand to the bandage on her head. 'Poor Keith. He quite adored that little girl.'

'Are you feeling all right?' Heidi asked.

'There's some cognac in the bureau over there.'

Heidi retrieved a small glass and bottle from a sideboard that supported a glass case of stuffed finches perched on a branch.

Octavia Goodhope screwed up her face and then took the cognac off Heidi, downing it in one hit. After a moment, she asked 'Do you have any idea who did this to poor Elisabeth? You think it was the intruder who pushed me over?'

'When did you last notice the spear?'

'It's hard to keep track of things. So many things. I've had thefts before, you know. Mostly the skulls and heads. The kids take them. In fact, that brother of yours—'

Brendan interrupted. 'Do you feel well enough to go over the attack?'

'Of course.'

'You said it was about six. You looked at a clock?'

'I can read the light, young man. It was dawn.'

'What happened?'

'I was up as usual, in this room, looking through some books. I must have become distracted for a moment. I can usually hear every spider's footstep in this house. He must have been quiet, or quick. I was standing by that table and the next thing I know I'm on my face and out. I must have hit my head on the edge. I drifted in and out of consciousness all day, then pulled myself up this afternoon and made it to this chair. I feel perfectly fine.'

She didn't look it. Heidi thought she looked shattered, despite her bravado.

'You didn't try to sound an alarm? You have flares, don't you?'

'To tell you the truth, I was ashamed. The last fool who came here to do me harm got the barrel of my father's service revolver up his nostrils.'

79

'Did you see your attacker at all?'

'I had my back to him. He was swift. I had a sense...'

'Yes?'

She hesitated. 'That he was young. I don't know what gave me that impression. Maybe because he was so quick.'

'Did you hear a powerboat? Anything like that at all?'

'No. He must have come by foot.'

'But it's two kilometres to the nearest road.'

'That doesn't concern some people.'

'Can you recall anyone who has expressed any particular interest in your weapons lately?'

'Only the director of the Oceanic Museum in Paris and I hardly think he'd leave with only one artefact.'

'Has anyone visited you recently?'

'No. Only those nice young brothers from the supermarket. They came last week with a delivery of food.'

'No other visitors at all?'

'Sorry. Can't help you.' Heidi picked up a note of evasion in her voice. She looked at Barton—she thought he had too.

'I still reckon you better come back with us and get checked out.'

'Absolutely not.'

'Then I'm going to send someone to watch over you.'

'Absolutely not.'

'We haven't caught the perpetrator yet. He might come back.'

'For another weapon?' she asked. 'Lord knows there's enough of them.'

'That's another thing.'

'Now, young Barton, don't start telling me I need a licence for all this stuff. It won't be worth the stink I'll kick up.'

'Yeah, I can imagine. Do you have someone you want me to call?'

'No one. Although you can give Keith my condolences. Don't

tell any of them I've had an accident, mind you. I'll be in my grave soon enough and my sister and her tribe can squabble over what's left of it after I donate the valuable pieces to various worthy institutions.' She smiled at him. 'I've already earmarked one of the shrunken heads for Lydia.'

13

'What happens now?' Heidi said to Brendan as she watched him hitch Octavia's dinghy to the Nullin pier. It was dark but light pooled on to the jetty from a houseboat moored close to shore. She could hear the evening news and smell fried bacon.

'The ambulance will take Elisabeth to the morgue at Nullin hospital. The body snatchers will probably arrive tomorrow and take her up to Sydney, to the lab in Glebe. The state coroner will have a look at her. We're not authorised to do that kind of thing here. The inspector will have been on the phone organising some blokes from Major Crime to come down. They'll set up a task force.'

'Carmel Bankston told me Elisabeth was missing last night. She didn't come home after the debutante ball.'

'Why didn't you tell me this earlier? Carmel didn't report it to us.'

'I told that other officer. Fraser.'

'If the spear was stolen at dawn, then she had to have been killed after that. I wonder who she was with before that.'

Heidi didn't say anything about the lover in the storeroom.

You won't tell Mummy, will you.

'Well, we'll know in a few days after the coroner's report.'

Heidi shivered as a brisk wind bit at her bare ankles.

'You better get home,' Brendan said. 'Your husband will be anxious.'

'Hell, I forgot to tell him I made a detour. He'll be worried. Or jealous.'

'I can understand that,' Brendan smiled.

'Should I be jealous?' Beckett was leaning against the kitchen sink, arms crossed. 'I called the station and they told me you'd gone off with Brendan Barton somewhere.'

'I'm sorry. It was sort of an emergency. Brendan needed a doctor.'

'You're not a doctor. You're not even a nurse. You've only played one on television.'

'I know my first aid.' She explained about Octavia Goodhope. 'I think you'd like her, Beck. She's your kind of crusty character.'

'You could have called. I would have downed half a bottle of whiskey if you hadn't have hidden it.' He stepped forward and put his hands on her shoulders. 'Anyway, what got into you? You shouldn't have been anywhere near that quarry. What if the murderer was still around?'

'Well, you were the one who took off up there to see those Blackpeters yesterday.'

'That was for work. And I'm a bloke. I can look after myself.'

'What's that cut on your face, then?'

He wasn't appeased. 'It's not the first time you've gone off and not told me where you were. I'm stuck in this house—'

She tried to work out what he was really saying. 'Beckett, you love this house. And you're not stuck in it.'

'I *never* know where you are.'

'You never knew where I was in Sydney.'

'Yes I did. I had spies.'

'Did you?'

'It's this place. It's *dangerous*.'

'And the city isn't? What's dangerous about it?'

'You had a car accident yesterday and today you get lost in

the bush when there's some axe murderer at large. God knows what danger you put yourself into going to strangers houses to give them massages.'

'Beckett, calm down. You run off pursuing enthusiasms all the time. I never ask where you've been. We've been married six years. We're entitled to do our own thing.'

'That's what I'm worried about.'

He was being irrational. She put her arms around his waist. 'Will sorry do?'

He held her face in his hands. 'For the meantime.' He kissed her. 'I don't know about you but I could do with that drink. It's about time we supported the local Leagues Club.'

'I'm exhausted, Beck. And I want to clean up. I feel filthy.'

'A drink will do you good. Have a wash and see how you feel.'

'All right. Just one.'

'Good. I intend to get thoroughly sloshed.' He was smiling now. 'I can't stand this much tension in a day.'

'I meant just one for *you*.'

The Nullin whale would have sunk in the Pacific but atop the Nullin Leagues Club it splashed in a styrofoam sea and spewed a fountain of water out of its plaster spout when anyone remembered to turn it on. It had frolicked on top of the club for forty years. The club had been built in the sixties to house poker machines and a bar, but the original cream-brick structure had been added on to several times over the years. It now looked like the local greengrocer had assembled it out of boxes. Extensions were built of different brick from the main building and the most recent addition, a sauna and spa, didn't even lie flush with the floor of the gym.

The poker machines had paid for the white terrazzo steps, scene of many a drunken slip, and the tinted sliding glass doors at the entrance. The carpet was a tan shag matted with age and spilled beer.

They took seats on stools at a vast bar that ran along a wall overlooking the poker machines. The wall behind the bar was covered in mirror tiles rippled with gold paint, behind bottled spirits and liqueurs. From an adjoining room, someone was calling a bingo game. The rough voice rose above a background noise of tinkling coins and clinking glass.

They decided that Stone's Green Ginger wine was the thing to order. Beckett sipped his and made a face. 'Nostalgia aint what it used to be.'

'I don't care what I drink,' Heidi said, downing hers. 'I'd even accept a Fluffy Duck.'

'How bad was it?'

'Horrible. It seemed like hours that I was sitting there with her. She looked so...lonely, cold. *Blue*, you know. I still feel numb. I can't imagine who would do that to a young girl.'

'A boyfriend? What about the boy you saw her with in the storeroom?'

'I don't even know if he was more than a one-night thing. But even if he were jealous, why kill her in that way? With a spear? And dressing her in that old coat...like some mangy animal. It was *sick*, Beckett. If he were jealous, he'd just strangle her, or hit her with a rock. But to go to all the trouble of...*arranging* her like that. He might have been discovered while he was doing it. He'd have to get her down there, whether she was dead first or alive.'

'But it's a pretty safe bet, isn't it? I mean, no one goes to the Nullin Void.'

'I had the feeling he wanted an audience, though.'

'What do you mean?'

'I don't know. It's like an ampitheatre down there. And we, the cops and me, we were the audience. The birds were an audience. It's like he had everyone's attention, even the worms. He was exhibiting her in that old coat, I'm sure of it.'

'Doesn't it remind you of something? Another dead skin?' he prompted.

'The platypus you mean.' She sighed. 'I thought of that straight away.'

'So the person who killed your platypus might have killed Elisabeth.'

'But why?'

'A natural progression. Bigger game. Think about it—all the animals that have been found have been impaled.'

'As far as we know.'

'And Elisabeth was speared that way too.' He tapped the bar with the coaster again. 'How many animals have been killed so far?'

'I don't know. Six or seven didn't you say?'

'Accepting your point that a jealous boyfriend wouldn't have gone to all the trouble to steal a native spear, drag Elisabeth into the Void, dress her in a fur coat, tie her up, then impale her and leave her for the crows, and assuming it's the same bloke who has been killing all these animals, then what's the significance of it? Maybe it's something religious.'

'You mean a crackpot is running wild around here making sacrifices for God? Stop being such a writer.'

'What did the old lady say?'

'That was funny, too. I could have sworn she knew who attacked her and stole the spear. Brendan thought so too, I could tell. But she denied it, except to say she thought he was young.'

'Maybe she wanted to put you off the track.'

'Maybe. She denied hearing any boats beforehand. And she's got sharp ears. She said as much.'

'Can you get to her by road?'

'Beats me how you could. Brendan said the road stops a couple of kilometres from the house and the only real access is by water. I suppose someone who knows the bush could walk it. It's weird, Brendan says she used to have Japanese slaves. Or that's the rumour. She's a pretty tough old bird. You'd have to be brave or stupid to confront her.'

'But the killer didn't. He was a coward. He pushed her, didn't she say?'

'Which means it probably was someone she knew, not wanting her to recognise him. Did I tell you she is Elisabeth Bankston's great aunt? No? Well, her sister Lydia is Keith's mother. Octavia doesn't speak to her apparently. Said she was leaving all her possessions to various museums. You should see it all. I bet it's worth a fortune. She's got all of Nullin convinced she's hiding buried treasure out there.'

'So the person who stole the spear might have been after something else after all?'

Heidi shook her head. 'Who knows? Look, I have to go to the loo. Try and solve the crime while I'm gone, will you? It's too much for me.'

Beckett signalled the barman for another round.

'What'll it be this time, mate?' the bartender asked. He had N-U-LL-N roughly tattooed across the knuckles of one hand and W-H-A-L-E across the other.

'It's time to hit the hard stuff,' Beckett told him. 'What's the house cocktail?'

'Mate, you'd have to come back during Happy Hour with the ladies. You'd be lucky to get a shandy out of me.'

'A shandy it is, then.'

The bartender returned with the beer and Beckett asked for peanuts. 'Thanks,' he said when a bowl was placed in front of him. 'My wife has asked me to solve a crime and I can't do that on an empty stomach.'

'What crime, mate?' The bartender mopped the bar.

'The murder down in the quarry.'

'Young Elisabeth? We just heard. Bad stuff that.' He scratched his head. 'But you're not a detective, are you? You're that writer from the old cheese factory, right? I heard people talk about you.'

'Oh, yes?' Beckett held out his hand. 'Beckett Versec.'

They shook hands. 'Neville Chamberlain. Bummer, isn't it? My folks were poms. Came out here after the war.'

'Did you know Elisabeth?'

'Yeah, she practically lived in here. Couldn't sell her booze when she was underage of course.' He winked. 'But she liked hanging out with the blokes.'

'A tomboy?'

'I don't mean to speak ill of the dead, but there are other words for it.'

'You'd think her family would bundle her off to boarding school.'

'I don't think Keith ever knew. No one dared tell him.'

'So what blokes did she hang out with?'

'See that mob over there?' He nodded towards a group in their twenties and thirties playing pool. 'And that mob over there?' He gestured towards a knot of men standing at the other end of the bar. 'And those blokes on the pokies? You get the picture?'

'And her parents didn't know? In a small town like this?'

Neville became terse. 'You'd have to ask Keith. Good luck with that, mate.' He turned his back on Beckett and starting opening some beers for the men at the end of the bar. Beckett noticed that Damian Hill was among them. He wondered who was looking after the kids.

'Don't look now,' Heidi whispered, coming up quietly behind him, 'but I've just seen the boy who was with Elisabeth in the broom cupboard.'

'Where is he?'

'Get up and go to the men's room. You'll pass him at the very end of the bar, drinking by himself. His hair's almost white. Take a look at his face. But please don't be obvious.'

'As I tend to be.'

Beckett came back a few moments later. He sat down on the barstool beside her.

'Well?'

'Looks like he's been in an argument with a garage door.'

'That's what I thought. One whole side is bruised. Don't you think that's suspicious? I mean, I see him fucking Elisabeth in the dark. Now she's dead and he's got a beaten-up face. Do you think I should go and tell Brendan?'

'You don't even know who he is.'

'I'll ask.' She called the bartender over. 'Do you know who that young man is?'

'Jaron?'

'That's his name?'

'Jaron Wignall. Runs the caravan park for Gray, that's his dad. Jaron's a good footballer. Pity about the old man.'

'Why?'

'Gets pissed all the time and likes to shoot galahs out of trees. Sometimes he tries it on people. The other day the whole bloody force had to go down there and take the shotgun off him. Took poor Mirna hostage. Something about her burning the bacon.'

'He's in jail?'

'Nah. He never has his day in court because Mirna won't press charges.'

'Jaron get into many fights?' Beckett asked.

'Well, he's a lad, isn't he?'

'He's got a big bruise on his face.'

'Didn't notice, mate. Probably got it during footy practice.'

'He's a member of the team?'

'More than that. He's our best back. Can I get you anything else?'

'Just the tab,' Heidi said. She nudged Beckett's arm. 'Let's get going.'

'Seventeen fifty,' Neville calculated.

Beckett placed a twenty-dollar note on the counter.

'Thanks, mate,' Neville said and palmed it.

'Don't you want to follow your suspect, see what he gets up to in the dark?' Beckett asked Heidi as they stood.

'Young Jaron's a suspect, is he?' Neville had been listening.

'Not at all,' Heidi said quickly.

'Cos if you're looking for a suspect,' Neville whispered conspiratorially, 'I reckon you'd have to follow the whole bloody bar.'

14

Heidi was woken with a start by the telephone. She checked the bedside clock. It was 8 a.m. When she sat up, her forehead felt like someone had placed a brick on it and hammered in tent pegs and rope to keep it down.

'Come soon, please,' said a husky voice on the end of the line.

Carmel Bankston.

Beckett groaned but went back to sleep.

She slipped out of bed.

She wasn't surprised to see two police cars parked behind the Bankston's house. As she rounded the path, carrying her massage table, she came across Michelle Bankston and Brendan Barton deep in conversation. Michelle was wearing a black, hooded cardigan over a black halter with gold chains and matching short skirt. Michelle's idea of mourning, Heidi thought.

'Carmel said for you to wait until the police are finished. It won't be long,' Michelle said.

'Have you found out anything?' Heidi asked Barton.

'A few things. We're waiting for the coroner to pinpoint the time of death, but it was probably early yesterday morning. Cause of death was ligature strangulation.'

'Strangulation?'

'Yeah. The spear didn't kill her.'

'Thank God for that.'

'Post-mortem hypostatic lividity was distributed over the posterior of her body, not in her feet, which you would have expected if she had been impaled alive. Plus there was no blood.'

'I wondered about that.'

'She'd been dead and lying on her back for a while before he stuck that spear in her. He must have had inhuman strength. Normally with impalings the spear is shoved through the anus while the victim is alive and the body's weight forces the tip to penetrate the organs.'

'Don't.'

'Sorry. Not that I've ever seen one before.'

'So he might have killed her before he stole the spear?'

'Probably. If the spear was stolen Friday morning at six, then he probably kept her somewhere overnight before he took her down to the Void. Or left her down there in the dark. No one goes there. He'd be pretty safe. She wasn't seen after the debutante ball, and we're still looking for her gown, shoes and handbag. We're going to set up a mannequin by the side of the road to jog some memories. Someone must have seen her. She was the kind of girl you noticed.'

'Did she have a car?'

'Yeah, a white BMW. But it never left the house. We're going over it now.'

'So the killer probably drove her there?'

'Or maybe she hitchhiked.'

'In her ballgown?'

'You're right. But now that Carmel's looked, none of her clothes were missing.'

'Did you find any clues in the Void?'

'Scientific has sent it all up to Sydney. But as far as I know just the usual used condoms and cigarette packs.'

'Kids use the quarry for sex?'

'I don't know.'

Michelle spoke up. 'Brendan! You *so* do!'

Heidi knew by his reaction that Brendan had been one of those kids, and Michelle too. Maybe together, at one stage.

'Pretty creepy I would have thought. And muddy.'

'It's a sort of local ritual,' he shrugged. 'You get dared.'

'So Elisabeth could have been meeting someone down there?'

'Possibly.' He put on his cap. 'I'm off. Tell your husband Stan's on my back to get him to come in and make a statement about his hat.'

'Why?'

'It's a piece of evidence. Who's to say your husband didn't forget it when he strangled her. You better come back too. It's just a formality.'

'That's what they say on "Prime Suspect".'

Brendan made a face. 'Take care, Shelley, won't you? You know where to reach me if you need anything.'

Michelle watched him go and then turned to Heidi. 'Come on, I'll take you in. I hope you don't mind a bit of a crowd. The cops have been talking to Pete, Charley and Diane. Oh, and me, of course. We can't tell them anything, though. We never really did see Elisabeth that much. She was hardly ever home.'

Heidi thought about the men at the Leagues Club as she followed Michelle around the path. If Elisabeth played around as much as Neville Chamberlain suggested, it was a wonder Carmel missed her at all. Surely the girl didn't come home some nights? She might have been accustomed to sexual trysts in all kinds of places, like the storeroom at the Masonic Hall. Had she regularly enjoyed doing it in the Void too?

Michelle led her into the marble hallway, where she directed Heidi to rest her massage table against a wall. Heidi could see several people in the sitting room adjacent. 'You might have to wait with everyone for a bit,' Michelle whispered. 'The police are going through Elisabeth's things upstairs and Carmel's helping them. Isn't it awful? I'd hate anyone to snoop through my stuff.'

'Well, Elisabeth would hardly mind now,' Heidi said gently,

although she wasn't quite sure of that herself. She believed that it was possible spirits attached themselves to things.

'Oh, I think she would. Like that ratty old coat she was found in. She'd hate that.'

'I thought that too. Do you know who the coat belonged to?'

Michelle shrugged. 'They showed us a photograph. None of us had seen it before. It was like *rat* or something. Brendan says that maybe it was home-sewn.'

'Not many people sew their own furs.'

'But it was old. Brendan said people did make their own coats out of possums and things during the Depression. Whenever that was.'

'So it didn't have a label?'

'Shit, they didn't show us the neck or anything. There was probably blood all over it. They say she was strangled and stabbed.' She put a hand to her mouth. 'Oh, but I forgot—you found the body didn't you? Was it really *grisly*?'

Disconcerted by Michelle's eagerness for the gruesome details, Heidi simply said 'yes'.

The room behind them had gone quiet. Several faces were turned towards them. Heidi felt guilty about being indiscreet. Had everything that she and Michelle said been overheard? Without missing a beat Michelle took Heidi's arm and stepped into the sitting room. 'Come in and meet Charley,' she said with forced gaiety. 'You'll love him.'

The policewoman, Cheryl Martin, was squeezed into a slender wing-backed chair, a cup of tea balanced on the meaty part of one thigh and a chunk of fruitcake poised at her lips. Opposite her, a woman of about thirty occupied as little of the sofa as she possibly could. With slim legs tucked one behind the other, she held onto the arm of the couch as if it were the edge of a life raft. This, Heidi assumed, was Peter's wife, Diane, who Carmel had accused of snatching up her eldest son along with a juicy property deal. She didn't look very aggressive now, with her

94

pinched expression and puffy eyes. At the other end of the sofa, with a placid red-haired girl of about three between them, was the dour-looking woman Heidi had seen on her first visit to the house.

The three men stood by the fireplace. Keith, in his turquoise polo shirt and cream trousers, was dressed more casually than his two sons, who both wore dark suits and ties, as if they were so worried about what to wear to the funeral they had dressed for it days ahead. Peter was taller than both his father and brother, with a narrow body that, whichever way it arranged itself while clothed, would always look louche. Charley, on the other hand, had a footballers body, thick and lumpy, his neck popping out of his tight collar. Michelle brought Heidi forward, ignoring everyone else to introduce the guest to her husband.

'Charley, this is Heidi,' she beamed.

Charley's grip was vigorous. 'So you're the one,' he said, a glimmer of eagerness in his eyes.

'And this is Peter,' Michelle said. He put out a hand. It was cool and finely boned with long fingers. Artistic hands, she thought. 'Pleased to meet you,' he said, but he looked through her.

'I'm sorry for your loss,' Heidi said, turning towards Keith too, who nodded and then grimly looked away out the window, where two detectives, probably part of the crime squad from Sydney, were conferring next to the swimming pool.

Michelle introduced her sister-in-law. The woman at the end of the sofa was 'Emily' and Heidi supposed she was the babysitter. The little girl next to her was Rebecca, Michelle and Charley's first child. Heidi noticed the girl was sitting huddled up to Emily, a cushion's length away from her aunt. Cheryl Martin grunted a greeting and mopped up the crumbs on her lap with damp fingers.

Heidi moved to a low ottoman that was tucked in one corner, feeling like an interloper.

'I'm going to check on Little Keith,' Michelle said. 'You be good with Emily, darling,' she said to Rebecca and left.

You could have boiled an egg in the time it took before someone spoke. 'You're here to give mother a massage?' Peter asked Heidi, as if it were his responsibility, as eldest son, to take over the role of host from his brooding father.

She was grateful he had broken the ice. 'I don't know if I can do much to help in the circumstances.'

'Oh, I'm sure you can help her.' Diane said. 'Carmel does like her massages.'

Peter gave Diane a black look. Diane tossed her head and looked away from him.

'This is all crap,' Charley said suddenly, either oblivious to the exchange or covering it up. 'You were the one who found Elisabeth,' he said to Heidi. 'Can you tell us about it? What did she look like?'

'Charley, for God's sake!' Keith roared, red in the face. He slammed his hand on the mantelpiece. 'This is hardly the time.'

'When is then?' Charley reddened too. 'She's my sister. I'm entitled to know. You're the one who identified the body, but you're not telling us a damn thing. Someone strangled her and then dressed her in that wretched coat and then stuck a spear in her guts and laid her out for everyone to see. And this...stranger finds her. It should have been one of us.'

'Don't,' Peter said.

'Why not? She would have wanted us to find her. Or *some* of us. Those who give a damn.'

'Don't talk such rubbish!' Keith looked like he might have punched his youngest son if Peter hadn't been standing between them. 'It's a bloody insult to all of us. Your mother's upstairs crying her eyes out.'

'And what were you doing all night? On the phone to the States, talking the colour of cheese.'

'The world has to go on, son. You do OK out of it.'

'I think it's someone she knew,' Charley said. 'That prick Jack Harding for instance.'

'Charley!' Peter looked horrified.

Keith spoke. 'Excuse my son, Officer Martin. He's had a bee in his bonnet about Jack Harding ever since the boy joined the company. If Charley had anywhere near the application that Jack has he wouldn't need to be so jealous.'

Charley looked like he was about to explode. Cheryl Martin jumped on it. 'Where is Mr Harding anyway?' she asked. 'We'll need to speak to him.'

Charley shot his father a triumphant look. Keith ignored it. 'Jack Harding is in Singapore. He took the eight o'clock flight from Moruya to Sydney yesterday morning. He'll be back on Wednesday, but I can help you in the meantime. Jack had packing to do the night of the ball. He left about eleven. It had been pre-arranged that Elisabeth come home with us. But when it was time to leave she was nowhere to be found. I told Carmel to stuff her and we came home without her.'

'You weren't concerned?'

'Elisabeth had lots of friends at the ball. They'd all gone by then. We assumed they'd gone off to the beach for a skinny dip.' He grunted. 'She was eighteen after all.'

'You know bloody well she wouldn't have gone for a swim,' Charley said.

Keith glowered at his son. Was there something Heidi had missed? Cheryl Martin picked it up. 'Why is that, Charley? Why wouldn't she have gone into the water?'

'Because, Cheryl, my sister was afraid of the water. You couldn't get her in the pool unless you went with her and held her hand.'

Cheryl Martin was as surprised as Heidi. 'That's unusual for a local, isn't it?'

Keith spoke up. 'My daughter was a quiet girl who preferred art to sport. She got dumped once too often by waves in the sea.'

Heidi thought of the photograph on Carmel's dresser of the Bankston children frolicking in the pool. Elisabeth had been about five, she recalled, and seemed perfectly at ease in the water then.

Keith looked at his watch. 'Anyway, I think we've done enough waiting around for one day. I'm off to work.' He took a pair of sunglasses off the mantel and pocketed them. 'Officer Martin? Stan can reach me at the factory if he needs me. You come with me, Charley. Stay here and look after your mother, Peter. Goodbye poppet.' He went over to the sofa and kissed his grandchild on the forehead. She looked warily at him. He nodded to Heidi and Cheryl Martin and exited through the kitchen. Surprisingly, Charley followed passively, stopping to kiss his child before he left.

Once they'd gone, Diane looked at her watch. 'I really have to go too. I've got to show Mr Nagoya the Mitchell property.'

'Do you have to do that, Diane, in the circumstances?' Peter said.

Diane tapped her fingers on the arm of the couch, a smoker without a pack of cigarettes. 'I should remind you it's my job. The day you start making some sperm that swim, I'll quit.'

'That's fucking outrageous.'

Rebecca started howling at the expletive. Emily picked up the child and lifted her onto her knee. 'Look what you've done,' she scolded Diane. 'You've upset her.'

'We're all upset,' Peter said.

'Not all of us,' Diane replied.

15

Michelle took Heidi upstairs when the police had finished with Elisabeth's room. She passed another detective on the stairs, gripping a cardboard box.

Carmel was sitting on the edge of her bed, dressed as formally as her sons were, in a soft grey tweed suit with a cream shirt, a silk bow at the neck. She was wearing pale hose and shiny two-tone Ferragamos. Carmel was the sort of woman who had a costume for every occasion, Heidi thought. This one was for audiences with police officers. There would be a version in black for funerals and in pink for charity lunches. It spelled out the terms under which Carmel was to be considered—with delicacy and respect. A grieving mother who could manage to button-up a three thousand-dollar jacket, choose snag-free pantyhose and polished shoes was not to be underestimated.

'This was my favourite photograph of Elisabeth,' Carmel said as soon as Heidi entered. She held up an empty frame, then dropped it back in her lap and said dismally, 'The police took it.'

'Do you have any others?'

'Not many recent ones. Keith was mad about taking photographs when the kids were young, but gave it away once the business grew. Being the youngest, Elisabeth missed out, especially after puberty...And she was so pretty...' Carmel's voice lost its battle for control of her emotions. She paused, then cleared her throat. 'I wish I'd paid attention to who her friends were. They might have some more recent pictures.'

Heidi wondered what kind of sedatives the doctor had prescribed for her. 'Will I set up now?'

'Go ahead.' Carmel smiled faintly. 'You know, I don't have anyone I can really talk to about Elisabeth. Would you mind if I talk about her to you?'

'Of course not. If it helps.'

'I feel you're part of this...because you found her.'

'I understand. Charley said the same thing.'

'He's not an idiot, you know.'

'I didn't think he was.'

'Keith does. He thinks both our boys are weak. Elisabeth was another matter. He thought she could do anything. Peter should have been the girl, it would have made him happier.'

'You'd never know it. He seems very self-assured.'

'I can't bear the way the men in this family keep their feelings bottled up.'

'Charley didn't look bottled up. It sounds as if he was particularly close to her.'

'Charley?' She sounded vague. 'Well, he was the closest in age.'

'Didn't she get on with Peter?'

'Oh, I didn't mean to give you that impression. They were always off together. Even once they'd grown up. They shared... a talent, I suppose.'

'Did Elisabeth have many school friends?'

'Oh, she was very popular. But I think she grew out of her school friends. It was a very good local girl's school, but she was more sophisticated, you know. A good imagination. She wanted to be a fashion designer. I was glad of it. It was going to get her out of here.'

Heidi laid out the towels. 'You would have missed her though?'

'Naturally. But you don't want your children around you all the time, do you? As much as you hate it, they've got to fly.'

'It must be nice for you having Peter and Charley and their families here all the same.'

'It has its moments.'

Heidi changed the subject. 'Would you like to get undressed now?'

Carmel didn't move. 'They won't know…' Her voice trailed off, her eyes liquid. 'They say they won't know if she's been sexually assaulted until the coroner's report.' Something defiant hardened in her expression. 'She had to have been assaulted, hadn't she? That had to be the reason he did it.'

'What do the police say?'

'They say they are *pursuing several leads*,' she said bitterly. 'Which means they don't know a damn thing.'

'They know where the spear came from. That's a start.'

Carmel snorted. 'Kids have been stealing things from Octavia Goodhope for decades. Look under any house around here and you'll find one of her gruesome objects among the old tyres and tin cans.'

'Apparently they're worth a fortune.'

'They are?' Carmel sounded bored. 'Lydia will be happy about that.'

'Brendan Barton says you're related to Octavia.'

'Keith is. She's his aunt. I've met her once or twice.'

'She seemed very fond of Elisabeth.'

'You know Octavia?'

'I went to see her with Brendan. We thought she might have needed medical attention. Someone attacked her and stole the spear that…they found with Elisabeth.'

'I didn't hear that she was attacked.' Carmel looked flustered 'Is she all right?'

'I think she's pretty tough.'

'So I believe.' Carmel tugged at the hem of her skirt, smoothing it down over her knees. 'I wonder what else they're not telling me.' She looked up again, her eyes full of pain. 'I didn't want to see her body. Is that very terrible?'

'No.'

'They say a person is fully developed by the time they're six. That whatever we do to them after that can't change what happened before. Do you think that's true?'

'I'm not a parent.'

'But you want to be?'

'Yes, I do.'

'Well, don't. From the minute the first one is born you can never be the same. You lose yourself...in the worry about them. You worry if they giggle all the time because you think they may be brain-damaged. And you worry when they cry because you think they might be in pain. And you worry that other people won't understand them or that kids will bully them or take advantage of them. And you worry that you're being too strict or too easy on them. And when they're older it's worse because there's drugs and sex and cars.' Carmel touched the bow at her throat.

'You never stop believing in them because, if you don't, who will? But you worry that it's your worrying that gets them into trouble. That by caring about them so much, you are asking for them to be taken from you. That if you didn't care, God wouldn't notice them at all. He would just pass on by and pick on another one...but you can't know what I mean. Only mothers know. I don't think even fathers get it.'

'But Keith seems shattered. He obviously loved Elisabeth very much. Surely he feels the same way as you do.'

'Oh, yes, she was everything to him.' Her face darkened. 'This time it's his fault. He loved her so much God stopped and took notice.'

'You don't believe in a very compassionate God.'

'Do you?'

'I think there's something compassionate out there. It may not be God. It might be Mother Nature.'

Carmel grunted. 'Mother Nature kills her babies too. You

haven't been in Nullin long enough to know. She drowns them in huge seas, or splits their skulls with lightning bolts...you don't think Elisabeth's killer wasn't a product of nature too? He wasn't made in a test tube. He's out there somewhere, the spawn of a mother and father who screwed him up before he was six. When they find him, that's what his defence will say.'

She gave a tight laugh and put a hand to her forehead. 'I'm going round in circles. I think we should do that massage now.' She stood up and started unbuttoning her jacket.

'What's your grandmother's recipe for heartache? I could do with an intravenous.'

16

'Here's your hangover cure.' Heidi carried a tray out to the back porch and placed it on the table next to Beckett. She handed him two halves of a cut lemon.

'What's this?'

'Place one under each armpit.'

'You're kidding.'

'It works. I'm doing it too.'

They sat together on the wicker couch, lemons tucked under their shirts. A flight of white cockatoos was pecking its afternoon meal of worms and bugs out of the grassy slope. Black-and-white cows munched on emerald grass. The soft rise of the hills surrounded them like bunting.

'I think Carmel's got a bad case of denial,' Heidi said, crossing her feet on the verandah railing. 'She's hired me less for my massage skills—which, as you know, are considerable—than for my therapist skills.'

'Which are also superb.'

'Thank you. But, really, Beck, she must know Elisabeth was playing around. Everyone else seems to.' She was quiet for a moment, watching the birds. 'Did I tell you the police think the coat Elisabeth was found in was handmade? Maybe some kind of feral animal. Although it didn't look like possum to me.'

'Do they think those Blackpeters made it?'

'Brendan didn't say. But they do skin animals for a living.' She shuddered.

'We've got a bunch of Cruella de Vils on our doorstep. All of a sudden this place has got much more exciting.'

'It's not exciting, Beck. It's horrible.'

'Sorry.' He squeezed her hand. 'You stay out of it.'

'What?'

'The crime detection. I'm the sticky beak in this outfit.'

'I found her body. I can't help being curious about it.'

He sighed. 'I'd like to know what that boy Jaron Wignall's story is. Did he look distressed that his girlfriend had been found in a pit with a spear through her chest?'

'Not really.'

'The other blokes didn't look that distressed either. Funny if they'd all had a poke at her.'

'Maybe they didn't respect her.'

'Or like her.'

'Or like her father.'

'Not hard to dislike him. Corrupt, I bet.'

'I don't even think his kids like him. Peter seems permanently pissed off. And Charley clearly hates him. There's some resentment of Jack Harding too. Keith seems to prefer him to his sons.'

'I'd put Jack down as suspect number one. Too smug for my liking.'

'It wasn't him. Brendan said the time of death was early Friday morning. Jack caught the eight o'clock flight from Moruya to Sydney Friday morning. He's gone to Singapore for a few days. If Octavia was attacked around six on Friday morning then Jack couldn't have possibly done that and then gone and dragged Elisabeth into the Void and stuck her with the spear and then driven to Moruya, flown to Sydney and caught the international flight.'

'Maybe he didn't get on the plane.'

'I don't think that's it, Beck. I just can't see him running around slaughtering all those poor animals. He doesn't sound like he'd have the time for it, for one thing.'

'What about the rest of them?'

'Let's see...Peter's wife Diane is a number. Sour about not producing an heir. He doesn't seem to care as much about that as she does. And there's Michelle. She seems oblivious of everything. It's either an act or she's thick as two planks. I'd go for an act. They named the kid Keith, which is smart. And Carmel's probably easier to live with when she's patronising.'

'Than when she's what?'

Heidi thought a minute.

'Vitriolic? I do wonder why Peter married Diane. They don't seem to get on that well.'

'How did you work that out?'

'Body language. Things she said. I get the feeling Peter doesn't pay a lot of attention to her and she's bitter about it. She's older than him too. Only a few years, but she seems a *lot* older. Very demanding.'

'Maybe she's a goer.'

'I knew you'd say that. He might have married her to spite his mother. Or father. Keith didn't send him to art school.'

'Did he resent Elisabeth because Daddy let her do what she wanted?'

'No. Everyone says they were close. Charley seems the odd one out. Hot-headed and emotional, I'd say. The others are pretty cool characters.'

'Aside from the family, any butlers who might have done it?'

'There's a housekeeper and gardeners. Probably a pool boy. Talking about pools, a funny thing, though. Charley said Elisabeth was scared of the water.'

'Maybe she had an accident when she was a kid?'

'Could be.'

'It would be nice to know *when* she became afraid of the water, especially if it was in the past few years. Put that on your list.'

'I'm not keeping a list.'

He ignored her. 'Now, what about that mad old woman up the river? She's on my list.'

'I don't think she's mad. Quite the opposite.'

'How many people round here know she keeps spears?'

'Just about everyone.'

'Which rules out an unpremeditated attack by a passing truck driver.'

'I get the feeling the police have done that.'

'We need to find someone who was screwing Elisabeth and knew about Octavia's collection of spears and was familiar with the Void.'

'Well, that narrows it down.'

'You know what?' He suddenly stood up. 'I've got the weirdest feeling.'

She looked up at him, startled. 'What's that?'

'Lemon juice running down my sides.'

17

Brendan Barton had his head in a thick cookbook when Beckett walked into the police station the next morning. The place was otherwise deserted.

'I came to give that statement.' Beckett offered him a sherbet bomb from a cellophane pack.

'I thought only kids ate these,' he commented, declining. 'How's the wife? She over the shock?'

'The wife's fine, thank you. Carmel Bankston's keeping her busy.'

'Yeah, I noticed her there yesterday. Glad someone's making something out of this crappy business. We're pretty stretched, even with three blokes down from Sydney. The last real murder we had round here—I mean a real mystery—was eight years ago. I was still at school. Fifteen-year-old girl stabbed and dumped, the bloke was caught weeks later. A milk trucker passing by picks up a hitchhiker, loses it, panics, sticks her with a screwdriver, dumps her body. The old superintendent, Ian Harmer, thought it was a local at first. Had everyone in town suspicious of the other. Until another truckie pipes up and says he saw this milk tanker parked on the highway not far from the scene, right timing, too weird to ignore. They got the bloke, a new driver on the Nullin–Melbourne run. No record, but they reckon he'd killed before.'

'Sounds like it's pretty dangerous to be a girl around here.'

'You should tell your wife to be careful. It wasn't very smart sitting down there with that body. The killer might have come back.'

'Do me a favour and pay us a visit some time. Frighten her a bit. She seems to think she's invincible.'

'Glad to be of service any time. Now, you better give me your statement about the hat.'

'Then can I have it back?'

'Unlikely. The killer might have found it and taken it to the Void when he murdered Elisabeth.'

Barton had started keying Beckett's statement into the computer when they were interrupted by the explosive entrance of a young man in rolled up shirtsleeves and hipster jeans, brandishing a mobile phone.

'Brendan, where's Stan?'

'At an area command meeting in Bateman's.'

'What the fuck's he doing there? I've got two of your goons up at Blackpeters with a search warrant.'

'That'll be Cheryl and Steve.'

'I *know* who they are. Laureen called me on one of their mobiles. Says they're trying to confiscate the tanning tools and hunting knives. Of course, Crock won't let them. He's got his shotguns out. If he fires one shot, I'll say he was aggravated. You fellows trying to turn this into a blood bath?'

'We're conducting a murder investigation, Andy.'

'And you pick on the Blackpeters because Keith Bankston told you to?'

'This has nothing to do with Keith.'

'Good old Keith,' Beck said under his breath.

The young man looked sharply at him. 'Who are you?'

'Beckett Versec.' He held out his hand.

'Andrew Eagan.' The young lawyer took his hand without enthusiasm. His own was surprisingly fine, given that the rest of his skeleton was upholstered with hard muscle. He had dark stubble rather than hair, a left ear punctuated with various hoops and stones, and a tanned, bony face that would have been intimidating if not for his sloe eyes fringed with black lashes. His bodyshirt looked like one of Heidi's op shop specials, as did the brown corduroy jeans strung below the navel with a wide riveted belt. Beckett took the time to look at Eagan's feet and noted the same trendy suede sneakers they wore in Darlinghurst cafes, where you could put your feet up on chairs while you read the paper with your macchiato and biscotti.

Eagan's mobile rang. Beckett thought he recognised a few bars of the theme from 'Robin Hood'.

'Yeah?'

Brendan raised his eyebrows at Beckett as Eagan cupped a hand over one ear and spoke into the mobile.

'Laureen, calm down. They *cannot* question Spaz without a lawyer present. What? For Christ's sake, get Crock to put those guns down. You're what? Look, they can take it. They've got a warrant. I'll take a look at it, but they can dismantle the whole fucking house if they want to. Yes, it's a mistake. I know. Make sure Spaz doesn't say anything until he gets here, will you? Go in the car with him if you have to. Calm down. They're *not* arresting him, OK? They're just bringing him in for questioning. I'm here and I'll get him home. I promise. Now, get in the car.'

He snapped his phone shut. 'Why the hell didn't someone inform me? Cheryl Martin could have had her head shot off. It's fucking irresponsible.'

Barton looked embarrassed. 'They had the warrant.'

'Wave a piece of paper at them and someone's going to shoot at it. Crock's only defending his property.' He sighed. 'Look, Laureen said your goons found a dead animal. What has that to do with Elisabeth Bankston's murder? The Blackpeters skin animals for a living, for God's sake. There must be hundreds of animal carcasses up there. Certainly smells like it.'

'Someone's been killing animals in the same way Elisabeth was killed,' Barton said. 'We think they're connected.'

'And you think Spaz has been doing it?'

'It's possible. He's pretty riled up about Sid being in jail.'

'Doesn't make him a killer.'

'Actually, I don't think he's a killer, either,' Beckett interrupted.

Eagan folded his arms, looked sceptical. 'Why not?'

'Because I saw him with a dead animal just the other day. He looked distressed to me. He didn't seem like the kind of person who would hurt a fly.'

'Precisely. Thank you.' Eagan turned back to Barton. 'How many dead animals have there been, Brendan?'

'Eight or nine now. I've checked around. The Animal Rescue had a wallaby and a blue-tongue. The sawmill got a bandicoot.'

'So, there's nine dead animals and one dead girl. I still don't see the connection. Did he use the same weapon?'

'We're not sure. The spear we found with Elisabeth was stolen from Octavia Goodhope Friday morning. Spaz knows where she lives.'

'All the local kids know where she lives.'

Beckett interrupted again. 'Of course it couldn't have been the same weapon that killed the animals. Unless he borrowed it and took it back and borrowed it again.'

'Yeah, you might be right.' Brendan scratched his head. 'But then, she wasn't killed by a spear, was she? She was strangled first.'

'And the animals were strangled?' Eagan asked.

'No, I don't think so.'

'So what is the connection, Constable Barton?'

Brendan looked startled. 'I'll have to think about that.'

'Make sure you do. I'm going to be back in twenty minutes to meet the Keystone Kops when they bring Spaz in. They better have a few more clues than you do.' He turned and slammed the wire door behind him.

Barton sighed. 'Knew I should have been a chef.'

18

Heidi juggled soy milk, washing detergent, toilet paper, two cans of tomatoes and a tub of yoghurt at the supermarket checkout. She was aware, more than ever, that people were staring. At the same time, they were giving her a wide berth, as if she were someone to be feared. The woman behind stood several steps back, hugging her red plastic basket to her as if it were a crucifix and Heidi was a vampire with an appetite.

The boy at the checkout actually blushed when she said hello. She supposed he imagined that she had strangled Elisabeth with her bare braids.

It was the same in the newsagent. The woman behind the register seemed to know all about her.

'You're a bit of a celebrity round here,' the woman confided, tallying the stack of magazines Heidi placed on the counter. 'Finding poor Elisabeth and all. I bet that was a shock for you.'

'It wasn't very pleasant.'

'Who do you think did it?'

'I have no idea. I'm sure you know the town better than I do.'

'The police were in here, you know. They had the coat with them. A disgusting thing it was. But I suppose you'd know...'

'Did they want you to identify it?'

'Yes. We all had a look. But we'd never seen it before. I don't know who would buy such a thing. It didn't have a label. They said it was handmade. It wasn't mink, you know.'

'I guessed that.'

'Not even rabbit. They got some expert to look at it. It was dog.'

'*Dog?*'

'Imagine that. Different kinds of dog. I never had much against those Blackpeters. They never troubled me. But that's disgusting.'

'You think it was one of the Blackpeters who killed Elisabeth?'

The woman shook her head. 'I don't know. I don't like the idea of it being *anyone* local. It makes me go all strange thinking that they might have come into this shop.'

'Did Elisabeth ever come in here?' Heidi asked.

'No, can't say that she did. Poor Carmel. Losing two.'

'Two?'

'There was young Keith. Oh, but you're new, aren't you, dear? No one ever says a word about him anymore. I heard Carmel went around the house and took down all his pictures. I suppose she's taken down all of Elisabeth's too. Funny bird, that one.'

'Young Keith?' Heidi nudged the point.

'Oh, yes. Keith, their oldest son. A difficult boy, I think everyone would agree. Drowned eight years ago now, trying to save Elisabeth from the rip in Hapless Bay. Peter and Charley and young Jack saw the whole thing. It was terrible for them. Keith was nineteen then, would have been, let's see, twenty-seven today.'

'They had another son?'

'Well, sort of. Carmel couldn't have children for the longest time after she married big Keith, so they adopted the young lad. And, as mostly happens with families that adopt, she fell pregnant with her own, Peter, not long afterward.'

'And he was "difficult"?'

She grunted. 'You heard things. He was in and out of all kinds of schools. A loose cannon, if you ask me. Peter seems a nice boy, always helps out at the Lion's Christmas party, but you'd keep your daughters away from young Keith. He was the type who'd talk a young girl into trouble and then leave her holding the baby. Not literally, of course, but I wouldn't be surprised. Still, it was a pity he had to die, doing the one good deed of his life. And now poor Elisabeth. It's too much for one mother to bear.'

The old man waiting behind Heidi had been all ears. 'You're a gossip, Gwen Marsh,' he said.

'You can talk!' The woman winked at Heidi, not offended. She took Heidi's money and gave her change. 'A lot of people round here owe their living to Keith Bankston, especially when the fishing went bad. You have to be careful what you say. But that young Keith broke his mother's heart. The whole town knows that.'

19

Laureen Blackpeter stood in the middle of the police station between her son and Stephen Fraser. She was at least a head shorter than both men but Beckett had no doubt she'd be like a cornered possum in a fist fight, all claws and teeth. She cast her eyes from Fraser's face to his crotch and Beckett could see the big guy shift in his shoes, even though his face remained impassive. Cheryl Martin hovered behind Fraser while Barton stood uncomfortably behind his desk.

'You fucking mongrel,' Laureen growled at Fraser. She had long jet-black hair, faded to grey near the scalp, tied back with a blue sparkle scrunchie. Her face was small and pointed, like a sugar glider's, with clear green eyes, her skin wizened from the sun. She might have been sixty, except that her body seemed girlish underneath the tight, acid-washed denim jeans and wraparound pink acrylic cardigan. She was wearing a padded, push-up bra, Beckett, a connoisseur of these things, noted.

Spaz cringed and ran his long fingers over his scalp in agitation. His black hair was scraggly and touched his shoulders. When he raked it off his face, Beckett could see the veins of his hands under his milky skin and the hazy colour of his irises, as if his eyes were swimming in cream.

'It's all right, I'm here,' Andrew Eagan announced as he re-entered the police station. 'You can relax, Laureen.' He addressed Cheryl Martin. 'Are you charging him?'

'He's here for questioning in relation to the murder of

Elisabeth Bankston and the discovery of the carcasses of several animals. Beyond that, I can't say.'

'Keith Bankston shouldn't be so careless with his own fucking children!' Laureen snarled. 'There's no reason to take mine off of me.'

Eagan ignored the outburst. 'On what evidence are you holding him?'

Cheryl crooked her finger at him and took him aside out of earshot.

'What are they talking about?' Laureen said to Barton.

'You'll find out soon enough,' smiled Fraser.

'Fuck you,' Laureen spat.

'Come on, Laureen, calm down,' Barton said.

'I'm calm. I know what you blokes are up to. You're trying to fit us up for resisting arrest. We came quietly.' Laureen spluttered into a fit of coughing.

'How's the lung cancer?' Fraser smirked.

'Shut up, Fraser,' Martin said, returning with Eagan. 'Let Andy speak with his client for a few moments.'

'Oh, the kid talks?' Fraser said.

'I c-can talk.'

Everybody looked at the boy.

'I c-can talk,' Spaz repeated, in the creaky cadence of a male whose voice has just broken. 'I know what you're saying about me.'

'And what's that, Spaz?' Cheryl Martin asked.

'Spaz's not answering any of your questions yet, Cheryl,' Eagan interrupted.

'You're s-saying I killed those animals! I didn't do that. It's wrong to kill animals. I keep telling me dad. It's wrong.'

'You see?' Laureen put her hands on her hips. 'You're all pissin' on the wrong tree. My son's as innocent as a newborn babe.' She coughed again. 'Do any of you bludgers have a smoke?'

'Here,' said Eagan, reaching into his back pocket. He emerged with a crumpled pack of Winstons. Laureen snatched it and gestured for a match.

'Outside,' Fraser told them.

Laureen lit up. 'So arrest me.'

'Let's talk on the porch,' her lawyer suggested diplomatically. 'I assume that's all right with you lot?'

'Be our guest,' Martin said.

Beckett went to follow them, but Eagan stopped him with a stern look.

'Interested in this case, Mr Versec?' Cheryl Martin asked. 'Or a friend of the family?'

'Let's say an interested observer. What makes you think Spaz did it?'

'I'm afraid that information is not for interested observers.'

'All those Blackpeters are sickos,' Fraser said, his eyes on Spaz and Eagan out on the verandah. 'He might have had help from one of those brothers of his, or the old man…Oh Christ, here comes more trouble.'

The girl did look like trouble, if you were of the opinion that young women were trouble. Beckett watched with the others as she strode down the driveway and stopped to talk to Eagan. She was wearing a tiny red tartan skirt over shredded black leggings and Converse sneakers, a pale blue hooded sweatshirt that barely reached her navel and a khaki satchel over her shoulder, into which she was delving with one hand as she spoke, pulling out a notebook. Her brown hair was cut into the unflattering bowl-shape that city teenagers had adopted as a jokey reference to the seventies.

'Who's that?'

Barton answered. 'The press.'

'*The* press?'

'Yep. One half of it anyway. Her name's Kirstie Olley and her dad Bruce owns the *Nullin Voice*.'

'So she's a reporter? She looks like she's barely out of high school.'

'She's older than she looks. Spent the past few years in Sydney doing a communications degree.'

'Now she's communicating all over the place,' Fraser grumbled.

'Always on the lookout for hard news is our Kirstie.'

'Or hard something,' Cheryl Martin said.

Fraser turned around and glared at her.

'Got a bit of a crush on our Steve,' Barton confided. 'But it isn't reciprocated.'

'I'd rather kiss your gran,' Fraser grunted.

'See? Anyway, Kirstie can turn a few local kids doing wheelies down the main drag into a three-part series about how the town is failing its young people. God knows what she'll do with this case. She reckons she's syndicating Elisabeth's murder to five interstate papers.'

'Here she comes, Stevie,' Cheryl teased. 'You better lock yourself in the loo.'

Fraser clearly wished he could do just that, but Martin's taunt now meant he had to stay and face the music. He shrugged, though Beckett could see he tried to make his large frame shrink as the petite young woman pushed at the door and entered the station.

She ignored Fraser and strode up to Brendan Barton. 'Have you arrested Spaz?' she demanded.

Barton was like a rabbit frozen in headlights. 'We've just brought him in for questioning.'

'On what basis?'

'We haven't questioned him yet.'

She wasn't about to give up. 'Why on earth would poor Spaz kill Elisabeth? What evidence do you have?'

'You'll have to wait for the press briefing.'

'And when will that be?'

'We don't know.'

'Come on, Brendan, you know me. I *am* the press.'

'We believe the same person who killed Elisabeth may be responsible for the recent deaths of several native animals. And Spaz was seen by a local resident carrying a dead kangaroo just before one was found on the golf course.'

'Who's your source?' She started scribbling in her notebook.

'Alan Rickards.'

'He's half blind. You took his licence off him.' Kirstie flipped through her notebook. 'Any news on the results of the autopsy?'

'Tomorrow.'

'What about cross-referencing the murder against other similar crimes?'

'Nothing's come up so far.'

'Any progress on her personal effects?'

'We're still looking for her clothes and handbag.'

'What kind of handbag was it? Expensive?'

Cheryl Martin looked at her notes. 'Louis Vuitton, brown with cream writing on it. Carmel reckons it was worth four grand.'

'Anything in it?'

'She always carried cards, but not much cash. There was a mobile phone. We've called it, and her voice mail answered at first, but we couldn't locate it. Battery's dead now, we think.'

'The talk round the pub is that she was tied with leather cords. Have you traced them yet?'

'We're not at liberty to discuss that.'

'Come on, Cheryl, this is me, Kirstie, you're talking to.'

'They're made of greenhide. Hand-braided.'

'Have you worked out what he used to strangle her? Someone suggested he used her dress.'

'Wait for the autopsy results. All we know was that it was something wide. A tie maybe.'

'What do her friends say?'

'We're questioning them now.'

'Family?'

'The boys and their wives didn't go to the ball. Peter didn't see her at all on Thursday. Charley saw her that morning. Keith and Carmel came home after the ball, only worked out she was missing the next morning.'

Kirstie closed her notebook. 'Where's that bloke who's head of the task force?'

'He's out.'

'Come on, Brendan. You don't seriously think Spaz did it?'

'*I* don't,' said Beckett.

She cocked her head in surprise. 'Who are you? A detective from Sydney?'

Before Beckett could say anything, Barton chipped in. 'Beckett? No, he's just a writer.'

'Thanks.' Beckett made a face.

Kirstie frowned. 'What paper?'

'No, no, I'm a *screen*writer. I'm not here to report on anything.'

She peered at him. 'Now I remember. I've heard about you. You're the movie mogul from Milk Mountain. My dad ran a small gossip item about you in the paper a few weeks ago.'

'I fled Sydney to escape gossip. What did it say?'

'I can't remember, but I got the impression Nullin was going to be the new hub of the Australian film industry.' She turned to Stephen Fraser. 'Did you hear that Stevie? Maybe you can audition for a role. They always want men with muscles like yours.'

'Yeah, sure,' Fraser grunted and kept staring out the window.

'When do you think you'll be finished with Spaz?' Kirstie asked Cheryl Martin. She looked at her watch. 'I've got to meet our photographer at Adelaide Harding's place in a minute. It's her hundredth birthday and she's got a telegram from the Queen.'

'Can't say. We have to wait for the Sydney blokes to question him,' Cheryl told her. 'You could call us at tea-time.'

'All right. I'll drop in later.'

As she went out the door, she patted Stephen Fraser on the bum. He scowled and turned crimson.

Beckett followed Kirstie Olley out of the police station. On the verandah, Andrew Eagan was still in deep consultation with Spaz. Laureen was stomping out a cigarette with the heel of her boot.

'Officer Fraser's quite a hunk.' Beckett watched Kirstie unchain her bike from a lamppost outside the milk bar.

She shoved the chain in a basket on the front of the bike, a faint blush on her cheeks. 'He's a lout. But as men go around here...'

'Not much choice?'

'Unless you like them with the stink of tuna on their hands or beer on their breath. Or with a wife.' She jerked the bike off the nature strip and started walking with it.

'Oh, I don't know about that. Jaron Wignall's pretty attractive.'

'Is that the best you can come up with?'

'That's what Elisabeth Bankston came up with.'

'Jaron? Really?'

'My wife saw them canoodling at the debutante ball.'

'I begged off from that one. Can't stand those right-wing retro events. Was she sure it was Jaron?'

'We found out his name later.'

'I take it you're proposing the theory that it was a jealous lover?'

'Well, it's hardly that poor Spaz.'

'You're right there. You sure you don't work for a newspaper?'

'Cross my heart.'

'What's your interest in all this?'

'I'm a writer. I can't resist a good story. It's exactly what I hoped for. A small town hiding a dirty secret.'

'Make that several dirty secrets. Some of them are not so secret, of course. And most of them are fairly pathetic. It's all about teenage girls getting pregnant and wives running off with the tradesmen and someone having his hand in the Lions Club till. You're lucky to arrive when we've had a murder. The first in a long time. They beat the shit out of each other here but it usually stops short of killing.'

'The last murder was pretty grisly. Brendan told me about it. The girl and the truck driver.'

'Valerie Harding?'

'Harding?'

'Yep. I went to school with her. Scared the crap out of us girls. We all stopped hitchhiking then. Well, for a few weeks, until they caught him. It's her great-grandmother I'm going to see, Adelaide Harding. They live just around the corner here.'

She turned into Emerald Street. The houses thinned out near the water, replaced by blocks of flats of varying age and condition, most of them built in the fifties and sixties. A lone beach towel hung on a Hill's hoist at the back of one building, testament to the change in season and the absence of holidaymakers.

On the corner of Emerald and Opal Drive a large pink stucco hacienda loomed, fringed by banana palms that would bear no fruit in this climate. He'd always assumed the building was a guesthouse, but Kirstie stopped outside the high wrought-iron gate and waved to a teenager with a camera bag standing inside. 'Well, goodbye,' she said, holding out her hand to Beckett and dismissing him.

He wasn't so easily dismissed. He shook her hand and held it. 'This is quite a place. Does the family come from old money?'

'Nah. Adelaide's husband, Wally Harding, was born in a humpy back of Speculator. Russ Harding, Valerie's dad, worked all his life for Nullin Cheese. You could say they got lucky when Valerie died—a British tabloid paid the family a quarter-million for the story because Valerie's mum, Sheila, is a pom. This was the old Tropicana Hotel. Russ pissed away all his money on it, moved Adelaide and the rest of the family in—Sheila, and Valerie's brother Jack—and then offed himself. They wouldn't be able to pay the council rates except that Sheila owns the cake shop in town and Jack's one of Keith Bankston's top men.'

'I know the cake shop.' He often dropped in there. They did a fine neenish tart. 'And I met Jack at the debutante ball. A bit stuck on himself, as they say around here.'

'He's done well, our Jack.'

Beckett watched her lock her bike inside the gate and then turned away. Huge grey cumulus clouds scuttled across the sky, pushed by an anxious wind. The last vestiges of sun warmed the boardwalk along Opal Drive, so he took a stroll. A flock of pelicans skidded along the smooth surface of the inlet. He threw them a sherbet bomb and didn't wait as the bird who caught the offering flapped its wings and squawked in indignation.

The rain came down, suddenly, as if summoned by the angry bird.

20

Heidi drove away from Nullin and the rain came down in sheets across the road. She drove slowly, careful of the wake thrown up by passing trucks.

On the highway she saw a police caravan parked on a muddy verge. She slowed down. A police officer she didn't recognise was dashing towards the van with a sodden department-store mannequin pressed awkwardly under his arm. The white gown trailed in the mud. The mannequin dropped a white sandal. She honked and pointed to let the startled policeman know.

A few hundred metres up the road, she passed the Nullin caravan park. It was visible from the highway, where it sat on the northern cliffs of the town, its grounds sheltered from the blustering sea winds by a copse of gnarled pines. This was one of the best views in the district, but out of season the cluster of aluminium vans had the same stubborn, disconsolate air of the last drunk in a pub at closing time.

Heidi pulled over and tapped the steering wheel. She turned the car around and headed back, stopping in the visitor's carpark outside the gates. Her sandals squelched in the mud as she made a run to the front office, covering her head inadequately with a bundle of the flyers she kept in the glove box.

As far as she could see there were dozens of vacant allotments, yet the sign over the door read NO VACANCY. She stepped up onto the narrow verandah, which was hung with mossy pots of something that had long stopped flowering, and turned a brass bell beside the wire screen door. Dogs started howling from somewhere at the back of the house. A woman's voice quieted them. It took some time, but eventually a shape ambled along the hallway, stopped short of opening the door and asked, somewhat suspiciously, 'Yes?'

Heidi couldn't make out the face in the back light of a sunroom at the end of the hall, but the woman was small with short, spiky hair. She was also wearing a neck brace. 'Mrs Wignall?'

The shape neither confirmed nor denied it. 'I'm not buying anything.'

Heidi assumed her friendliest voice. 'And I'm not selling. But I am just starting up my own small business in this town and I wondered if I could put up a couple of notices around here.'

'What kind of business?'

'I'm a massage therapist.'

She could hear the woman intake a heavy breath. 'Get off the property or I'll call the cops.'

Heidi cursed herself for not being specific enough. 'No, you don't understand. Not that kind of massage. I'm a medical practitioner. Look—' She stepped forward and placed a notice against the wire screen so the woman could read it. 'I've got a few patients who can vouch for me. Do you know Carmel Bankston?'

'Everyone knows Carmel Bankston.' The woman didn't budge, but Heidi thought she was reading the notice. 'You won't find many with the money for it around here,' she said. Her voice was slightly slurred. Pills, alcohol or brain damage? Heidi couldn't tell. 'Those that's on the dole spend it on cigarettes or booze.'

'There might be someone here with a sports injury, perhaps?'

'Well, that could be my son, Jaron. He's always hurting hisself, playing that stupid football. You can go and ask him if you want. Won't do much good, though. He hasn't got a penny of his own to scratch his arse with.'

'Where can I find him?'

'At the end of the first road on the right. You can't miss his van. The little bugger's tarted it all up.' The woman shrunk back into the hallway, then added in a whisper, 'Gray'll spew if you put those notices up around the place. He likes to keep the park neat. Be a good girl and just put one inside the ladies' toilets where he won't see it, will you?'

Where was Gray? Heidi suddenly had the distinctly creepy feeling that he was in the house listening to them. 'No problem,' she said.

Mirna closed the door.

Heidi stepped over a puddle. The rain had swept through the grounds as quickly as it had come. She shook the drops off her flyers and set off to find Jaron.

The road ran down near the edge of the cliff, ending, Heidi could see, in a sort of lookout over the water. In January, the village would be full to capacity with families who preferred the nostalgia of the place to the town's cheap motel rooms or seaside villa units. Kids would roam free, in packs, playing hide-and-seek in the communal toilet block or searching for sea monsters in the honeycomb of rocks under the cliffs, while their parents dealt games of canasta on card tables in their canvas annexes or poked at sausages frying on collapsible Portagas stoves. Towels would flap on makeshift clotheslines and wading pools slosh water on the balding lawns, the scent of Coppertone in the air.

Now, most of the lots were vacant, but Heidi could make out about ten caravans scattered around the property. Some of the permanent residents had attempted to make their homes sweeter by erecting striped canvas extensions, complete with plastic windows and doors, seashell rockeries, children's cubby-houses, basketball hoops and white picket fences around the perimeter. The most established vans boasted hanging plants, sun lounges positioned under plastic potted palms and metal letter-boxes. One resident had neglected to gather his flock of plastic flamingos and they were leaning higgledy-piggledy in the squally cliff-top wind.

There was a certain cheerlessness about the place that the grey concrete amenities did nothing to improve. Gray Wignall might have kept the lawns trimmed and the toilets clean but he'd made no effort that Heidi could see to do more than this. No kiddies' swings and slides. No communal barbeques. Not a single flowerbed or sign. The blue sky and the sparkling sea would be all the place needed in summer, but right now it looked as bleak as the exercise yard of a maximum security prison.

She turned into the first of two sandy streets and passed a woman who had started to hang faded floral sheets on a clothesline. 'Jaron?' Heidi asked. The woman, whose mouth was full of wooden pegs, nodded to where the road fizzled out in a clump of tea-tree. Heidi could see a red-and-black ute, a lawnmower propped in the back along with two surfboards.

Heidi had to push through the twisted trees until they opened out into a clearing. There was a caravan parked in the middle of it with an orange one-man tent pitched next door. A wide dirt track disappeared into the trees on the other side. She could see what Mirna Wignall meant when she said Jaron had 'tarted' it up. The side of the van facing her was covered with a lurid painting of a naked woman, her legs astride the van door and her hair floating around her head like kelp twisting in the sea. It was a clumsy attempt in terms of proportion and technique. The figure's genitals resembled her open mouth. Scraps of house paint had been used, judging by the limited colours. It wasn't a wall treatment you'd find in *Good Housekeeping*.

The caravan's windows had awnings and they were heavily curtained with an orange and brown fabric. Drips of water tumbled off the frames. There was no music, cigarette smoke or cooking smells coming from the van. If Jaron helped his father with the caravan park, then he might be out now in another part of the grounds. Or at football practice. She looked at her watch. It was after 2 p.m. She should have come earlier. Or later. Exactly *when* did you catch a young man at home? It was a long time since she'd had to think of that.

'Admiring the art work?'

Heidi might have jumped out of her skin-tight jeans, if they weren't zippered so firmly. She turned around. Jaron was standing outside the tent, a bath towel loosely gripped around his hips, scratching his head with his free hand. He'd clearly been sleeping.

'Sorry. I didn't mean to wake you,' she said.

'Are you looking for me?'

'Your mother said I could find you here.'

'You found me.' He clutched at his towel. 'Hang on a mo.'

He disappeared into the tent. She could hear him grunting and stumbling around. He emerged in a pair of jeans and a flannel shirt. She wished he hadn't. He was a fine specimen semi-naked.

'So what can I do you for?' he asked, picking up an empty beer can and crushing it in his hands.

'Did you do the painting?' she asked.

'It's pretty ordinary.' He ambled towards her. His hair, newly liberated from the pillow, was flattened over one ear, sticking up over the other. She could see now that the white was not chemically induced. The kids at school had probably called him 'Snowy'. His eyes were light blue, but his skin was tanned, partly disguising the fading bruise on his face, the purple turning a yellow-green.

'No. I think it's good. Who's the subject?'

He shrugged. 'No one.'

'I gather your mother doesn't approve.'

'She doesn't have to look at it.'

'What about your girlfriend?'

She could feel him shut down on her. His hand squeezed the beer can again. He suddenly threw it at a wire rubbish bin with more force than necessary. The can bounced off the caravan's side and dropped in a muddy puddle. 'Remind me why you're here,' he said.

Damn, she thought. I'm no good at this. I've got to connect

with him again. 'I hear you're a champion footballer.'

'Are you selling insurance or something?' He walked past her and opened the caravan door. 'I thought I'd seen you somewhere.'

'You saw me at the debutante ball.'

'Oh?' He stopped and turned. 'I was helping a mate out with the party hire. What of it?'

'You were in the storeroom with Elisabeth Bankston.'

'So that was you.' She was surprised to see he wasn't disturbed by this. 'We were just fooling around.'

'Don't you think that was a little bit unwise?'

'Fucking hell! Don't you people ever stop?' He slammed the side of the van with his fist. Heidi edged backwards. He then rubbed his hand and stretched the fingers, looking at them as if they'd acted on their own. He didn't look at her. 'You another cop?'

'No, I'm a massage therapist.'

He looked at her now. 'Is this some sort of joke? Did one of the blokes send you?'

'No. Your mum said you get sports injuries from time to time. I'm just touting for business. Look.' She handed him a flyer.

He took it, read it, then handed it back. 'Kim Blinko's the physio in town. He's not going to be too happy about you taking his business.'

'I only do massage. Besides, he must be pretty busy in football season with all you guys getting injured. That's a nasty bruise by the way.'

Jaron put a hand on the affected cheek. 'Yeah, ran into the goalpost.'

'It's a brutal game. Look, I'm sorry about Elisabeth. It must have been an awful shock.'

He stared right through her. The conversation was going to end if she didn't take a chance. She risked it. 'Was she going to tell her mother about you?' she asked gently.

'None of your business,' he said, still staring. 'I don't know why a bloke can't root a girl without everyone making a song and dance about it.'

'Her parents?'

'No, my fucking parents, if you really want to know. There's bad blood between Gray and Keith. Look around you. It's a fucking unreal spot isn't it? Keith's been trying to buy this land from under Gray for years. Dad's got a twenty-five-year lease, fourteen to go. But Keith, the bastard, is trying to get him evicted. Saying the property's run-down, not reaching its full potential, whatever. It's all bullshit. Keith and his mates want to build a casino and resort here. They're trying to turn the town against us, saying we're the only ones holding them all off from making a fortune.'

'What did Elisabeth say about it?'

'She hates her dad.'

'But it seems like he adored her.'

'Lizzie is good at making people adore her.'

Is not was. Heidi detected bitterness underlying his bravado. 'Who else adored her?'

'I can't say.'

'She was a pretty girl.'

'Lizzie flirted with everyone to piss off her folks. Carmel's got some bee in her bonnet about Lizzie getting pregnant to one of the local peasants.'

'And you were one of them?'

'I liked her and she was a good fuck, OK? Does it have to be any more than that? I'm not going to leave here and she wasn't going to come and live in a van with me, was she? So it was just fun.'

'So you were screwing the Bankstons in more ways than one. Why didn't your dad approve?'

'Because he thought she was a slut, the stupid fucker.'

'What if Keith won, and you all got turfed out of the park?'

'Then we'd have to find another one.'

'I can't imagine you're the sort of guy whose life ambition is to run a caravan park.'

'What do you know about me? I like it here. No one's in my face. I can go surfing whenever I want.' He turned and stepped up into the van. 'I don't need a massage, but I'll tell the other blokes.' He closed the door behind him.

End of conversation.

Heidi found her way back to the road, but not before she'd left one of her pamphlets under the windscreen on Jaron's ute. She went into the ladies' toilets and taped a notice to a cinderblock inside the door.

The dogs started up as she walked back to her car. She could see a dog run behind the Wignall house. Two pit bulls and a rottweiler were hitched together on very short leads, straining against them. She walked as close as she dared to the caged area. The dogs pulled at their collars and chains. She could see, even from a few metres away, that their collars had rubbed welts on their necks and that the skin was festering and pussy where the fur had been stripped off.

'Shut up you mongrels!' Mirna Wignall stepped into the yard and produced a can of some kind of aerosol, which she sprayed directly in their faces. The dogs yelped in pain and cringed. Heidi winced. Jaron's mum may have been a victim of her husband's violence but she had learned from him how to torment other creatures.

Had Jaron learnt the same lesson?

21

Beckett manoeuvred the Volvo over the slushy roads, peering through a windscreen obscured by fine spits of rain and the spidery crack where the Blackpeter brat's stone had landed. Something Eagan said had been bothering him. Nine dead animals, one dead girl. If you saw a connection, the girl was the tenth dead animal. And he was sure that number signified something. Ten, decalogue, decathlon...there was something there he couldn't put his finger on.

On a straight stretch of the Princes Highway ahead of him a woman with two small children were trudging in the long grass at the side of the road. The woman turned and stuck out her thumb. She was wearing a light summer dress and a brown cardigan, her dark hair plastered to her head from the rain. In the crook of her arm was a bundle. The children, a boy and a girl, both under five, were dressed in their Sunday best. The little girl wore a puffed sleeve pink satin dress with many petticoats and the boy had on pants with braces and a blue shirt. Beckett could see that the little girl's long white socks were splattered with mud.

He pulled off the side of the road.

The woman ran to catch him, dragging the children behind her. She pushed the children in onto the back seat then plopped herself next to Beckett. The bundle in her arms was a baby in a crocheted shawl. It gave a little cry and then settled down.

'Ta,' she said, without looking at him.

Beckett nodded and made a funny face at the children. The

girl, who looked not much older than two, was sobbing but brightened up at this. The little boy scowled. He seemed familiar.

'Nice day for a walk,' Beckett commented as he accelerated.

'Just took them to see their dads,' the woman said. 'Every month on the dot,' she added firmly, as if proud of her efficiency.

Beckett sneaked a sideways look at her as he drove. She was much younger than her dowdy clothing suggested, barely voting age. She had skin the colour of yellowing gardenias and tangled hair that was brown as malt. The children were both snowy-headed and tanned. Either this was genetic, or their mother didn't show much interest in the warnings about skin cancer.

'My name's Beckett.'

'Joey.' She kept looking straight ahead.

'Where are you headed?'

'Just drop us at the Speculator turn-off,' she said. 'We can walk.'

'I don't mind dropping you at your door.'

'S'OK.'

'Have you been walking far?'

'A few miles.'

'Mummy?'

Joey turned around. 'What?' she asked impatiently.

'Are you giving us away to this man?'

'Of course not.'

'Can I live with my daddy?'

'Me too. Can I?'

'I've told you. Your daddies can't look after you.'

'Why?'

'Why?'

'Why why why.'

'Shut up you little buggers!' Joey yelled and hit the back of the seat with her hand. 'Or I *will* give you away.'

The little girl started bawling and the boy began to kick Beckett's seat.

'Do you want to get in the back with them?' Beckett asked.

'Just ignore them,' she said. 'That's what works.'

'They have different fathers?' Beckett said this casually, but she took offence.

'So? What's wrong with that?'

'Nothing.' He took his hands off the steering wheel, a gesture of innocence. 'It's pretty common.'

'Yeah, well one of them's got a restraining order against me. But there's no harm in taking little Possum here, my boy, to look at his house. He gets the message.'

'He's not supporting you?'

'Not bloody enough. He reckons he's got enough mouths to feed.'

'What about the girl's father?'

'Same story.' She turned around and squeezed the little girl on one of her muddy patent-leather-clad feet. 'Isn't it, Petal?'

He couldn't tell if the children's names really were Possum and Petal. It was possible. 'What about the baby?' he asked.

'Hasn't seen his dad yet.'

'Do you want a blanket or something to keep him warm?'

'No. He's a tough little bugger.'

They drove in silence for a while. Past Hapless Bay he had to swerve to avoid the huge carcass of a red kangaroo splayed across the road. Joey whipped her head around and pointed it out to the kids. 'That was a beauty, wasn't it?'

Beckett had been slow to work it out. 'You're Joey Blackpeter, aren't you?' he asked.

She set her jaw. 'So, what of it?'

'I've met Possum before.'

'Oh?' Not very interested.

'He threw a rock at me.'

'Yeah, he's always doing that.' She looked at him. 'What did *you* do?'

'I was paying a social call.'

'You a cop?'

'Do I look like one?'

'Can't say you do.'

'I lost my hat.'

'Yeah.'

'It was found in the Void.'

'Lots of things end up there.'

'Elisabeth Bankston did.'

She shifted in her seat. 'Everyone uses the Void,' she said cryptically.

'But it's abandoned.'

'For fucking, stupid.'

'I heard they park up there.'

'Yeah. And their parents did it too. Probably their grand-parents.'

'Do you think Elisabeth took men up there?'

She shrugged.

He guessed something. 'Your brother Spaz goes up there all the time, doesn't he? Do you think he ever saw her?'

She clutched the baby so tight, it gave a little start. 'See, you've woken up the baby,' she muttered.

'I don't think your brother did it, you know.'

'Well, you're a bloody genius.'

'But he might have seen who she was with.'

She didn't say anything for a while. 'Look, you can drop us here, if you like,' she said as they went over the creek.

'At the turn-off?'

'Yeah. We're not far from where we're going.'

'I'll take you.'

'You bloody well won't.' She looked so fierce, he pulled over immediately. Possum started jumping up and down on the seat.

'But it's going to rain again.'

'Only water. Come on, ratbags.' Still cradling the baby, she opened the back door and the two small children spilled out. The

135

little girl fell into a puddle and muddied her dress. Joey bent over and smacked the back of her legs.

Beckett leaned over to close the passenger door and the young woman put her head back in. 'Don't need a kid, do you? I've got a spare. I could do you a nice price.'

As he watched her go he wasn't sure if she'd been joking or not.

22

Heidi, enraged by Mirna's treatment of the dogs, lunged against the wire fence and rattled it to get Mirna's attention. 'Stop that, please! You're only making them worse!'

Mirna turned but her eyes looked past her.

She didn't hear him come up behind her.

'Seen anything interesting?' She felt the hot breath on the back of her neck and the rancid smell of alcohol from his open mouth enveloped her. Too late, she tried to move out of his way. He grabbed her elbow. Hard. Pinching the flesh between the bones.

She twisted her arm away but he held tight. 'Leave me alone!'

'I said, seen anything interesting,' Gray demanded, his voice calm with true menace. She was surprised how young he was, about twenty years older than his son, not much older than Beckett, she guessed. He would have been good-looking if he'd shaved off his grizzled stubble, with the same white hair as Jaron, close-cropped like a pelt. Anger flushed his tanned skin; a blue vein bulged over one bloodshot eye. Somewhere along the way, he'd sheared off a bottom tooth and hadn't bothered to get it replaced. Maybe he knew it made him look more threatening. As did the metal blade of the lawn edger he had hoisted over one shoulder.

She tried to pull her arm away again but he yanked her towards him. 'I've got one rule in this place,' he growled, his face close to hers. 'No one mentions the Bankstons around here without a good thumping.'

'Get off me or I'll call the cops!' She heard the front door creak and Mirna Wignall appeared on the verandah. 'Mrs Wignall?'

Gray laughed at her. 'She won't do you no good. She's always getting the cops up here about some crap, aren't you, Mirna? Trouble is, she never presses charges. She's happy with things as they are. That right, love?'

Mirna said nothing, just held her arms crossed low on her stomach, a cigarette smouldering between two fingers.

Heidi made a lunge for his testicles, but he brought the garden tool between his body and hers in time. He laughed again. 'You all want the same thing, don't you, sweetheart?' Still pinching her arm, he pushed the wooden handle of the lawn edger up between her legs. 'And if you're very very good, you might just get it.'

She jerked her free hand away from her side and pushed the tool away. Gray let it drop. 'Don't you like long hard things, darling?' He pushed her back against the wire and grazed her neck with his rough stubble.

She tried to kick his ankles but her sandals hit air. She twisted her neck and tried to get Mirna's attention. 'Help me!'

'I see,' Gray said, sliding a hand up her thigh. 'You're shy. Why don't we go out back and get some privacy? Mirna won't mind. We might even ask her to watch.'

'You bastard!'

He pushed her up the steps and into the house. He forced one arm behind her back and held her waist tight, lifting her off the ground effortlessly whenever she tried to wriggle away.

The hallway was dingy and smelled of dog food. Out the back a verandah gave on to a dry yard scattered with building materials and rusting machines.

Gray took her to the gate of the dog run and held her to him while he opened the lock. She managed to get a decent blow to his shins, but it didn't shift his smile. He shoved her into the cage and followed, kicking the gate closed behind him.

The dogs were snarling at the other end of the stretch of dirt, straining on their chains. She didn't like the look of the flimsy railing to which they'd been tethered. She looked around for a toehold to climb the fence. There was an upturned bucket near a lean-to but it was hardly tall enough for her to use as a spring-board and she didn't want to excite the dogs any more. Mirna had stayed in the house. Heidi's only hope was that one of the other park residents would hear her voice and emerge from their vans.

Gray stood there, arms folded, smiling at her dilemma. 'Everyone round here minds their own business.'

'As soon as I'm out of here, I'm getting the cops,' she threatened. 'I'm not like Mirna.'

He snorted. 'I'll just tell them I thought you were one of them greenies. A bunch of 'em tried to free the dogs about six months back. That's trespassing.'

'Constable Barton knows I'm not a greenie.'

'But how do I? Mistaken identity then. Not enough to put a bloke in jail or even break out into a sweat. Now be a good girl and be quiet. The dogs don't like noise, it can make them very upset.'

He came towards her and she backed into a corner of the fence. The dogs were frenzied now, smelling her fear. There was nowhere else to go. She had to stand her ground.

Keep Gray talking.

'I was talking to your son about Elisabeth Bankston.'

'So?'

'I thought he might have known something about her death.'

'What's it to you?'

'I was her friend.'

'Never liked the bitch.' He smiled. 'Wish I could take credit for getting rid of her, but I can't.'

This outraged her. She forgot about the snarling dogs. 'But Jaron was mad about her. She was mad about him. Wouldn't that have pissed off her father? And that would have made you happy?'

'She was making a fool out of my boy with those other blokes.'

'A good enough reason to kill her.'

'It started long before Jaron stuck his oar in.'

'What did?'

'Keith was always careless with his children. Stands to reason.'

'What do you mean?'

He tapped his skull and smirked. 'I'm smarter than the lot of you. You've got to look at how the first one died.'

'The first one? You mean young Keith?'

'Yeah, the bastard.'

'He drowned accidentally.'

'I don't know about that.'

'You mean it wasn't an accident?'

'I'm just saying that maybe he was too much trouble. Like Elisabeth.'

'You think Keith Bankston killed his own children?'

'Not up to me to say.'

'But you're going to spread the rumours anyway.'

She'd been too familiar. Gray's face shut down, the same way Jaron's had. She was against the wire now. He grasped one of her braids before she could duck.

'Let me go!' She screamed in pain, clawing at his hand. 'If you touch me you'll be in deep shit whether I'm a greenie or not!'

'Let her out, Gray!'

Jaron was standing outside the dog run, at the far end, his fingers through the wire. She hadn't heard him, didn't know how long he'd been there. 'Jaron! Help me!'

'Let her out Gray!'

A bewildered look crossed Gray's face. He dropped his hand and shrunk back. She was shocked at the change in him. Jaron disappeared into the house and appeared again at the gate. Gray stood there passively while Jaron opened the gate.

'She's Keith Bankston's spy, son,' Gray said.

'Come on,' Jaron said, ignoring him, and held out a hand. Heidi took it and followed him through the house. Mirna was sitting at the kitchen table, grimly watching a small television set on top of the fridge. She didn't acknowledge them as they passed.

At Heidi's car, Jaron asked, 'Are you able to drive?'

'I'm fine.'

'It's my fault. He's paranoid. It's the booze. I just didn't realise...'

'Why don't you take your mother and leave him? Surely it would be safer for both of you.'

'I can control him.'

'I see that. But your mother can't.'

'She won't go. She's used to him like that.' He looked at his feet. 'It's their business.'

Heidi put her key in the car door. 'I can drive you if you like,' Jaron said.

'I'm fine. Really.' She paused for a moment. 'You said your dad's paranoid. How much do you think he knows about the Bankston family?'

'He's had a thing about Keith Bankston even before he started this shit about kicking us out. He goes into the library sometimes and looks at the old newspapers. What did he say?'

'Something about Keith drowning his son.'

'Yeah, his brain's addled. As if.'

'Your dad seems to think young Keith was trouble.' She wanted to add 'like Elisabeth' but didn't dare break his mood.

'I don't know. I was a kid. People don't talk about it much, out of respect.' He gave a bitter laugh at that. 'I do know that Mr and Mrs Bankston were overseas when it happened. They had to fly back. So what Gray says is more of his bullshit.'

Heidi turned her key in the lock. 'Thanks, anyway. I wasn't snooping, you know. I just wanted to drum up some business.'

Jaron reached over and opened the car door for her. 'Well, you might have found a customer.'

I was wrong about Jaron, Heidi thought. He defends women, not murders them.

They both turned when they heard a car come skidding towards them.

Beckett spotted Heidi's car from the highway. From where he sat, it looked as if Jaron was making a gesture of aggression. He couldn't see her face, but her body language suggested she was trying to get away. He floored the accelerator of the Volvo, caught the back tyres in some loose gravel and had to swerve to miss Heidi's Kingswood, sliding to a halt with the rear of his car facing hers.

He jumped out immediately and screamed at Jaron to back away. Heidi put her hands on her hips and glared at him. The blood was boiling in his ears and he didn't hear what she was yelling. He ran up to a startled Jaron, grabbed a handful of his shirt and pushed him. Jaron barely stumbled, caught Beckett's wrist in his hand and pulled it down by his side, as easily as if it were the arm of a poker machine. 'What's your problem, mate?' he asked, more casually than the situation would demand.

'Get your hands off my wife!'

'Beckett!'

'It's OK, Heidi. I'm here now.' Beckett wrestled his arm away.

'Very brave of you, Beckett, but Jaron wasn't doing anything.'

'I saw him attack you.'

'He was saying goodbye.'

'I've heard of jealous husbands,' Jaron said, 'but this is ridiculous.'

Beckett looked at both of them and rubbed his hand. 'Well,

why were you looking so…alarmed?'

'I wasn't. Jaron and I were just having a chat.'

'A chat?'

'Look, mate, I've got to get back to it.' Jaron put his hands in his pockets. He said to Heidi, 'You sure you're safe with this man?'

'Not entirely,' she said.

He looked confused for a moment. 'Sure thing.' He gave a sluggish wave and backed away until he got to the gate of the park then walked purposefully towards the house.

'Are you still mad at me?' Beckett made Heidi a cup of tea and put it in front of her on the kitchen table. She took it and said nothing. He sat opposite her. 'If you don't smile I'm going to go back and thump Gray right now.'

That got a reaction. She looked at him with blazing eyes. 'What good will that do? I was terrified but he didn't really hurt me. But he might lay into Mirna in retaliation.'

'So? She didn't raise a finger to help you.'

'Beck, don't be so neanderthal. She's the victim. She was frightened.'

'I don't believe that victim stuff. How could a decent woman stand by and watch her husband threaten another woman?'

'She thought I was to blame. Maybe she convinced herself I *was* a prostitute.'

'Maybe she convinced herself Elisabeth was a prostitute and went after her with a tie and spear?'

'Don't be flippant. Gray's the violent one in the family.'

'Not Jaron?'

She shook her head. 'He isn't a killer.'

'Just because he has a pretty face.'

'Not that. He pretends Elisabeth was only a fuck, but you can tell he's deeply wounded.'

Beckett gave a harrumph. 'He's a footballer. I'm suspicious of anyone who plays team sports.'

143

'I think there was a bit of a Romeo and Juliet thing going on there. Gray hates the Bankstons. Keith's been trying to take his caravan park off him.'

'So maybe Gray did it, then. To get back at Keith.'

'That's as far-fetched as everything else. Gray says we should be looking into the death of young Keith.'

'*Young* Keith?'

'The Bankston's oldest son. He drowned off Nullin Point.' She explained what the woman in the newsagency had told her.

'A horrible story, but what has a drowning eight years ago got to do with anything?'

'Gray suggested something about Elisabeth and young Keith being too much trouble. As if their father was responsible for both their deaths.'

'That's just crap to deflect the heat from himself.'

'Probably. Keith wasn't even in the country when his son drowned, apparently. But I got the feeling it was crap that Gray at least partly believed.'

'Which means you don't think Gray had anything to do with Elisabeth's murder.'

She tapped her fingers on her cup. 'I'd love to dob him in. He's a sadist and a sexual predator. But you should have seen the way he backed off when Jaron challenged him. Maybe underneath all that violence, he's a pathetic creature who can't get it up.'

Beckett made a grunt of frustration. 'He's a typical bully. Why do you always make excuses for people?'

'Because there's good in everyone. If you can just find it...'

'I don't agree. Some people are all bad. They'll never redeem themselves. Gray's one of them. You should tell the cops.'

'What are they going to charge him with?'

'I don't know. Assault?'

'I don't have any bruises. He could argue I was trespassing.'

Beckett banged his fist on the wicker table and sent a teaspoon flying. 'Bloody hell, Heidi, why do you put yourself in these situations? You sit in the quarry with Elisabeth's body when the killer might be watching you and you accuse a monster like Gray of murder when there's no one around to defend you.'

'Jaron was there. It was all right in the end.'

'One day it's not going to be all right in the end.'

'I know what I'm doing.'

'You don't have to be a crusader all by yourself.'

She reached over and put a hand on his knee. 'Look, Beck, I feel responsible for Elisabeth's death, that's all. I can't get over the sense that I could have done something. Maybe if I *had* told her mother that night what I saw, Carmel would have gone looking for her and things would have been different.'

'Things wouldn't have been different. Someone out there was set on killing her.'

'How do we know that? It could have been a crime of passion. By telling Carmel I could have broken the cycle.'

'Well, if you believe Gray, as you seem to do, something happened way in the past that set off that cycle. It was nothing to do with you.'

'Elisabeth wants me to be involved.'

'That's silly.'

Heidi took her hand off Beckett's knee. 'You can think that if you like. But sometimes it's strangers who have the clarity to solve things. We can see what friends and family miss.'

'Like what?'

'I'm intrigued by this stuff about young Keith. It's like he never existed.'

'Do we know anything about him?'

'He was "difficult". In and out of different schools. The kind of boy you'd keep your daughters away from.'

'So, did he get a young girl pregnant? Is that the trouble Gray was talking about? I'd hardly imagine Keith doing his young son in because he'd knocked up a girl. He'd ship him off or something, wouldn't he?'

'Or rip his likeness out of a family portrait. I think Carmel went round the house and did that.'

'Do you think there's some eight-year-old kid running around that's young Keith's?'

'Even if there is I still don't see what it's got to do with Elisabeth—unless you believe it's all some kind of Greek tragedy. Keith saves his sister from drowning, the only good deed in his life, and then, eight years later, she fulfills the destiny proscribed for her by dying anyway.'

'And being skewered on a spear, remember?'

'Then the gods weren't responsible.'

'Only someone who thought he was God.'

Heidi thought about that. She started to clear the teacups. 'How was your day, anyway?'

'Fascinating.' He told her.

'Do you really think Joey Blackpeter tried to sell you a child?' she asked.

'She certainly didn't seem too anxious about their welfare, carting them about in the rain like that.'

'I'm starting not to like this place.' She drained her cup and stared at it for a while.

'Reading your tea leaves?' Beck asked.

'I wish,' she sighed. 'If I could, I'd say it all looks murky from here.'

23

The goat farmer wrapped the crumbling block of soft chevre in yesterday's—Monday's—newspaper and exchanged it for a few dollars.

'Heard you stumbled on something unpleasant in the Void,' he said to Heidi.

'You've got a well-oiled bush telegraph around here,' she commented.

'Nope. A well-oiled wife.'

The woman at the farm stand where Heidi bought her eggs had more to say about it. 'Those blackfellas have been stealing my eggs for goodness knows how long. Them and the ferals. I'm not surprised that poor girl got killed, although the Lord only knows what her mother was doing letting her stay out like that.'

'It's a big leap from stealing eggs to murdering a teenager.'

The woman looked at her as if she were short of a few billion brain cells. 'There's the animals, too. All those farm dogs gone missing in recent years, now we know where they went. Thought the local Chinese had been serving 'em up, but looks like we were wrong about that.' She handed Heidi the carton of eggs and colour rose on her cheeks. 'I didn't mean you, of course, dear.'

Back home, she dumped everything on the kitchen table. She went to look for Beckett and found him on the back verandah staring at his laptop.

'Hard at work?' She stepped over the phone extension and sat on the wicker couch beside him.

He didn't look up. 'I think I've worked out the problem with Spaz. I typed "genetic defect" into Google and look what I got.'

Heidi bent closer to see a photograph of an extremely lanky boy with elongated arms and spidery fingers, his long face framed by large, pointed ears. His expression was distant, befuddled. In the background was a height chart. He was 200 centimetres tall. The legend underneath read: 'Boy, 13, Marfan Syndrome.'

'Spaz?' she asked.

'Almost exactly!' Beckett said, clicking the 'back' icon on his screen. 'You would swear it was him, even down to the expression. But this is a boy from Texas. He has this thing called Marfan Syndrome. It's quite common. One in ten thousand people have it. Even Mary Queen of Scots had it, apparently.'

'You're sure about this?'

'Listen.' He read from the screen. 'Marfan Syndrome is a heritable disorder of the connective tissue that affects many organ systems...affects both men and women of any race...serious problems associated with Marfan Syndrome include the cardio-vascular system...curvature of spine...abnormally shaped chest... loose jointedness and disproportionate growth usually but not always resulting in tall stature. I don't know about his heart, but this all sounds like Spaz. There's more...people with Marfan Syndrome are often near-sighted. It's usually inherited from a parent who is also affected but one quarter of cases occur sponta-neously, which would explain why no other Blackpeter, as far as I can see, has the same thing.'

'So how do you know that no other Blackpeter has it?'

'We don't. But I'd bet this house that Spaz has. That photo-graph could be him. Now something even *more* interesting—' He clicked the mouse again and searched for the right para-graph. 'Unlike most genetic abnormalities Marfan's does not adversely affect intelligence. It seems that you can have mild cases of it too. As well as Mary Queen of Scots, Rachmaninoff and Abraham Lincoln had it.'

'As well as all the subjects in Modigliani's paintings. I thought you said Spaz was a bit slow...retarded.'

'Actually, Brendan Barton said that. Seeing Spaz in the cop shop yesterday, he's not as stupid as he looks. Just overprotected by his mother. But I know who to call.'

Heidi went into the bedroom to change into her uniform while Beckett dialled information. He found the number he wanted and Andrew Eagan answered on the first ring.

Beckett told him about Marfan Syndrome. 'Anyone else in the family look like Spaz?'

'No, they're all runts,' Eagan said. 'None of them above average height. Solid, though.'

'Do you think Spaz has ever been checked by a doctor?'

'I'd be surprised. Is this condition dangerous?'

'No, but his heart could be damaged.'

'I don't fancy telling Laureen that. She thinks all her kids are perfect.'

'What's happening with Spaz anyway?'

'They're holding him on a minor charge. I reckon they're waiting on forensics and then they're going to do him for murder. So far all they've got on him, as far as I can see, is some circumstantial evidence from a couple of old farts that he was seen in the vicinity of the dead animals. No one's admitting to the coat and they can't prove any of the Blackpeters owned it. Even Laureen's got better taste than that.'

'Why did they bring Spaz in and not Crock or one of the others? They seem more likely candidates to me.'

'Because on top of everything some smart-arse farmer reckons he saw Spaz hanging around the Void a week ago.'

'He lives near there.'

'That's my argument.'

'I can't imagine that Spaz could be that violent.'

'Doesn't seem like it, but between us, he has what Laureen calls "episodes".'

'Fits?'

'More like tantrums. According to Laureen, he even thumped Crock one day a few months back.'

'But we still don't think he killed Elisabeth?'

'He had no reason to. He didn't know her as far as I can tell. Of course, he doesn't have any alibi, apart from his family. None of them do. The cops reckon Spaz found her waiting for someone, for a tryst maybe, and abducted her.'

'Then how did he get her all the way up to the Void? I assume he doesn't have a car.'

'Right. He walks most places. Sometimes gets a lift with his brothers.'

'Then they'd have to be in on it.'

'Spaz's the weakest link, though. The cops think they can pressure him. But thanks for the information on that genetic disorder. I can plead diminished responsibility if it gets that far.'

'Sounds like you've given up on him.'

'No way. I'm an environmental lawyer. I'm used to pushing shit uphill.' Beckett could hear him cover the phone with his hand, speak to someone. 'Look, I have to run. Keep out of mischief. You don't know half of what's going on.'

'Now you've made me even more curious.'

Heidi watched from the doorway as Beckett hung up the phone. 'Curious about what?'

'Curious how it could be that someone as beautiful as you would agree to marry me.'

'Very smooth,' she said, coming over and putting her hands on his shoulders. 'You're just trying to get back in my good books after yesterday.'

'True.'

'Well, any attempt deserves a massage. I can give you a quickie before I go to Carmel.'

'One of those ones where you pull my toes?'

'Or anything else you want,' she said.

24

Carmel appeared less of a whole person than a series of faint lines. Her bones felt delicate under Heidi's hands, her skin seemed to droop from her frame.

'You're not eating,' Heidi said as she pushed her thumbs into the side of Carmel's spine and made flat circles in the loose skin.

'I'll eat when they lock up Elisabeth's murderer and throw away the key.'

'I heard yesterday that they've got Spaz Blackpeter in custody. Doesn't that make you feel relieved?'

'I don't know what to think. He's retarded. They'll never be able to put him away.'

Heidi tried to keep her voice flat and soothing. 'Don't you think he did it?'

'Well, I wouldn't put it past Laureen.'

'What do you mean?'

Carmel seemed anxious to talk. 'I wouldn't be surprised if Laureen lured Elisabeth out there to get at *me*.'

'But why would she do that?'

'Because she's jealous of me.' She flapped a wrist. 'Of everything I have.'

'I can understand that. It doesn't sound like she's got much of a life.'

'She could have had a better life. It was her choice to shack up with Nino.'

'Nino?'

'Nino Blackpeter. Nino means nine. He's an old drunk, barely makes it out of the cave anymore. He's probably dead, come to think of it.'

Carmel's shoulders tightened and Heidi dug her thumbs along the lines of the muscles. 'I'm sorry if that hurts.'

'Nothing hurts anymore,' Carmel said.

Heidi worked silently for a while. She asked Carmel to turn over and laid the towel over her patient's hips and thighs. She began work gently on the stomach area.

'We can have Elisabeth tomorrow, you know,' Carmel said. 'They're sending her back from Sydney. Which means we can hold the funeral Friday. Will you come?'

'Of course, if I'm not intruding.'

'Intruding? The whole town will be out in their glad rags.'

'Glad rags?'

'Any Bankston event, wedding, birth or funeral brings out the gawkers,' she said.

Heidi took a breath. 'I heard about your eldest son, Keith,' she ventured. 'I'm sorry. No one should have to bury two children.'

'But we didn't bury Keith.' Carmel's voice sounded small and strained. 'The sharks got him. Not that they said so to *me*. They thought I couldn't take it.'

'He saved Elisabeth.'

'I can't remember. It's a blank. My husband took charge of everything when we got back. We were in Spain when it happened. I'll never forget that phone call in the middle of the night. It's every mother's nightmare.'

'I'm sorry,' Heidi said. 'What was your son like?'

'He was a lovely baby.'

Heidi thought that a strange thing to say. She wondered how to raise the issue of adoption. 'Did he look like Peter or Charley?' she finally asked.

'He looked quite like Peter. Tall and dark.' Carmel shifted her hips. 'You would never guess...He was adopted, you see. I thought

I couldn't have children. Then Peter came along, soon afterwards. It's the way, I believe. But I never thought for a moment that Keith was anything else but a Bankston. We should never have told him he wasn't. It was my husband's idea.'

'He didn't take it well?'

'He was the wrong age. Sixteen. The hormones were out of control.'

'Peter's only a year younger? Were they close?'

She sighed. 'When they were little. But later—Keith was more interested in Jack. They were thick as thieves at one point. Keith gave the other children a bit of a cold shoulder. I don't think he meant to. He just had other things on his mind.'

'Girls?'

'Girls, motorbikes, drugs. It was all a terrible cliché. I blame it on that Sid Blackpeter.'

'Sid?' Heidi was surprised to hear this name.

'Somehow Keith hooked up with him. Unbelievable, isn't it? I don't know how it happened. But he was a bad influence. The sick bastard knew Keith was sensitive, so he took him and...twisted him.'

'In what way?'

'Fed him rubbish about the world being a rotten place. About the rich living off the poor. He poisoned Keith against us.' She fell silent for a moment. Heidi stood behind her head and ran her fingers through her hair.

'That feels good,' Carmel said. She closed her eyes. 'I'm ashamed to say my husband used his fists on the boy. I know he seems brusque, but he's not a violent man—he's never *ever* touched the other kids, I'd leave him if he did—but he knew how to get under the boy's skin. They were like a train wreck together. I was powerless to stop them.' She shivered slightly. 'I got rid of all the pictures of Keith for his father's sake. He wiped the boy out of his mind because he couldn't live with the guilt.'

'Guilt?'

'He thought he drove him to it, you see.'

'Drove him to what?'

Carmel didn't answer.

Heidi heard raised voices on her way back to the car. She stopped under a trellis of withered grape, not wanting to walk into a brawl.

It was a man and a woman, arguing. The woman's voice was shrill. The man sounded pissed off. It didn't take long to work out the voices belonged to Diane and Peter.

She could hear broken bits of conversation.

'It won't work.' Peter was pacing, crunching on the loose gravel. 'It's a fucking waste of time!'

'Everything's a fucking waste of time with you, including fucking!' Diane's voice was more piercing. 'That's why we're in this situation in the first place.' She became more cajoling. 'You *agreed*.'

'I said...consider it.'

Heidi couldn't catch what Diane said next. She'd moved away from the house. 'Well, you're not...wait very long.'

Peter must have followed her. 'She's too much of a risk!...don't trust...'

'...legal.'

'What happens if she...him?'

'She won't if we pay her enough.' Diane paced back towards the house, only a few steps away from Heidi, who shrank back, embarrassed. 'Look, she wants to get out of this place. Let her get out. What do you think will happen to her as soon as she hits the city with money? She'll be dead in a King's Cross gutter in no time.'

'You sound like...would make you happy.'

'It would. What use is she?'

There was a pause. 'I don't know...Keith...'

'All we're doing is what he's done before...*Please?*'

Heidi couldn't make out what Peter was saying. She heard a

car door slam and an engine start. Then Elisabeth's white BMW backed up and swung out of the parking area, driven by a grim-looking Diane Bankston.

Heidi took a few steps backwards and walked around the side of the house as if she'd just come from inside it.

Peter looked more dishevelled than the other morning with the police. Today he was dressed in country clothes, an oilskin jacket, cord pants and mud-caked boots. His dark hair, which was short at the back but long on top, looked like it had lost the battle with the low branches of a tree.

'Hello.' She tried to sound bright. 'Slow day at the cheese factory?'

He looked dismal, as if his last smile had been a distant memory. 'I just came home to check on Mother. Is she all right?'

'As well as can be expected,' Heidi said.

'Good,' he said absently. He hesitated for a moment and then walked towards her. 'Look, I want to thank you,' he said, placing a hand on her arm.

The gesture reminded her of something, although she couldn't recall what. 'I'm glad I can help in some small way.'

'She likes you. Which is more than I can say for most people, including her family.' He removed his hand and raked it through his hair. 'Has she said very much?'

'She seems very proud of you and Charley.'

He grunted. 'They won't talk to us about it, you know. Keith still treats us like we're children and the facts have to be kept from us. And Mother...she's an expert martyr.'

'That seems a bit harsh. She's lost her daughter.'

'She should have paid more attention, then.'

'You think it's her fault.'

He gave a deep sigh. 'Of course not. But I think Elisabeth played Mother and Father off. She never listened to Charley or me.'

'So you think her death was directly the result of...lack of discipline?' Heidi didn't know how to say it without being offensive.

He shook his head. 'It's my fault. I should have known where she was heading. I was the eldest.' So he did know about his sister's promiscuity.

'You couldn't be responsible for her every move.'

'But I could be for some of them.' He didn't elaborate.

'I'm sorry you had to go through this twice. Carmel told me about your brother Keith. Do you miss him?'

She was surprised that he looked even more alarmed. 'Did she say anything to you about me and him?'

'No, not really. She mentioned that he was very different from you and Charley. A bit hard to restrain.'

'That's right. He wasn't like us. *Any* of us.' He rubbed his neck. 'Look, I better get going. I'll check on Mother and then I've got to get back to work. They're waiting for my decision on the colour of the words on our new packaging.' He gave a bitter laugh, remarkably like his mother's. 'It's *life and death*.'

A flashy red Mercedes sports car swung into the Bankston's parking area. It pulled up alongside Peter, kicking up gravel.

Jack got out, dressed casually in brown baggy pants and pale blue sweatshirt. He slammed the door and walked around the back of the car to Heidi and Peter.

'I thought you were in Singapore,' Peter said, his tone frosty.

'Just got back. Flew into Sydney at the crack of dawn, then on to Moruya. I've been driving since then. I'm buggered, but I wanted to see how Carmel was doing.'

'Carmel is doing fine.'

'Good.'

'Well, then, I'm going in,' Peter said. 'You can wait downstairs while I see her.'

Heidi caught his dismissive tone. Peter sensed this and remembered his manners. 'Heidi, have you met Jack Harding yet?'

'At the ball,' she said and smiled.

'Good to see you again,' Jack shook her hand.

'I'll leave you to it,' Peter said and strode stiffly away.

They watched him go, then Jack offered, 'Peter and Charley don't like me much. I suppose you've heard that from several sources.'

'I gathered it.'

'Charley resents me working there. Keith trusts me more than he trusts Charley. But I had to work hard to win Keith's trust and Charley thinks that should come automatically.'

'So you don't like him much either?'

'He's a bit dull, that's all.'

Heidi glanced around. No gardeners lurking the bushes. They were alone. Still, she kept her voice low. 'Carmel told me you were best friends with her son, Keith, the one who drowned.'

'Yeah, we knew each other.' Casual, but something flickered deep in his eyes.

'It wasn't more than that?'

'I guess we were mates. Looking back now, though, I don't know why I ever hung around with him. He was a real fuckup. He stole stuff, he tormented other kids, and I was the stooge who always got blamed. I should have worked it out before I did. The truth is, I'm a bit ashamed of those years.'

'What was he like?'

'Dangerous. He liked to push things right to the edge. He had certain games he liked to play and you had to go along or face his anger. And he could get very angry.'

'What sort of games?'

'You know, stuff like Truth or Dare.' He shrugged. 'It's funny, I haven't thought about him for a long time. Not until Elisabeth...'

'I'm sorry, you lost your sister too.'

'Yeah.' He pushed some gravel around with his shoe. 'I'm worried about Carmel. She's not as strong as she looks. Still, you can't treat her like a fragile piece of china, the way Peter does.'

Heidi thought about that. 'It seems a complicated relation-ship.'

'It's that all right.'

'What do you mean?'

'Nothing much. All families are complicated, aren't they?'

'Do you think he's jealous of your friendship with his mother?'

'It's not that. It goes back to when Keith was alive. We bullied him and he's never forgotten. As a result, he overcompensates and wants to control everything. His mother. Elisabeth. The business.' He shrugged. 'I'm in the way.'

'I'm surprised you're so honest about it.'

'Everyone knows. Even big Keith. Sometimes I think Keith even encourages it, to keep his sons on their toes.' His expression sharpened. 'My father was just an ordinary wage slave. Then he went and topped himself, which was shameful. To tell you the truth, Valerie didn't have the best reputation, and I wasn't an angel when I was younger. Until we got that big house we were no more than trailer trash to most people. Keith gave me a chance because I was his son's friend and I was good enough at what I do to rise in the company. My mum's got a business now. We've got a decent house and money in the bank. We're no longer trailer trash. But some people still think we've risen above our station in life.'

'You're not married?'

He smiled. 'Hey, I'm only twenty-seven.'

They heard a window being wound open and looked up. Carmel was waving from her bedroom on the second floor. 'Jack!' she called out. 'Come on up!'

Jack waved back. He winked at Heidi. 'I'm wanted. Gotta go.'

Carmel disappeared. As Heidi watched Jack's back, she thought about Carmel's pecking order of favourites. It was going to be Peter, not Jack, cooling his heels downstairs.

25

While Heidi was out, Beckett had spent the morning trying to concentrate on his writing. His laptop was set up on the kitchen table and he turned on the gas oven, leaving the door open to heat up the room. This wasn't enough, so he wrapped himself in an old blanket.

The phone rang and stopped. He contemplated it. It was an old mustard-coloured thing, a leftover from the cheese factory days. He could imagine a series of foremen grasping it in their meaty paws and shouting down the line. As he stared at it, it rang again. Rush hour on Milk Mountain. He picked it up.

'Don't hang up on me, you lazy bugger.'

'When have I ever hung up on you, Erv?' It was Ervan Ettiger, the producer of *A Small Death in Wollongong*. 'The connection's not so good way out here.'

'Funny thing that, the way your phone never works. Especially whenever I'm calling to see where my screenplay is.'

'It's here, Erv, where it's always been.'

'I'm not talking about the title page. I know you've done that. I'm talking about the rest of it. One hundred and ten pages I think we agreed.'

'Calm down. I'm almost there. It's just that I'm working on a new twist. I'm deep in research right now. I've got some inside information that's going to make it really authentic. You're going to love it.'

'I'm going to love anything that's on paper, the way things are going. But I guess that's the point, isn't it?'

'I'm not playing games, Erv. This will be the best thing I've ever done.'

'It better be. So what is the estimated time of arrival now? I can't keep the Roadshow bastards at arm's length for much longer.'

'May fifteen.' Beckett pulled a date out of his head. It *sounded* good.

'That's another three weeks! Christ! All right, you're lucky they're off to Cannes then.'

Erv hung up.

The best thing I've ever done. Hardly a risky statement, even in the screenplay's current state of pristine undoneness. Besides, Erv couldn't tell Pinter from L. Ron Hubbard. He'd present the phone book to the investors if it had the requisite number of car chases and simulated sex scenes.

The wire door creaked and Damian came in.

'Want a beer?' Beckett asked.

'Yeah, thanks, mate. That'll be my lunch.'

Beckett brought out two cans of Victoria Bitter. 'Damian, you're a man about town. What do you know about Joey Blackpeter? A couple of days ago I picked her up hitchhiking.'

'Lucky you.'

'So, you've met her?'

'The whole football team's met her, mate.'

'You too?'

'I don't deny I fucked her once or twice. I was lonely, you know, after Rosemary died.'

'I heard she's accused some of the local lads of fathering her children. You still see her?'

'Haven't touched her in years. She brought one of the little buggers around a while back. Tried to fob it off on me, after she'd tried the rest of the blokes. Barry Wicks has got a restraining order out on her. She stands outside his house with the kids and stares.'

'You're sure he's not your kid?'

'I used condoms. You never know with a piece of skank like that.'

'Condoms break.'

'These ones didn't.'

'Do you know who's the father of the baby?'

'Haven't heard any rumours. Could be anyone's.'

'She slept around that much?'

'What's it to you? Oh, I get it. She gave you a "reward" for picking her up.'

Beckett raised his hands. 'I'm innocent.'

'Yeah, why have mince when you can have sirloin, eh?'

'Elisabeth Bankston, she'd be sirloin, wouldn't she?'

'Didn't go there, mate.'

'It's just that Joey and Elisabeth seemed to have moved, I suppose you could call it, in the same circles.'

'Maybe she didn't fancy me.'

'So you did try?'

Damian shrugged and changed the subject. 'I'll tell you something, if you want to know. They reckon Elisabeth liked older blokes.'

'You've got any particular older bloke in mind?'

'Nah. I just heard it round the traps, that's all.'

'If I was looking for this older bloke, where would I look?'

'What's it to you?'

'I'm a writer, I'm curious.'

Damian nodded, as if that made sense to him. 'I'd look out of town.'

'One of the Blackpeters?'

'I can't say.'

'You seem to know a lot about this town, Damian.'

'Born here, wasn't I?'

'You would have known the Bankston's son, Keith, the one who drowned.'

'Yeah, I knew him.'

'What was he like?'

'A bit of a lad. He liked to shock people. Sometimes it could get a bit rank. His party trick was shitting on tables, but it was funny to us kids.'

'The adults didn't like him then?'

'Some of them didn't. Those with daughters.'

'I heard that. I also heard a rumour that he didn't drown accidentally.'

'Shit eh?'

'I heard his dad might have wanted to get rid of him.'

'Can't imagine it. Big Keith was always giving him things to keep him happy. He had so much *stuff*, you know. Computers and a mobile, even back then. He had dirt bikes, leather jackets, flying lessons, pockets of cash...shit, were we all jealous.'

'Was he happy?'

Damian shrugged. 'Who knows? He was always grinning, like it was all a big joke. Like he knew his dad was going to give him everything he wanted, so he wanted to push it as far as he could. But he was moody. Bipolar they call it now. He pissed off some people.'

'Anyone in particular?'

'A list as long as my arm, mate.' He held out an arm and examined his tattoos as if he hadn't seen them before. 'You could always talk to Jack Harding. They were best mates. His mum owns the cake shop.'

'His sister was murdered, I heard.'

'Yeah, but the lucky buggers got some money from the poms. Pissed it all away, though.'

'Did Jack see Keith drown?'

'Yeah, he was in the water.'

'You remember all this?'

'It was legend, mate. No one talked about anything else for months. It put the wind up all our mums, Keith drowning like

162

that. They started putting flags out at Hapless Bay after that.'

'That's where your wife drowned, isn't it?' Beckett asked gently.

'Off Nullin Point at the south end. But it was a shark that got her.'

'I'm sorry. It must be a dangerous spot.'

'The whole fucking coast's dangerous, mate. It's the undertow.'

The undertow, Beckett reflected, as Damian went back to work. There seems to be a whole lot of that.

Damian banged around out the front for a while, then Beckett heard him drive off.

Beckett went back to the computer and played a couple of games of Grand Theft Auto. He heard the crunch of real tyres on gravel and went to the front of the house, wrapped in his blanket.

'How!' Brendan Barton said, raising a hand.

'You may well ask,' Beckett said. 'I wish I knew myself.'

'You're working?'

'Non-stop. Want a cuppa?'

'Thanks.' Barton took off his cap and followed Beckett into the kitchen. He put his cap on the table. 'I was hoping Heidi was in.'

'She's gone off to give a back rub to Carmel Bankston. Then she's got two more pensioners. She's suddenly very popular. I suspect it's because they all think they can get some hot gossip out of her. Did you need her for anything in particular?'

'No, not really.' He reached into the inside of his leather jacket and pulled out a card. 'I wanted to catch her so she'd write in this card, for Mum. Say something like "this is a voucher for one massage" or whatever. I can leave the card, though. The birthday's not for two weeks.'

'Just leave it on the table,' Beckett said. He emptied a pack of Iced Vo Vos onto a plate. 'I must say, you don't act much like a cop, Brendan.'

'I don't feel like one much, either. I'm not real happy about working on a murder when I know the victim. And I don't like having Spaz locked up. We've charged him, did you know? This arvo he'll be sent to remand up at Goulburn. It's a tough place.'

'Is his brother Sid in jail there?'

'Nah. He's in the correctional facility at Bungalong.'

'What's Sid like?'

'He's as smart as a fucking tiger snake. He doesn't speak much, to cops anyway. Shuts his trap tight as a clam, although I believe he's quite the comedian with the other prisoners. Anyway, they didn't want Spaz near him.'

'Seems a bit unfair. Are you still convinced he did it?'

'The Sydney blokes have wrapped it all up and left us with sorting out the details. But you can't get round the fact he was seen with the animals. Scientific found a few hairs on the coat and they reckon they're his. DNA testing will sort it out. What's bothering me is his fingerprints weren't found on Octavia's spear. Lots of other prints we can't identify, but not one of Spaz's. And there was no semen. Not even any evidence of it around the site, so there's no DNA match there. Not that any of this is for publication, by the way.'

'Hey,' said Beckett, pushing his chair away from the table and leaning back. 'We're partners.'

'The Sydney blokes reckon Spaz was spying on Elisabeth. He's been seen in town more than usual lately. They'll add a kidnap charge to murder if we find the evidence.'

'Did you check out any of her boyfriends?'

'We spoke to her friends in town. None of them arranged to meet her. They all thought she was going home with her parents.'

'Maybe she changed her mind at the last moment.'

'Maybe. The boy she was seeing in Nullin—'

'Jaron Wignall.'

'You know about that?'

'Heidi saw them together at the debutante ball.'

'Did she? She could have told us.'

'She thought the relationship was common knowledge.'

'Not to me. Jaron was at the ball helping with the set-up. But his mum vouches that he was at the caravan park all night, after about eleven.'

'She's hardly reliable. I've heard she was a soak.'

'True. But there's no motive for Jaron to kill Elisabeth.'

'Unless he did it for his dad. I hear Gray's got a few things against Keith.'

'There's some bad blood about his lease on the park. I know Keith would love it if one of the Wignalls got in deep shit. It would strengthen his case to throw them off. But Jaron hates his dad. He wouldn't get involved in murder for Gray. Besides, try and tell the club that one of their best players is about to be arrested for murder. There'd be a riot.'

'So is the case closed?'

Barton sighed. 'Even if I had misgivings, there's nothing I can do about it. We don't have the resources without Sydney. Anyway, there haven't been any more dead animals since we got Spaz locked up.' He picked up his hat and put it on. 'That kind of proves it.'

26

This one is small and the size of a rabbit.

It struggles as you turn it over in your hands.

The belly is plump and pale, the top fur the colour of mulch. It hides in the forest, foraging for tubers and grubs.

But it can't hide from you.

You have waited at its nest all night, quiet as a fig root. It scurries back at dawn, drunk on fungus and insects.

An easy catch. Your hands around its neck, the sharpened stick ready. Impaled with one thrust, like shucking corn.

It shudders and is still. You hold a back foot between your fingers, examining the double claw. Three-toed they call it, although there are only two.

It is the most ancient kangaroo. Ten million years ago they were all this small. But while its brothers fled the rainforest, learned to stand upright and took giant bounds, this little mutant cowered under a tussock of grass. Evolution passed it by.

Wimp.

Its life is now pathetic, bounded by a series of little tracks that go nowhere.

Like yours.

Potorous tridactylus.

Long-nosed potoroo.

A rat with the hop of a kangaroo.

A freak of nature.

Like you.

27

The Warling Family Funeral Home was a low brown-brick building. A blue-carpeted reception area led on to a chapel, where urns
and baskets of white oriental lilies festooned every bare surface.
The casket, placed in an alcove in front of a pair of ominously
closed blue velvet curtains, was covered in a carpet of the same
flowers.

'I can't help thinking it looks more like a wedding,' Heidi
whispered as she bent to take a sheet of paper off her seat.

'Yes, but where's the groom?' Beckett whispered back.

Heidi acknowledged the stranger on her right, an ancient
man in a frayed shirt collar and musty plaid jacket, and sat.

Beckett took his place beside her. 'It does seem very festive for
a funeral.' It was true. The atmosphere was like that of a theatre
matinee crowd awaiting the curtain to rise on *The Sound of Music*,
an impression enhanced by the pan flute rendition of 'Climb
Every Mountain' which warbled from speakers placed around the
room.

'There's Octavia Goodhope,' Heidi said, indicating a head of
gossamer white hair seated front row left. 'And that, I bet, is her
sister Lydia,' she added, nodding towards a lavender rinse on the
right side, seated next to Keith.

'Elegant old dame,' Beckett said. 'Are those the Bankston
boys with her?'

'Yes, that's Peter and Diane at the end. Charley is next to
Michelle. The girl with the big, curly hair.'

'A bit overdone isn't it?'

'She's a hairdresser, she can't help it. I think that must be her sister Danielle behind, with Brendan Barton.' She indicated a girl with raggy blonde hair and a slash of bright blue in it.

'Yes, that's her. Who's the woman between Brendan and Damian?'

Heidi couldn't see her face but admired the wide-brimmed navy hat. 'I think that must be Brendan's mum.'

'Damian's the last person I expected to bother to turn up.'

'Why?'

'My money's on Damian having an affair with Elisabeth.'

'What makes you think that?'

'He's the type. And he denied it.'

'Well, I'd keep your ideas to yourself. I don't want my builder in jail.'

'Who are all those suits down the front with Keith Bankston?'

'Nullin Cheese blokes, I suppose. There's Jack Harding with them.'

A woman caught Heidi's eye and waved.

'Who's that?' Beckett asked.

'The newsagent. My new best friend.'

The room suddenly went quiet. Heidi turned, thinking the ceremony was about to start, and saw a man and woman enter the room. The woman was dressed in a fringed, red suede jacket and denim miniskirt and the man wore motorcycle leathers and a confederate cap. The couple looked like they'd been left behind by the carnival that took over the Nullin oval at Christmas, and had been wandering around town searching for their caravan ever since. Worse, they smelled like it. Fumes of alcohol, petroleum and dead animal rose from them and mingled with the sweet, cloying fragrance of the lilies and the undernote of dank sweat generated by the excitable citizens in the room.

Beckett had turned with her. 'Laureen Blackpeter,' he

whispered, 'and her eldest son, the irascible Crock.'

'The one who shot at you?'

'There's no mistaking that mug.'

'Why would she be here?'

'Paying her respects?'

'Or braving it out. Showing she believes Spaz's innocent?'

'Look. The rest of the family's shown up.' Beckett nodded at the door. Several young men reluctantly followed Laureen and Crock inside, to the consternation of the gathered mourners. The Blackpeter boys stood back sullenly. 'I wonder which is which.'

Laureen left her brood and trotted on high heels down to the front of the chapel. She approached Carmel and Keith. Carmel turned her head away, but Keith took Laureen's offered hand and shook it. The room burst into spontaneous chatter. Laureen turned and walked back up the aisle to the rear of the room, looking proudly ahead.

'I can't believe I just saw that,' Beckett whispered. 'Laureen sounded like she hated Keith the other day.'

'What did she say?'

'Something about him being careless with his children.'

'I thought someone else said that. But there isn't any bad blood between the Blackpeters and Bankstons is there? Apart from the fact Carmel thinks Sid corrupted her son Keith.'

'Not more than with anyone else in town as far as I know.'

'Carmel's looked away.'

'That's because of the smell.'

Heidi felt someone clutch at her arm. It was the ancient man next to her. 'Sorry, love,' he said, in a voice so soft Heidi had to lean so close his breath was hot and stale in her ear. 'I couldn't help overhearing. You got Laureen wrong, you know. Before she was a Blackpeter she was a Murchett.' He stopped, satisfied with this.

'A Murchett?' Heidi asked. 'Who are they?'

'Dairy farmers they were,' he said. 'The house was right in

Speculator, cows used to ramble all over the street. Days before tourists and ye olde shoppes. The farm got bought out by Keith's dad, old Albert, like most of the small dairies around here. Mitchell Murchett got a good price for it, Albert wasn't mean like some. But before that, Keith and Laureen were going together.'

'Keith and *Laureen*?' Heidi nudged Beckett, who had just spotted Andrew Eagan in the crowd of latecomers mingling at the back of the chapel in the vain hope of seats. 'I can't imagine it.'

'Oh, Laureen was quite a lady then, before she got mixed up with this lot. Schooled somewhere grand up near Canberra. He might've married her, except Carmel came along.' He gave an affected little cough. 'Of course, some say it was a union anyway, if you know what I mean.'

'What? He's a bigamist?' Beckett had picked up the tail end of the conversation.

The old man pursed his lips. 'That would be illegal.'

Before Beckett could question him further, the pan flutes subsided. A portly woman in a royal blue skirt and collarless jacket entered through a side door, her head down. She stood in front of the casket, hands clasped, and looked out over the congregation. 'I am here to perform a sad duty,' she announced.

'That'd be Carmel's idea,' the old man grunted. 'She always was one of them fermanists.'

'Let's get out of here,' Beckett said, as they streamed into the foyer, where groups of people stood waiting for the Bankston family to appear.

'I should stay and give my condolences.'

'Nonsense. You've done that already. Besides, Carmel won't remember you were even here.'

They escaped into the pewter light of the cold midday. A few others had done the same thing. The Blackpeter family was there, in a huddle, which made a few local citizens nervous. They found Andrew Eagan, with three other people.

'Perfect day for a funeral.' Eagan said as Beckett greeted him. He squashed a cigarette butt underfoot. 'Do you know Sara and Klas? And this is Martin Gondwana.'

Beckett introduced Heidi. Sara said, 'Oh, we're old friends.'

Beckett raised his eyebrows, but Sara didn't notice. 'Martin.' She grabbed the older man's arm. 'This is the woman who gave us the lift. The one who lives at the old dairy.'

'We're neighbours then,' he said in a drawl that was unmistakably North American. He took Heidi's hand and the warmth of his grasp tingled up her arm. He was a compact man of about fifty, with dusty grey dreadlocks caught into a thick bunch at the back of his neck and an even, golden tan that was a little too fresh for the time of year, suggesting a visit to the solarium or frequent trips to the tropics. He wore a padded linen vest over a striped shirt shot with gold and blue jeans that looked pressed. Even his toenails in their cradle of plastic sandal looked pearly and buffed, as if his followers took turns to wash them. She wondered about that. His presentation was immaculate, compared to the scruffy Sara, with her black feet, and Klas, whose hands looked red raw from his agricultural duties. She'd met men like him before—baby boomers who had gone 'alternative' in the seventies and eighties, only to luck out in the nineties when their hobbies, like designing surf wear or conducting meditation classes, turned into valid, money-making enterprises. Whatever the Gondwana scheme was, it was clearly a corporation now.

He turned over Heidi's palm and examined it. 'I can tell you're a healer,' he said.

'I'm a massage therapist,' Heidi said, taken aback.

'I thought so,' he said. 'It's this line.' He traced a finger down her hand.

Beckett didn't like that. 'Interesting name, Gondwana,' he interrupted. 'Doesn't sound very North American.'

Martin smiled. 'This land has been kind to me.'

'Oh? You obviously haven't been renovating a dairy and

taking cold showers in the morning. What line of business are you in?'

'Peace.'

'Can't be doing very well at the moment,' Beckett said.

'On the contrary,' Martin said. 'It's at a great premium.'

'We also sell honey,' Sara volunteered.

'I've heard you do a nice sideline in weeds, too,' Beckett said.

'Oh, yeah. You know...any time,' she said. 'We deliver.'

'So what brings you to the funeral, Martin?' Beckett asked him with a wry expression. 'A bit Christian for you, isn't it?'

Martin ignored that. 'We know Elisabeth. She's been up to the farm once or twice.'

'She was lost,' Sara said.

'Well, did you show her how to get home?' Beckett asked. Heidi wanted to kick him, but Andrew Eagan was between them.

'No,' Sara said firmly. 'She was looking for *herself*.'

'And did someone help her?'

'Of course. Martin did.'

I bet he did, Beckett thought. He looked at Heidi who was clearly thinking the same thing.

'I'd love to come and see your commune some time.' Heidi said.

'By all means,' Martin said, holding her eyes for a couple of beats. 'Now, if you folks will excuse me, I'm going over to pay my respects to the family.'

'We folks will,' Beckett echoed, as he watched the older man stroll off.

Klas touched Sara on the elbow. 'I think we should go now,' he said.

'We have to wait for Martin.'

'We can wait in the cafe.'

'He won't be long.'

Klas shrugged but said nothing more.

Beckett turned away from them and whispered in Eagan's

ear. 'That Martin seems a bit suspect to me.'

'Relax. It's just the tan.'

'You didn't have to be so hostile to him,' Heidi said, over-hearing.

'I can see I'm going to have to put you back in your chastity belt.'

Heidi didn't reply. She'd been watching Martin walk away. Most of the congregation had now gathered in the garden. The Blackpeters were still there, but they had been joined by the only person apparently willing to speak to them, the old man who had been sitting next to Heidi. Apart from Crock's hillbilly get-up, the rest of the boys looked little different from the other local lads. The tall one even had a beanie pulled low over his head as if he'd just come in from chopping trees. Maybe he had.

Across the garden, the Bankston family was accepting condolences from a line of sympathisers that snaked across the lawn to the street. Michelle held the baby and the nanny Emily took the hand of the little girl Rebecca. Diane stood beside Peter, who was holding the arm of his grandmother Lydia. Keith and Carmel stood stiffly together, looking shell-shocked. Jack Harding was behind Carmel. He looked like he was propping her up.

Then Charley appeared on the steps above the throng, with his great aunt Octavia on his arm. Octavia seemed bewildered at the size of the crowd and looked about in a dazed manner. All at once her legs seemed to buckle under her and she crumpled. Charley managed to catch her and guided her to a sitting position on the bottom step.

Several people noticed and rushed up. Heidi got there first. 'Put her head between her legs,' she said to Charley. 'Are you all right, Miss Goodhope?'

'Of course I'm all right. I was just coming out for air and I slipped on a stone or some such thing.' Octavia rubbed her right ankle, which was thin and delicate in its casing of black nylon. 'Now, help me to my feet.'

'I don't think you should—'

'Rubbish. I'm perfectly fine.'

Heidi took one arm and Charley took the other. 'Thank you,' she said, smoothing down her skirt. Heidi thought she looked rattled.

Charley did too. 'You should go home, Aunt Octavia. I can take you.'

'No you won't. Your mother needs you.'

'I'll take you,' Heidi volunteered. 'I was just leaving.'

'I couldn't let your father down,' Octavia said to Charley.

'He's got Aunt Lydia.'

The old woman chuckled. 'Yes, it is more Lydia's thing than mine. She can preside over the cream scones.'

'Come on,' Heidi said, taking her arm. 'Charley will give your apologies.'

'If you can take me to my dinghy, my dear, I'll be fine from there.'

'I can take you further than that. Besides, you'll be doing me a favour. You can show my husband your collection.' Heidi pointed in Beckett's direction.

'Who are those young people?' she asked.

'They're from the wildflower farm. The Gondwana tribe.'

'Oh, yes, I know who they are. And the other two?'

'The one in the blue and orange shirt is Andrew Eagan. He's a lawyer. And the other's my husband, Beckett.'

'The tall young man with the dark hair?'

Heidi nodded.

'In that case, you can certainly take me home. From this distance he looks very much like an engineer I had a blazing affair with in Western Samoa in, let's see, 1951.'

28

Octavia Goodhope moved some bones out of the way and put the tray of tea down on a table. 'How do you have yours?' she asked.

'Aren't you going to offer me some of your famous cognac?' Beckett teased her.

'All in good time,' she smiled. 'I don't know you well enough yet.'

The fine china cups rattled in their saucers as she poured the tea and handed it over. 'I'm afraid I don't have any biscuits.'

'Beck's sweet tooth needs curbing anyway,' Heidi said.

'I like my men big,' Octavia said, sitting down and pouring herself some tea. 'I was never a small girl myself.'

'This is a wonderful house,' Beckett told her. He had done a quick walk-through while she was preparing tea and calculated he'd need the best part of a year to examine every object.

'Oh, it's falling to bits.'

'Why don't you move somewhere closer to town?' Heidi asked.

'I've resisted all attempts to have me packaged up, sanitised and placed in a nursing home, young lady. I've had quite a life and I intend to keep living it.'

'But isn't it dangerous? You're vulnerable to the sort of attack that happened last week.'

'If he knows what's good for him, he won't be back again.'

'You sound like you know who it was,' Beckett said, watching her closely.

Her jaw set. 'If it's the same person who is the murderer of that child, then I certainly don't.'

Beckett wasn't content with that. 'Have any of the Blackpeters ever come here?'

'Only that poor young boy, the slow one. He used to trail along sometimes with the other kids.'

'Other kids?'

'The children who came for history lessons.' She saw that Beckett was surprised. 'It wasn't a formal thing. Most of them would have to be dragged kicking and screaming to any place where they'd get an education. But I let them play with the skulls and shrunken heads and while they were doing it I managed to get some information into their heads. Not that it did any of them much good. None of them took up tertiary education as far as I know. Except for the Barton boy, who went to police academy.'

'Did their parents know they came up here?'

She chuckled. 'Their parents came here when they were children! I remember very clearly that Keith Bankston was interested in Ancient Rome. So, now that I think of it, was young Keith...' Her voice trailed away.

'It was tragic that he drowned.'

'Everything about him was tragic, I'm afraid.'

'What do you mean?'

'He was bound to break his mother's heart one way or the other. He was adopted, you know. But that doesn't mean he wasn't loved.'

Beckett raised something that had been bothering him. 'I heard a theory it wasn't an accident.'

'I can see you've been listening to town gossip.'

'What gossip?'

'Oh, that he was distressed over young Valerie Harding's murder.'

'No, I didn't hear that exactly.'

'They were supposed to be sweethearts, you see. Young

Keith, Valerie and Jack were as thick as thieves. Keith and Jack used to finish each other's sentences, they were like twins. Used to play all kinds of mind games with each other. Valerie came here with them once, but she wasn't much interested in anything I had to teach her. More interested in getting Keith all riled up, if you know what I mean.'

'I hadn't heard any of this. She was only fifteen, wasn't she?'

'Fifteen going on thirty-five I'd say.'

'And you think Keith might have drowned himself over her?'

'*I* don't think so, young man. The boy didn't have that kind of self-reflection. And I'm not entirely sure he was as mad about her as everyone thinks. No, it was an accident all right.'

'I gather they didn't find a body.'

'I always thought that was a pity. Carmel needed a body to bury. But after the way they found poor Elisabeth...Still, many other poor souls around here have been taken by sharks.'

'Like Damian Hill's wife. Did Damian ever come here?' Beckett asked.

'Oh, yes. He was fascinated by the heads.'

'I imagine he was a bit of a ratbag as a kid.'

'He wasn't the best-behaved boy. He took a few things when he didn't think I was looking. Mind you, he never took one of the heads. I told him enough tales about witchcraft to frighten the life out of him.' She put her cup down and smiled to herself. 'The boys always loved the horror stories—cannibals, barbarians, Ghengis Khan, Vlad Tepes, Jack the Ripper. I could hold their attention for hours.'

'Was Jaron Wignall ever with them?'

'I don't know that name.'

'White-haired boy whose father owns the caravan park. He would have been about ten when Keith drowned.'

'The young ones don't come anymore. In young Barton's day they'd think it a great adventure to borrow a dinghy and putter up the river. Now they can't be bothered leaving their computer games. Not that I blame them. What I would have done to have a computer when I was a young girl!'

'You were an anthropologist?' Heidi asked to tease her out.

She nodded. 'I was the first female in my family to graduate from university. But then I went all "mental" as Lydia called it and ran off to the wilds of Borneo. I just didn't find the anthropology of dairy farming interesting enough.' She fixed Heidi with a shrewd look. 'But it's much more interesting these days.'

Before Heidi could ask her what she meant, Beck interrupted. 'You mentioned Spaz Blackpeter before.'

'The one with the genetic disorder?'

Beckett was surprised. 'You think so?'

'Well, it's quite apparent to my eyes. Some kind of recessive gene I would have thought.'

'I think it's Marfan's Syndrome,' Beck said. 'At least, I'm pretty sure it is. Do you have any idea which side of his family it might come from? Are any of the others afflicted like this?'

'I wouldn't know. Genetic mutations can be spontaneous.' She raised a scratchy eyebrow. 'Why are you interested?'

'The police have arrested him for Elisabeth's death.'

'Yes, I heard.'

'He used to hang out where the body was found. His family skin animals for a living and Elisabeth was found in a coat of dog fur. He knows your house and what it contains. He's free range. And he's a bit...disturbed.'

'It wasn't the Spaz boy who pushed me over. That much I know. It was someone quick...and wicked. And I can tell you as an anthropologist that the ritual involved in Elisabeth's murder takes a particular kind of mind and motive. I've told the police that. But those Sydney fellows won't listen to an old woman. They're too much in love with all their new technology. A body can only tell you so much. It's the sociology that matters. No, I'm sorry the police aren't looking further afield than that poor boy.'

'At the funeral someone told us that Keith Bankston used to

be romantically involved with Laureen Blackpeter, when she was a Murchett, I think they said.'

'I don't know about that. Could be.' She tightened her mouth.

'Have you had any dealings with the Gondwana family?' Heidi asked.

'Only once. One of them brought me some honey one day. But that was two or three years ago.'

'Can you remember who it was?'

'The American. He was very charming, although a bit intense.'

'We just met him,' Beckett said. 'He seemed a bit...phoney to me. Although Heidi seemed to be taken in by him.'

Heidi grunted. 'I'm reserving my judgment.'

'Oh, Americans are like that,' Octavia said. 'They hold you with their eyes. They're very direct. Besides, shamans in every tribe have the same sense of...theatrics. I've seen it hundreds of times.'

'You think he's a shaman?'

'Well, not precisely. But it's clear he's the tribal elder. There seem to be a few young ones under his spell...I'd like to know where they all come from.'

'I've met two of them,' Heidi said. 'The girl's as Australian as they come. The boy's Swedish or something. There are probably people from all over the world. I think some of them met at a demonstration in Melbourne.'

'Swedish, eh?'

'They seem to be the local suppliers of pot.'

'Do you think the flower business could be a cover for a booming drug cartel?' Beckett asked.

'Oh, I don't think so, my dear,' Octavia said. 'It's only a bit of grass.'

Octavia insisted that they take her dinghy back down the Bilba River, where it would be collected and returned to her by the grocer's delivery boys.

'What a place to live!' Beckett enthused as he steered the boat under low-lying mangroves. 'I can see why she's resisting a nursing home.'

'She's too isolated up there,' Heidi said. 'She doesn't have a phone and now we've taken her boat.'

'But don't you get the feeling she's very comfortable with fate? If she's murdered in her house, so be it. I admire that kind of attitude.'

'I think it's foolish. I'm going to make the point of visiting her more often.'

'Not a hard thing to do. She's an absolute font of local knowledge.'

'But she's holding back, isn't she?'

'Or is she leading us on?'

'What do you mean?'

'I don't know, but I've got a feeling she wants us to find out something.'

'Why didn't you ask her, then?'

'I didn't know the right question.'

Heidi put her hand on his knee. 'Beckett, darling, I think we asked it. We just don't know which one it was.'

29

The Nullin library was housed in a brown brick building, possibly built with leftovers from the Warling Funeral Home. Inside, the staff had tried to brighten the place up, hanging mobiles of whales and birds and dotting the walls with cheery posters. Artwork from the Nullin primary school was proudly pinned to a felt-covered partition, the stick figures drawn in frantic gestures like supporters at a Whales match. The young woman behind the counter had two-tone black-and-canary-yellow hair and was wearing a woolly zip-up cardigan, which seemed a bit excessive in the cosy central heating.

'If I want to find something in an old newspaper, where do I look?' Beckett asked her.

'Local or city?'

'Local. Do you have any back copies of the *Nullin Voice*?'

'How far back?'

'Eight years.'

'Do you want to read about Valerie Harding's murder?'

He was surprised. 'Yes, actually.'

'A few people have been asking for them lately.'

'Why is that?'

'Well…it's because of Elisabeth Bankston's murder, I suppose. It reminds them of Valerie.'

'Who are "them"? The cops?'

'Not just the cops. Lots of people in town are interested. It's kind of exciting.' She lowered her voice. 'Some of them reckon the Yowie did it.'

'What's the Yowie?'

'You know, that old big-foot that lives in the bush round here.'

'First I heard of it.'

'There's a whole family of them, from Cooma way. People up there have seen them for years. They're about seven feet tall, covered in hair and hunt with spears. Some people reckon they stuck Elisabeth with a spear and then they dressed her in that fur cos they thought she was one of their babies.'

'Why did they leave her then?'

The girl looked blank. 'I dunno. Like, they're not very smart?'

'You look like you're about Valerie's age. Did you know her?'

'A bit...we went to the same school, but she was a year older. My sister Mandy used to hang out with her sometimes.'

Beckett guessed as much. Stop anyone on the street in this town and they'd have some relationship with Elisabeth or Valerie. 'And?' he probed. 'What did *you* think about her murder?'

'Are you a detective or something?' She sounded hopeful.

'I'm new in town. I like murder mysteries.'

'Yeah, so do I,' she said. ''Cept it's harder when you know the body...the person.'

'I understand.'

'I wasn't shocked that Valerie was killed. She was as thick as Bob Murphy's breakfast sausages, as my dad used to say.'

'Stupid about boys?'

'Guessed it in one. She was a real slag. Of course all the papers made her out to be innocent. But no one round here makes fifteen and is still innocent, if you know what I mean.'

'Wasn't she young Keith Bankston's girlfriend?'

'As if. She used to boast about it, but it was crap.'

'How long after Valerie's death did Keith drown?'

'The papers will say somewhere. It was only a few months later. Around the time that truckie got off.'

'The truckie got off?'

'Yeah. He was released on a technicality. Upset a lot of the old ducks, I can tell you.'

'I assumed he was safely locked away somewhere. So he didn't do it?'

'We all reckon he did it, all right. There were traces of Valerie in his truck cabin. But the chain of evidence or whatever they call it was corrupted. They don't get many murders around here, see, unless you go back to the goldfields.'

'Is the truckie still around?'

'Lots of people were worried that he'd come back and do it again. Then a couple of years ago he rolled the tanker in some fog at Bulli Pass. He's a quadriplegic now. Do you want me to dig up those papers as well?'

'No, that's OK.'

'Hang on a mo, then. I'll get the others.'

She returned a moment later with a stack of newspapers and placed them on the desk in front of him. 'There's some *Herald*s too. The murder even made the Sydney papers.'

He picked them up. 'Thanks...'

'Carrie.'

'Like Stephen King's Carrie?'

'Duh,' she said with exasperation. 'Like Carrie Bradshaw.'

'Who's that?' he asked.

'From "Sex and the City",' she said. When he still looked blank, she added, 'On TV.'

'I don't have a TV.'

'You're kidding, right?'

Beckett remembered Octavia Goodhope's lament that the local kids didn't visit her anymore. This one could use a few history lessons from the elderly anthropologist. And she worked in a library—what were the rest of the kids like?

He suddenly had a flash of something relevant to Elisabeth's murder. But the thought flew straight out of his head again.

He took the newspapers and found a table. For about five weeks during that November and December the *Nullin Voice* had featured the murder on its front page. The bylines in each case were credited to Bruce Olley, Kirstie's father.

Valerie had been found beaten, stabbed and dumped on 6 November. Her body had been abandoned in the Nullin Void, Beckett noted with rising interest. It was about twelve hours before the body had been discovered by a farmer looking for a lost calf. Valerie was last seen on the highway hitching to a friend's place. Her parka had been found on the Speculator Road.

The police had determined that Valerie was beaten with fists, stabbed with a screwdriver and tied up with something, possibly the elastic used by surfers to lash boards to their van's roofs judging by the marks on her skin. The screwdriver and the straps were standard, according to the superintendent, Ian Harmer. 'Like finding a needle in a haystack, everyone round here's got that sort of thing in the shed.'

The similarities with Elisabeth's death seemed to be restricted to the place where the bodies were found and the fact both girls were tied up. But Valerie's death seemed more frenzied. Her body had been dumped, not displayed.

He flipped to an issue dated late November. THIS IS THE FACE OF A KILLER read the headline. Below it, a jowly, unshaven middle-aged man stared dully from a police mug shot, a murderer straight from Central Casting. Josef Passer, fifty-six, milk-tanker driver, of Sunshine, Melbourne, married, father of two, was arrested for Valerie's murder after evidence linked him to the crime. Passer had admitted that he had picked up the victim hitchhiking along the highway at about 9.30 on the relevant evening but only drove her as far as the Speculator turn-off. When questioned why he had left a teenage girl by the side of the road in the dark late at night, he said that she had insisted she was meeting someone there and, besides, she looked older than fifteen. What was he supposed to do?

Forensics had found hairs, fibres and skin cells from the girl in the truck's cabin. Witnesses saw his truck parked on a shoulder of the highway just south of Speculator but Passer explained that he had pulled over after dropping the girl and taken a nap, as he had driven the Melbourne–Gerringong run and then back down the highway that day without a rest stop. No one who passed the truck could remember seeing him in it, but he argued that he always lay flat down the seat, so how could anyone see him? The police did not accept his explanation and on the strength of the forensic evidence arrested him. He was remanded to Goulburn prison, without bail.

Beckett searched the pile and found the issue that expressed outrage at Passer's release, dated late January.

HE'S FREE: VALERIE SUSPECT RELEASED ON TECHNICALITY!

On examination of new evidence brought to light by Passer's crown-appointed defence lawyer, Harry Chen, Justice Cameron Allen of Goulburn Magistrates Court, has rejected the prosecution's claims that forensic evidence collected at the scene can be used at the trial. Justice Allen believes there is now sufficient reason to allow that the evidence might have been tampered with prior to Passer's arrest. Arresting superintendent Ian Harmer denies any misconduct but admits that the evidence could not be accounted for at one stage in the process and that there were other inconsistencies. 'It's just a technicality,' he said. 'We will continue to pursue other avenues in bringing this perpetrator to justice.' Passer has been on remand in Goulburn since 29 November, pending a trial set for 12 August. 'I said I was innocent all along,' he told reporters at a press conference on his release. 'I never touched that girl.'

The article went on to describe the outrage expressed by Valerie's family. 'The police have stuffed up,' said Valerie's father, Russ Harding, a longtime employee of Nullin Cheese. 'I'm going to spend every quid I have proving Mr Passer done it. And if he didn't I'm going to track down the real killer, you can count on it.'

Beckett flipped through the six or seven other papers. In an issue of late February, below the top story of the Nullin Cheese Fair and a photo of a girl in a hat made of cardboard cheese, a headline read NEW CLUES IN VALERIE'S MURDER. 'New Nullin police superintendent Stan Lewis revealed today that police are "vigorously" pursuing new evidence that has come to light in the Valerie Harding murder case. Sources close to the police say that elastic straps possibly used in the murder of the 15-year-old have been found in a shallow hole in the bush and that the family of the victim is being questioned again.'

There was nothing in the next week's issue, but in the following edition a brief column appeared on page three. 'The trail has gone cold,' Lewis was quoted as saying. 'We have found no new suspects. We have questioned friends, family and acquaintances and we cannot connect anyone to the scene. We believe the identity of the murderer is no secret, but we lack tangible evidence.'

In the same issue, the front-page story was BANKSTON BOY LOST IN TRAGIC DROWNING. The photograph under the headline showed a family snapshot of a lanky, narrow-shouldered boy in board shorts, crouched on a rock with snorkelling gear beside him. He grinned from under dark hair cut into a shaggy fringe. In his hand was a large crab that he held up for the camera. Beckett looked more closely at the boy's pale, stringy arms. There was a mark on one bicep that looked like a simple tattoo. Beckett went and asked Carrie for a magnifying glass. She didn't have one, but an elderly woman filling out a reservation card handed him her reading glasses. 'Use these love, if you want.' He thanked her and returned to the page. The mark was clearer now—a 'V' in medieval lettering. Valerie. So much for Keith not being that interested in the girl.

The article outlined the events of the drowning. Elisabeth had got into trouble with her boogie board, swept up by the rip, and Keith and Jack had swum out to save her. Keith reached her first and passed her over to Jack, who had taken her back to shore, where Charley and Peter were waiting in the shallows. They all watched as Keith pushed the boogie board up onto some rocks and then dived back under. He never came up. Jack swam back out to look for him but gave up after about twenty minutes when the police, who had been called by a bystander on the shore, arrived. The verdict was that he had been taken by a shark, although there was no sign of blood in the water. Experts suggested that the shark might have grabbed hold of a leg and dragged him under the water and out to sea. His father and mother were in Europe at the time but flew back immediately. 'Please respect the family's privacy,' was the official comment from an employee.

Valerie Harding was mentioned, but only in the context that it was a tragedy two close friends could be lost within months. 'That Nullin has to mourn two of its brightest young stars is more than a tragedy, it's a travesty,' waxed Bruce Olley. Brightest young stars? Beckett thought. That's something of an exaggeration.

The final paper on the pile trumpeted TRAGIC VALERIE'S FAMILY IN $250,000 WINDFALL.

> The *Nullin Voice* has learned that the family of murder victim Valerie Harding has received a windfall payment from British newspaper the *Daily Mirror* for the exclusive story of tragic Valerie's life and death. Mrs Sheila Harding was brought up near Birmingham, England, and her parents emigrated to Australia when she was seven. It is believed the *Daily Mirror* was particularly interested in her point of view as a person who came to Australia seeking the good life and struck tragedy. Mr Russ Harding would not comment on the payment, which is believed to be in the $250,000 vicinity, except to say that he would use the money to buy his wife 'the big house that she always wanted' which would, nevertheless, 'not make up for Valerie's loss, no way'. When asked if he still held any beliefs on who killed his daughter, Mr Harding said, 'We all know who done it but he got off scot-free.'

Beckett returned the glasses to the woman at the desk. 'Do you have any issues later than March?' he asked Carrie, handing her the stack of papers.

'They're upstairs in the paper room,' she said. 'Did you find out anything?'

'Too much,' he said.

30

'I'm going to Melbourne for a few days,' Carmel told Heidi, as she slipped the two fifty-dollar bills into her hand. 'I'm indulging in some retail therapy.' She held up a wrist and slapped her diamond watch back on it. ' It never works, of course.'

Heidi drove into Nullin to collect her mail from the post office. Then she drove a few blocks to the police station. Not bothering to lock the car door, she walked up the station path, Brendan Barton's mother's birthday card clasped in her hand. Stephen Fraser almost knocked her over on the way out of the station as he scrambled for his squad car.

'What's up?' she asked Brendan, who was working at a computer. 'It looks like an episode of "Law and Order".'

He didn't look up. 'Octavia Goodhope's been assaulted and has been taken to the hospital. Fraser's gone to take over from the detectives who went with the ambulance. I'm just setting up an incident report now.'

Heidi felt ill. 'My God, Beck and I were just with her Friday. I knew we shouldn't have left her alone. Is she all right? What happened?'

'I dunno. She was unconscious when the grocery boys found her.'

'Do you think it was the same person who attacked her over the spear?'

'Possibly. But she's still out to it.'

'Here's your mother's card,' she said quickly, placing it on the desk. 'What's the best way to get to the hospital?'

'Take a right after the footy ground on Wallaga. But—'

She didn't wait for him to tell her it was none of her business.

The Nullin and District Hospital had ten beds, which were most often filled by fishermen with deep cuts to their legs, footballers with broken ribs, tourists with acute sunburn and the odd yachtsman pulled from the sea en route to Hobart in the annual race.

Heidi ran into the foyer and asked the woman at the desk to direct her to Octavia's room. Expecting resistance, she was surprised when the woman nodded and explained the way to intensive care. As she dashed down the corridor, Heidi remembered that she was wearing her nurse's uniform. The receptionist had assumed she was an extra hand called in for the emergency.

So did the male doctor in charge. 'Get rid of these,' he commanded, handing her a kidney dish full of gauze bandages before she fully entered the room. Stephen Fraser was sitting on a chair in a corner, head down, hat in hand, looking at the floor. He hadn't noticed her.

When she returned the doctor was seated, rather touchingly, at Octavia's side, holding her hand. 'I'll stay with her if you like,' Heidi offered.

The doctor looked relieved. 'Thanks. We're badly understaffed and we've got an emergency caesar on the slab. It never rains but it pours.' He got up. 'Her vitals are steady. The head wound's deep but clean. She'll come round in a while. Just make sure *he*'—he nodded at Stephen—'doesn't disturb her. No questions until further notice. Good day, officer.'

Fraser looked up as the doctor left. He started at seeing Heidi there. 'Hey, you can't—'

'It's all right.' Heidi didn't quite lie. 'They need an extra hand.'

'You're a nurse?'

'Don't I look like one?'

Fraser ignored her, fortunately. 'How's the old lady? Can I talk to her yet?'

'Look at her. What do you think?'

He grunted. 'Looks like I'm going to have to stay here all night.'

'I can stay.'

'Yeah, but you can't take a statement. In fact, you're still a suspect in this case—'

'Who says? I thought you'd locked up Spaz.'

'You might be an accomplice. I reckon it was unnatural the way you stayed with that body after you found it. Killers are the only ones that ever hang around. Innocent people run off screaming and have nightmares the rest of their lives.'

I will have nightmares the rest of my life, you big dope, Heidi thought as she took the chair by Octavia's bedside and picked up the old woman's hand. It felt like a lump of ice. She wore a turban of bandages and a corsage of drips. She seemed to be breathing shallowly but steadily.

Heidi stroked the hand and stared down the officer. 'Well, if that's the case Sergeant Fraser, you're going to have to stay awake and make sure I don't slip anything into that drip, aren't you?'

The two small rooms above McGillop's Tackle Shop were occupied by the *Nullin Voice* and accessed by a covered exterior staircase that was cluttered with bound stacks of newspaper. A white cat slept on the landing.

Kirstie Olley was shuffling some photographs, her feet up on a desk. The room was otherwise empty—except for overflowing filing cabinets, unruly stacks of boxes and two messy desks covered with spiked papers, books and an assortment of stone-age computer monitors, only one of which seemed to be plugged in.

'I've walked into a scene from *My Girl Friday* and you're Hildy Johnson,' Beckett said.

Kirstie didn't look at him but fluttered her fingers and said, 'Hi Attractive Married Man. You're just in time. We have a new development in Elisabeth's murder, if you're interested.'

'Which is?'

'They've found another skewered animal. A potoroo. You know, they're little kangaroos. Killed the same way.'

'Where did they find it?'

'At the back of the Leagues Club, in an old beer crate.'

'So Spaz couldn't have done it?'

'That's right, it's only a few days old. Spaz has been locked up for a week. It certainly didn't wander there by itself.'

'Then that proves he can't be Elisabeth's murderer.'

'Exactly, though the cops have dismissed it as a copycat.'

'Have you got a theory?'

'Not really. But come and look at these.' She waved the photographs at him.

He took some files off a chair and rolled it over to her.

She kicked her legs off the desk, pale in ankle socks and short red tartan kilt. She caught him looking at her thighs and smiled. 'So you've left your wife for me.'

'I thought you stayed away from married men.'

'Whatever gave you that idea?'

'You seemed pretty depressed the other day about the slender pickings in this town.'

'Ah, but now you've come into the picture things have taken on a rosier glow.'

He changed the subject. 'What clan is that?' He pointed to her kilt.

'Not sure. The Olley family are descended from Lutheran sword-makers who fled Germany to escape religious prosecution.'

'No wonder you're sharp.'

'Not original, Boris.'

'Beckett.'

She smirked. 'I know.' She held up a photograph. 'Take a

load of this. The crime scene.'

He took the photographs from her. He flipped through them without looking too closely.

'Nasty, aren't they?'

'The police give these out?'

She smiled and tapped her forehead. 'I have my ways.'

'Fraser?'

'He'll do anything for me.'

'Anything to get away from you, more likely.'

'Don't be like that. Am I that unattractive?'

'Notice I'm keeping a safe distance?'

She laughed. 'I've got the autopsy report too.' She dug around in a drawer and came up with a sheaf of photocopies. 'Did you know her brain weighed 1300 grams?'

'What does it say?'

'In layman's terms? Let's see. Time of death was approximately 2 a.m. That's when she was strangled. A ligature strangulation with something wide, probably a tie or scarf. The fibres they found were silk not twine.'

'Spaz doesn't wear silk ties.'

'Or scarves. There was no semen but that doesn't eliminate condom use. It was impossible to tell if she'd been sexually assaulted beforehand, with a bottle or something. There was some horrible tearing by the look of it, although that could have been the spear. She had fingermarks on her arms. But there was little debris under her nails. She didn't put up much of a fight. Her blood alcohol level was point one.'

'Drunk?'

'Looks like it.'

'So he took her for a drink somewhere?'

'Don't be sexist. It could have been a she.'

'It would have to have been a very strong she to push that spear through her organs.'

Kirstie put the report down. 'There's more.'

'What?'

'The cops took the tapes from all the Bankston family's answering machines the day Elisabeth's body was found. They didn't find anything of interest on any of them.'

'So?'

'The morons didn't think to check the cheese factory. Peter, Charley and Keith all have voice mail in their offices. It turns out Elisabeth did leave a message—on Peter's machine. About midnight on Thursday, the night she disappeared.'

'Why didn't she call him at home?'

'Don't know. She probably didn't want to wake him up.'

'And?'

'And she sounds all mysterious, but excited. In high spirits, a little bit slurred. But it's brief. She says, "It's Lizzie, I'm going to find out tonight. I'll tell you everything tomorrow." And that's it. Then she's either cut off or she's in a hurry.'

'Peter didn't check his own machine?'

'He says he hasn't checked it since the murder. Deliberately. He said he expected it to be full of do-gooders and ghouls.'

'I find that hard to believe.'

'Me too. But if he's covering up something, why didn't he just wipe the tape?'

'Hmm. Why didn't he? Did he say he knew what the message meant?'

'He says he hasn't got a clue. Maybe she wanted Charley or Keith and dialled the wrong extension. She might have if she was pissed.'

'What did they say?'

'They haven't a clue, either.'

'I don't believe Peter.'

'I agree it's suspicious. But it still comes down to who she was meeting. It obviously wasn't Peter. And what on earth would Spaz know, if it was him?'

'I can't imagine. Look, I've just been to the library. I was checking up on Valerie Harding's murder.'

She looked surprised. 'Valerie? What's her murder got to do with anything?'

'I was trying to connect the dots between Valerie's death, young Keith's drowning and Elisabeth's murder.'

'You're not going to get very far with that. Valerie's murder was completely different from Elisabeth's, except that they were both found in the Void.'

'Both were strangled. Neither appears to have been sexually assaulted. Your father covered Valerie's murder, didn't he?' he asked.

She nodded. 'I had to fight him for this one. Fortunately—or unfortunately, I suppose—Gran is moving into a nursing home this week and he's up in Bateman's. I get the gig.'

'The main suspect was released. The cops still thought he did it but there was some problem with the chain of evidence, or so your dad wrote.'

'Yeah. It was a total fuckup. They collected fibres from Valerie's cardigan in the bloke's rig, but somewhere between here and the lab in Sydney a couple of alien hairs got into the evidence bag. Of course, Harmer sat on it, but the truckie's lawyer's own forensic expert worked it out pre-trial. It cast doubt on their entire case, so they had to let him go.'

'The police found other evidence later, though. The elastic straps, buried in the bush.'

'Oh, yeah? But nothing must have come of it.'

Beckett was thoughtful for a moment. 'I wonder if you'd humour me for a bit.'

She cocked her head. 'That sounds appealing. What would you like?'

He ignored her flirting. 'This money the Harding family got from the London paper. Did your dad keep a copy of the *Daily Mirror* story on the Hardings?'

'Hmm. I suppose he did. I could call him—but, wait a tick, I know where he keeps his old stuff.' She stood up and smiled. 'Underneath the newer stuff.' She disappeared into the other room and emerged with a thick file. 'Let's see.'

The Harding file contained police reports, scrawled notes of interviews, clippings from the Sydney papers—but nothing from the *Daily Mirror*.

'The story must have been published a few weeks after that Passer guy was freed,' Kirstie said. 'Dad mightn't have kept it.'

'I wonder,' Beckett said.

'Wonder what?'

'Do you think the paper would keep archives?'

'Now you've got me curious.'

'How do I find out?'

'Go online, I suppose. They've probably got a website.'

'Of course. I'll get on to it.'

'Oh, no you don't. Let's look it up together. Here. I don't want you out of my sight until I know what you're up to.'

'I think we can be certain that I'm up to nothing,' Beckett said.

31

Octavia made no improvement for hours. It was after 5 p.m. when Heidi called Beckett from the hospital payphone, explaining where she was and not to expect her home until late. 'I'm not leaving until she wakes up.'

He sounded a little miserable at the prospect. 'Come as soon as you can. I've lots of news. I'm going nuts telling it to the refrigerator.'

Fraser was making a hash, by the sound of his grunts, of the *Woman's Day* crossword. Heidi went back to her chair next to Octavia's bed and took the frail woman's hand again, trying to warm the bone chill out of it. All of a sudden Octavia gave a little cough, gripped Heidi's fingers and opened her grey eyes.

Heidi looked to see if Fraser had noticed. He was chewing on the end of a biro, frowning at the page.

Heidi squeezed her hand back. 'Octavia, it's me. Heidi Go.'

It took a tremendous effort for Octavia to turn her head a few degrees, but she managed it. She squeezed Heidi's hand again.

'Are you in pain?' Heidi whispered.

Octavia gave a small nod.

'Look, here's a clever device on your finger. Press it...like this...and you get a shot of pethidine. That should do you.'

'Never did like the stuff.' Octavia's voice was croaky but strong.

Fraser looked up. 'Did she say something?'

'Just a moan or two. She's in a bit of pain. But she's gone back to sleep again.'

Octavia closed her eyes tight in complicity.

'Feeling better?' Heidi whispered.

'No. But I will, dear...'

'I think someone attacked you. Can you remember anything?'

She moved her head slightly. 'No.' She clamped her mouth tight. A tiny trickle fell from her closed eye down her cheek. A tear?

'You should tell, you know. They might go after someone else.'

She shook her head more vehemently. 'I don't know...'

'You do,' Heidi said. 'I want to know too. I want to help.'

Fraser looked up.

'Don't mind me,' Heidi told him. 'I'm reciting poetry to stop her from going into a coma.'

After a few moments, Octavia gripped her hand again. 'How long...'

'How long have you been here?'

A muffled 'No'.

'How long will they keep you here?'

A nod.

'I'd say at least a couple of days, maybe more.'

She shook Heidi's hand. 'No!'

'You've had a serious head injury. I don't know what else...'

Octavia mumbled something.

'What?' Heidi bent her head closer.

The old woman sounded like her mouth was full of cotton wool, but Heidi could make it out the second time. 'Look...'

'Yes?'

'Look for the...brother...'

'What brother?' Heidi asked, too loudly.

Fraser got up. 'What brother? What did she say?'

'She wanted her brother,' Heidi told him. She was damned if she was going to let him get any information for free.

'Who's he?' Fraser asked. 'I didn't think she had one.'

Heidi looked down at Octavia. She had closed her eyes again. A tremor ran through her hand.

Something had frightened her very badly.

Beckett was on the phone when Heidi got home. She kissed him on the neck and went into the bedroom to change into a sweater and jeans. Beckett had three bar heaters on and the oven door open and it was still draughty.

When she walked back into the kitchen, Beckett was heating some milk on the hot plate. 'Hot chocolate?' he asked her. 'We've run out of soy.'

'No thanks.' She opened the fridge and took out a tub of yoghurt. 'I'm going to have a banana with this.'

Beckett poured the hot milk into a mug and then dropped five marshmallows on top. He sat opposite her, stirring the drink until the marshmallows melted. 'How's Octavia now?' he asked.

'She doesn't look very good, but she came round for a little while. I don't think she's suffered any brain damage, she's just a bit confused, that's all. Do you know what she said when I asked her who attacked her?'

'What?'

'She grasped my hand tightly and said, "Look for the brother".'

'Her brother?'

'No, she definitely said *the* brother.'

'Have you any idea who the brother is?'

'The only brothers I can think of are Charley and Peter.' She started slicing the banana into her yoghurt.

'But she must know dozens of brothers. They breed like rabbits around here. What about Spaz, Crock and the rest?'

'That's true, I didn't think of them. Spaz visited her with the other kids.'

'But if that's the case, why didn't she just say a name? Why be so mysterious about it?'

'Maybe she wants to set us a challenge.'

'Maybe. I'm up for it.'

Heidi put down the knife and looked at him. 'You've found something out.'

He told her what Kirstie had said about the message on Peter's answering machine. 'So Elisabeth had arranged to meet someone that night.'

'Peter must be in on it.'

'He claims he hasn't a clue what she meant.'

'I find that hard to believe.'

'Me too. But the best is yet to come.' He explained about his search for the newspaper article about Valerie. 'We went on the *Daily Mirror* website and we couldn't get into the archives. Then Kirstie remembered she had a friend from journalism school in Sydney who works on the *Independent* in London. That was Kirstie on the phone then. Her friend just spent three hours doing a search of the story in the *Daily Mirror* and all other British tabloids, just in case the information was wrong. And she came up with *nothing*. There was no story on the Hardings in any British tabloid in that year and she searched the next year as well.'

'Maybe it was in a regional newspaper.'

'Nope. She searched there, too. I doubted all along the British papers would be interested in a small murder down here.'

'But Valerie's mother's English.'

'She came here when she was a kid. It was hardly a truck driver targeting British backpackers.'

'Then who paid them the money? *If* they were paid.'

'They were paid all right. That house must have cost a bit, even eight years ago. And they bought the cake shop. Russ Harding was just a storeman. I reckon both places cost more than $250,000. It's a wonder none of the locals called them on it.'

'Maybe Valerie's dad robbed a bank. There must be a reason why he wanted to cover up the origin of the money.'

'Because it was given to him by Keith Bankston.'

'That's a bit of a leap.'

'Think about it. Not many people in the district have that much money to throw around. Russ Harding worked for Keith. And, remember, Harding's son Jack got a decent job at the cheese factory not long after.'

'So it's a payment for something? But what?'

'Russ did something for Keith. It has to be.'

'Or he was blackmailing him. Russ committed suicide a while afterwards, didn't someone tell you? Maybe it was out of guilt?'

'Possibly.'

'Or how about this—what if he didn't commit suicide? What if he was murdered? Blackmail is a pretty certain way of getting thumped.'

'If that was the case, then you'd have to point the finger at Keith Bankston, wouldn't you?'

Heidi stared at him. 'Shit.'

'The question is, what did Keith do to be blackmailed?'

'You don't think it has anything to do with Valerie?'

Beckett nodded. 'Think about it. What if Keith murdered Valerie? There's all that stuff about the contaminated evidence. Maybe he got one of his cop cronies to try to frame the truck driver? He's got enough power.'

'Keith's not a pleasant bloke but, really...'

'Maybe young Keith found out the truth about Valerie's murder.'

'Keith wouldn't kill his own son.'

'His *adopted* son.'

'How would he do it? There were witnesses to the drowning.'

'All kids. He could have had a frogman waiting by the rocks...'

Heidi slapped her hand on the table. 'Really, Beck, if you would only put this much imagination into your screenplay! In the first place, why would Keith Bankston murder Valerie?'

'Maybe he was having it off with her.'

'With his son's girlfriend?'

'*Droit de signeur* and all that.'

'Beckett, we live in a modern town in New South Wales, not some feudal backwater in twelfth-century France. I wouldn't be surprised if Keith has a few mistresses tucked around the place, but a fifteen-year-old girl? Don't you think there'd be gossip?'

'Exactly. He might have murdered her to shut her up.'

Heidi sighed. 'Or maybe Carmel murdered her in a jealous rage. Or maybe Peter and Charley drowned their brother at their father's bidding.' She stood up and took the empty yoghurt cup to the sink. 'Don't screw up your nose. It's all equally ridiculous.'

'Well, there's one person who might enlighten us.'

'Who's that?'

'And the bonus is, she's a really good cook.'

32

Sheila Harding came out from the back of the shop when the chimes over the door signalled Beckett's entrance. She'd been indulging in a cigarette given the wafts of smoke that accompanied her through the bead curtain. He was reminded of Carmel Bankston and the generation of older women who grew up believing cigarettes to be elegant accessories and who were now paying the price for that vanity in the deep lines around their mouths and yellowing tips of their fingers. There were other lines on Sheila Harding's face, but he supposed these were from sorrow. That her hair was short, curled and jauntily yellow did nothing to offset the weariness in her manner.

She smiled faintly, recognising him. 'The neenish tart man,' she said in an accent that still betrayed North Country roots. 'How many will it be today?'

'I've got to watch my waistline,' he joked. 'How about four? And four of those delicious vanilla slices while you're at it.'

She constructed a cardboard tray and arranged the cakes on it with the help of a pair of tongs. 'Having a tea party?' she asked him and then started coughing violently, turning away from the cakes. 'Sorry,' she said, as she slid the tray into a paper bag and put it on the counter. 'That'll be, let's see, eighteen dollars eighty.'

He took some folded notes out of his pocket and peeled off twenty dollars. 'A small price to pay for the best neenish tarts in the district.'

'Thank you,' she nodded.

'I suppose you've been baking all your life.'

'I have. People always complimented me so I decided to set up shop about seven years ago.'

'Must have cost you a pretty penny. It's a nice shop,' he said, gesturing towards the frilly Liberty print curtains on the window and other homey details, like the cuckoo clock on one wall.

'I don't have much else to do,' she said.

'Family left home?'

'My husband died not long after I opened the shop. I lost our lass some time back. My son still lives at home but he works long hours.' Some small vanity compelled her to add, 'He's an executive at Nullin Cheese.'

'Oh, yes? What's his name?'

'Jack Harding.'

Beckett pretended to think. 'Ah—I met him at the debutante ball. Good-looking lad.'

She seemed pleased. 'He's done very well. My husband Russ was only a storeman there. Jack's so important he travels overseas all the time.'

'Keith Bankston must think highly of him.'

'And so he should. Jack's a smart boy. He was always very determined as a lad. And he was such a lovely brother to Valerie. When they were kiddies he'd make her lunch and brush her hair. She had lovely hair.'

'She was the daughter you lost?'

'She was murdered, the same way as poor Elisabeth. She was only fifteen.' She looked away for a moment and then back at him, moist-eyed. 'I tried to call Carmel to offer my help, but I couldn't get through. I sent Jack to the funeral. I just couldn't...'

'I understand. Was Jack a friend of Elisabeth's?'

'He knew her, played when they were kids. He was more involved with the other lad, Keith. You heard about young Keith I suppose?'

'Yes. It's tragic that Carmel has lost two children.'

'It used to be tit for tat,' Sheila Harding said vaguely. 'We'd lost one each.'

Beckett thought that was an odd way to put it. 'What do you mean?'

'Oh, just that we were equals then. Now she's out-tragicked me.'

Sounds like a competition, Beckett thought. Maybe this lonely woman misses the attention she received when her daughter died. 'I think I remember hearing about your daughter,' Beckett ventured. 'Valerie, did you say?'

'Yes,' she sighed. 'Full of life, she was. Not the easiest girl in the world, but what teenagers are? I told her not to go hitchhiking. Not once, a hundred times…I wasn't a bad mother.'

'Of course not. Kids do what they like, don't they? You can only tell them so many times.' When she looked at him gratefully, he went on, 'I can't imagine how awful it must have been for you…' He broached the subject carefully. 'I heard you had a bit of a windfall afterwards.'

She scowled. 'I never did agree with that. Russ talked me into giving that newspaper our story. I said to him, this is making money over our Valerie's dead body. He thought I'd be happy with a new house and the shop I'd always wanted, that it would make up for…everything. I hate that wretched pink house, but I keep it because it reminds me of Russ. It never did make him happy. The stupid bastard hanged himself a while afterwards.' Her voice faltered. 'He never could take things like I could.'

'But Jack's still with you, at least. How did Jack take it?'

'It was worse for him. Not only did his sister die, and his best friend but then his dad too. He was in a black hole for a long time. Keith Bankston got him out of it. He gave the boy responsibility. And it turned out, after me worrying myself sleepless what was going to become of him, that he ended up being good at business. He's turned into a leader, our Jack.' She gave a sad smile. 'In some ways Keith Bankston replaced his son with mine.'

She looked at Beckett with shining eyes. 'But I don't mind, really. I'd have given Jack to Beelzebub if he could have guaranteed my boy would make something of himself.'

'I imagine the Bankstons felt the same way about young Keith. From the way they talk they seemed to have loved him very much, even though he was a bit of a wild one. He was adopted, wasn't he?'

'Yes, but when you've given up hope of ever having one of your own, you love the child wherever it has come from. Even when, as it often happens, you end up having children of your own blood later. Carmel was so happy to have that child, she used to take him in his baby carriage down the street for everyone to admire, like the Queen with a young prince. It was only later, when she started having the other kids, that she kept to herself, got a bit stuck up. She never did have much to do with me, even when Jack and Keith were as close as brothers. I like her though.'

'So do I. It wouldn't be easy living with big Keith.'

'That's what Russ used to say.'

'Your husband didn't like him?'

'Hated him, if you want to know. But he was a lowly worker and Keith was his boss, so that was normal.'

'Jack doesn't have a problem?'

'No, he slotted right in from the start. If I hadn't've given birth to him myself and remember the night of his conception I would have said he was a Bankston.'

33

The weather had taken a colder turn in the past week. The mornings were no longer fresh and crisp but misty and damp, with soft-bellied fog draped over the valleys and on the shoulders of the naked hills. Easier to stay in bed than get up.

At least that was Beckett's argument when he reached over and pulled Heidi back down beside him as she tried to slip off the bed.

'I've got an appointment, Beck,' she argued.

'It won't take long.'

'Is that a promise or a threat?'

Heidi dressed silently while Beckett went back to sleep. She had an eleven o'clock appointment at a pensioner's house, a woman who had called her nervously and asked three times if her services weren't one of those 'sex things'. She pulled a corner off one of the vanilla slices Beckett had brought back from the cake shop the day before and washed it down with some tea.

She loaded her table and bag of towels and oils in the back of the station wagon. But when she tried to start the car, the engine wouldn't turn over. She tried again. Not a sound, not even the usual squeal and cough. She waited and tried once more. Flat battery, she deduced.

Beckett wasn't amenable to being woken up. 'I don't have any jumper leads,' he mumbled, his face still wedged in the soft down pillow.

She pulled the covers off him. 'You'll have to drive me, then. It's after ten.'

He groaned, but pulled on some clothes while she made him a coffee.

He was still half-asleep when he dropped Heidi at a small house with an enormous dry lawn.

'Pick me up in an hour,' she said.

With time to kill, and it being opening time, he headed for the Leagues Club. The bar was open, but Neville Chamberlain wasn't anywhere to be seen. Beckett gestured to a gap-toothed youth, who took his order. At the end of the bar, a lonely drunk was gesticulating for the bartender.

'Where are ya, you bludger?' The drunk flopped his head on the bar and then yanked it back up again, flaying his arms about and knocking over his beer. 'Look what you done, you little bastard,' he said to the wall of bottles.

'Hold your horses, Gray, I'm coming,' said the bar man.

'Is that Gray Wignall?' Beckett asked.

'Yeah. Came in pissed a few minutes ago. He bothering you?'

'No, just curious, that's all.' Beckett's instinct was to leap on his wife's attacker and punch him in the jaw. Instead, he ambled down and took a barstool beside him. 'Easy on there, mate,' he said. 'I'll get you another one.'

Gray looked at him as if he were Santa Claus.

Beckett called the bartender over. 'Get him another beer.'

'I don't think it's a good idea,' the young man said.

'Just do it,' Beck said. 'I'll be responsible.'

The bartender scurried off, mistaking Beckett for one of the detectives from Sydney. He came back a moment later with two beers.

'There you are, friend,' Beckett said, pushing the glass towards Gray and dropping a note on the bar.

'Much obliged,' Gray drawled. He looked at the beer but didn't pick it up.

'You're Gray Wignall, aren't you?'

'Yeah? Who wants to know?'

'I've been wanting to speak to you.'

'What about?' He continued to stare at the beer.

'Keith Bankston.'

Gray snarled. 'Get the fuck out.'

'Don't get me wrong,' Beckett persisted. 'I'm no friend of the Bankstons. It's just that I've been doing some research into Keith's business practices—'

'Why would you wanna do that?' His head snapped up. There was a suspicious gleam in his eye.

'Because I think there's something peculiar about the money Russ Harding got after his daughter died. It was supposed to be from a British newspaper but I can't find any evidence the story was ever published.'

'Sheila's got a copy of it. You should ask her.'

That surprised Beckett. He'd been convinced the newspaper story didn't exist. He tried another tack. 'Russ Harding bought a house and shop with that money. And his son got a job out of it, at Nullin Cheese. I was wondering if that was a bribe...from Keith Bankston.'

'Search me,' Gray said, stubbornly.

'And I was wondering what it was a bribe *for*. And why Russ Harding killed himself not long afterwards. And if he were blackmailing Keith for something.'

'Blackmail. You don't want to get into that.' He shook his head slowly.

'I think you know, Gray. I think you're maybe planning to do the same thing.' He took a sip of his beer. 'And I don't blame you. I dislike developers. A bloke works hard building his business up, has legal entitlement to the land, and the fat cats think they can ride roughshod over the law—'

'They don't ride roughshod over me.'

'Any normal bloke would try to stop them any way he can. I'd do the same thing. And Keith Bankston's been lording it over this town too long.'

'He got his comeuppance.'

'You mean his daughter's death?'

'That too.'

'What else?'

'You're asking the wrong bloke, pal.'

'Who should I be asking, then?'

He looked cagey. 'I'm not tellin' ya for nothin'.'

'What will you tell me for?'

'Let's see.' Gray licked his lips. 'What about a case of Resch's?'

'Done,' Beckett said.

Gray shifted on his stool.

'Well?' Beck prompted.

Gray looked sideways. 'Sid.'

'Sid Blackpeter?'

Gray nodded. 'Keith Bankston reckons he's so fucking smart, but Sid Blackpeter went and made a fool of him. And the funniest thing is, Keith doesn't know it. I piss my pants whenever I think of it.'

'What did Sid do?'

'That's for me to know and you to find out.' He smiled triumphantly at Beckett. It was hard to believe he was only about forty, with his broken teeth and sun-lined face. He chuckled. 'And you'll never find out because Sid's locked up in jail.'

'If it's so amusing, why don't you tell Keith yourself?'

'Oh, I intend to do it, mate. But I'm saving my amnunition...' He stumbled on the word. He then held up his glass swirling the contents. 'Cheers,' he said. 'The ute's out the front. You can toss the case in before you go.'

The old woman counted out her dollars on the laminate table. She only had coins and an ancient two-dollar note. When she reached twenty-eight dollars and twenty-five cents, she looked at Heidi with milky eyes and said, 'You don't mind, do you, love? That's all I've got till me pension comes through.'

Heidi put her hand over the money and picked up a few coins. She pushed the rest towards the woman. 'Actually, Mrs Cooper, I've overcharged you. We didn't get round to those feet of yours because of the chilblains.'

Oh well, Carmel can subsidise that one, Heidi thought as she closed the flyscreen door behind her. She walked down the broken concrete path to Casuarina Drive, one of the back streets of Nullin without either sea view or sea air. Mrs Cooper's fibro house was typical of the neighbourhood, a patchwork of paint and hasty repairs with a lawn the colour of toast scrapings that even the recent rains couldn't bring back to green.

When Beckett pulled up she got in. He filled her in on his conversation with Gray Wignall. 'It appears as if Sid Blackpeter is implicated in this after all.'

'Sid? But he was in jail when Elisabeth was killed.'

'It doesn't mean he didn't orchestrate it from there. Gray was adamant Sid had made a fool of Keith Bankston in some way Keith didn't know about.'

They passed the golf course. The gates to the Bankston property loomed to the left. Beckett slowed down and then stopped to let a white BMW join the highway. A woman drove and another sat beside her. 'Did you see that?' he asked.

'Diane Bankston? Yes, she seems to have helped herself to Elisabeth's car.'

'No. Not her. The girl beside her.'

'I didn't recognise her. She looked like she had a baby over her shoulder.' Then she worked it out. '*That* was Joey Blackpeter?'

'Unlikely companions, don't you think?' Beckett drove for a

kilometre or so then asked, 'Do you think Joey's trying to point the paternity finger at old Petey?'

'Then why would she be in a car with Diane?'

'Diane wants children.'

'God, you're right.' She thought about the conversation she'd overheard between the couple. It now made sense. 'They were talking about Joey. Of course. They were going to pay her for the baby. It's not that far-fetched. She tried to sell it to you, after all. And I think Diane is desperate enough do something like that.'

'Maybe Pete is the father.'

'I can't imagine it.'

'If I remember rightly, you told me Diane said that fucking had gotten them into trouble in the first place. So presumably that means Peter has spread his seed around.'

'I'm not sure she said that. I think it was more that *not* fucking had done it.'

'As in, they rarely have sex?'

'I think so. Peter didn't sound remorseful, just wary. Like Joey was trying to con them into something and he didn't trust her. They seem to have a problem with infertility, remember. Obviously Diane wants to adopt the baby and Peter doesn't.'

'And they don't want Keith to know.'

'I'd bet on it.'

'Sounds risky to me. Joey is pretty indiscriminate. Can't imagine her keeping it secret for long. And I can't imagine any of the Blackpeters keeping that sort of secret if they found out. They'd have to want to use it against Keith. There'd be mileage in it.'

Heidi remembered more of the conversation she overheard. 'It sounded like Diane had it all worked out. Give Joey enough money and she'd clear out of town, never to return. Then I imagine Diane and Peter could go up to Sydney for a while and return with a baby that they could say came from a legitimate agency.'

'Why wouldn't they do that anyway?'

'Shortage of white babies, Beck. Don't you know that? A lot of couples end up adopting an abandoned girl baby from China as a last resort. The Chinese dump or murder them because they only want boys and there's a one-child-per-couple law.'

'Well, then, Peter and Diane should do that. It's morally more responsible.'

'Can you imagine Keith wanting a Chinese in the family? He can barely bring himself to talk to *me*.'

'But he wouldn't want a Blackpeter either.'

'Diane's logic is that he's not going to find out.'

'All this talk about people not having sex is making me feel I should be making my own contribution.'

'You've made enough of a contribution for one day.' She flicked him under the chin.

'Don't. I'll have an accident.'

She stared at the road for a while. A new thought came to her. 'I've remembered something else. Diane said they were only doing what Keith had done before.'

'So he and Peter did sleep with Joey.' He smiled.

'I don't think she meant that. They want to adopt Joey's baby. Young Keith was adopted.'

'So Keith could hardly object to them adopting a baby too.'

'Yes, but it was more than that. Like they were doing *exactly* the same thing as Keith.'

'I don't get it.'

'What if young Keith was also adopted from—'

'Joey?'

Heidi glared at her husband. 'Beckett I could throttle you! Keith couldn't have been Joey's baby, because she's younger than him, you dolt.'

'Then what?' Beckett looked hurt.

'It still doesn't mean young Keith wasn't a Blackpeter baby. He might have been Laureen's.'

Beckett said casually, 'He might have even been Keith and Laureen's.'

Heidi looked at her husband appreciatively. 'You're not so addle-brained after all.'

34

The local NRMA serviceman was Mick Black. He managed to get Heidi's car started but he was more interested in the Volvo.

'Nice car, this,' he said to Beckett. 'You ought to get that windscreen fixed but. The cops'll pull you over in no time.'

'I had a run in with the Blackpeters last week.'

'Yeah? You wouldn't be the first. One of 'em tried to pinch me van a few weeks ago. I chased him off. That scary one I think it was.'

'Spaz?'

'No, his big brother. I've shooed him off before. The one that's called Scary.'

'I've met Spaz and Crock. But Scary sounds like he belongs in the Spice Girls.'

'Never heard of 'em. Bloody refugees are they?' Mick Black asked.

Heidi changed into jeans and a mohair cardigan which came down to her knees. She drove to the hospital to check on Octavia Goodhope. The old woman was sitting up in her hospital bed, giving the nursing aide hell. 'This is a hospital. Don't you know about hospital corners?' she admonished.

'That sounds more like it,' Heidi said, placing a bunch of tulips on her lap. 'Let me find a vase.'

'Don't worry, dear, I'm going home in a minute. If I can talk someone into releasing me.'

'How are you going to get home?'

'Charley is coming to take me.' She shifted to one hip and untangled her nightgown from beneath her. 'They don't know how to make beds anymore,' she lamented.

'Are you better?'

'Perfectly well. They've done all the tests. This old skull needs more than a whack on the back of the head with a brick to crack it.'

'Is that what he used?'

'Something like that.' She patted her bandage. 'They tell me I have eighteen stitches.'

'Are you sure you'll be all right at home?'

'They're giving me one of those mobile phones, although frankly I don't think it's going to work up at my house.'

Heidi took the chair beside the bed. 'Octavia, you said something to me the other night.'

'Did I?' The old woman looked cagey.

'When I asked who did this to you, you said, "Look for the brother." Which brother was that?'

'I don't recall saying it.'

'But you must know what you meant.'

'Delirium, my dear.'

'I don't think so,' Heidi said firmly. 'I was looking at you when you fell at the funeral. You saw someone. And I think that someone saw you seeing him. And he came along later and attacked you.'

'Not so, I'm afraid. I'm sorry I was babbling. You mustn't go running off on wild goose chases. You might get yourself into trouble.' She raised a hand and placed it on Heidi's. 'I thought your husband was the one in the family with the imagination.'

Beckett sat at the kitchen table and spread out the *Nullin Voice*. Already Elisabeth's murder was reduced to a single column, although the article pointed to coverage of the funeral inside.

On page three, under a photograph of a kickboxing class for

senior citizens at the Fishermen's Recreation Club, was a story which trumpeted an impressive export deal for Nullin Cheese with Libya and Cuba. Strange world. And mixed fortunes for the Bankston family.

He flipped through the paper, thinking of the piles of old copy he had gone through looking for information about Valerie Harding's death. Nothing much had changed in eight years. Bingo prizes. Whale watching announcements. Holiday rentals. And then he realised what had been gnawing at him since yesterday.

Something Gray Wignall had said.

Sheila Harding had a pair of tongs in her hand and was crouched low arranging chocolate eclairs on a shelf. When Beckett entered she stood up and smiled. She dipped back down again and came up with an eclair in her tongs. 'I just broke this one. Would you help me out and eat it?'

It didn't look very broken to Beckett but he willingly took it. 'Do you often give out free samples?'

'Only to discerning customers.'

'Actually, I've come to ask you a question.'

'Oh?' She looked rather more interested than necessary. He thought then about how lonely she must be. Her mother-in-law, at 100, was probably more of a chore than a companion. And Jack was probably too busy travelling for Nullin Cheese to be much comfort.

How was he going to phrase it without arousing her suspicions? If the *Daily Mirror* article existed, it would make all his speculation wrong-headed. He decided to be honest. 'Since we spoke the other day I've been thinking about your daughter, Valerie,' he began.

She looked disappointed. 'You're not the first person who has asked me about her since Elisabeth died.'

'No, no.' He wanted to distance himself from the local ghouls, even if that distance was only a hair's breadth in reality. 'I don't want to know about her death. I'm sure it's nothing to do with Elisabeth. I'm much more interested in her life. I was wondering if you had any pictures you could show me.'

'I don't have a good photo,' she said, playing with the edge of her apron. Her voice was softer now, all traces of suspicion gone. 'We never did take up with cameras in this family. They ran one of Jack's Polaroids in the paper, but it didn't do her justice.'

'Is that the British paper?' he asked carefully.

'That too. I've got a copy. Do you want to see it?' She looked hopeful, as if he would say yes.

'If you don't mind,' he said, trying not to betray too much interest.

'Hang on a tick.' She disappeared through the bead curtain. It was only a moment later when she returned. She handed him a tabloid-size page, laminated. 'Russ got that done,' she explained. 'Propped it up on the sideboard for all to see.'

It was the front page of the *Daily Mirror*, dated 2 February eight years before. The quality was a bit fuzzy.

'Photocopy?' Beckett asked.

'Yes. They never sent the real thing, even though Russ wrote to them.'

The same photograph of Valerie that had been used by the *Nullin Voice* was run at quarter-page size. She looked tentative, demure even. 'How old is she here?' he asked.

'About thirteen. Before she became a handful.'

'Pretty girl,' he lied. She had a pugnacious look, all chin and pout. But her hair was fair and cut in a heavy fringe. Probably her best feature. Under the masthead, the heading screamed at him in one-inch caps: AUSTRALIA KILLED MY DAUGHTER. Under that, in slightly smaller letters: BROKEN-HEARTED BRIT MUM TELLS ALL.

Beckett started to read and then stopped. 'They interviewed you by phone?'

'Yes. That's his name there.' She pointed to the byline. Bill Bertram.

'A Londoner, was he?'

'No, he came from the Midlands.'

'Did you sign any contracts?'

'Yes, why?'

'I'd hate to think you were ripped off.'

'It was hardly that. I couldn't believe they'd pay so much money for such a thing.'

'There were follow-ups?'

'They ran it over three days. Russ showed me copies. I don't know where they are, though. It's all a bit of a...daze.'

'Thanks,' Beckett said, handing the page back to her. 'It must be comforting to know someone cared over there.'

'They didn't care,' she said. 'They wanted to make fun of Australia. Make it out to be full of convicts and thugs. I wish I'd never spoken to them.'

'But you wouldn't have this shop.'

'I'd rather have my self-respect.'

'But you didn't destroy the article?'

'Russ was proud of it.'

'I understand.' He smiled at her for a moment and hoped he looked sympathetic, not patronising. He liked her and thought she didn't deserve the short straw she'd drawn in life.

'I think I'll go out back for a fag,' she said at last. 'Could you turn the "closed" notice around when you leave?'

'Okay,' he said. 'Take care.'

As he turned, she said in a wistful voice, 'Do you think I should have talked to the *Mirror*?'

'Yes, I do,' he said.

She nodded.

He turned the notice and closed the door behind him.

He hadn't lied. There was nothing wrong with what she'd said in that article.

It was just a pity it was fake.

35

As Heidi drove home from the hospital she thought about Elisabeth's funeral. Octavia *had* seen someone, she was sure of it. She tried to remember who was in the crowd on the lawn outside. The Bankston family, accepting condolences. The Nullin Cheese blokes and their wives. Andrew Eagan and the Gondwanas. The Blackpeters, of course.

Beckett was convinced that Sid was up to his neck in it. But maybe the person who alarmed Octavia was one of Spaz's *other* brothers. She tried to recall their faces. Five boys, each of them like the other. But she wasn't sure that Octavia looked directly at them. On the other hand, she *was* sure Octavia had looked in her direction, at Eagan and Beck, Klas and Sara and Martin Gondwana walking towards her.

Elisabeth had known Martin, he'd admitted that much. By the sounds of it, she had also confided in him. He'd come to the funeral, so there was some kind of emotional connection. How deep was it, she wondered? He was an attractive man. Charismatic. A vulnerable teenage girl could easily fall under his spell.

She changed her mind at once about going home. She turned off the highway towards Speculator, as usual, but veered onto an old concrete road a kilometre or so before the village. The road crossed Chinaman's Creek a few kilometres out and then ran beside it and disappeared into the hills. She vaguely remembered which way Sara and Klas had directed her the last time. When she spotted a bunch of wildflowers tied to the trunk of the tree, she recognised the track and turned into it.

The forest was scrubby and still charred where a bushfire had gone through it some years before. The canopy overhead became denser the further she bumped along the road. She knew her instincts had been right when she came across a beaten-up Kombi van parked in a clearing. She pulled in beside it and got out of her car. The Kombi van's side windows were covered in slogans and decals. Someone had painted cannabis leaves on the side and airbrushed in block letters LEGALISE POT. A sure way to get pulled over by the cops, she thought. But it was on blocks, so it probably had been retired from active duty for some time—the 'Free Nelson Mandela' sticker on the windscreen confirmed this.

Heidi followed a path that ran downhill from the clearing. Among the trees she could see square shapes that she took for beehives. The air became damper as she descended. Wet leaves and bark stuck to her boots.

Someone nearby was playing drums and the sound was getting closer. A moment later the bush opened up to reveal a small valley hemmed in by tall timber, dominated by a large rush-sided structure, similar to an Indonesian long house, with a stream circumventing it. A huge pit of stones gave off smoke as if someone had been tending the fire, but there was no one in sight, unless you counted whoever was drumming—and that was above her head. She looked up and saw a platform wedged between the trees three metres above. From this angle all she could see were a pair of huge dirty feet and the bottom of a tall African-style bongo. He didn't miss a beat of whatever tune he was pounding out—her presence hadn't been detected.

She looked beyond him and spotted a series of platforms at different levels, throughout the treetops. Some of the structures were covered with tents, erected from sticks and protected by waterproof fabric. Cosy. She couldn't imagine what it would be like to spend a winter there in the bone-chilling, dripping rain.

She didn't hear Klas come up behind her. 'Do you like it?' he said softly, touching her elbow with the same proprietorial gesture he had displayed in her car.

She recognised the accent at the same time that she remembered the gesture. She spun around, tugging her elbow from his cool grip, irritated, then relieved to see a familiar face. 'Where is everybody?'

He looked at her as if she were certifiable. 'It's the third Thursday of the month. They have taken the honey to the Speculator farmer's market.'

'What are you doing here then?'

'It is not my turn.'

'How many are you?'

He shrugged. 'There are about ten now. But in the season we have thirty, forty.'

'What season?'

He said blandly, 'Whenever there's a protest being organised.'

'They come to hide out here?'

He glared at her as if she'd crawled out of a World Bank vault.

She looked around. 'Has Martin gone to Speculator too?'

'No. He is doing the taxes.'

'*Taxes?*' Heidi was taken aback. 'I thought you didn't believe in the system.'

He shrugged again. 'Martin says the way they get you in the end is always through the taxes.'

Heidi thought of Al Capone. 'He might be right. Can I see him?' When Klas hesitated, she reminded him that Martin had said she could come at any time.

He gave a sharp nod and disappeared into the lodge. She wondered if they stoked fires inside at night and ran around sweaty and naked.

He came back out a moment later. 'Wait here,' he said and walked off up the hill.

Rude, she thought, feeling unsettled.

A breeze ran like a shiver through the camp, ruffling the little flags of hand-written fabric strung on a rope that ran from the eaves of the long house to a stake carved like a totem pole. The drummer had slowed his beat. The tinkle of bellbirds created an entirely different rhythm.

Her reverie was broken by the appearance of Martin at the entrance to the long house. He strode over to her and shook her hand. 'I'm glad you honoured us with a visit, Heidi.' He didn't let go of her hand, but clasped it between his and led her to the fire. 'You look cold.'

'I am.' She took her hand away and wrapped her arms around herself. 'I can't get used to this damp.'

He took her elbow and drew her closer to the fire. He sat on a damp log and gestured for her to do the same. 'But it's beautiful. The scent of wet leaves in the gully. That's still exotic to me, coming from the West.' Americans always thought their west was the only west. He moved his head closer to hers. His proximity made her uneasy. 'Wait up. You've got something on your neck.'

He touched her neck and looked at his hand. 'A leaf. I thought it was a leech.'

'God, you don't have any of those around here, do you?' She looked worriedly at her feet.

'Thousands.' He smiled. Unlike his other, all-embracing smiles, this one was very much focused on her. 'You're here to find out about Elisabeth,' he said abruptly. 'You were curious at the funeral. I didn't think it would be long before you came to us.'

'I didn't know her. But I care about her...for lots of reasons.'

'Of course. You're an empathetic person. Her pain was transferred to you when you found her.'

'You said she'd come up here once or twice and you'd helped her. "Find herself," I think Sara said.'

'When you come from a family like that you need help. Fortunately, Heidi, Elisabeth was a smart girl. She knew where to look.'

223

The way he said her name disturbed her. It was as if he had assumed an intimacy she had no intention of giving him. 'And how exactly did you help her?'

'I see you're suspicious of me. I helped her in the regular ways. I listened.' He paused. 'If you're thinking it was anything more, it wasn't.'

'But you're in a position to influence a girl like that.'

'I wouldn't abuse it. I've been chaste for three years. I don't expect the others to be, but it works for me.'

'Why three years?'

'That's when my dot com went bust and I found myself here.'

She had to suppress a snort at the matter-of-fact way he said this. 'That's a pretty radical reaction to failure isn't it?'

'I didn't fail. It's not a word I recognise, Heidi.'

'But you had a spiritual awakening because of it?'

'It's easier to do when you've got no money. For many years I had too much money. It distracted me.'

'And now you've gone into the business of simplicity?'

'Very good. It's an excellent way to put it. We need very little here. Everyone pools what they have.'

'Like tithing?'

'No, talents. Sara's here for her personality. Nelson up there contributes his musical skills. We have horticulturists—'

'For the crop?'

'You don't approve?'

'It's a bit dubious.'

'Not at all. We're not big producers. We're waiting for the substance to be approved medicinally. Then we can do some good. You'd be surprised, but there are dairy farmers who have turned to growing cannabis to subsidise their farms.'

'What about Elisabeth's skills? She had quite a lot to contribute—financially.'

'We didn't want her money. But I don't wish to talk about her in detail.'

'She'd want you to help find her murderer.'

'They've arrested someone I believe.'

'But he didn't do it.'

'Oh? Well, all I can say is I can't help you. She only talked to us about her family.'

'But I think the murder *is* something to do with her family.'

A shadow of concern passed over his bland expression. 'What makes you say that?'

'I think she found out something, and someone tried to stop her telling it to anyone else.'

'Something about her family?'

'Yes, though I don't know what.'

'I don't see how it would make any difference.'

'How *what* would make any difference?'

'Anything she found out about her family.'

'You *do* know something.'

'Not really. It's not indiscreet to say that a lot of her turmoil stemmed from her sense of self, or lack of it.' He stared at Heidi, weighing up what to say, testing how far he could trust her. 'I'll tell you this. But you must promise to keep it to yourself.'

'I promise.'

'Elisabeth found out her brother had a different mother and she wondered if she did too.'

'She'd only just found it out? I thought it was common knowledge that Keith was adopted.'

'No, not that brother. I'm not being clear. Another one. The eldest.'

'Peter?'

He nodded.

'Peter isn't Carmel's son?'

'Elisabeth wasn't one hundred per cent sure. Some local busybody had said something to her.'

'But I'm sure you could find a dozen Nullin residents who saw Carmel pregnant with Peter.'

'I suggested that. I asked her to think about *why* she believed the rumour so quickly. Was it a kind of wish fulfilment, that she didn't want to belong to her family and was looking for a way out? Many teenage girls secretly wish for a parallel life. A mysterious birth mother waiting to be found could become the hub of a rich and tantalising fantasy. She could blame all her failures on that.'

'So Keith Bankston was their father but they had a different mother? Did she say she thought that their mother was Laureen Blackpeter?'

He gave a brief nod. 'You already know her suspicions.'

'I worked out that the eldest boy, Keith, was the child of Keith and Laureen, but I don't know about the other two. Or three, if you throw Charley into the mix. What was her reasoning?'

'She didn't say.'

Heidi thought for a minute about what Beckett had told her earlier. It was starting to make sense. 'Elisabeth left a message on Peter's answering machine the night she disappeared that suggested she was going to meet someone who would provide some kind of evidence. I think that evidence was about their real mother.'

'And you think that someone is the murderer?'

'It's possible. But why would they not want her to find out, especially if it's town gossip anyway?'

'The murderer may not be rational. Do you know the old test?'

'No. What's that?'

'Let me ask you a question. A young woman goes to her mother's funeral and meets a very handsome man there without finding out his name. The next week she murders her sister. Why?'

Heidi didn't know. 'Is this one of those puzzles with two bodies in the room and broken glass and they turn out to be fish?'

'No, not at all. Give up?'

'Yes.'

'She wanted to meet the man again.' He smiled. 'A psychopath would give that answer straight up every time. It's how their minds work.'

'God. Thank goodness I failed.'

'The motive may not make sense to a rational person.'

'For such a spiritual man, you're very tuned into the machinations of the real world.'

'I was a shrink in another life.'

She wasn't sure whether he was talking about reincarnation or something he had done in this life. He saw that. 'I practised in California for a while. I attended med school first. Then I did law. Then psychiatry. I'm a fully qualified Doctor Feelgood.'

'You sound restless.'

'Oh, yeah,' he laughed. 'I even played in a rock band once. We had a modest hit.'

'So what was your dot com?'

'A video delivery service.'

'Really?'

'Really.' He opened his palms. 'It could have been anything, Heidi. It was only ever about the money. And we never made any. Lost a couple of million.'

'How did you meet Elisabeth?'

'She met Sara at the farmer's market. Sara's a magnet for troubled souls.'

'She bought pot too?'

'She was a normal teenager.' He looked up at the trees. 'It was difficult for her in Nullin. Her folks made her claustrophobic.'

'I understand that. Her mother seemed more afraid that she'd get pregnant than anything else. The word out at the Leagues Club is that she slept around.'

'They're probably saying the same thing about you.'

Suitably chastened, Heidi blushed. 'You're right. I shouldn't be so quick to believe local gossip.' She thought about Valerie Harding. 'There was another girl who was murdered eight years ago and the town also painted her as a slut. I wonder if it was true.'

'Small towns are full of small minds.'

They said nothing for a moment. Heidi noticed that Klas had been sitting further up the hill watching them. She felt a shiver of dread. 'I better go,' she said.

'But you should see the property.' He looked put out.

'Another time. You should get back to your taxes.'

He sighed. 'What is it they say? They're inevitable. Like death.'

She looked at him sadly. 'But death shouldn't be inevitable for an eighteen-year-old girl.'

36

Peter is the only one who can help me with this, Heidi thought as she drove away. He must have known Elisabeth's suspicions about them being adopted. He might know if it had something to do with her death.

The main building of the Nullin Cheese complex looked like a cube of ricotta in the middle of a concrete platter. Perhaps it was intentional. The whitewashed, rendered two-storey building was about fifteen years old, judging by the post-modern slits that served as windows. It might have been a hospital, if it weren't for the huge illuminated sign across its roof and the yellow-painted tourist kiosk in the shape of a wedge of cheddar in the middle of the carpark outside the entrance. A parking area for tour buses had been set aside and a line of about thirty elderly people in walking gear lined up patiently, like cows waiting to be milked.

'Welcome to Nullin Cheese,' drawled the young girl behind a vast reception desk covered in brochures and novelty items like pins and cheese-shaped pencil sharpeners. 'Can I help you?' She looked about as curious as a sleeping lizard.

'Peter Bankston, please.' Heidi tried to sound businesslike.

The girl picked up the phone. 'Do you have an appointment?'

'Yes.' Heidi gave her name and waited.

'Your name isn't in his diary,' the girl said.

'Tell her I'm a friend.'

The receptionist spoke and then reported back. 'Mr Bankston is elsewhere on the premises at the moment. You'll have to wait until his assistant finds him.'

'Fine,' Heidi said and sat on a black leather sofa next to a coffee table piled with more brochures. She picked one up and browsed. It was expensively produced with misty-edged photographs of the heritage buildings in the complex and the surrounding lush countryside. Someone had strung a daisy chain around a cow's neck in one of them. Keith Bankston, surrounded by beaming yellow-suited employees, stared from another. Even for a promotional brochure, he couldn't manage more than a gruff frown. She wondered what had made him so hard.

Heidi read that Nullin Cheese was a wholesome, family-owned business with three hundred happy, profit-sharing staff and a co-operative of jolly dairy farmers who pumped one hundred million litres of milk into the factory each year. Butter had been produced in the district as early as the 1860s, but then it was only good enough to send back to England as axle grease. Nowadays, one thousand tonnes of 'international award-winning' cheddar were produced annually for markets in China, Saudi Arabia and Brazil.

Someone coughed. It wasn't Peter, but Jack Harding.

'I heard Belinda on the phone up to the processing plant looking for Peter,' he explained. 'I thought I'd entertain you until he got here.'

'Thanks,' she said, genuinely pleased. Jack had been Elisabeth's friend. He might know as much as Peter.

'So now you know all about us,' he said, nodding at the brochure. 'I don't need to do the grand tour.'

He was dressed fashionably, immaculately, in a single-breasted grey suit, dark grey shirt and pale pink tie. He watched her appraise him. 'There's a delegation from Hong Kong coming in this afternoon.'

'I like it,' she said.

'Come on, I'll get you a drink.'

She followed him through glass doors, down a white corridor

and up a flight of stairs. 'Quicker this way,' he explained.

His office was white and beige, with a beige leather sofa and a coffee table. She was surprised the narrow windows let in as much light as they did. The view from here was partially obscured by a stainless steel storage container but she could still see across the valley to the blue mountains beyond.

He motioned for her to sit. 'What can I get you to drink? Milk?' And then he laughed. 'Something stronger? We can do beer, wine or whiskey.'

'No, just some water, thanks.'

'I'm disappointed in you.' He put his head into the corridor and called out instructions. Soon, a blonde in a black pantsuit brought them iced water in tall glasses. Altogether too chic for Nullin, Heidi thought.

'You have business with Peter?' he asked when she'd gone.

'No...he offered to show me around some time.'

His face relaxed. 'It's not the best day. We have the delegation. And things are a bit behind since...'

Heidi nodded. 'I realise that.'

'You know, even the cleaning staff were devastated. Elisabeth used to play here when she was younger. One of my first jobs when I joined was to make sure she didn't get into any mischief when she came up here.' He smiled. 'It pissed me off then, to tell you the truth. I didn't think I'd been hired as a babysitter.'

'But you were friends.'

'Yeah. She used to come in here sometimes, put her feet on that coffee table and chew the fat. She was always entertaining.' He looked down. 'It's hard to believe she won't be doing it anymore.'

'She confided in you?'

'Just girl-talk. Angst about her parents. Boyfriends. I suppose I was like a brother to her.'

'You were in a way. Being her brother's best friend.'

'Yeah.'

'Did Keith ever talk about being adopted?'

'Once big Keith told him, when he was about sixteen, that's all he talked about. All the time, like a broken record.'

'Did he ever say he thought he was Laureen Blackpeter's child?'

Jack looked genuinely amazed. 'No shit?' He cleared his throat. 'Sorry. It's the Nullin in me coming out. No, he never did say that. Only how he wished Keith and Carmel hadn't adopted him. *Is* Laureen his mother?'

'I don't know. It's an idea.'

'It's probably crap. He started hanging around with Sid Blackpeter just before he died. I warned him the bastard would screw him up. I bet Sid told him that to mess with his head.'

'You were there when he drowned?'

He gnawed on his bottom lip. 'He was gone by the time I swam out. A shark must have got him, he disappeared so fast.'

'That must have been devastating for you.'

He nodded. 'I was pretty pissed off with him by then, all the bad stuff he was doing with Sid. But it was still horrible. The poor bastard.'

'People in town say Keith was disturbed after your sister's death, which was a couple of months before, wasn't it?'

He gave her a mocking look. 'Never listen to local gossip, Heidi. My sister was a kid who hung around with me. It was *me* who was his friend.'

'My husband saw a photo of him with a tattoo of a "V", which I assumed was for Valerie, on his arm.'

His expression hardened into something more intense. 'It was years ago.'

She tried to make it sound insignificant. 'I thought it was sweet that he'd have a tattoo celebrating his girlfriend.'

'I said Valerie wasn't his girlfriend.' He shifted tone. 'Look, he was just fooling around. Teasing, as usual. She meant *nothing* to him.'

'So it isn't possible he committed suicide over her death?'

He laughed. 'There's been some ridiculous gossip around this town over the years, but that's the stupidest. It was a terrible accident, but not the kind that's unknown around here. I saw him drown. So did Peter, Charley and Elisabeth. He was skylarking as if he didn't have a care in the world beforehand and then he was gone.'

'Did Elisabeth ever tell you she thought she was adopted too?'

Surprise registered on his face. Before he could say anything, the blonde assistant put her head around the door. 'Peter's back in his office. Whenever you're ready—'

Jack jumped up. 'Good. I'm sure she's had enough of me.' He turned to Heidi and took her hand, shaking it. He smiled ironically. 'Come back another time and I'll show you round. We've got a new sterilisation unit that's *really* fascinating.'

37

Peter also had on a suit for the Hong Kong delegation but his collar was crumpled, his tie askew. 'Belinda didn't say why you were here. Is it something about Mother?'

'No, not at all. Nothing has happened,' she reassured him. A thought occurred to her. 'Are you worried something might?'

'No, no,' he mumbled. 'Spending money in Melbourne will cheer her up.'

'She's tough.'

'I suppose she is. Tougher than me. I can't help thinking something else is going to happen...When you lose two siblings like *that*...you're never sure of anything again...' His voice trailed off and then he made an effort to sound cheery. 'Do sit down and tell me why you're here. I've got a meeting in an hour, but I can show you around if you like.'

'No, not today. Jack said you had important visitors.' She sat down on a black leather chair by the desk.

'We have to do our dog and pony act for the Asian market. It's a bit pathetic when all we're selling is cheese, isn't it?'

'You don't belong here do you?'

He sat on the edge of his desk and fiddled with a pen. 'Is it that obvious?'

'Why don't you leave and do what you really want to do?'

'Elisabeth kept telling me that. My father expects me not to have the gumption to stick it out. So to spite him I stay on.'

'And spite yourself?'

'I'm not an artist. I'm a moderately educated rich boy.'

'You sound like you resent that. Do you have a difficult relationship with your father?'

'No, he has a difficult relationship with *me*. I'm not...I don't know...enough of a ratbag. He only loves bad boys. Charley and I are too wishy-washy.'

'Why do you think that is?'

'My grandfather Albert. The old bastard made him stick with the family business when he didn't want to, so he's revisiting the sins of his father...'

'What did your father want to do?'

'He wanted to be a commercial pilot.'

'And he wanted to marry Laureen Blackpeter?'

She'd thrown that in to shock him, but he accepted it smoothly. 'It's no secret they went out for a while,' he said evasively. Then he laughed. 'Well, "went out" is hardly the word for it.' He made a face. 'I don't know how he could do it. Have you seen her?'

'She's had a hard life. She might have been different when she was younger.'

'She's a slag. Thank God the rest of us have Carmel for a mother.'

Heidi was shocked at his language. But she had an inkling why he was disgusted by Laureen. 'You said the "rest of us",' she prompted.

He looked confused. 'I meant all of us.'

'But Laureen was young Keith's mother, wasn't she?'

The colour ebbed from his face. 'What makes you say that?'

'It isn't hard to work out. When did you know?'

'I *don't* know for sure. No one said anything to us when we were kids. *Anything*. Not Mother or Father. Elisabeth asked Mother recently and she denied it.'

'Maybe she doesn't know. Maybe your father has never told her the truth.'

He snorted. When he didn't say anything more, she went on.

'Peter, Elisabeth thought you and she were Laureen's children, too, didn't she?'

'What makes you think that?' He'd gone paler, if possible.

'I heard she left a message on your answering machine the night she disappeared about finding out something.'

'And you think that something was that we were adopted too?' There was a new note in his voice. Relief?

She knew that she'd missed something. 'It makes sense. What else could it be?'

His eyes scanned her face, summing her up. 'All right, I'll tell you. I don't know why, except that I trust you. But you must promise not to let it go beyond these walls.'

She nodded.

He frowned. 'That's not good enough. You have to promise.'

'I promise,' she pledged.

He took a deep breath. 'All right, Elisabeth did think we—she and I, not Charley—were Laureen's children.'

'Someone told her?'

'Yes.'

'Who?'

'She wouldn't tell me. Whoever it was, they told her about my father and Laureen having a relationship when they were younger and about him taking up with Laureen again, after...About my brother Keith being Laureen's child—'

'That's true?'

'I don't know for sure. But it makes sense. I'll tell you why in a minute.' He picked up a paperclip and started twisting it. 'This person told Elisabeth she only had to look at Spaz Blackpeter and photos of my big brother to see the resemblance. And she only had to look at herself and *me* to see the resemblance too.' He threw the paperclip angrily down on the desk. 'We do all resemble each other, you know. We're all long and pale but with dark hair.'

'Lots of people look like that.'

He brushed that comment aside with his hand. 'It was more

236

than that. Spaz Blackpeter has a genetic mutation—'

'Marfan's Syndrome?'

He looked at her sharply. 'Is that what it's called?'

'I think so.'

'Then you know more than us. I'll have to look it up. Elisabeth said that we might have it too, in a milder degree. She said that's why Diane couldn't keep her babies. That my sperm was no good. And that's why Elisabeth—' He stopped.

'What, Peter?'

'Lost her baby.' He looked distressed. 'She was pregnant the Christmas before last. Mother and Keith didn't know, so you mustn't—'

'I won't say anything. Who was the father?'

'She never told me.'

'But you can guess?'

'No, I can't. It's irrelevant anyway. You see, with my wife losing her babies as well, she thought there was something wrong with the genes. She wanted me to get tested.'

'But it could all be a coincidence. Carmel couldn't have babies at first either. It might be nothing to do with the genes.'

'Look, I agree. Carmel's even got our tags from hospital, there are our birth certificates. But Elisabeth was insistent that all these things could have been faked.'

'And you don't know who fed her all this information? Could it have been Gray Wignall?'

'The father of that boy Elisabeth got messed up with a while ago? Why him?'

'He hates your father.'

'I don't think it was him. But it was a "he" and he was probably right on one thing. About our brother being Laureen's son. He said that my father had gone to Laureen when Carmel couldn't conceive and he used her as some kind of surrogate. I don't know if it was accidental or deliberate. He must have paid Laureen to give up the baby to keep Mother happy.'

'So Carmel must have known?'

'Not necessarily. The baby could have come from anyone. But if this guy was right about this, why wouldn't he be right about the rest?'

'Peter, you know how far-fetched this sounds? It's rubbish. I know your father's a powerful man, but he could hardly get a birth certificate faked, fake all those local hospital records.'

'That's right. I looked into everything. I told Elisabeth that this person was talking bullshit to disturb her. He succeeded.'

'Have you asked your mother?'

'Elisabeth did and Mother said it was nonsense.' He paused. 'She also said our brother Keith being a Blackpeter was nonsense too.'

'You still have some doubts, don't you?'

'Not really.' He sighed. 'I do think Keith was Laureen's son.'

'Your mother wouldn't lie to you unless she was trying to protect you.'

'Or protect herself. She loved my dead brother more, despite him not being her own child. Despite being lied to. Both of them did.' He added, with frustration, 'It's no use being nice in this world.'

Heidi didn't know if he was referring to his mother or himself. 'Do you think Keith knew Laureen was his mother?'

'I'm sure he did. Sid told him.' He slid off the desk and paced. 'I've only just worked this out. Keith was moody towards the end. You couldn't get close to him. It wouldn't have been much fun learning your true family was a pack of...mutants.'

Heidi nodded. That tallied with everything she had heard from Carmel and Jack. The young, impressionable Keith's inexplicable attraction to Sid. He thought he was his brother.

Look for the brother, Octavia Goodhope had said.

One thing was bothering her, though. 'If you proved to Elisabeth that most of this couldn't be true, why was she still pursuing it before she died?'

'She wanted to believe it, I suppose. She was cross with

Mother. Carmel pretends she wanted Elisabeth to have a full life but she kept tabs on her all the time.'

'Not all the time.'

He stopped pacing. 'Not all the time.' He was thinking, like Heidi, that Carmel had failed to keep her daughter out of precisely the kind of trouble she feared.

'Look,' said Heidi, 'I know that Elisabeth told at least one of her friends she thought she was adopted. Her theory may not be as secret as you think.'

He looked ill. 'Which friend?'

'It doesn't matter. She might have told everyone for all we know. The thing is, you should talk to your mother about it. She must be feeling guilty on some level.'

'Who isn't?' He then did something that Heidi hadn't seen a person do before—he actually wrung his hands. They turned bright pink from the friction. 'I should have stopped her. It was a stupid wild goose chase.'

'You told the police you didn't know what Elisabeth's message meant.'

'No, I said it didn't make sense to me. I lied to protect...all of us.'

It still doesn't make sense, Heidi thought. Why would the killer want to keep Elisabeth quiet about something so many people already knew and which was conjecture? And if it were Gray who told her about Keith being Laureen's son in the first place, was it Gray who was with her the last night of her life? Or was he just a malevolent meddler?

'You did the right thing,' Heidi reassured him. 'Elisabeth's misguided thinking that you and she are adopted had nothing to do with her death.'

'You don't think so?' He sounded like she'd thrown him a lifeline.

What she didn't say was, *but that wasn't why she called you that night. And you know it.*

239

38

Kirstie looked up from her computer when Beckett walked in. She rolled her chair back and stretched, showing off an expanse of smooth flesh between cropped sweatshirt and hipster jeans. 'You've just made my day. I need some distraction from writing about foreshore development.' She hugged a knee. 'And I find you *very* distracting.'

He leaned against the doorjamb, a suitable distance. 'Then pay attention. I just saw Sheila Harding and she showed me a copy of the feature she'd sold to the *Daily Mirror*.'

'The one that doesn't exist?'

'The one we couldn't find. But she had a laminated copy, complete with journalist's byline. Bill Bertram.'

'We could try and contact him, then.'

'No need. It's a fake.'

'What do you mean?'

'Someone did a really lousy job of faking a front page. The type wasn't even set straight. The text—what I could read— was barely literate. I don't think the *Mirror*'s standards had slumped so badly that the subs wouldn't pick up a misspelling of scandalous. S-c-a-n-d-u-l-o-u-s. I suppose only a writer would notice that sort of thing. I'm sure Sheila thinks it's genuine and that she spoke to a genuine journalist. She said he was from the Midlands.'

'So someone set it up to cover up the source of the money. Russ?'

'He had to have known about it. But was he that smart to act alone?'

'No.'

'Jack, then? He gained a cushy job.'

'He's smart but he was a nasty lout before he reformed. Who could supply him with all that money, unless he was involved in some kind of larger crime, like drugs?'

'Do you think Jack might have been blackmailing Keith?'

She shook her head. 'I don't think Jack could have pulled it off. He might have dreamed up the idea, but it's hard to imagine him keeping it secret. And I truly think Valerie's death shook him up so much, it shook him back on to the straight and narrow.'

'Well Sheila thinks she sold her soul to the devil over that story. She still feels guilty.'

Kirstie thought for a moment. 'It was an English journalist who interviewed her? I bet it was someone local, play-acting. There can't be that many poms around here.'

Beckett remembered. 'A few work for Nullin Cheese. I met them at the debutante ball.'

'Nullin Cheese? You think Keith could have talked one of his blokes into playing a journalist?'

'Could be. I know he's connected somehow. His fingerprints are all over this.'

'It's a pretty elaborate ruse to cover up a loan—or a blackmail payment.'

'But the payment must have been about a quarter-million. That's not the kind of money a boss throws at a modest worker.'

'True. Let's assume Keith *did* pay Russ that money. We're back to why again.'

'Blood money,' Beckett said.

Kirstie whirled her chair full-circle. 'I think you're right.' She paused. 'But whose blood?'

Beckett was chopping onions when Heidi came up behind him and kissed the back of his head. 'Pumpkin risotto?'

He kept chopping.

'What's wrong?'

'Where have you been?'

'I went to see Martin Gondwana.' She pulled out a chair.

Beckett waved the knife in his hand. 'What the hell were you doing up there?'

'Put that down before you cut yourself,' she told him. He flung it into the sink and she went on. 'It was *fine*. I didn't get into any trouble. Martin was helpful.'

'I don't trust anyone over forty with dreadlocks.' He wiped his hands and sat down opposite her. 'So tell me what happened.'

She outlined what Martin had to say about Elisabeth's suspicions. Then she told him about her conversations with Jack and Peter.

'Any one of them could have been the murderer, Heidi.'

She ignored him. 'I'd say Sid Blackpeter definitely told Keith he was his brother. That would account for Keith's weird behaviour before he drowned.'

'And Gray—or someone else—knew this somehow and taunted Elisabeth with it, to get back at big Keith?'

'He must have bailed her up one time when she was visiting Jaron.'

'I wonder if Jaron knew what his father had done.'

'He didn't sound like it. He seemed confused about his relationship with her. It was on and off by the sound of it. I think she was a bit mixed up about herself and Gray's information didn't help.'

'Peter believes Keith was Laureen's son?'

'I think it's pretty clear.'

'Yet he told Elisabeth that the other rumour about them also being adopted was nonsense?'

'He *proved* it. There's plenty of evidence they were delivered by Carmel. It's too far-fetched to think otherwise.'

'Well, then, why didn't Elisabeth believe him? She left that message before she died.'

'But, Beck, this is the thing. I don't believe that was what the message was about at all. It was something else she was excited about. And Peter knows that very well.'

'You think he's lying?'

'Being evasive, anyway.' She shivered, and it wasn't just the chill evening air.

Beckett noticed. 'I'll get you a blanket.'

'Thanks.'

He brought one back from the bedroom and slipped it over her shoulders. 'I've got the creeps about this, Beck.' She took his hand as he sat again. 'What kind of person is Keith Bankston? He starts up an old relationship with a woman just to produce children, by the sound of it. Then, after his eldest son drowns, he transfers his affections to a boy who was nothing more to him than the friend of his dead son. This makes his own boys, Charley and Peter, feel discarded. He's a toxic father.'

'Even more toxic than we think,' Beckett said. He told her about his visit to the cake shop. 'He got one of his henchmen to play journalist and convince Sheila Harding that she'd earned herself a quarter of a million from selling her story to the *Daily Mirror*. That means Russ *was* being paid to keep quiet about something.'

'And part of the deal was giving Jack a job. Although I really do get the feeling that Keith is fond of Jack.'

'Could Jack be Keith's son?'

'I hadn't thought of that. Could he?'

He squeezed her hand. 'I'm just being a devil's advocate here. I like Sheila Harding. I don't think she's the kind of woman who would have had an affair with Keith.'

'But she told you Russ hated Keith. Maybe that was the reason.'

243

'We've had Keith involved with Valerie, Laureen and Sheila so far.'

She relaxed. 'It's stupid, isn't it? We might as well add Gray's wife, Mirna, and Joey Blackpeter while we're about it.'

'But by this logic, Joey could be his daughter too, couldn't she?'

Beckett got up from his chair and stood behind his wife, tugging her braids gently. 'Great detectives we make. We're completely on the wrong track, aren't we? All this snooping around and we come back to Keith, principally because we don't like him.'

'It's his fault, though. I'm sure of it. Even if he never laid a finger on anyone.'

'I think Sid Blackpeter has the answers.'

'Don't you dare, Beck.'

'He's in jail. What could go wrong?'

'Please don't,' she said. She stood up and put her arms around him. 'I'd hate this to be your last meal.'

Beckett waited until Heidi went to bed and then dialled Andrew Eagan's home number. 'Hang on a mo,' said a young voice of the male sex. '*Andrew*!!!!'

'Who is this?' Eagan sounded less than friendly.

Beckett told him.

'Oh, yeah, the Marfan's man.'

'I need a return favour.'

'At this hour of night?'

'You sound like you were up.'

'So to speak. Go ahead.'

'You're Spaz Blackpeter's solicitor. Does that mean you're Sid's as well?'

Eagan sounded wary. 'Not exactly. I represented him in his last court case.'

'He could afford a lawyer?'

'There was a problem with legal aid. I'd been working on a treaty with local Aborigines and heard about him. I volunteered. Why do you want to know? Sid's away for a few years.'

'I'm writing a screenplay about Aboriginal youth in custody.' Beckett elaborated his credentials and those of the producers. 'I thought talking to Sid might give me some special insight into the problems—'

'Is there any money in it?'

'What do you mean?'

'I said, is there any money in it for Sid?'

'Well, I hadn't exactly—'

'Because Sid won't do anything that doesn't involve money.'

'Surely it's of benefit to him to have his story told sympathetically?'

'Listen, the last thing Sid needs is his story told. And I doubt you or anyone would be sympathetic.'

'How much is it going to cost me?'

'I'll get back to you.'

39

The last thing Beckett expected Sid Blackpeter to be doing was smiling.

But there he was, standing in the middle of the visiting yard in his green boilersuit, with his arms crossed and grinning as widely as if his dog had come in first at Harold Park.

Beckett knew this was Sid by the wide berth the other prisoners and their visitors had given him. The guard at the gatehouse hadn't needed to point him out at all.

The next surprise was that he was so small, smaller than all his brothers. Most of the women visitors would tower over him, and some of the children too.

Sid had seen him but Beckett stood for a moment at the gatehouse and took in the scene. A six-metre-high granite wall enclosed the yard, casting most of it in shadow. There were watchtowers on two corners and a central control tower, which looked into other areas of the prison. An open-sided shed provided shelter to visitors if the weather turned nasty. About twenty prisoners and twice as many visitors huddled in small groups, with the occasional rogue child breaking away to try to engage the guards in play. One little boy stood statue-like, staring goggle-eyed at a watchtower. The air was moist as a morning fog rolled out.

Sid's grin had stayed attached to his face but even from a distance Beckett could sense the threat in the way he'd dropped his shoulders. Beckett had been granted what was known as a 'contact' visit, but now hoped there wasn't going to be too much of that.

Nor did he feel too comfortable peering down at the black stubble on top of Sid's head, but the eldest Blackpeter son seemed not the slightest bit perturbed. 'Mate,' he said in a coarse voice, as Beckett reached him, and raised his right hand only as high as his thigh, so that Beckett had to stoop to shake it. Beckett admired the way Sid used his low centre of gravity as a weapon, forcing his opponent off-balance.

The prisoner's hand felt as rough as sandpaper. Beckett made eye contact, but all he could see were murky brown irises in a yellow-tinged pool, the lids heavy as if they'd learned to droop that way after years of too many legal or illegal mood-altering substances. He was slighter than his brothers, without the barrel chest and meaty necks that characterised them. This surprised Beckett because he imagined the fearsome Sid would have been built like an armoured tank, especially after a few months of prison bodybuilding. Most of the other prisoners were twice his weight, a fact that seemed not to have cowed the cocky Sid one bit.

'Bit of a pussy name, Beckett, isn't it?' Sid said, taking his hand away and looking at it suspiciously. 'You're not a poof, are you?'

'Never gone in for it.' Beckett didn't smile.

'That's right. You've got a pretty wife, I hear,' Sid beamed, making it clear he knew all along.

Beckett didn't like it. Sid's comment was full of threat. *I know where you live.* He tried to defuse it. 'That Andrew Eagan's a pretty sharp lawyer by the look of it.'

'Yeah, not bad for a pillow-muncher. The judge took pity on me and sent me here. Beats that fucking hole Bathhurst.'

'You've been there?'

'Twice.'

'What for?'

He shrugged. There was a tattoo of a swallow on his neck. 'Offensive conduct, three months. Stock theft, eighteen months. That was a while ago. Then they opened this place. Closer to home. That faggot Eagan argued it was easier for me poor ma and pa to visit me here. And they fell for it. Ma's been once and Nino never comes. He's legless most of the time, lost count of his kids. And superstitious, like the other boys, thinks the minute he steps in the nick he's gonna get stuck here. Joey's come and shown me her rugrats. Me nephews and niece.' He sounded proud of that.

'What are you in for now?'

'Malicious infliction of grievous bodily harm. A six-year stretch. I'll be out of here in three, no worries. I'm a model prisoner.'

'What did you do?'

'Questions, questions. But I'll tell you for nothing. Even though I'm innocent, of course.' He pulled at his chin and Beckett could see he was missing two joints of his ring finger. 'That towel head who runs the fruit palace down in Nullin reckoned someone jumped him in the backyard and smashed the back of his skull with a brick. Awful messy it was. But the little prick shouldn't have looked all funny at that someone when he was playing pokies at the club the night before. He should have kept his goggle eyes to himself. So what if that someone was emptying other people's cups of change when they'd gone to the bar for a beer? Shouldn't have left them unguarded, should they? There are some bad types hanging round there.'

Beckett felt uncomfortable standing over him. 'Do you want to go and sit?'

'No, mate, I reckon we can do our business here. Did you leave the two spot for me?'

Andrew Eagan had suggested Beckett might get further with Sid if he contributed to his prison account. 'Yes, it's there.'

'Good. That'll keep me in stick books for a bit. It's fucking impossible to get a hard-on here without 'em, unless you're a hock. You should bring your wife next time, do me a service. I'm thinking of getting married to one of them do-gooders who write to cons. Then I could have conjugals. Don't matter what she looks like, does it? As long as it's tight and wet.' His eyes challenged Beckett to contradict him. 'But you're not here to talk about me stubby little dick. What do you want?'

Beckett wondered how best to ask his questions. His eyes went to a couple of security guards having a conversation near the wall. Sid caught the look and smiled again. 'I wouldn't count on the Gestapo, mate. They got respect for me. What are you afraid of? I'm a nice guy.'

'You mightn't like my questions,' Beckett said honestly.

'The last person whose questions I didn't like necked himself. But don't let that put you off.'

'All right, I won't. I'll get to the point. What do you know about Elisabeth Bankston's murder?'

Sid's eyes widened. He hadn't been expecting that. Then the hoods lowered again. 'Lovely girl, I hear. Gave it up all over the place.'

'You didn't expect me to ask about her.'

'Thought you were here to help me with the fillum I'm writing about me life. That's what Eagan said.'

It was the first Beckett had heard of it. 'You don't want to talk about the murder?'

He shrugged. 'As if I care. Go ahead.'

'Your brother Spaz is the leading suspect.'

'Yeah, well, the local constabulary is a pack of ponces. They got me for throwing a brick but there was worse things they missed.'

Beckett let that go. 'Do you think he killed her?'

'Not a smart question to ask, mate.'

'All right. Did you ever meet Elisabeth?'

'Can't say I did. Saw her, maybe.'

'There's a rumour going around she found out something about her family that the killer didn't want her to find out.'

'So?' But there was a glimmer of interest.

He decided to give the unlikely version. 'That she and her brother Peter were not Carmel's children. That they were the issue of Keith Bankston and your mother, Laureen, and they were adopted secretly.'

Sid threw back his head and guffawed. His laughter bounced off the prison walls and made heads turn nervously. The security guards froze. Sid slapped his sides and chortled. He turned to the guards. 'It's all right, fellas,' he called out. 'I've got a comedian here.' He turned back to Beckett. 'I haven't heard such a good one for yonks.'

'But it's true her brother Keith was your half-brother.'

Sid's face drew in. He didn't like it. 'Who told you that?'

'Peter seems to think so. He seems to think you were the one who told young Keith about it.'

'What would he know? He was always a little twerp.'

'But you were friends with Keith?'

'He used to hang around with me. Lots of kids did. I have char-*is*-ma.' He grinned at that.

'*Was* he your brother?'

Sid rolled his shoulders. 'What if he was? Ma had too many kids. One of them might as well as get on the rich man's rort.'

'But the Bankstons didn't tell him. So you felt obliged. Maybe you thought there was some money in it eventually?'

'Look, I didn't give a shit whether he had bucks or not. It was obvious to a blind man that the kid was one of us.'

'In what way?'

'He didn't fit in with that nelly life. He had *character*.'

'You mean he had criminal instincts?'

'*You* could say that. *I* would say he had life in 'im.'

'But he drowned.'

Sid rolled his shoulder again, didn't say anything.

'Do you know anything about that?'

'Me? I wasn't there. Poor bugger, taken away from all that filthy Bankston lucre, in the prime of life.'

Beckett knew there was a lie underneath this. 'Some people say he was distressed over Valerie Harding's murder.'

'Who's she when she's at home?' But his smile said he knew very well.

'His girlfriend. He had a tattoo of her initial on his arm. A "V".'

'I don't think it was that, mate.'

'What do you mean?'

'Dunno.' But he was still smiling.

'She was murdered around the time you were friends with Keith.' He tried something out. 'Some people might say that was too much of a coincidence. Maybe someone wanted to get Valerie out of the way. Someone was jealous.'

'Well, that would be the slag's brother, then.'

Beckett honed in on this. 'So you *do* know about her murder.'

'Can't say I do. Except now you've jogged me memory. She had a ponce for a brother. He was too keen on Keith for his own good.'

'But Jack says that you were the bad influence.'

'That's his name, is it? They've been saying that about me since I was born. That I was bad influence on me teddy bear.'

Beckett took another tack. 'So you believe Keith's death was an accident?'

'The sharks got him.' Sid showed a set of broken teeth. 'Nothing anyone could do. Tragedy, wasn't it?'

'Had he seen Laureen before he died?'

'No.'

'He didn't want to meet her?'

'That he did. But it wasn't right.'

'Why not?'

'She'd already gave him up.'

Beckett thought that had some logic. Laureen may not have wanted to be reunited with her son. 'Elisabeth found all this out. Is there anyone you can think of who was upset or threatened by that?'

'Don't know, mate. You'd have to talk to her parents. They're the ones with the most to lose. Their bloody reputation. Imagine it, having a Blackpeter bastard in their family.' He shook his head. 'That wouldn't go down well.'

'You hate Keith Bankston because of what he did to your mother, don't you?'

'The pussy dumped her cos his dad Albert didn't like it. And then years later he starts screwing her again. Maybe she was missing it, Nino couldn't get it up no longer. But the silly bitch, she should've kept her legs closed. And when she got up the duff, he bought the baby off of her. The boy was one of us, that riles me. She shouldn't've done it.'

'Shouldn't have given him away?'

'Done any of it, mate. But we got Keith back.'

Beckett thought of what Gray had told him, about Sid doing something to get Keith Bankston back for adopting young Keith. 'Gray Wignall said you did something to Keith Bankston, Sid. Something that made a fool of him.'

Sid raised his eyebrows. 'Gray said that, did he? He's a smarter bugger than I thought.'

'So you did?'

'It's not hard to make a fool of a bastard like that.'

'Are you going to tell me what you did?'

'Nope. You can work it out.'

'Give me a clue.'

'I gave you plenty.'

Beckett thought about the chronology. Keith marries Carmel. They try unsuccessfully to have babies for several years. In the meantime, Laureen gave birth to Sid, Crock…what were the other names? But she must have had five children in those years, because Spaz and Joey came later. Then she takes up with Keith again. Beckett couldn't imagine how the affair started or where it took place, but it raised some more questions.

He decided to risk Sid's anger. 'How do you know that none of the rest of you are Keith's children?'

Sid showed no emotion. 'I'm not going to get offended at that, mate. We all look like Nino. Little human dynamos, aren't we?' He chuckled.

'Keith junior didn't look like any of you.' He paused. 'And neither does Spaz.'

That irritated him. 'Don't you start talking about that poor bugger. He got dropped on his head or something.'

'Then he must have got stretched too. Spaz was no more dropped on his head than you. It's a genetic mutation, Sid.'

That got the reaction Beckett feared. Sid leapt at him and grabbed his trousers at crotch level, bunching the fabric in his fist and yanking upward. A nauseating pain seared through the core of him. Tears stung his eyes and he tried to twist away. Sid held firm. Out of the corner of his eye Beckett saw the guards turn away. The little thug could have his way with him and no one would care. He heard himself squeal.

'There's nothing wrong with us, you fucking poof!' Sid yelled, his neck reddening and a blue vein in his temple throbbing underneath the tanned skin. 'You fucking eat your words or I'll clock you. And you won't get up.'

Beckett doubled up, feeling like vomiting. 'I didn't say there was anything wrong with your family.' He cursed the tremble in his voice. 'If both Spaz and young Keith have a Bankston father then it's likely the mutation came from that side.'

Sid loosened his grip, curious now. 'You mean Keith Bankston's the dud root?'

'Sort of,' Beckett said, backing away from him, catching his breath. 'Peter Bankston looks a bit like Keith junior too. That's why Elisabeth thought he also was your brother.'

'There you go again. He fucking well isn't.'

'All right, I accept that. But Octavia Goodhope—'

'Who the fuck's that?'

'The old lady who lives up the river.'

'Oh, yeah, got some ace stuff from there once.'

'Not a spear by any chance?'

'No, a machete and some other tools. Stuff like that.'

'OK,' Beckett nodded. 'Octavia Goodhope has her suspicions about who killed Elisabeth. She said to look for the brother.'

'What brother?'

'That's what I want to know.'

'Well I don't give a fuck. There are brothers and then there are *brothers*. I've got a few bros in here.'

Beckett challenged him. 'I thought you knew everything, Sid.'

'What I know is you don't have a fucking clue. None of you do.'

40

Heidi was pushing some hyacinth bulbs into a patch of soil in the back garden when she heard a car come rattling up the drive. She threw off her cotton gloves and investigated, expecting it to be Beckett, worried about his trip to Bungalong to see Sid Blackpeter.

Damian got out of his ute and slammed the door. He took a short aluminium ladder from the tray at the back and carried it over to where Heidi was standing on the old concrete loading bay.

'Hubby out?' He dropped the ladder at his feet and stretched his arms above his head, loosening up after the drive from town. Despite a stream of wind that seemed to have blown straight up from the Antarctic, he was wearing his usual uniform of navy singlet, shorts and work boots. His chest muscles expanded provocatively under the blue cotton. Heidi remembered that in some places they called those singlets 'wife beaters'. God, she thought, I've got my very own Chippendale in the front yard. Beckett better get home soon.

'Beck will be back soon if you want to talk to him,' she said.

'Not really. Just noticed the car missing. I've got some work to do on that wall.' Then he reached behind his neck with an arm and groaned. 'Trouble is, I've done my neck in. Can hardly move it one way or the other.'

'Then you shouldn't be working.' She regretted that as she said it. Another excuse for Damian to walk off the job. The house would never get finished. She bet he laid his tools down if he cut himself shaving.

He groaned some more and twisted his shoulders. Standing at the top of three steps she was slightly taller than him. He looked up at her. 'I was wondering if you could give it a bit of a bang about. I've heard you're good with your hands.'

Not a good idea, Heidi, she told herself. Your relationship with Damian would be much healthier kept at a distance. Then again, fixing his neck would get him back to work quicker. 'All right,' she sighed. 'Sit on that bottom step.'

'I don't have to take off all my clothes?'

She gave him a look of mock disgust. 'Sit, Damian.'

Heidi made herself comfortable on the top step while Damian crouched two steps down. 'I can feel those knots,' she said, pressing her thumbs into his shoulder blades. His skin felt slick, as if he'd been pouring baby oil into it. 'What have you been doing?'

He shrugged. 'I dunno. Fixing a mate's shed. Taking the new bike up to Cooma and back. Having a few beers down the club. Buying the ladies a drink.'

'There can't be too many available ladies around here.'

'You volunteering?'

Heidi gave him a swift chop at the base of the neck.

'Ouch!'

He tried to wriggle away from her but she held his shoulder firm with one hand.

'Stay still, Damian, you're making it worse. You're very tense.'

'Nothing wrong with a little tension. There are parts of me that are *very* tense.'

'Then maybe I should stop.' She took her hands off his neck.

'No. Don't.' He twisted around and put his hand on her forearm. 'It's just I'm not used to getting this kind of attention from a lady.'

'A likely story,' she said, taking his hand off her arm.

He looked offended. 'You think I'm joking? I couldn't get any of them to boil me an egg.' He sounded wistful. 'Your husband's a lucky man. How long have you been hitched?'

'Six years in June.'

'So you're still doing it a couple of times a week.'

'None of your business.'

'Don't worry, seven year itch is coming. When it does, I'll be here, willing and ready.'

'Thanks, Damian, I'll sleep better knowing that.'

'I just want you to know there's back-up.'

She smiled and started work on his shoulders again. He gave a few appreciative groans. After a few moments working in silence, she asked, 'How well did you know the eldest Bankston boy, Keith?'

'We mucked around a bit. Why?'

'Something Jack Harding said.'

'Well, Jack was his best mate. He knew him better than me. What do you want to know?'

'Keith had a "V" tattooed on one of his arms. I thought it must have been for Valerie but Jack tells me I'm wrong.'

'Didn't Jack tell you what it meant?'

'No, he didn't say...I suppose I didn't get around to asking him.'

'There was no secret about it.'

'You mean you *do* know?'

He shrugged. 'Yeah. Sure. Keith was a bit of a weirdo, had this thing about that bloke they named the vampires after.'

'Dracula?'

'No. Dracula wasn't real but this bloke was. Vlad the something.'

'Vlad the Impaler?'

'That's it. I haven't thought about this for years. Keith reckoned this Vlad was really sharp. He had all these books about him. That's why he had the tatt on his arm. "V" for Vlad. I mean, it was a bit sick. The rest of us got tatts of whales or whatever. I've got a beauty.' He started to unbutton his fly. 'Want to see it?'

'No thanks, Damian.' Heidi knew a little about Vlad the Impaler herself. She guessed most kids did. Keith Bankston wouldn't have been the first young man to have been titillated by stories of Vlad's predilection for skewering his enemies' bodies on spears.

Skewering his enemies' bodies on spears.

She felt her intestines liquefy.

'It's not that bad,' Damian said, looking at her curiously.

'What?' she asked weakly.

'My tattoo. You've gone all pale.'

'I'm fine,' she told him, recovering. 'I think someone just walked on my grave.'

'A whole crowd by the look of it.'

She tried to sound lightly curious. 'So Keith was obsessed by Vlad the Impaler? I remember Octavia Goodhope saying you kids loved her stories. Did Keith only talk about Vlad...or did he act anything out?'

'Like what?'

She could see that Damian was several steps behind her. Better he stayed that way. 'Oh, just that someone said Keith was a bit...cruel.' She didn't want to put too fine a point on it.

'Yeah, he teased the younger kids all the time. He went a bit far sometimes. I reckon we all did.'

'What sort of things did he do?'

'Oh, you know, putting his cigarette out on someone's skin to see what would happen. Once he nailed Elisabeth's kitten to a cross.'

'That's more than going a *bit* far.'

'Yeah, but you don't understand. He was curious. Like he wasn't really bad, he was trying to see what it would be like to be bad.'

'He hurt animals. I don't know how anyone can do that simply to experiment.'

'You're a city slicker. This is the country. Animals get hurt all the time. Trapped, shot, hit by cars.'

'Stabbed.'

'That too.' He still wasn't getting her point. 'Keith liked to experiment on people more.'

'Oh? Like who?'

'Like his brothers. Like some of the slags around town. He started a boy's club called the Order of the Dragon and only let girls in if they showed him their pussies.'

'Who was in this club?'

'A few of us.'

'*You* were in it? You liked humiliating little girls too?'

He shrugged, but was unapologetic. 'It was like playing doctors. Nothing different from what they did behind the shelter shed in Year Six.'

'Was Valerie Harding part of this?'

'Can't remember. But she followed him around like a dog.' He tapped his head. 'Course. I understand now. She thought that "V" was for her. I bet the mean bastard told her that.'

'Didn't Jack look after his little sister?'

'I can't remember. He didn't pay her much attention, I don't reckon. He did have a big blue with Keith, but that wasn't until after Valerie died, so it can't have been about her. Actually, I don't know much more than that, because that was when Mum put the brakes on. She'd had enough of me mixing with "riffraff" as she called it.'

'The riffraff being?'

'The other boys I suppose. I was a perfect angel you see.'

She smiled. He was incorrigible. 'Stay there,' she said and stood up. 'I need to rotate your neck.'

She stepped down and stood between his legs, facing him, taking his head gently in her hands. 'Relax.'

'You're making it a bit hard...if you know what I mean.'

'*Relax.*'

He closed his eyes. 'Hmmm.'

259

She eased the neck in circles. With a sudden movement, she pulled upwards and cracked the vertebrae.

'Ouch!' He put both hands on her legs to steady himself.

'Nonsense, that didn't hurt at all,' she said.

Beckett chose that moment to accelerate the Volvo into the driveway. Heidi turned to look at him, Damian's hands around her knees.

Beckett jumped out of the car and pushed past both of them, disappearing inside without a word. Heidi followed but he slammed the door to the makeshift bedroom. She called out to him. He didn't answer.

'Sorry about that,' Damian said, when she went back outside. 'I suppose it didn't look too good.'

'He'll get over it,' she said. 'I'm going back to the garden. Help yourself to a beer.'

'I don't think I'll be doing that,' the handyman said, looking nervously at the front door. 'I need some more undercoat. I'll come back in the morning.'

Damn. Heidi guessed Damian wouldn't be back tomorrow and knew she'd have to persuade her husband to make a gesture of peace before he did. The way things were, with her home tumbling down around her ears, handymen were more valuable commodities than husbands.

The afternoon sun had trained its beams on some other lucky spot. It was getting dark and colder. She went into the house and made Beckett a cup of hot chocolate. She knocked on the bedroom door again, juggling the hot chocolate and a packet of Tim Tams. 'Chocolate delivery,' she called out.

He didn't answer. She pushed the door inwards anyway. He was sitting up on the bed, his eyes trained on the words of Deepak Chopra, an author she enjoyed but he usually scoffed at.

'Gone over to the other side?' she teased, but he didn't acknowledge her. She sat on the bed next to him and put the hot chocolate on a side table. She threw the biscuits at him, which forced him to drop the book. 'Are you sulking?' she asked.

'I haven't heard any words of apology yet.'

'What for?' She'd be blowed if she was going to make it easy on him.

'You know.'

'No, I don't. You came up the drive like a lunatic and then almost pushed me over in your rush to get inside the house. Sid must have been really awful to put you in such a foul mood.'

'Sid's a gentleman compared to that little prick Damian. The one you were cavorting with the minute my back was turned.'

Did he realise how much he sounded like a third-rate daytime soap? Probably. But when the Irish temper flared his Serbian pig-headedness always got him into more trouble. He could stew for a while. 'Actually, Damian's a big guy,' she said blithely. 'He's almost as tall as you. And he's built. It was smart of you to come and hide out here. I wouldn't like to be at the other end of Damian's fists.'

Beckett threw the packet of Tim Tams at the wall—which meant he was really mad—and glared at her. 'That's it!' he growled, but didn't move.

'Don't you want to know what Damian told me?'

'I don't care what you two got up to.'

She ignored his petulance. 'He told me that the "V" you saw on young Keith's arm stood for Vlad the Impaler, not Valerie. Keith had a thing about old Vlad.'

Beckett folded his arms. 'So what?'

'Think about it.'

Beckett shrugged. 'Vlad the Impaler. Fifteenth-century Romanian warlord, heir to the Wallachian throne. A Christian who fought off the advancing Turks of the Ottoman Empire. First-class sadist. Nailed turbans to the heads of captured Turks. Killed most of his victims by impalement. Slaughtered thousands of peasants at a time by driving them off cliffs into beds of spikes...' He stopped.

'You should try out for trivia night at the Prince of Wales.'

'Keith was obsessed with this joker?' Now he was interested enough to forget that he wasn't talking to her.

'It wasn't a secret, apparently.'

He sat up straighter on the bed. 'Sid knew about it. He told me the "V" didn't stand for Valerie.'

'What else did he say?'

'A lot...and nothing. He confirmed young Keith was Keith and Laureen's son and that he'd been the one to tell him. What Gray said was true, Sid *had* done something to get Keith back for that. But I couldn't find out what it was.'

'What about murdering Elisabeth? The Bankstons took a Blackpeter child, so the Blackpeters took a Bankston one in retaliation?'

'But Sid was in jail.'

'Another brother then?'

'Could be. Although I got the feeling it was something else. He was too cocky for it to be straightforward.'

She tucked her legs underneath her. 'Beckett, if young Keith was obsessed with Vlad the Impaler and Elisabeth's body was found impaled, do you realise what that means?'

'That it's a copycat? Someone who knew Keith. Someone who knew about Vlad. Someone who wanted to point the finger at him.'

'I think it's more than that, Beck. What if it were young Keith himself who did it?'

He'd forgotten all his anger at her now. 'He died eight years ago.'

'He *disappeared*. They never found a body, remember. Maybe he ran away.'

'Then where has he been all this time?'

'That's a good question.'

'You'd think someone would have seen him.'

'Maybe a lot of people have seen him. Maybe he changed his

appearance. He could have grown his hair, changed his voice.'
She was getting an idea.

Beckett shook his head. 'No way. In a small town like this?
Someone would know.'

'He might be very clever.'

'It was eight years ago. No one could hide out for that long.'

'Maybe he went away. He might have had help.'

'Who from?'

'Beck, it's as plain as that big nose on your face. You visited
him today.'

'You think that's what Sid did to Keith to pay him back?
Helped his son run away?'

'Keith junior hated his family. He was probably desperate to
get away from them—bitter about being adopted and angry that
his real mother was hidden from him.'

'But where did he go?'

'Probably as far away as possible. Sydney. Overseas perhaps.'

'With what money, my dear? I can't imagine Sid having
enough for an international airfare.'

'He might have been stashing money of his own away for a
while. No one would have noticed.'

Beckett rubbed his chin. 'Russ Harding had money. Keith
senior gave it to him.'

'You're confusing the issue, Beck. We have no idea what
Keith Bankston's payout to Russ has got to do with his son's disap-
pearance. If anything at all.'

'Or if it's got anything to do with Valerie's death.'

They were silent for a moment, each following their own
piece of mental string through endless loops and knots.

Beckett finally spoke. 'Even if all this were true, why would
Keith kill his sister?'

'He was a psycho. Twisted. He wanted to get back at Carmel
and Keith...it could be lots of things. There's the dead animal
connection too. He had the kind of mind that enjoyed torturing

defenceless creatures. Damian said Keith once nailed Elisabeth's kitten to a cross.'

Beckett felt the bile rise up again. 'Damian seems to know a hell of a lot all of a sudden. It wouldn't surprise me if he were the copycat.'

'Damian's not the type. He's a hedonist, not a killer.'

'And you would know, wouldn't you?' Beckett leaped off the bed. 'I'm going out.'

'Where?'

He didn't answer.

41

Beckett didn't know where he was going, but he wasn't going to sit around the house and let his blood boil. He put the Volvo into first, then second, and roared off down the driveway, the back wheels sliding in the gravel. He knew he was being an ass but he couldn't help it. He always joked about his wife's friendships with other men, but secretly—or less secretly whenever his temper blew—hated every one of them.

What he feared most was that she would tire of his inadequacies and exchange him for some other man. At the same time he knew, acutely, that his greatest inadequacy was that very fear.

But Damian...he was more than a threat to their marriage. He had his callused mitts on her, that was for sure. If there'd been any inkling in Heidi's manner that his advances had been unwanted, Beckett would have ripped into him. Heidi, however, had smiled at her husband as if Damian's hands on her legs was the most natural thing in the world. He kept his foot hard on the accelerator. Damian was in too many places at once. He had too many connections to Elisabeth's murder. He most likely had had some grubby sexual relationship with her; he'd certainly had one with Joey. And he'd stolen objects from Octavia Goodhope, he knew what she kept in her house. Octavia Goodhope had been attacked by someone familiar. Someone she was protecting. Would she protect Damian? Possibly. But she'd told Heidi to 'look for the brother'. As far as he knew Damian wasn't anyone's brother. He took the highway into Nullin. He thought of stopping outside the

Nullin Voice offices on the off-chance Kirstie was at work. He had the idea of luring her out for a drink, but feared where that might lead in his mood. Kirstie seemed the sort of girl who was up for anything and after a few drinks he might be too.

By the time he pulled into the Leagues Club carpark Beckett's brain was swimming with revenge fantasies. The Nullin Whale had gained a few strokes of blue paint since the last time he was there: REFFUGEES OUT. AUSTRALIA—LOVE IT OR LEEVE IT.

The carpark was full. It was Happy Hour, after all. Damian's ute was not there.

As he had hoped, Neville Chamberlain was at the bar. 'Hit me with a double Jack Daniels, straight up.'

'Bad day?'

Beckett nodded. Chamberlain put the whiskey in front of him. Beckett tossed it down. 'Might as well line them up,' he told him. 'But before I get thoroughly pissed, I want to ask you something.'

'Fire away.'

'Does Damian Hill have a brother?'

Chamberlain looked at him curiously. 'Sure.'

Beckett felt his spirits soar. 'Well? Who is he?'

'The young cop.'

'I haven't met a cop called Hill.'

'That's because he's not called Hill. Norma Barton was married to Paddy Hill before she divorced him and set up house with Colin Barton.'

Maybe it was the bourbon, but it took a while for this to register. When it did, Beckett was appalled. '*Brendan Barton's* his brother?'

'Half-brother. Younger by two years.'

'You'd never have guessed it.'

'Yeah, Paddy was black Irish and poor old Colin had a touch of pom.'

'And Brendan's the good guy and Damian's the crook.'

'Damian's no crook, just a bit of an opportunist. What makes you think he is?' Neville was looking at him intently.

'Nothing.' Beckett held up his glass. 'I'll go for a triple this time.'

Heidi couldn't sleep. The illuminated numbers on the clock seemed to penetrate her brain even with her eyes closed. She was thinking of pale, skinny boys with tattoos on their arms, of kittens nailed to crosses, of the platypus with its throat cut. She was thinking of Valerie stabbed with a screwdriver, Elisabeth hunted with a spear, young Keith taken by a shark. The lost children of Nullin. She worried that Beckett had got himself into a fight with Damian and was lying dead in some Nullin back street. Or that he'd got drunk at the club and wrapped the Volvo around a tree. The clock flashed on 12.17 and she couldn't think of anyone to call.

At 1.09 she heard the wire door creak, followed by a thump and a muffled stream of abuse. She heard water in the sink and a rustling in the cupboard. A chair scraped along the floor. Then the inevitable crumpling of cellophane as a packet of biscuits was ripped open.

The sound of Beckett drunk and in need of a sugar fix.

Relieved, she rolled over and slept.

The morning mist rolled in, bringing with it droplets of moisture as fine as a baby's sneeze. She sat up and looked at Beckett who was clinging, his back to her, to the very edge of the bed. She knew better than to wake him. She crept into the kitchen and boiled some water. The water went into a bucket and she washed herself, as quickly as she could, with a bar of lavender soap and a torn piece of towel. She rummaged quietly around in a trunk in the bedroom until she found cord pants, long-sleeved tee-shirt and a crocheted poncho rescued from another op shop in another life.

She dug out a pair of old motorcycle boots and pulled them on. She snatched her handbag from the table and hooked it over her shoulder, car keys in her hand. She scribbled a note for Beckett, telling him she'd be back later.

Then she went to the rusting biscuits tin where she kept the cutlery. She took out a small paring knife and put it in her bag.

If young Keith was a killer she might need it.

The fire in the pit was smouldering, dampened by overnight rain. The wet hadn't deterred a group of Gondwanas from gathering near the hissing pit, their shaved, mohawked and braided heads bent in concentration as they tied lengths of elastic to chopped-off elbows of wood. They looked like a troupe of clowns making essential repairs to their rubber chickens and unicycles before the next performance under the big top. One girl even held a dilapidated parasol over her head, which looked comically unsuitable to protect her from any kind of rainfall.

It was Sara, dressed in an eighties vintage purple-and-red mohair sweater, a pink Indian wedding skirt scattered with gold sequins and rubber boots. 'Hi!' she said brightly. 'Martin said you came the other day.'

Heidi scanned the seated Gondwanas for other familiar faces. 'What are you all doing?' she managed to ask casually.

'There's a WTO meeting in Brisbane on the weekend. We're going up in a bus. We're just preparing some stuff.'

'Like what?'

'Oh...' She waved her hand vaguely. 'Just slingshots.'

Heidi thought of the leather cords that had bound Elisabeth and her heart did a nervous flip. 'Is Martin here?'

'No, he went up to Brisbane ahead. Do you need to see him?'

Yes, she thought to herself, I do need to see him. But it can't be helped. 'It's all right. I thought I'd just drop in as I was driving by.'

You could hardly drive by the Gondwana camp but this didn't seem to register with Sara.

'Is Klas around?'

'Why?' Sara sounded less friendly now. Possessive.

'When I was here the other day he said he had some problem with a shoulder,' she lied.

'He hasn't said anything to me.'

'I thought I might as well look at it.'

'Suit yourself,' Sara said. 'He's down with the crops.'

'How do I get there?'

Sara pointed out a clearing in the forest. 'Take that track downhill as far as you can go.'

'Thanks,' Heidi said. 'If I don't come back in half an hour, come looking for me. I'll be lost.' Or in another kind of trouble.

'Sure,' Sara said. 'Be careful of the bees.'

Beckett awoke with the sensation that someone had performed brain surgery on him and had left the instruments sewn inside. The back of his head felt as if that same person were hacking at it with a bone saw.

He eased himself off the bed and stumbled around until he found some trousers and a shirt. Then he staggered into the kitchen. There was a note on the table. She'd gone out. He wanted to see her, to make things right. All of a sudden he felt overwhelmingly remorseful.

And then he remembered. Damian Hill was Brendan Barton's brother. Damian was a brother. *The* brother. If he proved it, it would be a vindication. He would have been right to be angry about Damian's attentions. Heidi might have been in danger, standing there with his hands on her legs. She might have been his next victim. When Damian was locked up she'd realise and be grateful.

He thought about what to do next. He could hardly bowl up to Brendan Barton and accuse his brother of being a killer. Damian would deny it.

But he could get Octavia Goodhope to admit that it had been Damian who had attacked her.

42

The greenhouse sat in the crook of a valley embraced by a shallow creek, which wrapped itself around the small wedge of cleared land. Hills rose sharply on all sides, with the sludge sky a patch above, giving Heidi the sensation that she was an insect in a bell jar. The valley was unnervingly quiet, except for the trickle of water over stone and a low hum like a sect of monks chanting underground.

Bees. A couple flew around her head, investigating, before darting off into the eucalypt forest. Bees had never frightened her before but when she saw what lay ahead in the clearing, she gave pause. The greenhouse, which was made of wooden frames and clear plastic sheeting, was completely surrounded by hives. Dozens of boxes of them, stacked four or five high, standing like rickety sentinels. Stacked there, she realised, to keep anyone interested in the cannabis plants at bay.

At first she didn't see Klas but as she approached he appeared from the far side of the greenhouse with a small cage in his hand. He was so intent on whatever it was he was doing, he didn't notice her about fifty metres away.

She watched him amble over to a stack of hives, put the cage down and take off the top box. He opened it up and pulled out a frame. Even from where she stood, she could see it was covered in writhing bees. He wasn't wearing either a veil or gloves. Her grandmother's remedy for bee stings came back to her. Slit open a cigarette, moisten the tobacco and pack it on the sting. For a brief moment she wished she smoked. She tucked her arms under her poncho and was glad she was wearing boots.

Something in that movement attracted Klas' attention. He looked in her direction but made no sign that he recognised her.

She stopped about three metres from him. It was as close as she dared. She could see the bees climbing up his arms, studding his red handknit sweater, alighting on his face and buzzing around his dreadlocks. He didn't exert a muscle to brush them away.

He wasn't happy to see her, but when had he ever been? She tried to rustle up some warmth towards him. 'Aren't you afraid they're going to sting you?' she asked.

'They sting me all the time,' he shrugged, the movement sending a squadron of bees into the air. He put a hand out to show her the red welts. 'It's no big deal.' The other hand steadied the frame.

'What are you doing?'

'I'm looking for the queen,' he said in his heavy Scandinavian accent. Too heavy? she wondered now.

'What are you going to do with her?'

'Kill her.'

She was shocked by his tone. 'Why would you do that?'

'Because I'm introducing a new queen. If I don't kill the old one, the other bees in the hive will follow her.'

'That seems such a waste.'

'She's served her purpose.'

'Just like your sister did?' she asked.

Klas smashed the frame down on the hive and hundreds of bees shot angrily into the air.

Beckett knew that Octavia Goodhope hid the key to the ignition on her dinghy under the vinyl padding on the front bench seat. She'd asked him to leave it there that day after the funeral. He wasn't the greatest expert on boats, but he started the outboard and made a not-too-wobbly exit from the dock up the river.

He gave a wide berth to boatsheds, a fleet of trawlers and a houseboat covered in a jungle of cultivated vines. Further up the tributary, an oyster fisherman was cleaning his trays. Soon, however, the mangroves closed in and he had the water to himself, except for the statue of the Virgin with the twisted head that looked puzzled by his presence as he steered the boat past the old mission.

The gunmetal sky made the water reflect a dark stain like an oil slick. So viscous was the river's appearance that he imagined it smelled of oil too. It was only when the motor started spluttering that he realised it *was* oil and that the outboard was leaking.

The engine cut out and the dinghy drifted towards the mangroves. Beckett looked about for oars and found there weren't any. Probably stolen from the dock. He thought Octavia's house might be around the bend, but all the bends had looked the same. He couldn't risk swimming it; God only knew what lurked beneath the dark water. Perhaps even sharks lost their way up here.

He let the boat drift against the low arms of the mangrove. He grasped at a branch, and then another, and pulled himself along the shoreline, occasionally getting tangled in roots and paddling with his hands to get out of them. He wished he were in better condition. Slowly, he managed to ease the boat around the bend.

Octavia's carved warriors stared across the water. He felt as if he were a spy slipping into shore beneath their gaze. He wondered if they'd spot him and turn, creaking, their abalone-shell gaze reducing him to jelly.

He tied the dinghy to the dock and stepped on the jetty, shaking his wet sleeves. The row of shrunken heads wound in the breeze. He had the unpleasant feeling he was being watched—as indeed he was, by the glass eyes of a wild boar's head nailed above the door. He stepped through the open front door and called Octavia's name. A faint voice responded from inside.

The rattan blinds on the front windows had been raised and he could see the room more clearly this time. She was sitting upright in her armchair by the low table, dressed formally in a white frilled blouse, tweed skirt and elastic hose with lace-up shoes. Under the gauze bandage that wrapped her head, her frown was dark with suspicion. But it wasn't the fury in her eyes that bothered him—it was the barrel of an old revolver she had trained on him.

He stopped in the doorway and raised his hands. 'It's all right, Octavia. It's me, Beckett. Heidi's husband.'

At first she looked as if she didn't believe him but she was squinting, trying to make him out.

'I'll come closer,' he said, taking a tentative step.

She kept the gun trained on him. There was a slight wobble in her wrists but her voice was clear and accusing. 'I didn't hear a boat.'

'Your dinghy broke down round the bend. I had to paddle up.' He shook his arms so she could see they were wet.

'Come closer,' she commanded. He took a few more steps. '*Closer!*'

He was now an arm's length from the short nose of the gun.

'You *do* look like whatsisname. My romance in Borneo.' She lowered the gun.

He realised he had been holding his breath. 'Are you all right? Has someone tried to break in again?'

'No. I wasn't expecting you, that's all, young man.' She dropped the gun into her lap.

'May I make you a cup of tea?'

She became animated again. 'Where are my manners? Sit down and I'll make you one!' She began to push herself out of the chair.

'No, I'm happy to do it. Everything easy to find in the kitchen?'

She nodded. 'There are biscuits in the tin on the counter.'

He went out the back to the kitchen, which seemed to have been untouched since before the war. There was an old Kooka oven and shelves full of Bakelite containers labelled with names like sago and barley. The biscuit tin which held shortbread was a souvenir from the Coronation in 1953. He found a large iron kettle, a dusty canister of black tea, some UHT milk, sugar and a blue and white striped teapot, complete with knitted cosy. The teacups were as fine as eggshells.

He poured Octavia a cup of weak tea and then shovelled sugar into his cup. He took an armchair across the table from her and reached for a shortbread. 'I hope someone has been visiting you regularly,' he said.

'Oh, I don't want them to go to the trouble. It's out of every-one's way.'

'Have you thought any more about who attacked you?'

She looked down. 'It was just a bit of foolishness. Some school kid on a dare, no doubt. Get the silly old witch up the river. It's a wonder it hasn't happened more often over the years.'

If she were so untroubled she wouldn't have had a gun. He decided to press on anyway. 'I want to ask you something impor-tant, Octavia. After you were attacked the second time, you told my wife to look for the brother.'

'I was concussed.'

'I don't think so. I think you wanted her to know who attacked you.' She started to protest but he held up his hand. 'Hear me out. Maybe you wanted to warn her and then you became frightened she might find herself in danger, so you retracted it. But whoever attacked you was someone you knew. Heidi sensed it the first time, when the spear was stolen.'

'I would have told young Barton if I knew.'

'But you wouldn't have if your attacker was Barton's brother.'

'Barton's brother?'

'Damian Hill.'

He had expected her to bluster and deny it, but he hadn't

expected her to laugh, a bright, ringing laugh that sounded delighted—and relieved. 'Goodness me, you do have the wrong end of the stick! Or spear, I should say.'

He knew by her reaction that he was way off course. 'Are you sure? Damian has taken stuff from you before.'

'When he was twelve. I haven't spoken to him for years, but Brendan tells me he's settled down and made something of himself.'

'He's got a bad attitude to women.'

'That doesn't surprise me. You could say that about most of the lads around here. I had to go off to the jungle to find a decent man.'

'It's more than that. I think maybe he pursued Elisabeth Bankston and she turned him down. She was going with a local boy and she didn't have time for Damian. I think Damian tried to lure Elisabeth to a rendezvous by feeding her some secret about her family and killed her when she rejected him. He covered up the murder with the spear to make it look like someone was seeking revenge on the Bankstons.'

Octavia smiled at him benignly, as if he were a five-year-old who feared monsters under the bed. 'You don't like Damian, do you? Did he make a pass at your wife?'

Beckett was about to deny it but Octavia's wry smile let him know that would be foolish. 'Yes.'

'Let me put your mind at ease. I don't know much about Damian these days, but it wasn't him.'

'Who was it then?' Throwing out the challenge.

'I can't say.'

'Or won't say?' When she didn't answer, he felt intense frustration. 'Why are you protecting him? He's a murderer.'

She wiped it aside with a flap of her hand. Then she dropped the hand to her lap where it tightly grasped the other. He waited until she spoke. 'You said Damian tried to lure Elisabeth to meet him by telling her some secret about her family. Can you tell me what it was he was supposed to have told her?'

'Only if you tell me about Vlad the Impaler.'

Alarm registered on her face. 'What about Vlad the Impaler?'

'Young Keith Bankston was fascinated by him, wasn't he?'

'Yes he was. So were the other boys. What has this got to do with anything?'

'The way Elisabeth's body was arranged. The spear through her body.'

'The decimation, you mean?'

Beckett felt his heart rise in his throat. His cup rattled on its saucer. Decimation. That was the word he was looking for. 'Decimation?' he asked.

'Yes. The Romans used to kill every tenth captive. Vlad the Impaler liked to do the same thing. Every tenth victim was impaled on a spear.'

'Nine dead animals and Elisabeth the tenth body.' He thought aloud. 'Why didn't you tell the police?'

'I thought Brendan would have worked it out by now. He was there at the lessons.'

'You don't want them to find the killer, do you?'

'I don't know what I want!' She raised a hand and then let it fall on the arm of the chair. She examined his face. 'Now, it's your turn to tell me the secret about the Bankstons that lured Elisabeth to her death.'

'You're changing the subject.'

'Maybe not.'

So she wanted to play games. 'OK. She found out that young Keith was Laureen Blackpeter's son. She thought she was adopted too.'

Octavia looked genuinely amazed. 'Silly girl!' She put a hand to her brow. 'Oh, but I suppose it's her father's fault. Not setting her straight about Keith's real mother.'

'So you knew Keith was Laureen's son?'

'Of course I did. I encouraged it.'

It was Beckett's turn to be amazed. 'How?'

'Keith didn't have any children and Carmel was getting broody. I always liked Laureen. She had character. But she'd fallen on bad times with that Nino Blackpeter. Keith met her again at a council meeting. She'd turned up to protest about a road going through their land or some such thing. I think Keith felt attracted to her again. I suggested that he could solve all his problems and hers.' She looked brightly at him. 'That's when the shit hit the fan, if you'll pardon my expression. Lydia found out about it and hasn't spoken to me since. I'm sorry Elisabeth thought she was adopted too. It was only ever Keith.'

'But it turned out to be a cruel thing, Octavia. He never felt as if he belonged. Sid Blackpeter was the one who told him who his mother was.'

'That's his father's fault, not mine. I was only trying to guarantee a continuation of the line. Primitive cultures do this sort of thing all the time. The males seek out the fertile females.'

'But you weren't observing chimpanzees in a forest.'

She looked away.

'Keith didn't tell Carmel either.'

'He's a flawed character.' She leaned forward. 'But he does love his children. He's been a good father.'

He knew she was using this to justify her actions. He wasn't in the mood to cosset her. 'I don't know if Peter and Charley would agree.'

'He's hard on them because he's afraid they'll turn out like young Keith.'

'Which is how?'

'A murderer.' All her stiffness left her body. The effort of saying what she'd held to herself for so long suddenly made her limp.

Beckett jumped off his chair and knelt beside her, taking her hand. 'Keith's alive, isn't he?'

'I don't know,' she said.

'You saw him?'

'It can't be. He drowned.'

'What if I told you he didn't? That his drowning was faked?'

Her grasp was like iron. 'It's impossible.'

'You know it isn't. You saw him with your own eyes. You recognised something about him when he stole the spear. And he's the one who attacked you last week.'

She nodded. 'I was more sure of it the second time.'

'He saw that you recognised him at the funeral?'

She nodded again. 'I still don't believe my own eyes.'

Heidi had been right. Sid had helped Keith fake his own death. 'Where is Keith, Octavia?'

She shook her head.

He thought of Heidi's note and her certainty the night before that Keith was alive. Driven by jealousy, he'd gone off after Damian. 'You have to tell me,' he implored, tugging at her hand. 'You see, I'm worried that my wife has gone looking for him.'

'Where?' she asked faintly.

'That's the problem. I don't know.'

43

'I don't have a sister.' Klas banged the frame again and more bees flew into the air. Some of them landed on his sleeves and face but he didn't react. He peered at the cells of wax and honey and ignored Heidi.

Yes, you do, she thought. That accent's phoney. Keith Bankston had Scandinavian relatives. She remembered the photograph on the mantel. You probably got it from them. Sara met you in Melbourne, where Sid had smuggled you after the fake drowning. You probably paid him to do it. You must have had someone down there who supported you. Or maybe you slept rough, merged with the street kids, blended into the big city. You turned your anger against society, became an activist. Met the Gondwanas and became intrigued by Nullin again. Lived on the fringes with them, making trips into town, maybe observing your family from a distance. Safe in the knowledge that if you came across any of them, they wouldn't recognise you under the dreadlocks. Anyone else in town would be distracted by the accent. Besides, everyone thought you were dead. You were safe unless you chose to show yourself. But Elisabeth recognised you...

That was Elisabeth's message on the machine. Heidi realised now, why she'd sounded so upbeat. She'd found out Keith was alive. *I'm going to find out tonight.* Keith had lured her to the Void, to silence her.

Octavia had been looking at the Gondwanas when she had stumbled at the funeral. Heidi was sure of it. She'd been looking directly at Klas. He was tall and pale and long-armed. Octavia alone had recognised her great-nephew. Klas. Keith.

There was a way of proving it.

'Could I see your arm?' Heidi stepped forward as Klas banged the frame again. This time, the alarmed bees flew in her direction, as if the flowers on her crocheted poncho were the real thing. She tried to brush off the few that swarmed around her face, but they alighted on her hands. She flapped her wrists but the bees continued to creep over her skin.

'Don't move.' Klas was still concentrating on the frame. 'They won't sting.'

'Did you hear me, Klas? I'd like to look at your arm.' She was close enough now to touch his left arm, but didn't dare disturb the bees that massed along the red wool up to his shoulders.

He put his head up and looked blankly at her. 'Why?'

'I want to see your tattoos.'

'Why?'

His stubbornness made her impatient enough to forget the bees. She grasped his wrist and tried to push the woolly sleeve up past the elbow. Klas dropped the frame and stumbled backwards, registering shock. 'What do you think you are doing?' He caught his balance and pulled his arm away. Bees circled, buzzing frantically.

Heidi ignored the prickle of bee feet across her cheek. 'You've got a tattoo of a "V" on your arm.'

'What?' he said. It was a good performance of looking puzzled.

'Show me, then,' she demanded.

'All right, all right, crazy lady.' He pushed the loose sleeve of his sweater up to his shoulders, watching apprehensively as she stepped forward to scrutinise his arm.

The bees were delighted at the scent of naked skin and became more frenzied. Unafraid now, Heidi brushed them aside and examined the arm. As she remembered, the skin from clavicle to elbow was covered with an elaborate pattern of dark blue gothic lettering. She could make out a 'U', a 'K' and a 'P'. Wound around the letters were curlicues and scrolls that she could see now were tiny creatures, like medieval dragons and newts.

'Show me the other arm,' she commanded, thinking that perhaps the photograph of Keith's arm that Beck had seen had been reversed. But this arm was simpler, a work in progress. A few dragons, a sword through a heart and the letters 'S' and 'G'.

No 'V'.

No scarring where a 'V' may have been removed. No letters or dragons that might have been drawn over it. There had never been a 'V' tattooed on Klas' arms.

'Did you find it?' He was irritated, pulling down his sleeves roughly.

'What are the letters for?' she asked, confused.

'Per and Ulrike, my father and mother. K is for Klas, naturally. S is for Sara. G is for Gondwana.' He was oblivious to a bee crawling across his left eyebrow.

'Where were you born?'

'In Gothenberg.' He pronounced it *Yottaborya*. 'Do you want a birth certificate?'

She stared at him, couldn't think of anything to ask.

'Why are you doing this?' He made the odd gesture of putting a hand to his pocket as if feeling for something. She realised then that he probably didn't have the correct papers or a valid visa. That's why he was circumspect in his behaviour.

'It's all right, Klas,' she reassured him. 'I don't give a damn whether you're here legally or illegally. I mistook you for someone else, that's all.'

'Is it someone I know?'

Before she could answer, she felt something red-hot pierce the skin near her right thumb.

'Shit!' She shook her hand wildly. 'I've been stung.'

He took her hand, examined it and found the sting. 'The bee

dies now,' he said morbidly.

'Do you have any tobacco?' she asked. 'It helps draw out the pain.'

'No,' he said, 'but I have something better.'

'Octavia, where is Keith?' Beckett had both her hands in his. They felt as light as dried seaweed. 'My wife might be in danger.'

The old woman looked away from him. 'She'll be all right. He's too clever to be found.'

'Is he one of the Gondwanas?'

'Who?'

'The tribe of hippies. You said you met Martin, the American.'

'Oh...yes. I must be losing my mind.'

'*Is* he hiding out with the hippies?'

'I'm not sure.'

Beckett was losing his patience. 'He's a murderer. He needs to be brought to justice.'

Octavia gave a sigh so deep that Beckett feared it was a death rattle. 'It's his father, you see. He'll never get over it. Those people got him back.'

That expression again. Sid had said it. The Blackpeters had their revenge on Keith Bankston for taking Laureen's son. *They got him back.*

Back...Everything was now clear. He spent his life with words, but he'd missed the ambiguity.

There was a mobile phone on the table next to Octavia. 'Can I use that? I have to make a call.'

'You can try.'

He picked it up and dialled. There was no response.

'It doesn't work.' Octavia shook her head.

He threw it back down on the table. 'Damn.'

'No need to swear,' she chastised him. 'What else do you expect from fucking Telstra?'

He looked at her in surprise.

'I better tell you how to get out of here,' she said.

Heidi sat behind the wheel of the stationary Kingswood and thumped the dashboard with one fist. Damn.

She'd been totally, embarrassingly wrong about Klas. If he hadn't been tall and skinny, if his name hadn't started with K, if his arm hadn't been a mass of writhing tattoos, if Octavia hadn't been looking in his direction when she stumbled—she wouldn't have been misled.

He'd been fine about it in the end, even putting some moist cannabis leaves on her hand to draw out the sting. The leaves had worked, too, and she silently thanked her grandmother again. Her hand had erupted in a bruise but that was the worst of it.

Sara had stared at her as she'd run back up the hill to the car. She hadn't time to explain her hasty exit. Keith was out there somewhere and she might be the only one who knew he was alive. Except poor Elisabeth. Who had told Peter. The realisation washed over her like warm water.

She put the car in gear and reversed quickly. Peter knew, she was sure of it. It wasn't Elisabeth's suspicions that they were adopted that had made him edgy. He was haunted by the knowledge that Keith, the troublemaker—and now the murderer—had come back to life. Peter was probably torn between denial and the desperate need to protect his family from the truth.

She'd demand from him where Keith was.

She took the turn into Speculator a little too soon and narrowly avoided a ditch. She slowed down, trying to calm her racing pulse. A flat-bed truck passed, toting bales of hay. She waved at the driver, who waved back. A kelpie balancing on the hay yelped at her. Further along the road, a red kangaroo lay in a bloody lump by the side of the road. Its head was spread like paste on the bitumen, its shoulder almost sheared off by the impact with whatever had hit it. She wondered how soon it would be before the Blackpeters sniffed it out.

Blackpeters. Spaz, Sid, Joey, Crock. What were the other names? The Seven Dwarfs the town called them. All of them short except Spaz, who had a genetic defect.

Her mind wandered to Elisabeth's funeral, where she'd seen five of the seven children, all boys, all alike with their heavy beards and cropped heads. Spaz hadn't been there. Nor Sid. Joey the only girl...

It struck her like the slap of a cold hand. There had been five brothers at the funeral. There should have been *four*. Spaz, Sid, Joey and four others made seven. But she was sure there had been five.

There was an eighth dwarf.

She pulled over and sat staring at the road, her mind scanning the group of Blackpeter boys standing at the back of the funeral service and later on the lawn. Four beefy short stops and one tall one.

One tall one. Not Spaz because he was in Goulburn.

She eased her foot back onto the accelerator and did a U-turn. She roared up the Speculator road trying to find a way into the Blackpeter camp. Here somewhere. She turned onto a promising dirt track but fifteen minutes later ended up back on the main road at the same spot where she had veered off. She knew this by a cow that hung its head over a barbed-wire fence in a paddock across from the T-intersection. It flicked its ears to get rid of the flies and looked solemnly at her as if to say, I told you so.

Heidi figured that there must be another point of entry to the mountain road further north. There was pasture on one side and forest on the other and some of it looked familiar. But, then, most of the countryside had this mix of cleared land and deep rainforest. All paddocks and all trees looked the same to her.

Frustrated, she slammed her foot hard on the accelerator and took the next bend at a speed which might have given a rally driver pause. As she straightened up something flashed across her peripheral vision. In the millisecond it took to catch her breath, the object collided with the hood of the Kingswood on the passenger side of the car and the impact sent Heidi flying sideways against the door handle, her head smashing the window and her hand jolted from the steering wheel, as a violent centrifugal force wrested control of the car from her grasp. She barely had time to register danger as the car sailed across the road into an impassive ironbark. The passenger's side crumpled like a box of crackers under the wheels of a supermarket trolley. The hood flew up and a torrent of hissing water sprayed the windscreen.

She was still upright and conscious. She felt no pain. The driver's door opened easily. She pushed it and stumbled out into a ditch. It was only when she straightened to full height that her legs collapsed like skittles. The last thing she saw was a smear of sky and shimmering leaves.

44

Beckett plunged into the forest behind the old woman's house with only his instinct to guide him. Octavia had stood on the closed-in back verandah and pointed due west, explaining that one of the dirt roads that led into the hinterland ran parallel to the river about two kilometres inland. If he took that road north another two kilometres it intersected with the bitumen road to Speculator. There he was more likely to come across a car to take him back into town. He guessed if he travelled north, on the bitumen road he'd come across recognisable signs of the Blackpeter camp. It would take him hours to walk it, but he was hopeful of hailing down a co-operative local with a sense of adventure.

Octavia had insisted he take the mobile phone. 'Useless here anyway.' It jangled against his car keys in his pocket as he pushed through the scrub. The vegetation was mostly brush and tea-tree, with scraggly stringybark gums and older ironbarks creating the canopy. The bracken and creepers that looped underfoot were more treacherous than the saw-tooth leaves of the banksias and the spokes of the rough tree-ferns that scratched his face as he stumbled past. He fell once, the impact softened by the downy growth of maidenhairs and tussock grass that covered the forest floor. Creatures slithered and scurried away as he approached; something shot across his face, feathers flapping, and disappeared into the brush. He was reminded that he hated nature, even as his nostrils drew in the delicate lemon, salt and eucalyptus fragrance.

Heidi used a soap that smelled exactly like this.

It was the thought of his wife and the possibility she had gone after Keith that spurred him on. He fervently hoped that Heidi hadn't drawn the same conclusions he had. But the sick feeling at the pit of his stomach told him she'd been a step ahead all along.

Sid Blackpeter had been right. He'd told Beckett the truth, only Beckett hadn't recognised it. *We got him back.* The Blackpeters had got their boy back and in doing so had got Keith senior back. What had Gray said? *Keith Bankston reckons he's so smart, but Sid Blackpeter went and made a fool of him. And the funniest thing is, Keith doesn't know.*

Keith had faked his own drowning with the help of Sid. Laureen had taken him back. What had she said when they arrested Spaz? *Keith is careless with his own children.* The young man had hidden out there for eight years, rarely showing his face in town. Even if he had been seen with his half-brothers, there was little chance he'd be recognised, especially under a Blackpeter beard. And he *had* been seen in town, but everyone thought he was Spaz. Keith and Carmel believed he'd drowned, as had the whole town, with the exception of Gray. They'd blacked him out of their minds.

Blacked out. A Blackpeter again.

Keith had killed his sister and set up his brother, poor Spaz, to take the rap for Elisabeth's murder. And Laureen let him do it. He was persuasive, a charmer, everyone said that. He must have convinced her he was innocent.

What kind of monster was he? A monster with a taste for impaling dead animals and beautiful young women.

And the dead animals were appearing again.

Was he going to wait until he got to ten this time?

'Big roo, but,' Heidi heard a voice in the sky say. 'Wonder she's not mincemeat.'

A softer voice said something that was blown away on the

wind, like dandelion spores.

Heidi tried to concentrate but the right side of her head from brow to jaw felt as if it had been filled with heavy stones.

'What'll we do with her?' she heard the male voice say. With his words came the waft of something long dead.

'Take her to the highway and dump her on the side of the road. Someone'll come along.' It was a female, young and harsh.

'We could leave her outside the hospital.'

'No fuckin' way. The kids need their tea.'

'Let's leave her, then.'

'Pick up the roo and let's go.'

'Don't!' Heidi was surprised to hear herself speak. Her mouth didn't feel like it had moved. She was aware of a raw sensation across her midriff where her ribs had been whacked by the door handle. She tried to prop herself up. 'Don't leave me!'

'Bad luck, sister.' The woman again. Heidi could sense her moving away across the road.

'Joey—' She tried to say it loudly but the words flopped out of her mouth like a limp rag.

The man heard her, though. 'She knows your name,' he called out. 'You didn't say you fuckin' knew her.'

The woman's voice came closer again. 'Shutup, I don't.'

'Joey...take me to see...'

'What she fuckin' say?'

'She said your name.'

'I told you I don't know the cow!'

'Keith.' Heidi clutched her side, feeling with her fingers to find if any of the ribs were broken. Her side felt bruised but she was breathing easily.

'What?'

'Take me to see Keith.'

'Keith-fucking-who?'

'Your brother.'

Beckett's hands stung with a dozen cuts from prickles and sharp leaves, and he'd made the mistake of grasping a tall sedge that cut through his right palm, but the anxiety in his heart made the pain in his hands seem negligible.

He noticed that the forest floor had become littered with old soft-drink cans, polystyrene hamburger boxes, blue plastic shopping bags, shreds of blowout tyre rubber. Signs of civilisation. With mounting determination, he pushed on through the forest. The dirt road that opened up before him was corrugated with loose stones and potholes, but it could have been the Yellow Brick Road, he was so overjoyed.

Joy soon turned to disappointment as he trudged north down the centre of the road. This was one of a network of lanes that laced the hinterland, built once as bullock and coach tracks but bypassed for decades by ribbons of bitumen that took a more direct route between town and city. He doubted if a car had been along here for months. There was no sign of any tyre marks in the soft mud by the side of the road. He would have to walk the two kilometres to the main road. No, he would have to run.

He picked up his feet but it was more a shuffle than a gallop. Within twenty minutes he found himself jogging on smooth bitumen. He could have dropped to his knees and kissed it.

He didn't need to. No sooner had he started north again when he heard a car engine behind him.

He turned and waved frantically.

The car pulled over and stopped.

Beckett jogged towards the silver Magna. The driver's door opened and a dark-haired young man got out. He wore a casual zip-up jacket over suit pants and polished shoes, an odd combination. Beckett felt a jolt as he recognised the man as Peter Bankston. What was he doing up here, miles away from Nullin, Speculator and the cheese factory?

'I can't take you back to town,' Peter said, even before Beckett could speak, 'but are you hurt? I can call someone.' He dug a mobile out of his pocket. Then he dropped it on the ground, as if his hands were greasy. He seemed jittery.

Beckett realised he must have looked like he'd been in a fight with a razorback. He bent down, picked up the phone and gave it back. 'I'm fine. I got stranded in the bush. Long story. I'm Beckett Versec, by the way.' He held out a hand, and saw that it was bleeding.

'I know,' Peter said. He didn't take the hand. 'I'll get a towel.'

'Thanks.'

Peter knelt on the driver's seat and reached into the back of the car, finding a ragged blue towel. Beckett took it. It smelled of oil but a corner was clean.

'Sorry, it's not the cleanest. I've got some electrical parts back there.' Peter took the towel back from Beckett when he was finished and tossed it into the car.

His skin had a waxy green look. 'I've really got to be off,' he said, nervously. 'I'm sorry I can't take you. I'll call an ambulance.'

Beckett dug Octavia's mobile out of his pocket and held it up. 'No need. Where are you going?'

'North.'

'Is someone expecting you?'

'Just some...relatives.' Peter put a foot back in the car.

'Odd,' Beckett said. 'I'm going to see them too.'

45

Heidi slouched against the rails in the back tray of the flatbed truck. The endorphin rush had subsided and now her ribs hurt like hell. The truck had turned onto a dirt track and the corrugated surface ensured a steady bump and grind. She held her ribs tightly but with every jolt a stabbing pain drove into her side.

She bit her lip and tears of frustration filled her eyes. She'd been a complete idiot mentioning Keith's name to Joey. What had she been thinking? That Joey would have been pleased with her? That she would have happily escorted her to have a chat and a cup of tea with the secret brother? More likely Joey would do what Heidi feared she was doing now—carting her off to face a very angry, and possibly lethal, kangaroo court of brothers. The Blackpeters had protected Keith all these years. Why would they give him up now?

Her mind betrayed her attempt to focus it on escape. She shuddered and thought of the roo heads on fenceposts, the impaled native animals, Elisabeth strangled and violated with a spear. All the Blackpeters were killers. They lived steeped in blood. And no one knew she was here. She'd gone off blindly, stupidly, thinking she was invincible. And soon she would be dead, like Elisabeth. Worse, they might never find her body. She thought of Beckett rattling around alone in that big old cheese factory, always wondering if she would come home.

She snapped herself out of it and tried to focus again. She should try to get away now, while she could, before she had to contend with a whole family of killers. But it was useless jumping off the truck. Joey and the baby were in the cabin with her brother, the one the kids called Uncle Shank. Possum and Petal sat in the back, on an old tyre, staring at her. If she jumped, she had no doubt the kids would sound the alarm. Joey and Shank would turn back for her, throw her into the truck more roughly next time. Her side ached at the thought of it.

The kangaroo that had been annihilated by its collision with Heidi's Kingswood lay between her and the children. By the looks on their grubby faces, they thought that she was roadkill too.

Maybe that's all I am.

Her handbag, which she'd managed to snatch from the front seat of her ruined car, was lying at the feet of the children. She eyed it and said, 'Pass my bag,' with as much authority as she could muster.

Possum, wide-eyed, picked up the fabric bag and tossed it at her. She rummaged in it for her vial of Rescue Remedy, squirting several drops on her tongue and spilling more of it as the truck ploughed over a pothole. Her hand briefly closed around the handle of the paring knife. She kept the bag close as she took her poncho off and pulled up her tee-shirt, tenderly running her fingers along the ribs again. She gestured for Possum to throw her a bit of cloth crumpled in a corner, which he did obediently. It was an old sheet and she ripped a long strip, then wound it tightly around her torso, tying the frayed ends in a knot. She managed to lift her arms to get the poncho back over her head. The pressure of the bandage supported her ribcage and relieved some pain.

Heidi smelled the Blackpeters' place about five minutes before the truck pulled up at a mesh gate topped with rolls of razor wire. The reek smacked her in the face—the metallic, earthy scent of drying blood, the putrid odour of decaying flesh, the rotten-egg stink of tanning hides. She found a piece of leftover sheet and pressed it against her nose. It didn't help.

Shank got out of the truck and opened the gate. They were hemmed in by trees but the road past the gate seemed recently graded. Shank drove through, closed the gate and they rattled down the hill for another couple of hundred metres.

Three skinny dogs snapped at the tyres and a couple of chickens flew out of the way as they drove past dozens of roo skins stretched over wire frames in the clearing by the road. Clusters of forty-gallon drums gave off foul chemical odours. Bile rose in her throat.

That's where I'm going to end up.

She slid her hand into the bag and felt for the knife.

A shack appeared in front of them.

Heidi turned with some difficulty and looked at it over the side of the truck. As shacks go, it was palatial in size. The place looked like it had grown upwards and outwards over many years and was made of materials scavenged not only from the forest but the local tip. Most of the structure was formed of irregular planks of timber and split trunks of trees, but some of the walls were thatched with palm fronds and others covered in corrugated iron. Pellets of compressed newspaper and cardboard served as bricks. Junkyard car parts formed windows and doors. An old Mobil bowser stood at the door, along with a refrigerator that seemed connected to something, perhaps a generator. A blackened drum lay on its side on a trestle, filled with smouldering coals.

In another life Heidi might have admired the Blackpeter's ingenuity. Right now she knew if they got into that house, she might never come out again. Except in a barrel. The wooden shaft of the knife was small comfort in her hand.

Shank jumped out of the truck. He was not much taller than Heidi but he swaggered with a bow-legged gait. 'Mum! Get out here!' he yelled. 'We got a fine piece of roadkill.'

He wasn't talking about the roo.

Joey slammed her door and came around the back, hoisting

the baby over her shoulder. The baby she hoped to sell to Diane Bankston. Heidi eyed her warily. She sensed a reptilian calculatedness underneath Joey's mask of indifference.

The girl opened the tailgate and said coldly, 'Get down.'

How far would I get if I ran? Heidi wondered. She exaggerated her struggle to stand, clutching her bag behind her so Joey didn't see it.

She climbed awkwardly down from the truck. The children ran off into the house giggling. Another Blackpeter brother appeared, scratching his head. Shank went inside and came out a moment later with his mother.

Laureen looked bleary-eyed from where Heidi stood. It was early afternoon, but she was wearing an old beige nylon slip and filthy sheepskin boots, as if she'd just tumbled out of bed. Certainly her tangled hair looked like it.

Laureen made an unsteady lurch forward. 'Who the hell is this?'

'I dunno,' Shank grunted. 'Joey knows her.'

'She's here to see Keith,' Joey said.

Laureen snapped her eyes in Joey's direction. Joey shrugged. Then Laureen turned back to Heidi and glared. 'There's no Keith here.' Just a hint of slurring on the 's'.

'She knows, Mum.'

Laureen stared right through Heidi. 'I said there's no Keith here.'

'She wants to see him,' Joey insisted. 'She's come all this way, Mum, why not let her?'

Heidi wondered what game Joey was playing, but she didn't like it.

'Who the fuck *are* you?' Laureen folded her arms around her breasts and jutted a hip out.

'I'm Heidi Go.' Her voice sounded thin, distant.

'So? What the crap have we got to do with you?'

What was she going to say? She thought it wise to leave the

Bankstons out of it for a moment. 'My husband is a...friend of your son Sid.'

'Sid's got no friends.'

'My husband visited him in jail yesterday.'

'Lots of people visit him in jail. Cops, for instance.'

'My husband's not a cop.' She hesitated. Laureen looked like she would snap her fingers and set the boys on her with little provocation.

'I met him, Mum,' Joey said. 'He gave me a lift. Tried to put his hand up my skirt.'

It was the smirk on Joey's face that made Heidi step over the edge. Maybe she was never going to get out of there, but she had to know. 'Your son Sid told my husband everything. That Keith's been alive all these years.'

She gambled that Laureen would believe Sid would spill an eight-year secret to a stranger. It paid off.

'What business is it of yours?'

'You should give him up.'

'Why would I want to do that?'

'They've got Spaz in jail, but he didn't do it.'

'I know that.'

'Keith did.'

Laureen waved her thin, macadamia-brown arm. 'That's crap. None of my boys are murderers.'

'If he's not a murderer, we should take him into town and let him prove it.'

'I don't fancy anyone's chances of talkin' him into that.'

'Laureen, it's over. You can't protect him now. Elisabeth Bankston found out about him and told her brother Peter. My husband knows. It won't be long before the police do and they come looking for him.'

Laureen was so quick Heidi hardly had time to register that she'd moved. She was upon Heidi in an instant, grabbing her right arm and twisting it up her back under her poncho. Heidi screeched with pain. Laureen's breath was right in her face, a sickening blend of sweet whiskey, sour milk and cheap violet scent.

'People in town think we're all bad,' Laureen snarled. 'But we're just makin' a livin'. I got seven good kids and we keep to uselves. If any of 'em have gone off the rails for a minute, it's the townfolk who corrupted 'em, not the other way around.'

Heidi could hardly breathe for the pain in her twisted arm. She tried to free herself but the struggle was more excruciating than Laureen's grip. The nausea welled up inside her and she tried to hold it down. No good. She turned her head and vomited all over Laureen's boots.

'Filth!' Laureen screeched, releasing Heidi's arm and shaking her feet. The boys stepped forward.

Joey starting laughing hysterically.

Heidi's arm flopped to her side. She was still clutching her bag in her other hand. She raised that forearm to her mouth and wiped the foul taste away.

'I'm going to piss myself,' Joey guffawed.

'Shut up!' Laureen yelled at her. And then she shivered, whether from booze, the cold or dark memories, Heidi couldn't tell.

'Why did you give Keith away, Laureen?' Heidi managed to get the sentence out but every breath tore at her side. She braced herself for another attack. It didn't come.

'I shouldn'ta let him go in the first place. It was a sin.' Laureen scratched at an arm. Heidi could feel the others suddenly tense. 'Keith Bankston is the devil. It was his idea. Nino said we could do with the money, which Christ knows we coulda back then with all them babies. He drunk it all up in six months.' She looked through Heidi to some imaginary tableau from her past. 'I never went into town from that moment on, in case I saw him with her ladyship in his pram.' She clutched at a tarnished locket around her neck and Heidi instantly knew whose picture was inside it. Her eyes focused on Heidi again. 'But he was different when he came back.'

Heidi struggled to keep talking. She wanted more than anything to fall into a deep, comforting blankness. But she'd be dead the minute she dropped to her knees. 'He was different?' she asked. 'In what way?'

'He was all full of Bankston cockiness,' she said grimly. 'They should've took care of him better.'

'How?'

'Given him some discipline. All my boys got the stockwhip when they acted up and they're as good as gold now.'

Shank was standing behind his mother, arms folded. The other brother had a checked shirt hanging out over camouflage pants and a tongue hanging out over a drooping bottom lip in the kind of hungry stare Heidi had seen whenever she'd walked past a construction site. They didn't look good as gold.

She had to keep Laureen talking, win over her sympathy. 'I understand how you feel. You wanted a better life for Keith. And the Bankstons didn't love him like you did. But hiding him away isn't going to help him. He needs to face who he is.'

'Who he is, is a Blackpeter,' Laureen said defiantly.

'Can I talk to him?' Heidi wasn't sure she wanted to do this at all now, but she needed to buy some time.

'Didn't you hear what Mum said?' Shank took a step forward. 'It's none of your fuckin' business.' He started towards her.

Heidi stepped backwards.

'Where are you goin'?'

'I can find my way back to the road, thanks.'

'I wasn't offerin' to show you.'

She felt the bullbar of the truck at her back. 'Let me go, please. Laureen?'

Laureen had the glazed look again.

'Dingo and me haven't finished with you yet.' Shank put a hand over his crotch and tugged. 'We're sick of the slags in town. Nice to have somethin' fresh.'

'My husband knows I'm here.'

'Yeah? Well maybe he'd like to join in. We don't mind, do we Ding?'

All she had was the knife. She glanced at the handbag she was clutching. Joey caught the look. 'What's in the bag, bitch?'

'Nothing.'

'Fuckin' give me that!' Joey commanded.

'It's just a bag.'

'Oh, yeah?' In a flash, Joey dumped her baby into Laureen's arms and threw herself at Heidi. Heidi pressed the bag behind her body but Joey grasped her wrist and peeled her fingers away. Joey plunged a hand into the bag and came up with the knife, holding it up for her brothers to see. 'Piddling little thing, isn't it, Shank?' She turned back to Heidi. 'Think you're going to cut us all to pieces with this, do you? Shank here uses blades like these for toothpicks.' She lunged at Heidi with it, making little stabbing movements close to her face. Heidi put up her hand and her thumb connected with the blade. She sucked on it but didn't cry out. Be damned if she was going to let Joey know she was hurt.

'You think that's a cut?' Joey taunted her. 'Wait until you see what the boys have in store for you.'

'Now, now, let's not be rude to visitors.' Heidi whirled around at the sound of a new voice behind her. It was Crock, confederate cap cocked over one eye and a shotgun slung over his shoulder. She hadn't even heard a twig snap. 'I say we let her find the boy.'

'Yeah, let her, Mum.' Joey urged again. 'I'll take her.'

'Quit it, Joey,' Crock said. His eyes were shiny black marbles reflecting a cruel humour. 'No one's taking her. If she's smart enough to get the nasty bugger to talk to her, she's smart enough to find him.'

Laureen's expression dulled and she shrugged. She patted the baby's back like any good grandmother. 'No skin off my nose.'

'But there's a catch,' Crock said to Heidi, smiling through a tangle of rotten teeth. 'We're gonna give you a ten-minute start. Then we come looking for you.' The rifle slid into his hands and he pointed it at her. 'We give all the animals a bit of a start, other-wise it's no fun.'

A muscle over Peter's eye twitched. 'What relatives are you talking about?'

'The Blackpeters.'

'I don't know what you mean.'

'I went to see Sid at Bungalong yesterday.'

Peter was uncomprehending. 'Why would you go and see Sid?'

'Because Spaz didn't murder your sister and I don't like injustice. Sid told me about Keith.' He paused. 'That he's alive.'

Peter started to say something and then closed his mouth.

'Elisabeth found out, didn't she?'

Peter looked like he was about to deny it, then nodded.

'So he needed to silence her.'

'You don't know that.'

'But *you* do.'

'I...I don't know. Why would he do such a thing? She was his *sister*, for God's sake.'

'Maybe he hated you.'

'But why did he hate us? I always treated him like my big brother! He didn't need to run away.' He shook his head angrily. 'How could he do that to Mother?'

'Does she know he's alive?'

'I didn't have the heart to say anything. Until I knew...for sure. I picked her up from the airfield a couple of hours ago. She's been in Melbourne. It did her good. She seemed...not so sad. If I find Keith and talk to him, maybe he'll come home with me. I don't want Mother to find out from a third person.'

'Peter, who told Elisabeth that Keith was alive?'

'I don't know.'

'She never told you?'

'It was a secret. Some kind of game. She thought it was

exciting.' He gave a choked laugh. 'It was exciting for someone.'

'Do you think it was Keith himself? That she met him somewhere?'

'I don't know! She refused to say.' He swallowed hard. 'I did get the feeling it was someone she was...involved with, though.'

'Romantically?'

'I don't know.'

'You don't think that person was Keith?'

'That's the thing—she *wouldn't.*'

'Not even for kicks?'

'No. And when I find Keith he'll explain everything. He'll have an alibi.'

'But, if you knew about Keith being alive, why did you leave it until now to come looking for him? Why didn't you tell the police?'

'Don't you think I hate myself for that! I should have looked for him the minute...'

'The minute Elisabeth was missing?'

'I couldn't believe it was him. I didn't even know it was true. Then your wife came to me. I let her think Elisabeth was worried that we—she and me—might be Blackpeters too. I could tell the way that she looked at me, she knew there was more. I wanted to ask Mother today...about everything. But I couldn't.' His eyes held Beckett's. 'It's my responsibility to bring him home.'

'You can't go up there alone. He might be your brother by blood, Peter, but even if he isn't a killer, what about the others?'

'I can look after myself.'

'I'll come with you.'

'No way. This is family business.'

Peter moved quickly back to the car. He slipped into the driver's seat and slammed the door. He turned on the ignition and the engine roared. He put the car into reverse. Beckett vaulted to the rear and tried to block him. The back door was unlocked and he yanked it open. Peter put his foot hard on the brake.

Beckett ducked his head and slipped into the back seat. When he looked up again, Peter was staring at him coldly. So too was the single barrel of a high-powered rifle.

Two guns pointed at him in a day. It was a record.

46

Crock raised his rifle to the sky and discharged it above the treetops, away from the shack to the left. 'Just givin' you some help, darlin'. He's that way.' He cocked the gun again, lowered the sight and trained it on her. 'Get a move on, possum. The clock's tickin'.'

Shank and Dingo looked at Heidi hungrily. Joey smirked, hands on hips. This was a game they had all played before. They would track her down, however fast she ran. And if they didn't...there was Keith, waiting for her out there somewhere. Keith who'd murdered Elisabeth. Keith who would do the same to her.

Heidi had no choice but to take her chances in the bush.

Crock raised his shotgun again and fired. She didn't hesitate now. All fear and no thought, she hurtled into the scrub. She felt unco-ordinated and wrong-footed. There was no path and branches sprang at her as she crashed through the trees, catching in her hair and snagging her poncho. She risked losing a moment to struggle out of it, the effort tore at her smarting ribs and she had to bend over double to catch her breath.

She stood upright again and something brushed against her head. She looked up. The carcass of a possum swung above her, one foot roped to a tree. She started to scream but swallowed it. Keith would hear her. He could probably already smell her fear.

She started off again. She had no idea where she was going, except that it was up. She took the incline powerfully at first, driven by the fear of being blown to smithereens by Crock's shotgun. Soon her thigh muscles were tight wires. Her hamstrings seized up. And each breath was accompanied by a lacerating pain in her side.

Her boots kicked something solid. There was a loud snap. She stumbled and came to a halt. She looked down on the now closed jaw of a large, rusting trap that had just missed her foot. *Shit.* She hadn't thought of that. How many fur traps were there set around here? She had to be more careful.

The bush looked untouched in any direction. No clue that Keith was anywhere close. She hoped that she wasn't running into another kind of trap, caught between a murderer and a madman.

The madman had given her a ten minute start.

She looked around her wildly, needing to move on, not knowing where to go. The putrid smell of the Blackpeter camp had been replaced by something else, something dank and earthy lingering under the scent of gum and myrtle. She tried to put a name to it, but couldn't. She set off uphill again, her instincts told her there might be a road at the crest and she galvanised her mind and every muscle in her body to find it.

A shotgun blast shook the treetops further down the hill. A crow flew across the sky shrieking.

Her ten minutes were up. Unless she got lucky, so was her life.

The blast made her thighs go to water. She grasped the branch of a tea-tree to steady herself. The pain in her ribs now seared through her skull. The ground beneath her feet rose upward to meet her.

A twig crunched. It jolted her out of the blackness. She whipped her head up and was startled to see a shadowy human face staring down at her. The body exuded the dank odour that permeated everything out here. It came to her in a flash what it was—the stench of old graves.

God, no.

Keith.

He was like nothing she'd seen before.

He stood there like a black ghost, his indigo eyes locked on her with feverish intensity. She took in the long, dark, matted hair that brushed his pectorals, the beard that sprawled across his face. In his cracked and shredded bike leathers he looked like he had barely survived the same holocaust that had felled a blackened tree nearby.

She stepped backwards.

And then he did something shocking. He spoke and his voice was as clear as creek water. 'Follow me,' he said. He sounded cultured, not crude like his brothers.

Crock's shotgun blasted somewhere down in a gully. The bush around them quivered. Even the insects made a commotion.

Keith turned and ran in confident, loping strides. She could follow his direction by the movement of the branches as he crashed through. He might take her to a road and then she might escape them all. Or he might lead her straight into the jaws of an iron trap.

There was no choice. Whatever kind of killer Keith was he didn't have two barrels trained on her.

She staggered after him across the spur of the hill, he was a dark, thin figure, like a burnt match. After a few minutes the branches stopped snapping back, the forest floor went quiet and she thought she had lost him. But there he was, standing still as a ghost gum, waiting for her.

They travelled like this for a few hundred metres. Keith kept stopping and watching her, waiting for her to catch up. She was past caring about his motive. He could have killed her by now if he wanted. She had no defences. Without him, she would be at the mercy of Crock and the other brothers.

Keith disappeared over the spur. Heidi clumsily followed, taking a diagonal path. The land plateaued over the crest. The trees were sparser here, scrubby bushes more prevalent, as if the forest had been cleared at some point. It was easier landscape to cross, but her legs had long since turned to blocks and the memory in the muscles was the only thing that drove her onwards.

Keith stopped again about a hundred metres from her, standing in a bamboo forest of spare, straight stalks. As she dragged herself closer to him, she became aware that the stalks weren't bamboo at all but pale, stripped sticks crowned with odd shapes. She instinctively slowed down. And then a tremble started up in her body.

Keith's long body, in its covering of raven leather, was framed by a grisly garden of skulls driven through with sharpened stakes. Some of the skulls were bleached, but scraps of flesh and fur still clung to many of them. She could make out possums, dogs, a kangaroo, something that looked like a rat.

There was no way she was following Keith into this lair.

Beckett watched Peter's car slide away in the gravel and roar north up the road.

Damn.

The idiot had a rifle. He probably didn't know how to use it.

And Heidi was out there. Somewhere.

He didn't want Peter to get into a shooting match with the Blackpeters and have Heidi caught in the crossfire.

He tried Octavia's mobile. A signal.

Further up the road he could see that the bush on one side petered out to cleared farmland. He dashed towards it, pressing redial.

It was pointless running. Heidi saw the black fury in his face. It was the face Beckett had shown her on the Internet—Spaz's long face, but without the big ears and the transparent expression.

He pulled at her good arm. She could feel the amazing strength of him in his intense grip. She tried to shake him off, but it was futile. She went obediently limp.

Another gunshot rent the air.

He stared at her for a moment then pulled her back towards the skulls.

'No!' she yelled. 'Not in there!'

He ignored her and she tripped behind him locked in his grasp. Things crunched under her feet. She looked down. Bleached bones.

They came through the spear forest and into a clearing. In the middle stood a shack. Not any ordinary shack.

It was the size of a doll's house, barely tall enough for Keith to stand in. To understand what she was seeing, Heidi's brain seized on images from the European fairytales her mother had told her when she was a child. The Gingerbread Man and his little house in the woods. Hansel and Gretel lured into the witch's cottage.

And then the resemblance struck her. It was a miniature of Octavia Goodhope's house, constructed of bleached, distressed timber slabs scavenged from some old building. The narrow verandah that wrapped around the shack was strung with animal heads in various stages of decay. Seashells and animal bones were scattered along the path and more sticks, sharpened and carved to look like spears, were propped against the railing as if it were some medieval battlement.

Keith let go of her arm, his back to the shack, watching her reaction.

'It's beautiful,' she said, and meant it. It was, in a ghostly, ghastly way.

It was the right thing to say. He bowed his head.

Crock emptied his barrel into the trees again. He was much closer now. She could see the tops of the trees shake.

Keith's head snapped up. He held her eyes for a minute and then disappeared round the back of the shack.

She took a deep breath and started after him again. Then she stopped and pulled one of Keith's spears out of the dirt.

She would need it.

Breathing was difficult—she had to stop and start. She used the spear to support her failing legs. The terrain was flatter, the vegetation light. They were nearing cleared farmland. Crock's next gunshot sounded more distant. She could imagine him cursing as he came upon the empty shack.

I'll get away from both of them and find a farmer with a phone, she resolved, aware that she was, absurdly, pursuing her pursuer.

Keith picked up his pace. The path was now sandy, easy to traverse, but her gait had slowed down to a hobble. Her leg muscles, her ribs and shoulder had gone beyond pain. It was the pain in her feet that now tore through her with every step.

She limped round a bend and saw Keith had stopped. His back to her. He was looking at something.

And then she saw.

He was looking across the Nullin Void.

47

Beckett didn't know what road he was on but he could see the red roof of a farm. Octavia's mobile had only one number stored. The direct line to the Nullin police station. Cheryl Martin had taken the call and he'd described as best he could where he was. He mentioned something about a gunman. That was all.

Twenty minutes later a white Holden Rodeo kicked up gravel as it turned the corner. Beckett walked into the middle of the road and flagged it down. The truck had barely stopped before Brendan Barton and Stephen Fraser jumped out with rifles in their hands.

'He's gone,' Beckett told them.

'What's the story?' Barton asked, keeping the gun by his side.

'Peter Bankston pulled a rifle on me. He's gone off half-cocked. And I think Heidi's up there too.'

'Where?'

'At the Blackpeters.'

'Why would they be there? With guns?'

'Because young Keith Bankston's alive. He's your killer.'

'Hang on a minute,' Fraser said, looking bemused. 'Who says young Keith's alive?'

'Sid Blackpeter.'

Fraser laughed. 'Well, then, we all better run round with our tongues hanging out if he says so.'

'You don't have to believe me. Octavia Goodhope knows. So does Gray Wignall. Elisabeth worked it out. That's why she's dead. He didn't drown. He faked it and hid up here…Look, we don't have time to argue. Heidi might be in danger.'

'If that's the case,' Fraser insisted, 'how come we never worked it out before?'

'Good question.' Barton shot him an ironic glance.

'Well, I'm not going up to the Blackpeters without good reason. Fuck it.'

'Shut up, Steve,' Barton snarled at him. 'Peter's got a gun and it sounds like he might use it.'

Beckett climbed in behind the two police officers and told what he knew as they sped along the road. Fraser huffed and snorted at first but soon went quiet.

'Keith killed Elisabeth because she'd found out about him?' Brendan asked.

'Seems like it.'

'I don't believe it. She was his sister.'

Beckett was about to respond when they turned a bend. 'Stop the car!' he screamed, thumping his hand on the back of the seat.

Heidi's Kingswood was lying in a ditch on the other side of the road against a tree, front doors flung open, hood up.

Brendan jumped out first but Beckett beat him to the car. 'She's not here!' He ran around the vehicle desperately. 'Maybe she walked off into the bush?'

'Calm down,' Brendan said. 'She wouldn't do that. She'd wait by the side of the road. Someone might have picked her up.'

Beckett pulled her keys out of the ignition. 'But she would have taken her keys.' He checked the back seat. 'Her handbag's gone.'

Brendan was examining a bloody dent on the passenger's side. 'Looks like she hit a roo.'

'Then where is it?' Fraser walked across the other side of the road and back, shaking his head. 'Someone must have picked it up.'

'I reckon that someone picked up Heidi too,' Brendan said. 'No guessing who that might be.'

Heidi imagined the howling wind was full of the cries of all the innocent animals Keith had killed.

She stood facing him at the edge of the Void, white knuckles grasping the spear. She could see the parking area a couple of hundred metres away across the other side of the quarry. It was empty. No one to call out to. No one to help. Cold sweat ran down her spine. The wind pulled stray hairs across her eyes.

Keith started to climb down a pathway hewn into the side of the rock.

'No, Keith! Don't!' There was no way she was going to follow him.

He stopped.

She had said his name.

He stepped back up the path towards her.

Please don't let him kill me now.

He held out his hand.

'I'm not going there.' She shivered.

'Why?'

'No.' She shook her head. She jerked the tip of the spear at him. 'Don't come any closer!' She could smell acrid sweat mixed in with the other body odours. He was repulsive. And yet—she felt alarmed at this—there was an undeniable wild beauty about him. She was horrified at the connection she was feeling with him. He was a killer but she sensed something soft in him.

You always make excuses for people. Was it that?

He was now so close she could smell the death on him again. 'I saw you,' he said.

'Saw me when?'

'Down there.' He turned his head towards the Void.

The hairs on the back of her neck spiked. He'd seen her with Elisabeth's body. 'I thought someone was watching,' she said, trying not to show him how scared she was. 'I thought it was Spaz.'

'He brought the coat. She was cold.' That elegant voice

again. If she closed her eyes it could seduce her.

She felt herself begin to swoon. With an effort, she snapped out of it. 'She was your sister.'

This had an astonishing effect. He took another step towards her. 'She wasn't my sister!' he growled.

Her arms trembled as she poked the spear at him. She struggled to get her mind on track. 'She was your half-sister, then.'

He shook his head angrily. 'No. She was not.'

'But Keith adopted you because he'd had an affair with Laureen and you were his child.'

'Laureen is a liar.'

She tried to judge what he might do next by his eyes. They were feverish, evangelical. He believed this. 'She lied about you being his child?'

'I am not *his* child.' He spat it out. 'Laureen lied to make them want me.' He spoke slowly, as if talking was something strange.

She forgot her fear for a moment. 'But Laureen told me it was Keith Bankston's idea.'

'It was Laureen and Nino's. I was their boy. They wanted money for me.'

'She told you this? When?'

'When she was drunk.' He spat the word out, disgusted.

'Then how do you know it's true?'

'Spaz. Spaz and me are the same. Everyone says so. We're freaks. Freaks like all the animals around here. Possums with duck bills. Deer that stand on their tails. Rats with wings.'

'You're not a freak,' she said gently. 'You're just a boy that other people did some very bad things to.'

'No, they all said it. I am a freak.'

With growing alarm, she realised he was disconnecting from her. He looked at her as if she were an animal in a trap and he was working out how to seize her by the throat without being bitten. She grasped the shaft of her spear more tightly. He shifted his eyes from her face to what was in her hand. With a gesture too swift for her to block, he put his hand around the flint of the spear and wrested it from her in one quick movement. When he took the shaft in his other hand and tilted it towards her, she was horrified to see that the blade had made a cut right across the palm. Bright blood dripped down his fingers but he seemed not to have noticed. He was more intent on watching her squirm.

Brendan Barton got out of the truck surprisingly casually, Beckett thought, given that Crock and two of his brothers had shotguns pointed at him. Beckett stood by the truck with Fraser, who seemed jumpy, even with a rifle by his side.

Barton raised his hands to show he'd left his rifle by his seat. 'It's all right, Crock. I'm not looking for any Blackpeters. I just want to know if you've had any visitors lately.'

Crock smiled. 'Only the odd stray animal.' He gestured to some kangaroo skins nailed to a frame.

'I was thinking of Peter Bankston.'

'Who?'

'You know who. He's armed.'

'I'm quaking in me boots.'

'What about the young woman, Heidi?'

'Don't think I know her. Wouldn't be too smart for a young woman to come wandering in here, would it, with some of these blokes not seen a fresh female on two legs for some time.'

'You bastard!' Beckett tried to launch himself at Crock but Brendan hoisted him by the arm and restrained him.

'Let me handle it,' Brendan warned. 'Mind if we take a look around?' he asked Crock.

'Now that would be inconvenient,' Crock said. 'Laureen's just having a lie down. There's been too much excitement around here lately, you can't blame her. Come back tomorrow.'

'Can't do that, Crock. We've got good reason to believe the people we're looking for have been here in the past couple of hours. Maybe we should wake Laureen up and ask her.'

'I said I haven't seen 'em. A Blackpeter's word is a Blackpeter's word.'

At that moment Possum chose to run around the side of the house with his little sister, Petal, stumping after him on her short legs, rubbing her eyes and bawling. In Possum's hand—what Petal wanted—was Heidi's bag.

'Then what the fuck is that?' Beckett yelled at Crock, enraged. He shrugged away from Brendan and chased Possum into the scrub. He picked the child up by the scruff of his good shirt and yanked the bag from his flailing hands.

'This is Heidi's bag,' he shouted. He turned to Crock, heedless of the Blackpeter brothers' combined firepower. 'What did you do with her?'

'Nothin'.' Crock put down his shotgun and rested his arms on the barrel. Beckett could see that one arm was scarred with a handmade tattoo of a kangaroo and shiny welts that looked like burns. 'So many fuckin' animals in the bush these days, you can't expect me to remember all the mongrels that get away.'

Beckett could smell a faint whiff of discharged gun. It had been fired recently. Crock had said something about 'getting away'. He clung to the hope that Heidi had.

'Right,' Barton said, stepping between them. 'You're either coming in with us, Crock, or your memory's going to get miraculously better. Right now.'

Crock made a point of slowly taking his confederate cap off his head and scratching his scalp slowly. He was probably only thirty, but his hair was so thin on top it looked like a scrape of Vegemite across brown toast. 'Funny, you know.' He smiled with tobacco-stained teeth. 'I reckon there was something like what you're lookin' for here a while back. Ran off into the bush with hardly any encouragement. We didn't follow, did we fellas? Couldn't be bothered. There are plenty of traps out there. It's probably got its leg caught in one now, screamin' with agony.'

Beckett no longer cared about the guns pointed at him. He balled his fist and it connected with the side of Crock's jaw.

Crock reeled back and put a hand to his face. Then he smiled. 'You better get a move on before the dingos sniff it out. They love Chinese food I hear.'

48

Keith lifted the tip of the spear and nudged her elbow with it.

Heidi stepped back.

He didn't move but flicked the spear at her again. Playing with her. Reminding her who was the hunted.

She had to keep his mind engaged. This was the human part of him. The rest had become feral, instinctive. 'Keith, did Elisabeth find you? Did she talk to you?'

This upset him. He jabbed the spear. It didn't touch her.

She tried again. 'You saw her?'

'I saw her dead.'

'Yes, I know. You and Spaz put the coat on her. That was kind.'

He didn't respond. 'You went to Elisabeth's funeral. I saw you. Carmel might have recognised you. Why did you go?'

He looked at her as if the answer were obvious. 'To see him.'

'Keith Bankston?'

He shook his head. 'No, my brother.'

Heidi didn't understand. If he believed Laureen, Peter and Charley weren't his blood brothers, who was he talking about? It was too hard.

She tried another tack. 'Octavia Goodhope had a spear. Someone stole it and stuck it in Elisabeth. Why would they do that when they had spears of their own?'

'It might have been a sign.'

'What kind of sign?'

He gave a small grunt.

'Someone hit Octavia with a brick when she recognised them. Why would they hurt her?'

'Tell her he's sorry. He didn't mean to.' He had taken her lead and slipped into the third person.

'She wasn't going to tell anyone about him. But Elisabeth was.'

'It's his fault. She came with him.'

This confused Heidi for a moment. Then she realised Keith was not talking about himself. 'With a boyfriend?' she prompted. Her eyes slid across to the carpark. She thought she caught a glimpse of silver in the trees.

'He's not a boyfriend.' Keith said.

Heidi thought about Elisabeth's message to Peter. Someone had told her about Keith. Has that person brought her to the Void? 'Does he have a name?'

He suddenly got cagey. 'If I tell you it spoils the game.'

'What game?'

'An eye for an eye.' His mind seemed far away. The arm with the spear had gone limp. She thought about grabbing it. It was then she noticed that his hands were covered in angry red welts. 'What happened?' she asked. She stepped forward. 'I can heal that.' She reached out to touch his hand.

He pulled it back as if he had been burnt. 'No!'

She shrunk back. 'That's fine.'

He seemed to be looking through her again, then cocked his head as if he had sensed something move in the bush.

She froze, hearing nothing herself, but fearful it might be Crock.

A large skink coloured like a coil of tarnished copper ran between their feet.

Before it could scurry to safety, Keith slammed his spear through its back.

The speed and brutality of the action appalled her. He lifted the spear to display his kill and her disgust must have shown on her face. 'It's all right. It's a freak,' he said. 'It doesn't deserve to live.' He pulled the warm body off the spear and threw it into the bush.

'Like the platypus and all those other animals you killed?' She spoke before she thought, angry now. 'Like Elisabeth?'

'Why do you keep talking about Elisabeth!' It wasn't a question.

'Because you killed her and dumped her body in the Void.'

She stood her ground, expecting the worst, ready to fling her body into the brush if he raised the spear at her again.

'Dumped her body?' He looked puzzled. And then she could see something change in his face. Acknowledgment. 'I did dump her. She deserved it.' He was angry.

'Why?'

'She said I was a Blackpeter. Abo trash.'

'When was that?'

'She brought me here. She said everyone did it in the Void. She said we could too. She said she'd never done it with an Abo before. I didn't want to. She made me mad.'

'Then what did you do?'

'I shook the lie out of her. I stabbed her. I tied her up. She was an animal.'

'What happened after that?'

He seemed surprised at the question. 'I drowned.'

Fraser drove, while Barton called for backup. 'We'll get the helicopter up here. They better get a hurry up, though. It'll be dark in a couple of hours.'

'Why aren't we going through the bush looking for her? She's not going to be out here.'

They were back on the Speculator Road, driving north.

'Unless she hid in the bush, she's hopefully found her way to the main road. With a bit of luck, she'll be up here somewhere.'

'What if she ran into Keith?'

Brendan turned around in the front passenger's seat and looked at him. 'We still don't know there is a Keith.'

'Believe me, there is.'

'Yeah, and there's a Yowie,' said Fraser, from behind the wheel.

'The thing I don't understand is why Octavia didn't tell me,' Brendan sighed.

'She didn't want to believe it,' Beckett said. 'You boys were like her children.' He had the window of the Rodeo down, elbow out, scanning the bush. His every instinct was to jump out and run, yelling Heidi's name. But Brendan had reasoned with him and he was right. What point was there in both of them being lost in the woods, perhaps kilometres apart? Heidi could have gone anywhere, in any direction. She might already have found the road and been saved by a passing motorist. Or the motorist who picked her up might have been Peter Bankston.

'Where are we going? She can't have travelled this far in an hour.'

'We're heading for the Void. That's about as far north as she could have gone in the past couple of hours. Then we'll circle back. There's a dirt road that runs between the Void and the Blackpeter's property. We can try that.'

Fraser slowed down around the next bend and indicated to turn. 'Void coming up.'

They bumped along a dirt track for a couple of hundred metres. Beckett's mind flashed on Heidi's description of Elisabeth's body. He prayed to the God he only believed in when the mortgage was due, or the plane he was sitting in took off. Please let her be safe and hiding in a cave somewhere.

'There's a car!' Fraser slowed down, cautious.

Beckett was electrified at the sight of the silver sedan. 'That's Peter Bankston's Magna,' he shouted.

'I can't see anyone,' Barton said, his hand back on his rifle.

Fraser put on the hand brake and jumped out of the car, rifle high.

Brendan followed suit, stepping out from behind the open door only when he was sure Bankston and his weapon weren't in the immediate vicinity.

Beckett didn't think about precautions. Barton yelled at him as he shot out of the truck behind them and ran straight to the edge of the Void.

He looked down into it.

There was no one there.

And then he heard the crack of a gunshot, shocking the crows out of the trees and into the sky, like the black wings of death.

Keith's face expressed the turbulence of his memories. His eyes flickered like those of a person watching a film in a darkened room. She wondered what episode in his own cinema he was scanning now. The humiliation of being told he was adopted, by a man he hated? The bravado of the fake drowning, diving under the rock shelf and swimming towards a new life? Some kind of clash with Crock or Sid that made him an outcast even from the fringe-dwelling Blackpeters? Laureen's drunken outburst? Elisabeth's taunts? Or something even darker from his childhood, the games he played, even then, with the lives of small things?

Games...

She watched him carefully. He looked through her. She kept her breathing steady, calming herself. She prepared for flight, inching backwards, wary of any sound, however small, that might jerk his mind back to the present.

She covered a couple of metres this way. If she could now just slip sideways into the bush...

There was a snap of foot on twig. Her heart threw itself against her ribcage.

Keith's eyes flashed.

Now he saw her. Not as a person, but an animal.

Like Elisabeth.

To be hunted.

Too quickly, he released the spear and it caught her on the clavicle. She could hear the awful sound of the bone cracking but the spear didn't penetrate and slapped to the ground.

She lost her balance and fell backwards.

He loped towards her and picked up the spear again.

She scrambled to her knees, holding her shoulder, keeping her eyes on his face, afraid to make any quick movements in case he reacted. Make it personal she told herself. Let your captor know you are a breathing, feeling human being. 'Keith!' she yelled at him. 'My name's Heidi! I'm your friend!'

But of course, she wasn't.

She dropped her bloody hand to her side and cautiously felt for a rock on the path. Her hand closed over something flinty.

'You're a freak,' he said.

'I'm not a freak!' She was screaming now. 'I'm Heidi. I live in the old dairy over the hill. I do massages for a living...'

'You're a freak. You've got slanty eyes and white hair. You don't belong here.'

Despite herself, her mind raced back to an incident in Sydney. Three teenage boys. Pissed, out for a night of gay-bashing, but she would do. A back lane in Surry Hills at midnight. Trying to unlock her car before they turned nasty.

One of them slamming his fist against hers so she dropped the keys. Another pushing himself into her from behind, grabbing her by the waist, flinging her to the road like she was a slab of beef. The third one putting his foot on her back, bending to pull her hair, hoisting her to her feet so that he could throw her against the car.

A hand down her pants and one over her mouth so hard she could taste blood.

She had been called freak before.

She raised the sticky hand with the rock and his eyes locked on it. In the second when she knew she must throw it hard and realised she didn't have the strength, Peter Bankston crashed out of the bush.

Peter held a rifle ready to fire but she could see his arms were trembling.

She saw the puzzled look on Keith's face.

'Peter! Don't shoot!'

Peter stepped forward, ignoring her. They were alike, these two. Pale, tall, tortured. They had to have a genetic connection.

Peter thrust the rifle into Keith's chest, his face a mixture of awe and disgust. Keith pushed himself forward against the gun barrel. 'You murdered *Elisabeth*,' Peter said, as if the act were still unbelievable. 'Our sister.'

'Elisabeth?'

Keith's question hung in the air as Heidi found her last functioning sinew and launched the rock.

It hit Peter on the side of his head.

But by then he'd fired his shot through Keith's heart.

49

Heidi was aware of the blades of a helicopter hacking through the air above and of shouts across the chasm. She lay against a boulder in the scrub, her legs beneath her and every nerve ending sparking with pain.

She couldn't move to save herself but there was no need. Peter had flung his rifle away and was on his knees, head down in submission and grasping the slain man's boots as if reaching out to rescue him from the abyss.

The abyss. The Void. Not a hole in the ground but a burial ground for years of hurt, betrayal, disillusion, sorrow. Carmel's dead daughter. Laureen's lost son. Spears, tattoos, war games...love? Was love in here anywhere? Heidi thought so...but she couldn't find it through the fog of pain.

Her head spun. Dazed, she lay staring at the empty sky, hearing Beckett's voice now, but captive to visions that moved in and out of focus.

'V' for Vlad. 'V' for Valerie. Valerie Harding stabbed and bound. Lover. Sister. Brother. Killer...

Something wrong about that.

She couldn't think.

The angry Void had reclaimed them all.

And now it was sucking her in...

Beckett was saying something. The words spurted like dirty water out of a rusty tap. Not clear...

Beckett saying her name. Urgent.

White. A curtain rail. The yellowing plastic covering on a ceiling light.

Her hand being squeezed.

'Beckett?'

'Garbo talks!'

She turned her head. A dull thud in the front of it, but no pain.

Beckett, in focus now, stood up and reached to kiss her where it throbbed.

She was in bed.

'Where am I?'

'In Nullin hospital.'

She tried to sit up but dizziness defeated her. 'Can I have a pillow?'

He found two and propped them against her back. Then he helped her sit up. 'Is that OK?'

Heidi found one arm was strapped to her chest in a sling. 'How long...?'

'Are you in pain?'

'A bit.'

'You had an accident.'

I had more than that, she thought.

'Your clavicle is cracked and your shoulder lacerated. You've got bruised ribs and a nasty bump on the head.'

'The Blackpeters...'

'Did they hurt you? Do you remember...?' He was tentative.

'Yes. Everything. No, they didn't hurt me.' It was lie, but she didn't want Beckett going thundering off into the bush after them.

He squeezed her hand tighter. 'Christ, Heidi, I'm sorry. I thought it was Damian. I went to Octavia—'

She didn't care about Damian. 'Where's Peter?'

'In the holding cells. It's OK. Keith Bankston's got an army of lawyers on it. He hasn't been charged, at least not until they speak to you.'

'Why not?'

'Why not? He saved your life. It was self-defence or at worst manslaughter.'

'He didn't save my life, Beck.'

'But Keith had a spear.'

'And Peter had a gun.'

'I know. I ran into him on the road.'

'How...?'

'Never mind. I called Brendan. We found your car. But Keith would have killed you if Peter hadn't been there. We wouldn't have made it...God, I feel bad about this. If I hadn't been such an ass about Damian you would have told me how you worked it out. I wouldn't have let you go up there alone.'

'Shut up about Damian. I went to see Klas. I thought Klas was Keith.'

'Klas? What, that Nordtrash hippie guy?'

'He had tattoos. His name started with K. I thought...' The thud in her temple was cranking up its tempo. 'What medicine have they got me on?'

'They gave you a local anaesthetic when they sewed up the cuts.'

'An operation?'

'Eight stitches.'

'What else? I feel weird.'

'A tetanus shot and some antibiotics. Oh, and some steroids.'

'Steroids?'

'It's a precaution.'

'How long have I been here?'

'Four hours.'

'It's dark outside?'

'It's about 8.30.' He wove his fingers through hers. Her thumb was bandaged too. 'Look, if you thought Klas was Keith, then how did you wind up at the Blackpeters? What happened to your car?'

'I ran into a roo. Joey picked me up. But I was going there anyway.'

'To provoke them. Why the hell do you always do that?'

She sighed. 'Someone has to act, Beck.'

'But why should it be beautiful, petite you? There are plenty of big, strapping cops around.'

'I'm sorry. I promise I won't do it again.'

'And you won't because there isn't going to be another time. Stick to interfering in your patients' diets from now on.'

Not another time...She shifted her hips, trying to get more vertical. She was more awake now. Thinking through the fog of interconnected memories. 'There were eight dwarfs, Beck. That's how I worked it out. There couldn't have been six boys at Elisabeth's funeral if Sid and Spaz weren't there.'

'Yeah,' he nodded. 'Scary Blackpeter.'

'Scary?'

'That's what the NRMA bloke told me. People knew there was another Blackpeter. I bet they'd even seen him sometimes. But they thought he was Spaz. Or this one called Scary. No one counted.'

'How did you work it out?'

'Octavia Goodhope recognised him. It was to do with the games Keith played as a child. Decimating animals. Killing every tenth one.'

She shook her head. Not a good idea. Fingers of pain gripped the back of her neck. 'He didn't seem like that, Beck. He was so sad.'

'He was a killer. He killed his sister. He almost killed you.'

'I'm not sure she was his sister.'

'What do you mean?'

She told him as best she could about Laureen's revelation. 'I think that set off the killing of the animals. He saw himself as a freak, like the animals. It was a kind of suicide.'

'I don't believe it.'

'What?'

'What Laureen said. She was pissed, after all. She might have said it to be vindictive.'

'Do you think?'

'Look, Octavia arranged the adoption. More than that, she seemed to have encouraged the affair between Keith and Laureen in the first place. I think it happened. I think they did have an affair, whether out of rekindled lust or for producing a child, I don't know. Nino's sons are all short and stocky. Then there's the Marfan's. I bet Keith has a touch of it.'

'But we're back to where we were. Keith and Spaz are alike.' She felt the familiar tug of confusion. 'And so is Peter.'

'You think they're *all* Keith's sons? Why wouldn't he have adopted Spaz then?'

'He'd already had Peter with Carmel. Maybe he couldn't deal with Spaz's extreme disability. It must have been evident when he was born.'

Beckett shook his head. 'The Marfan's is probably on Laureen's side, not the Bankstons. It's just a coincidence Keith and Peter look like that.'

Heidi sighed. 'I suppose we'll never know.'

'There's DNA testing. Keith could insist. In fact, maybe the prosecutor *will* insist, if it has a bearing on the case. If Peter shot his brother...'

'But we get back to one thing. If Elisabeth *was* Keith's sister, why did he kill her?'

'According to you, he didn't think she was.'

'You're right. God, my head aches.'

'I'll get you some Panadeine.'

'No! I left my bag at the Blackpeters, but—'

'I've got it.' He picked it up from the floor.

'Bless you. Find my Rescue Remedy.'

'Darling, that stuff's not enough. You need proper drugs.'

The old argument between them. She ignored him. 'I need

some milk thistle to counteract the effects of the drugs. Do you think you can go home and bring it back?'

'I'm not going to leave you.'

'Look, I'm fine now. Call the nurse if you like. When you get back you can stay and hold my hand all night if you want to be a martyr.'

He stood. 'Are you sure?'

The phone by the bed rang. Beckett picked it up and spoke for a minute. He put the phone down. 'That was Cheryl Martin. They'll leave you alone until the morning.'

'Thanks. Now please go get that milk thistle. And bring me a bottle of lavender oil. Oh, and my headache tea. It's in a tin—'

'I know where it is. But you've got to promise you won't do any fretting in the hour or so that I'm gone. The case is closed. The bad guys are all where they should be.'

She nodded, not at all sure of that.

She watched him search in his pockets for his keys and pull them out. 'Shit, I forgot. I left the car at the dock. I'll be a little longer.' He took her head gently in his hands and kissed her on the mouth. 'I'm sorry I was such an idiot,' he said. 'I can't believe I thought it was Damian.'

'Why did you, anyway?'

'Because he's Brendan's brother. Octavia told you to look for the brother.'

'You're not kidding, are you?'

'Nope.' He looked pleased with himself.

She lifted her hand to wave goodbye.

That word again.

Brother.

50

Heidi drifted back to sleep. It seemed as if she had only closed her eyes for a moment when she heard someone come into the room and close the door.

He opened the curtains, took a seat by the bed.

Beckett?

'Did you get the...?'

Aftershave. Beckett never used aftershave.

She turned her head. It felt so heavy...

Keith Bankston's face loomed close to hers, his neck and face flushed, a sheen of perspiration covering his skin. She didn't like the expression in his eyes. Anger. Something thwarted.

She tried to sit upright, but a searing pain shot from her neck to her hip. She pushed herself up on one elbow and gritted her teeth. 'What are you doing here?' She didn't care if she sounded frightened. He was the bad guy. Adulterer. Bully. Hateful father.

Keith leaned forward and put a hand over hers. She pulled it away. 'Don't worry. I've spoken to the nurse. She won't interrupt us.'

'I need painkillers.'

'You'll have to wait. I've sent her off on a tea break. You're the only patient here and I assured her I'd take care of you.'

She glanced at the table by her bed. His eyes followed hers. He put his hand on the telephone and smiled.

'My husband will be back soon.'

'I don't think so,' he said.

She felt her stomach sink. 'If you've done anything to him...'

'Take it easy,' he said, clamping his hand on her wrist, firmer this time. 'You're in no condition to get up. The nurse said the blisters on your feet will make it hard to walk for a few days.'

She twisted her wrist away. 'What have you done to my husband?'

'Nothing. Just a bit of car trouble. So that we can talk.'

'You bastard.' She had known in her heart it wasn't over. That Keith's death hadn't solved anything. That she couldn't simply go to sleep and wake up with it all behind her. 'Then why are you here?' She managed to give her faint voice some edge.

'I've been to identify my boy. They have a morgue in this hospital.' He gave a deep snort. 'The Lions Club raised the money.'

His sanctimonious tone made her sick. 'Lucky, isn't it?'

His voice remained calm. 'Why didn't you come to me when you found out Keith was alive? This could have all been avoided.'

'What? Your embarrassment?'

It wasn't the smartest thing to say. His face was a blister of rage. 'Listen to me young lady...'

She didn't want to have this conversation. Not now. Not alone. She couldn't think it through, feared that she would strike out at him to hurt. But she would be the one who would hurt.

Try harder. Think.

He yanked his striped tie away from his shirt collar as if he had been choking. He shifted in the vinyl chair and it squealed under his weight. Not fat, but powerful, the meaty shoulders and thick neck of a man built to rule the playing field. She could feel the heat coming off him like a charge. When he spoke again his voice was even. 'I can see you blame me.' He sighed and folded his hands on the bed in front of him. Playing the reasonable man. 'You're misguided, like the lot of them. My only concern is for my wife. Keith's dead now and his poor mother hasn't a chance to find out why...'

His hands were huge.

She pushed herself upright. Her headache was almost blinding. She wanted to scratch it out of her skull. But it was a torment she could direct at him.

Use it.

'Keith hated you,' she said. She kept her eyes on his hands.

'He was adopted. It's a bloody difficult thing.'

'You bastard. You knew you were his real father.'

He hadn't expected this. 'Who told you that?'

'Never mind. I know you think you got Laureen pregnant. But she lied.'

'Bullshit.'

'Keith didn't think it was. He told me that Laureen confessed he'd been Nino's child all along. That she fooled you for the money.'

'He thought that?' He shook his head. 'That bloody Laureen is a menace.'

'Yes.' And so are you.

He paused. 'She was a good sort before she became a drunk. I would have married her but she dumped me for that Blackpeter scum. She was a fool, I could have given her everything. But she was attracted to danger. When she realised what a lousy choice she'd made, she came back to me, begging. I'd found Carmel by then. I wouldn't have her back.' He pulled off his necktie.

'But you did. You had an affair with Laureen after you were married.'

He was silent for a minute. 'She came on strong with me after a council meeting. I drove her home. We parked at the Void for old time's sake. It was a mistake.'

'And you thought that one time had produced a boy?'

'I had no reason not to believe her. And Carmel wanted a child. It seemed to be for the best.'

'You could find out if you're Keith's father, you know. There are tests.'

'To what end? It won't help Keith now.'

'It might help Peter.'

He misunderstood her. 'That's why I'm here. When you tell them what happened, they won't prosecute.'

'How do you know what I'm going to say?'

'Peter told me. He said Keith was about to attack you. That he admitted to killing Elisabeth.'

'That wasn't what happened, Keith. Peter went up there to kill him long before he stumbled over me.'

'Listen to me, young lady. Peter went up there to bring Keith home. He had the fool idea the boy would come. You should be bloody grateful he turned up when he did. And you're going to tell the authorities that.'

'Are you threatening me? Or are you going to give me hush money like you gave Russ Harding?' The question had just popped into her brain. Under the tight band of headache, her subconscious was kicking in, like an evil stranger sitting on her shoulder, urging her into danger.

'What the hell has Russ Harding got to do with this?'

'I don't know. You tell me.'

'You're suggesting I bribed Russ Harding?'

'You did something. After Valerie's death he was quarter of a million or more richer.'

'Nothing to do with me. They sold their story to a British newspaper.'

'It was a fake. I have proof. My husband has proof.'

'Then they all fooled me.' Innocent.

'You gave Jack a job. A good job.'

'He's a talented young man.'

'And then Russ Harding killed himself. Over something. I guess it was to do with Valerie.' *That's right*, she remembered. The realisation had struck her in the Void.

It wasn't about Bankston genes at all. It was all about Valerie.

But what about Valerie? A wall had gone up in her head again.

Keith said nothing. He stared through her. Young Keith's stare.

'Wasn't it?' she prompted.

'Keith told you about Valerie.' It was a statement.

'Yes,' she said, pretending, not knowing where this was going.

'Then you're more of a nuisance than I thought.'

'You're threatening me.' She kicked one leg to the edge of the bed, ready to flee.

He noticed. 'You think I'm going to hurt you?' He followed her eyes to the tie in his hand. 'With this?' He shoved it in his pocket.

'You threaten everyone who doesn't do what you want. If that doesn't work, you bribe them.'

He laughed, as if she'd satisfied some opinion he had of her. 'How much do you want?'

'I don't want your money.'

'You must have a price. It must take quite a bit to fix up that old factory of yours.'

'We're doing fine, thank you.'

'Of course, my family used to own that old place. I'm not so sure the papers were in order when it was first sold, back in the fifties. I could ask my lawyer to look into it. It would be a pity if you had to call in your own lawyer. They cost a bomb, I believe.'

Now she was really mad. 'Is that why Russ killed himself? You threatened him too?'

'What are you talking about?'

'The money you paid them. To hush them up.'

His tone was self-righteous. 'I paid for *her*. For Valerie. I couldn't see Russ suffer like that. Poor Sheila. Their only daughter.'

His false compassion enraged her further. 'Why did you pretend they'd got the money from a newspaper then?'

'Sheila wouldn't take it if she knew, Russ said, so we got Bill to invent the story. She got a house and a cake shop out of it.'

'But it wasn't enough?'

'She lost her daughter. I still had my son. When my son drowned, it was an eye for an eye. I thought it was God's work. Now I know the bastard ran away to save himself.'

An eye for an eye. Keith had said that.

'Save himself?' she prompted.

'If you know the whole story, you'll understand what you have to tell the police. There are a lot of innocent people who could be hurt.'

'But Keith wasn't one of them?'

'No. The police found the straps. They were his. They might have been traced to him.'

What straps? Elisabeth had been lashed with straps. Then she recalled something Beckett had said. It felt like a decade ago. She tried to drag it to the front of her brain.

The truck driver accused of murdering Valerie had been released on a technicality. Later, the police had uncovered some new evidence. The straps that bound her. They had been closing in on the killer.

The straps had been young Keith's.

'Why did he do it?' she asked. But she knew.

She teased me. She said I was a Blackpeter. Abo trash...She said she'd never done it with an Abo before...I didn't want to. She made me mad.

He'd been talking about Valerie, not Elisabeth. Valerie had found out that he was a Blackpeter. She had teased Keith about it. Octavia had said that Valerie liked to get Keith 'all riled up'. He'd reacted violently and strangled her.

Keith shrugged. 'It was about sex. Rough play. An accident. Boys will be boys.'

His casualness sickened her. 'Stabbing the life out of a girl was just rough play?'

'Listen.' His voice took on a frustrated note. 'Keith came home a few minutes before me that night. I'd been out. Alone, thank Christ. The silly fool tracked blood into the house. I followed it into the kitchen. He was sitting at the table drinking a glass of milk, covered in the girl's...A glass of milk!'

'Did he say why he did it?'

'We didn't speak. I didn't know what he did. I thought it must have been a fight. A bad fight. I made him take off his clothes and go shower. I cleaned up. I burnt the clothes. I cleaned his car too. He never told me. The next day I knew what he'd done.'

'But you couldn't have cleaned up everything. The police must have found traces of blood or hair in his car.'

'They didn't look. Keith was never a suspect.' One of his fists was balled in the other. 'All I did was clean up my boy's car after he got in a fight.'

Not a cover-up in Keith's mind. But it was still a sin of omission.

'But the police must have questioned him.'

'They did. Jack provided the alibi.'

'*Jack* provided the alibi for his own sister's murderer?'

51

Keith had come to bully her, to stand over her, to bribe her. All that mattered to him now was getting his son out of jail.

For Carmel's sake. And for his own standing in the community.

But also, she knew, for his love of Peter. It was only a faint pulse but it was there.

She wondered if Peter would ever know.

When she got the chance, she would tell him.

'Jack gave Keith an alibi for Valerie's murder?' she asked, astounded.

'Jack told the police Keith and he had been playing CDs at Jack's place, that he was there until the early hours of the morning. They didn't doubt him.'

'He was the murdered girl's brother. Why should they doubt him?' She pushed her way through it. What had Octavia said? Something about Jack and Keith finishing each other's sentences. But they'd had a falling out after Valerie's death. Now she knew that was because Jack found out that Keith had killed her. Still, though, he covered up the crime. 'Jack should have been exposing Keith, not protecting him.'

'I never understood what went on between those two.'

'But you work with Jack. You gave him a job. Haven't you ever asked him over the years?'

'No. Keith died for me when he killed that girl. There was nothing to discuss.'

'*Never?*' They had never talked about it? That was the sickest thing of all, Heidi thought. Two grown men with a terrible secret between them. All these years, Jack exploited Valerie's death. He had a cushy job. He'd become the substitute elder Bankston son.

If he had gone to the police with the knowledge that Keith was the killer, the Bankstons would have shunned him. So he'd sold his sister out to get on in life.

Keith brushed off her outrage. 'Jack was just trying to make it easier on us. Keith was a bully and a pansy. A coward. He murdered young Valerie. And then the bastard murdered Russ too.'

'What do you mean?'

'Russ didn't have the guts for it in the end. He topped himself.'

'The guts for what?'

'Knowing who did Valerie. Not telling. Taking my money. As if it were *poison*.' He saw the look on her face. 'What is it, girl?' he demanded.

'If Jack hadn't lied, if you'd gone to the authorities straight away, Keith wouldn't have faked his own death and he'd probably be out of jail now. It was a crime of passion, he was a teenager. They would have been lenient, especially with your influence.'

He shrugged. Not wanting to face it.

'Elisabeth wouldn't have gone looking for Keith, she wouldn't be dead.' Her mind was now sparking and leaping like a live electrical cord. 'And Peter wouldn't be in this trouble. He thinks Keith killed Elisabeth.'

'He heard the bastard confess. That's why he shot him.'

'I was there. It wasn't like that. He confessed to Valerie's murder, not Elisabeth's.'

'He killed her because she found out he was alive—'

She saw the confusion on his face. 'You thought Keith had murdered Elisabeth all along, didn't you?' She paused. 'You *knew* he was alive. When did you find out?'

'I didn't bloody well *know*. Elisabeth came to me and said she'd found out he hadn't drowned. I didn't want to believe her, so I blew her off. She must have gone back to him to find the proof. Proof for me. And then he killed her.'

'But he didn't kill her.'

What she was saying finally registered. He pulled the bunched-up tie out of his pocket and wiped his forehead with it. 'What do you mean?'

'He didn't kill her. He told me.'

I stabbed her. I tied her up...I drowned.

He'd 'drowned' after he'd killed Valerie. There was nothing about Elisabeth.

Or was there?

She thought of all the animal heads on spears. 'She was dead before he found her. He just displayed her. It was a sign.'

'That's horrible.' Keith put his head in his hands. 'He did it to show me.'

'It wasn't about you.'

He wasn't listening. 'What did I ever do to him to deserve this?'

He still didn't know.

He dragged a hand through his hair and said wearily, 'I'll go to the police tomorrow. The boy's dead. It won't matter anymore. It'll prove Peter did the right thing.'

In his mind, his runaway son had killed his daughter too. He couldn't see beyond that, despite what she'd said.

Then he did a strange thing. He reached down and took her hand again. She flinched but he held it firm and placed his other hand on top. 'Peter saved your life. Please don't forget that when the police come calling.'

She watched him leave.

He hadn't told her. He had asked her. *Please.*

That must have been a first.

52

Heidi pulled the telephone receiver off its cradle. She dialled with trembling fingers.

Keith had done something to Beckett.

Her home phone rang until the answering machine picked up.

The sense of panic returned. *Answer, damn you.*

She dialled again. The machine kicked in. Her own voice wobbled back at her over the line.

She tried to remember the number of the police station. Damn. As she was thinking about dialling 000, the phone rang.

She pounced on it.

'Was that you calling?' Beckett sounded flustered.

'Are you all right?'

'Yes. I just came in. Why?'

'I was...worried.' The last thing she was going to do now was tell him about Keith's visit. 'You said you'd be back.'

'Yeah, sorry. Some bastard towed my car. A guy on the pier told me a truck came and took it away around 8.30. The taxi that dropped me off had gone, so I had to find another one. Have you ever tried to get a taxi in Nullin? I think there's only one.'

'You're not hurt?'

'No. But I can't get back tonight. The taxi guy's coming at eight to pick me up. He's the brother of the NRMA bloke.'

'Eight? That's a real sacrifice, Beckett.' Some of her humour had returned.

'Glad you appreciate it.' She could hear an intake of breath. 'Hey, you're OK, aren't you? You sound odd.'

'No, I was worried, that's all.'

'Well, I'm fine. Get some sleep. Wish I were with you. Maybe I can sneak between the covers in the morning.'

She smiled. It hurt. She hung up.

The nurse came in, checked her vital signs and gave her two painkillers. Where were you when I needed you, she thought, but took the pills gratefully.

She lay her head on the pillow and tried to get comfortable. The sling made it difficult. The dressing on her right shoulder made it difficult. Every part of her body was tender. She found the position that ached the least.

But she couldn't sleep. Things were becoming clear, despite the drugs, despite her weariness.

She thought of Keith alone in the hospital morgue with only Keith Bankston to claim him.

But she was part of it, too. If she had turned her car around and gone to the police Keith might still be alive and reconciled with Carmel. She had pursued him to his death.

Beckett would say it wasn't her fault, that Peter and Keith would have confronted each other without her. There *was* a terrible synchronicity in it. Some instinct had driven Peter to the Void at the precise moment Keith had led Heidi there.

Destiny?

Completion.

But it wasn't complete.

She closed her eyes and tried to make her mind go blank, but she couldn't banish Keith's accusing eyes. She felt his pull as if he had reached out from the grave and tugged her hair. She thought of his pale skin and the hands red with welts. He'd spoken with a voice that had grown hoarse without practice.

You poor, sad, lonely creature, she told him.

Freak, he said. *You're a freak like me.*

You're right, I am. She had always felt that way. She remembered her white grandmother: *It would be lovely to have grandchildren that looked Australian.*

So you understand, he said. *What family can do.*

She sat bolt upright, her nerves frayed. She was having a conversation with a dead man. The room was dark, but light spilled in, washing everything in cool blue. Ominous shadows hung in the curtain folds. She could hear the faint hum of a generator and a clicking sound, like someone stacking plastic. Her hair was alive with static electricity. She put a hand to it and felt something cold retreat, as if he had been stroking her crown and was stung by her heat.

But he was dead. He was in the morgue.

She had to see for herself.

Gently, she pushed herself upright and swung her legs over the side of the bed. Her toes were swollen, the only thing familiar about them the purple nailpolish she had applied a week before. Someone had bandaged her ankles. There were plasters on her soles where blisters had burst.

She stood, carefully. The pressure wasn't too bad. She looked around for her clothes. There was nothing in the drawer of the table beside her bed. But there were paper slippers on the floor. She wriggled into them.

She shuffled to the door and put her head into the corridor, feeling cold and exposed in her hospital gown and panties. A male nurse was standing at the nurse's station reading a clipboard. She wasn't quick enough. He spotted her.

He hurried down and asked her if she needed anything. 'You've got a buzzer,' he pointed out.

'I need to go to the bathroom.'

'Do you want assistance?'

'No thanks. Just point me at it.'

The ladies' room was three doors down. She went inside, waited, then checked the corridor. The place was deserted.

She shuffled down the corridor to a set of scratched plastic doors. Her paper-clad feet slid on the shiny linoleum and she reminded herself not to hurry.

Keith wasn't going anywhere.

She'd been in enough of these places to know the morgue was easily accessed by ambulance, tucked away from the living.

She slipped through the doors into a darkened corridor. A pale light glowed at the end. She could make out a trolley and a trio of wheelchairs facing each other in ghostly conference. A forest of apparatus hung with tubing and empty plasma bags clustered behind the chairs, as if eavesdropping. Her senses heightened, she breathed in the clinical, metallic smell of chemicals and ammonia, the smell that masks germs, disease and death.

She stopped, wanting to turn back, needing to go on. She reached the light at the end of the corridor, but it revealed only a storage room for technical equipment. A closed door across the hall was illuminated. She rattled the handle. It was locked.

There was another closed door where the corridor came to a dead end.

She knew before she opened it that some wit had made this the morgue.

She stood with her hand on the handle and felt she was about to fall into a black hole. She hesitated and then summoned all her willpower.

Let me fall.

The handle turned. She pushed the door open a fraction and peered into the black. A sulphurous smell assaulted her nose and eyes. She felt for a switch. Two fluorescent tubes kicked on and the room was bathed in a hard light that made her wince.

Everything was gleaming with newness. There was a stainless steel table backed against a new row of sinks, its irrigation hoses and suction tubes jumbled on top. A head of circular lights was fixed to the centre of the ceiling. A cluster of cardboard boxes on a bench suggested that someone had been interrupted in the process of unpacking.

They could keep their oscillating saws and instruments of dissection. None of it would be any use to Keith. He'd be sent to Sydney in the morning for the coroner to make the cut. This room would have to wait for a less controversial death.

She needed to see Keith dead. To see him as a corpse, in the cruel, hard light of reality. Otherwise he would haunt her sleep forever.

The back room was the size of a large kitchen. Heidi stood in the doorway. A huge steel refrigerator stood against a wall to the right, flanked by two tall cabinets with glass doors, these partially stacked with plastic containers. She stepped towards the big stainless steel door. There were fingermarks on the shiny surface. She knew why. Keith would be on a tray behind it. She prayed that there hadn't been another death in Nullin today.

She took a deep breath and closed her hand around the handle. It took some effort to pull the door open with one arm. A rush of cold air moved through her thin cotton gown.

He was in the middle drawer, his plastic shroud unzipped to the neck. All she could see was some matted blood in the wild hair on the back of his head where he'd hit a rock when the life had been exploded out of him.

She heaved the drawer out. He was so close. Even disinfectant couldn't mask his smell. She studied his face. The frown was still heavy on his brow. His jaw was clamped rigidly. Deprived of its spirit, his body had not given up the anger that characterised him.

Seeing his face wasn't enough. She needed to look at the wound, to make sure it had been real. She gently unzipped the heavy plastic down to his waist and separated it.

The gunshot was like a small, ragged star splitting his chest, blowing apart a forest of black hairs. But it wasn't the violence of the shot which horrified her.

Like his hands, his body was covered in abrasions and welts, white now that the blood had started to settle in purple stains to the underside of his torso and arms. So much of his body had been mutilated that the welts joined in places and formed their own crusted surface, like he'd put on a ragged shirt of scar.

Then she pulled the plastic apart to examine the tattoo of the 'V' on his arm. It was covered with a cross-hatching of scars, like those made by a razor blade. Had he been trying to hack it out?

She touched his hand. It was cold as frozen chicken, the fingers stiff. His knuckles were crusted with a landscape of scabs. She stared in disbelief. *Who did this to you?*

'Don't touch him.'

She whirled around.

Jack was standing at the door, his suit jacket folded neatly over his arms as if he'd popped in to check on the packaging of the cheese. 'The silly bugger used to scrub himself with steel wool. He'd rub the skin until it was like a river of blood.'

She was conscious of her flimsy gown. 'What are you doing here at this time of night?'

'Carmel asked me to identify the body.'

'Keith did that a while ago.'

'Did he? We must have crossed wires.' He tossed his jacket on a trolley and took a step towards her. His eyes were on her, avoiding the body of his boyhood friend. She could smell sweat under the verbena of his cologne. He looked her up and down. 'You'll catch your death of cold in that outfit.'

She felt vulnerable. This was Keith's best friend. The man who had given his sister's killer an alibi. This was not the place to find out why. 'I was just going back to my room.'

'I heard you almost got killed out in the bush,' he said. His eyes were flat as the back of tacks.

She tried to brush it off. 'Keith was never going to kill me.'

'I wouldn't count on that.'

He was blocking the door. She tried to move past him. In an instant, he had her wrist. She was so bewildered, she gave a small yelp, but he held fast and pulled her towards Keith's body. 'Let's see what Keith says about it.'

He was stronger than she imagined. And she had nothing physical left. Jack wanted to hurt her. Whatever hatred was inside him came out fast and sharp as a switchblade. And it was directed at her. She didn't know why.

He pushed her stomach against the lip of the tray. Her gown had ridden up and she felt his fingers dig into the tender spaces between her ribs.

Fingers. Poking, twisting, scratching, thrusting. A Surry Hills street. One streetlamp, blurred. A dog's thin bark. Then the impact of a fist on bone. A male fist. Her bone.

She tried to kick out but he pressed his body hard against her back. When she managed to force a foot between his legs he crunched down hard on her toes with his shoe. She twisted away but he grabbed her good arm and pulled her back.

She screamed. 'Let go of me!'

He ignored her. He was staring at Keith's body, his jaw slack. 'It doesn't even look like him,' he said. 'Fucking idiot.'

'Please let go of me,' she begged. 'You're hurting me.'

He clamped her elbow. 'He always had such beautiful hands. He could break an animal's neck just like *that*.' Then he looked away from Keith and gave her a hollow smile. 'You're lucky he didn't break yours.'

'He wouldn't have.' She tried to shake her arm loose.

His grip firmed. 'I might have to do it for him.'

'Why? What have I done to you?'

'Nothing, as far as I know. I'd like to finish Keith's work.'

'Like you used to finish his sentences?'

'We liked to share.' He yanked at her arm. The tray rolled back a few inches. He pushed her sideways, hard against the glass door of a cabinet. '*Don't touch him!*' he snarled. He clamped his hand over her nose and mouth and she couldn't breathe. She kicked out, but he wedged his body against hers, pinning her.

She bit his hand. He dropped it, cursing. As she tried to pull away, she watched him slam his elbow against the glass door and shatter it. Shards of glass crashed to the floor. He swiftly bent and picked up a long piece of glass and struck at her. She turned, but an edge caught her neck. She watched appalled as blood ran down his arm. He'd sliced his hand. She thought of Keith grabbing the flint of the spear.

'Don't cut me!' She jerked her head away from the shard he was holding. She could feel the stickiness of blood on her neck. *Please don't let the cut be too deep.*

Jack's hand was slashed and his elbow was bloody but he didn't seem to notice. He lowered the glass and dragged her back to Keith's body. 'Why? Don't you want to end up like this?'

'Not in front of Keith,' she begged.

He looked at her strangely again. 'But that's exactly what I'm going to do. I'm going to show him.'

'Show him what?' But she knew. Show him the kill.

He'd done this before.

The morgue was too remote for her shouts to be heard. It was a place for the dead, not the living. She was about to join them.

She couldn't even hope that Beckett would stumble down here. Damn Keith Bankston for towing his car.

Jack stood over Keith, forcing her to cower beside him. He hardly seemed to be breathing. She kept still, afraid any movement might set him off. He was staring at Keith's network of scars. His eyes betrayed a glimmer of tenderness but when he spoke, his voice sounded hard. 'Don't you want to know why he did it?' he demanded. He shook her again.

She obeyed. The inside of her throat felt like dust. 'Why, then?'

'To prove that he wasn't ordinary. That he was braver than all of us.' His words were sour.

She took a chance. 'He hurt you, didn't he?' Her voice came

out raw. 'When you found out he'd been hiding all these years?'

That stung him. His fingers dug into her flesh. 'The bastard could have confided in me. I wouldn't have told anyone.'

She tried to sound sympathetic. If he thought she was on his side, she might have a chance. 'You proved your loyalty before. You gave him an alibi for Valerie's death. Even though she was your sister.'

'That's right. Ungrateful bastard.'

'And then he deserted you.'

He started to get agitated again. She could feel a current of anger run through his body. 'He tricked me into thinking he'd killed himself. I knew he couldn't drown. He was too good a swimmer. I fucking *knew* it. For eight years he sat out there in the bush and watched me make a fool of myself. He never would have put on a suit and worked for his bloody father like I did. He tricked me into having the life he never wanted.'

The hand around the broken glass was loose by his side, a dark smudge of crimson. Heidi didn't take her eyes off it. 'But then you realised he was alive. It wasn't today, was it?'

'When the freaking animals started turning up. I heard about them. And then he left one at the back of my house. A vampire bat. It was a sign.'

'That he wanted to resume the game?'

'He used to pretend he was Vlad the Impaler. I played along. No harm in it.'

'But you slaughtered innocent animals.'

'*I* never slaughtered anything innocent.'

'Elisabeth was innocent.'

She'd gone too far. His eyes flickered. He turned them on her. 'What makes you think she was so innocent?'

'Nothing,' she said and held her breath.

In a flash the shard of glass was at her throat. 'Fucking tell me! What did he say about me and her?'

'Please,' she begged. The long edge of the glass was pressed against the soft part of her jaw. She could hardly choke the words out. 'I'll tell you.'

He released the pressure on her throat.

He was like two people. A wild, dangerous teenager, hurt, lashing out. A cold, calculating killer, wanting to show off his skill. One of them was going to kill her. She had to appeal to the other. But how? Flattery?

Adrenaline surged through her body and focused her mind. 'Keith wanted you to know he was alive. He sent you a signal by impaling the animals.'

'I responded.'

'Yes you did. It was clever of you. You tormented Elisabeth with what you'd found out, that her brother had never died. I bet you were the one who teased her about being adopted.'

He nodded.

'Then you lured her out to the Void on the promise of seeing him. Somehow you made sure Keith knew you'd be there. You wanted Keith to see you strangle her. You knew he was watching.'

Jack was pleased with this. 'I showed him. Just because I'd been a suit all these years didn't mean I couldn't do it. He never had enough faith in me. He was the wimp, hiding out all this time. I was the one who'd been strong.'

'But he didn't accept that, did he? He stuck Elisabeth on a spear to show you that he didn't care. That Elisabeth's death meant nothing to him. That the game wasn't finished.'

Jack shrugged. 'He always was a sick fuck.'

'And Elisabeth? What was wrong with her?'

'She was a pest. She had the hots for me for years. I didn't reciprocate. She didn't give up. Always running off with the local boys to make me jealous. As if.'

'She was more to you than that. She was *his* sister. Did you do it because of Valerie?'

He laughed. 'I never cared about Valerie. She was a silly little slag. The only good she ever did was to die and make Keith

Bankston owe us big time for it. That fool on the slab did us a favour, if you want to know.'

'Why kill Keith's sister, then?'

'It wouldn't have counted if it had been anyone. Any local slag.'

She at last saw what he meant. To surpass what Keith had done to Valerie, Jack had to sacrifice someone important to him. To both of them.

An eye for an eye.

Elisabeth for Valerie.

She forgot about his hand around her arm, the shard in his fist. It was all so...pathetic. 'What was the point, Jack? He's dead. They're going to take him to Sydney and cut him open. Then Carmel is going to bury him like she couldn't before. Like she buried Elisabeth. Like your mother buried Valerie.'

Jack shook her violently. 'The point is he didn't believe I could do it. He was always so superior. Vlad the fucking Impaler! It sounds like something out of boy scouts. Look at him, he's a joke. A slab of rotting meat. A stupid kid who ran away while I stayed and did the man's work. Stupid, fucking, mutilated idiot!'

She pulled away from him and this time he let go. The shock of release made her stumble backwards and her feet crunched on broken glass. She thought he was going to come after her but he turned back to Keith's body.

She could have run but found herself transfixed. Jack had taken the sharp glass and was pushing it in and out of Keith's chest. He was methodical rather than frenzied.

Now it was her turn to grab his arm. 'Stop it, Jack! You didn't need to prove anything. It's always braver to accept your responsibilities in life than run away. You looked after your mother. You tried to make something of yourself.'

He pushed her away. 'You think so? Every fucking nobody looks after his mother. Every fucking nobody gets a job. Every fucking nobody wants a house. I kept swimming but he drowned. I could never do that.'

With his free hand he yanked the zip of the body bag down to Keith's knees.

Criss-crossed scars ran down Keith's chalky abdomen. The black pubic hair looked brittle and wiry as the steel wool he had used to scrub away his anger. His penis lay bloodless across one thigh. It had been spliced underneath the shaft until the skin opened like a burst sausage. The scars had healed in hard ridges.

Heidi forgot her fear. 'God. What is that?'

'The trick is to butterfly the penis so that the urethra remains intact and functional. Lovely, isn't it?'

'He did that to himself?'

Jack's tone was envious, tinged with sadness. 'You see, I could never do that.'

And then the teenager departed and the man came back. Before she could react, he snatched her round the neck again and pressed the glass against her cheek. 'But I can do you.'

53

'No, you couldn't do that.' The voice was frigid.

Jack swung round, dragging Heidi with him. The shard of glass in his hand wavered close to her eye. She jerked her face away from it.

Carmel stood in the doorway, a black cardigan over her shoulders. 'You couldn't ever be him. I shouldn't have let you try.'

Jack didn't seem surprised to see her. 'I thought you didn't want to come,' he said neutrally. He tightened his elbow under Heidi's neck, choking her. She tried to prise it away with her hand. The sharp glass bit into her cheek. She stopped wriggling, afraid he would take her eye out.

'I changed my mind.'

'Come and look then.'

'You don't think I can?'

Carmel stepped forward, her eyes locked on Jack.

It was as if Heidi wasn't there.

Carmel looked down and sadness washed over her face. 'I should have protected him. He was just a baby. I was too passive. I didn't stop any of it. I saw it happening and I didn't stop it.' Without looking up, she said, coolly, 'Put that thing down, Jack.'

He released the pressure of his arm on Heidi's throat but kept it against her body. The shard glimmered under her eye. 'She'll get away.'

'She doesn't count.'

'Keith hasn't finished with her.'

Carmel now looked at him and her eyes were implacable. 'I will not have another thing killed.'

Jack's breathing was shallow. Heidi thought he was preparing to strike out again, but he relinquished his grip and pushed her towards Carmel. The older woman grasped her wrist. Heidi doubled over, coughing, the bile rising from her stomach.

'I'm sorry I let this get so far,' Carmel said. 'Has he hurt you?'

Heidi stood up and felt her cheek. Her hand came away with a slight smear of blood. 'I don't think so.'

'It's all my fault.'

'It's not your fault,' Heidi said. She looked back at Jack. He was standing still, watching. 'It's your husband's. He deceived you.'

Carmel appraised Heidi, her eyes now shining like wet shale. 'And you think I didn't know it?' Something proud flashed across her face.

Heidi kept Jack in her sights. 'You knew all along that it was Keith and Laureen's baby?'

'Of course I did. Why do you think I named him Peter? I wanted Keith to know I knew where our first son came from. Black Peters.'

'Why didn't you just tell him?'

'It would have ruined our marriage.'

'And you love being married,' Jack said.

Carmel ignored him. 'I would have had to have left Keith. And if I hadn't left him then, I would have had to leave him later when I found out that he'd hidden the boy's...crime from the police.'

'You *knew* he killed Valerie?' Heidi was aghast at her complicity.

'A mother can never sleep until her children are all in bed. I heard my son come home that night. I heard his father clean up after him. My husband has never cleaned a thing in his life.' The laugh caught in her throat. 'I watched Keith use the murder to

351

exert power over the boy, just as he found other things to humiliate his brothers. I watched while my son made friends with that criminal Sid, knowing where it would lead. And as for you,' her eyes switched to Jack, 'I knew you were corrupting him. I didn't stop that either.'

'You didn't mind a bit of corruption yourself.' Jack was now examining the glass in his bloody hand, like another person might study their nails.

Carmel's skin had been as waxy as the rope of pearls around her neck but now the high points of her cheekbones flushed with colour. 'You murdered my sweet Elisabeth. How could you?'

He looked up. Heidi was poised for a violent reaction, but Jack's voice was bland. 'I had no choice. Keith started the game.'

'And so killing Elisabeth was the logical conclusion? After all we'd done for you?'

'Done for me? What I'd done for *you*. *I* protected Keith from the cops. *I* played sonny boy to make you happy when he ran away. You knew damn well he'd killed Valerie. You knew damn well your husband had paid Russ off. I kept quiet about it all these years.'

'You kept quiet because it suited you.'

Heidi could see Jack's fist closing around the glass again, yet something about Carmel's manner kept him in check.

Jack pointed to the corpse. 'Look at him. Poor bastard. You should have left him in the bush when he was a baby. I hate you meddling rich people.'

'It's a class war now, is it Jack? How many excuses can you invent to delude yourself that you're not a murderous little shit?'

'Your "son" didn't stop me.'

'How could he do that?'

'He was watching. I could feel him. I used to watch when he killed but this time he was watching me. He thought what I was doing was beautiful. He didn't have to say it. He dressed her up for me. If he could speak, he'd tell you so.'

Jack was standing between Carmel and the body. She calmly stepped past him and gently touched Keith's arm. 'You pale into insignificance compared to the convergence of...horrors that led my son to *this*.'

'Don't touch him!' The anger erupted. He was so swift, Heidi had no time to react. He jerked his bloody wrist upward so that the point of the glass was directed between Carmel's eyes. His arm was trembling.

'Jack, stop it!' Heidi yelled.

Carmel didn't blink. 'I don't care,' she said to him. Her voice was steady.

'Either do I,' Jack answered. And then his arm shot upwards and back towards his body like a sprung bolt, the glass slicing into his carotid artery.

Carmel gave a slight gasp but didn't move.

Seconds later, Heidi was crouched on the floor, pressing a palm and all of her weight against Jack's neck, trying to stem the blood flow.

As the hot blood spurted into her eyes and mouth, she turned and looked up at Carmel. 'Get help! Get a doctor!'

Carmel walked out of the room.

'You fucking idiot!' Heidi screamed at Jack as the life poured out of him. 'It's not a competition.'

But it was and it was finished.

54

There were some advantages to not being able to raise your arms, Heidi thought, as Beckett untied the sling and slipped off her jacket.

It was cold in the bedroom, even though Beckett had solicitously switched on a heater and lit the oven for warmth. She sat on the edge of the bed, her bruises yellowing and her cuts melding under the lashing of bandages. She felt less sore than weary, glad to be out of the hospital and yearning for the familiar sag of her own mattress.

Beckett was kneeling between her thighs. He stretched and kissed her on the forehead as if she were a child. 'How are you feeling now?'

'Not too bad. Just a little tired.'

He started unbuttoning her shirt. 'I've asked Damian not to come around for a few days.'

'Why not?'

'You don't want him banging about while you're trying to rest.'

'Not much chance of him doing that, knowing Damian. Anyway, I'll be fine in the morning. I've got things to do.'

'No, you haven't. I've taken care of everything. I've even done the shopping. You're not leaving this bedroom ever again.' He smiled, but she knew that it would be the case if he had his way.

'You were an idiot about Damian, you know.'

He shrugged. 'I know. But not half as much an idiot as you.

You had most of the male population of Nullin wanting to kill you.' He started counting on his fingers. 'Gray Wignall. A whole brace of Blackpeters. Young Keith. His father. That Jack. God knows who else.'

'There's no one else.' She said it in such a way that he took another meaning from it.

He squeezed her hand and then dropped it. 'Sorry.'

'It won't break.'

'Your thumb, though. Joey cut it.'

'I have another one.'

He unbuttoned her cuffs. 'I do have some good news. Brendan gave me my hat back. Now I can finish that draft.'

'Just as well, Beck. We need the money. I'm not going to be able to work for a while.'

She could tell he was mulling over saying something. He carefully took her shirt off. She hadn't worn a bra because of the stitches on her clavicle. Her nipples hardened in the cold. He reached across the bed and found the top to his pyjamas. He slipped her arms into it. It was huge on her. As he was doing the buttons up, he said, 'I wish you'd think about doing something else. It's dangerous going into strangers' houses.'

'Nothing has ever happened to me in a stranger's house,' she said. It was strictly true.

'You got involved with the Bankstons. I wish you never had.'

'And seen Spaz go to jail for Elisabeth's murder? You were just as involved as me.'

'He would have got off.'

'You think Andrew Eagan would have won the case? I don't. He's not a criminal lawyer.' Beckett closed every button on the pyjama top. It reminded Heidi of something. 'Spaz did dress Elisabeth in the coat. He was part of it in one way.'

'Young Keith would have manipulated him. He was the one with the sickness for killing animals. Spaz is a gentle soul. He must have hated the whole thing.'

355

'He probably idolised Keith too. That's why he didn't dob him in to the police.' She watched Beckett fold the sleeves back. 'I wonder why Keith lived apart from the Blackpeters.'

'Maybe he was too peculiar even for them.'

'Laureen thought he had been spoiled by the Bankstons in some way.'

'Think about it. It must have been a huge shock to find yourself among those thugs when you'd been leading the life of a wealthy young man. Sid must have really twisted his mind. And I believe him capable of it.'

'You should have heard Keith's voice, Beck. It was beautiful, cultured. I know he was a killer, but there was something sensitive about him.'

'Sensitive? He strangled Valerie. He bashed Octavia Goodhope.'

'He was sorry about that.'

Beckett slipped his hands into her waistband and began to unzip her jeans. 'Don't be such a bleeding heart.'

'At least I've got a heart.'

'Yeah, one that almost stopped beating.' He yanked her jeans down to her hips.

'He did a lot more harm to himself than me. You should have seen the scars. He scrubbed himself with steel wool. He tried to gouge out his tattoo. He slashed his penis...I don't know how he could have done that.'

'I read about it somewhere. It's a manhood ritual of some Aboriginal tribes. They cut the underside of the penis and let it bleed into the fire for purification. It's called a butterfly cut.'

'But why?'

'To create a one-time male menstruation, in sympathy with the female.'

'*Sympathy?*'

'I'm no psychologist but I bet Keith did it after Sid told him they were brothers.'

'And after he killed Valerie. She turned on him for some reason, called him an "Abo".'

'Because he didn't want to fuck her that night in the Void?'

'Maybe. Jack insists Keith had no interest in her at all.'

He was quiet for a moment, peeling her jeans off. 'I still don't understand why the cops didn't consider Jack. He's got away with a hell of a lot over the years.'

'Remember, Beck, he went to Singapore the next morning. He couldn't have stolen Octavia's spear.'

'And the police thought the person who stole the spear was the killer.' He touched her hand again. 'You're not going to defend him, too, are you?'

'No, Beck. He tried to kill me. He really wanted to. Carmel saved me.'

'So what was their relationship?'

'I don't know.'

'Lovers?'

'I'm not sure. It was more like she was a domineering mother.' She shuddered, remembering. 'Thank God for that, though. He obeyed her.'

'Maybe he took on Keith's life in every way. Including substitute mother...But he still lived with Sheila, so he hadn't rejected her.'

She remembered Jack's tender expression when he looked at Keith's body. 'He was like two people at once. He hadn't ever thrown off the kid who was Keith's best mate. He was really hurt when Keith drowned, but it was worse when he found out he hadn't.'

'So he played a drawn-out game with Elisabeth in revenge.'

'She had a crush on him.'

'Like Valerie had a crush on Keith.'

She thought about it. 'I wonder if he encouraged Elisabeth for that reason.'

'Jack was the one who told Valerie Keith's secret about being adopted. I bet he stirred her up to tease Keith. If it hadn't been for that maybe Keith wouldn't have been driven to murder her. And then he did the same thing to Elisabeth. He told her he knew Keith was alive and where to find him. Then he made a rendezvous to show her, after the ball.'

'He met her outside the hall?'

'Probably somewhere nearby. He didn't want people to see them leaving together. Maybe they had a few drinks in his car before he took her up to the Void and murdered her—in front of Keith, we presume. But how did he know Keith would be there?'

'I don't know. Instinct? Peter knew he'd be there too.' She shivered.

He stroked her legs to keep them warm. 'It's all very Leopold and Loeb.'

'Who are they?'

'Two homosexual students in Chicago in the 1920s who killed a fourteen-year-old boy to see if they could commit the perfect crime. Hitchcock made a film about it called *Rope*. Remember?'

She nodded. 'I do. Still, it's a bit simplistic to say it was a homosexual thing. I'm not even sure they were. I got the impression they shared girls.'

'And kills.'

'No, Jack only watched. Until Elisabeth.'

'But they did cruel things for each other's benefit.'

She sighed. 'I was even wondering if Jack could have been the father of Elisabeth's lost baby.'

'It could have been anyone by the sound of it.'

'Will we ever know?'

'Probably not. The two of them are dead.' Beckett found his pyjama bottoms. He lifted Heidi's feet and threaded them through the legs.

'Four. We can't forget the girls, Beck.' She wriggled to help him pull on the pants. 'You know, I met Elisabeth once. I heard all the gossip about her and I've spoken to people who love her…yet I still can't get any sense of what kind of person she was. She seemed so confident when I met her at the ball, but she must have been a very confused girl underneath.'

'That's the sad thing about murder victims,' Beckett said. 'Once they've died violently it becomes the most important thing about them.'

Heidi watched him roll up the cuffs of the pyjama legs. 'Are you finished?'

He sat up and took her hands in his. 'Yes, except for the sling. Ready for bed?'

'I was thinking, I'm not all that sure about these pyjamas. I think you might have to take them off again.'

Beckett enthusiastically obliged.

On the morning of September 11, 2001, I sat at my desk in downtown New York and began to write the murder scene in this book. Usually at this time on a Tuesday I would have been a few blocks away, buying vegetables at the farmer's market under the World Trade Center. But that morning I forced myself to stay home and nail the scene. Moments later, a plane roared overhead and ploughed into the Twin Towers, right before my eyes. I was propelled out of New York and back to Australia, where, after much disruption, I finished the book. Writing a book that contains so much death might seem morbid given the circumstances, but I found it therapeutic to fold dark thoughts between covers and to invent the kind of neat ending that doesn't always happen in life.

Any mistakes in this book are my own but I would like to gratefully acknowledge the assistance of Senior Constable Jake Buckley of the Ballina police and Dr John Clifforth of Melbourne. I am indebted, as always, to Michael Heyward and Melanie Ostell for their brilliant editing skills, and all at Text Publishing for their continuing support. To Ramona Koval and Maureen McCarthy, thanks for the cups of tea and companionship.

I wish, finally, to thank my dear friends in New York for their courage, compassion and loyalty. You know who you are. Bless you.